THE
CHOSEN SEED

THE CHOSEN SEED

The Dog-Faced Gods
BOOK THREE

SARAH PINBOROUGH

GOLLANCZ
LONDON

First published in Great Britain in 2012
by Gollancz
An imprint of the Orion Publishing Group
Orion House, 5 Upper St Martin's Lane,
London WC2H 9EA
An Hachette UK Company

A CIP catalogue record for this book
is available from the British Library

ISBN 978 0 575 08954 9 (Trade Paperback)

1 3 5 7 9 10 8 6 4 2

Typeset by Input Data Services Ltd,
Bridgwater, Somerset

Printed in Great Britain by
Clays Ltd, St Ives plc

The Orion Publishing Group's policy is to use papers
that are natural, renewable and recyclable products and
made from wood grown in sustainable forests. The logging
and manufacturing processes are expected to conform to
the environmental regulations of the country of origin.

www.sarahpinborough.com
www.orionbooks.co.uk

For Jules

'*There is no truth. There is only perception*'

Gustave Flaubert

Prologue

He pulls his coat tighter around his thin frame and tucks his chin into his chest. The year is starting to die and its bitterness at that fact is clear in every bite of the wind that attacks him. The young woman in the doorway gazes up, her eyes already bleary. There is a mixture of awe and confusion in her expression. Soon, he is sure, there will be something else.

'For this is the word of your God,' he says, smiling softly. 'Spread it.'

She opens her mouth for a moment but he turns and walks away before she can blurt out whatever it is she wants to — there will not be anything original to hear. The muttered thanks of the junkie doorway-dwellers is always the same; he's seen enough of them to know that, this night, and the one before, and the one before that. He has been busy spreading his word in the alleyways and under the bridges, where the invisible congregate. It gives him a quiet sense of satisfaction that eases his own bitterness.

He leaves her — high, and now dying — and strolls through the city streets. It's creeping towards midnight, but the capital never sleeps. He watches the smiling, bright faces around him. Perhaps now is the time to spread his word a little wider.

A couple laugh and lean in to each other. The man is smoking, which is why they are out in the freezing night rather than enjoying the warmth within, but the cold doesn't appear to affect them. Both wear wedding rings, but he doubts they are wedded to each other. There is a flush of a drunken office flirtation surrounding them, and he can see in the woman's face that her own husband is a million miles from her mind. This man's hands and touch and charm are all she wants tonight. She's feeling young and sexy again, herself, not just a mother and wife.

He goes inside and buys himself a drink, the same brand of beer that the woman is drinking, and stands behind them. No one pays him any attention. It's late and the world appears to be filled with good cheer. Here and there he sees a flicker of gold, but the Glow is so weak it's almost an embarrassment. The woman and man have none.

Their drinks are sitting on the windowsill of the pub and it takes barely a second to do what needs to be done to her beer. He waits patiently, and after a moment her companion goes inside to find a toilet and she reaches for the bottle. He watches her swallow and then comes alongside, smiling as if he too is having the time of his life, which perhaps, in some perverse way, he is.

'Happy Hallowe'en,' he says, and clinks his bottle against hers.

She smiles and then drinks.

'For this is the word of your God.' He doesn't smile, and her own expression wavers. 'Spread it.'

'What did you say?'

He doesn't answer but turns and walks away, dropping the half-full beer bottle in a bin as he does so. He feels satisfied. He's found a new market.

Chapter One

Cass didn't turn around until he heard the tentative steps coming through the doors behind him. The church was quiet and he'd picked a row near the back, away from the two old women busily arranging flowers and polishing silver. Not that they were paying him any attention; he'd lit a candle and now he was moving his mouth silently and that was enough for them to think him one of the fold. It didn't take much these days – the Church was a club desperately in need of new members.

He raised his hand to the elderly man clutching a small suitcase, but even then it took Father Michael a couple of seconds to recognise him. He hurried over, looking nervous.

'Cass,' he said, his eyes searching Cass' face for some trace of guilt or innocence. 'You've lost weight. And the hair—'

'Looking like Cass Jones might get me unwanted attention. And having a hole blown through your shoulder can make you drop a few pounds.'

'Of course, of course.' Father Michael looked apologetic. 'But are you okay? You just disappeared— I was worried. I was surprised to hear from you, but I can't say that I wasn't pleased . . .'

'A friend's been looking after me,' Cass said, then, 'I'm getting there.'

There was a moment's awkward silence where all the

allegations hurled at Cass via the world's press hung between them.

Cass broke the silence. 'Thanks for bringing the stuff. I appreciate it.'

'It's fine.' Father Michael smiled. 'The police haven't been back to the house, not since your troubles started. I presume they were just checking to make sure you weren't hiding out down there – as if you'd be that stupid. As if you'd killed those people— I wonder sometimes if anyone ever knows anyone at all.'

'You don't think I'm guilty?' He tried to hide his surprise.

'Not for a moment, Cass.' Father Michael was looking at him with something close to pity. 'You have to ask?'

'Everyone else does.'

'People can get blinded by evidence.' The old priest winked. 'Why do you think no one believes in God any more?'

Cass almost laughed aloud as an unexpected warm rush of gratitude flooded him. He hadn't wanted to call, but he hadn't been able to come up with any other way to get the photographs and documents out of his dead parents' house. He'd expected suspicion, but on reflection maybe he had just been blaming Father Michael for his own father's crimes, simply because the priest had been his father's friend, and one of the few people close to him still alive.

'I brought you something else.' The priest tugged at his pockets. 'Two things actually. The first is this.'

'A cashcard?' Cass stared at the plastic. 'I can't take that.'

'The account has a few thousand pounds in it – it's not a lot, but enough to get you going. I didn't want to take the money out of the bank in case the police were watching me – they've gone quiet, but you never can tell, can you?' He gave a wry smile. 'I've learned to be a little more wary,

4

this past few months. And yes, you can take it: your father left me this money and I've never touched it – I always wanted to give it to your children – yours and Christian's. The pin is zero zero zero zero – easy to remember.'

'It was my dad who gave Luke away.' The words were bitter, but gave no real indication of the rage Cass felt inside.

Another silence, then, 'Castor Bright?'

'Who else?'

The priest let out a long sigh. Cass wished he had been a little more surprised – how much did Father Michael really know – or suspect – about Mr Bright and the Network? He'd been there, all those years ago, when Cass' parents had been brought together by the elusive, ageless man. He'd seen Alan Jones change from ambitious war correspondent to quiet, religious village-dweller, and he'd stayed close to both Alan and Evelyn Jones.

'Sometimes,' the priest said, his eyes wandering over to the flickering candles around the nearest pillar, 'situations get out of control. People make promises they have no intention of keeping. The future is a long way away.'

'Did you know?'

'No, but I knew your father.' The lines in the old man's face deepened. 'Since Christian died – and with everything that's come after – I've thought a lot about your family. Christian was increasingly fatalistic, those last few times I saw him – and your father was too, after he'd discovered his faith. At the time I thought it was just the peace finding him, but now I'm not so sure: now I think he was simply *resigned*. As Christian was.' He looked at Cass. 'They didn't have your strength, and I think Christian knew that.'

'Christian was a good man.'

'Goodness and strength are two different things.'

Cass noted that the priest didn't try to persuade him of

5

his own goodness. He didn't care – he knew exactly how far into the grey spectrum between the black and white of good and evil he had ventured.

'So what are you going to do?' Father Michael asked.

'Find Luke.' The answer was fast. Cass had spent the past two months thinking about what he was going to do next. 'Go after Mr Bright and fuck him and his Network up. Do my best to keep the others off my back until it's done.'

Father Michael nodded. 'Well, you always were the over-achiever of the family.' He smiled softly. 'And you know where I am if you need me.'

'Thanks.' Cass frowned. 'You said you brought two things?'

'Ah, yes – brain's not what it was.' He handed Cass a folded piece of paper. 'This man, Dr Stuart Cornell: he had an obsession with your father for a while. Used to go through phases of calling incessantly, and turning up at the house, shouting at your dad that he needed his help to expose the truth. He might just be a crackpot, but he used to be a pretty eminent theologian at one time, and with all this madness surrounding you – well, he may be worth a visit. Can't do any harm.'

'Thanks.' Cass stared at the name on the paper, then tucked it into his jeans pocket.

'So what now?'

'Now you go first. I'll give it fifteen minutes or so before I leave. I think we're safe – if anyone *had* followed you, I'd be arrested by now.' He sounded more confident than he felt. It wasn't only the police who were looking for him. He was sure that Mr Bright hadn't lost interest in his well- or not-so-wellbeing, not to mention the strange girl and old man who had rescued him after he'd been shot.

The awkwardness returned as the priest fumbled for an

appropriate goodbye. Cass could sense that the older man wanted to hug him, but he couldn't bring himself to relax into the gesture. Instead he held out his hand. 'It's good to see you,' he said, meaning it. 'I'll keep in touch.'

'Make sure you do, Cass Jones. Make sure you do.' The priest gave him another smile before heading to the aisle. He faced the altar and made the sign of the cross, then turned and left the church. He didn't look back.

Twenty minutes later, and Cass Jones was strolling through Loughton, heading up the High Street towards his most recent home. He'd been here for two weeks and he was itching to get on with what he needed to do. He was almost healed – if he ignored the constant ache in his shoulder and the sparking pins and needles in his mainly useless left hand. The movies made a shot to the shoulder look like a scratch, but the reality was different: Cass was pretty sure he was lucky be alive at all, and thankful the joint itself hadn't been shattered, otherwise no amount of physio would give him the use of his arm back.

As it was, his grip was so weak it was barely there, and that didn't look like it would be changing any time soon. His memory of Brian Freeman was now tinged with a greater respect: the man must have nearly bled to death sitting in the back of that snooker hall all night with the Yardies. Cass wasn't sure whether that made Freeman either brave or stupid, but it did make him one fucking hard bastard. And maybe that made Cass either brave or stupid for having been the one to send him away all those years ago.

The December wind blew through the darkening night, and it felt strange to have it lifting his grown-out hair – the usual dark number 3 crop had given way to a shaggy light brown, thanks to a bottle of Just for Men. What with that and the weight he'd lost over the past two months, he wasn't sure even his own mother would recognise him, let alone DS Armstrong or Commander Fletcher. Still, he kept his head down and his back curved as he walked, changing his natural shape: even out here on the edge of Epping Forest, a corner of north-east London that was more Essex than the city, it was better to be safe than sorry.

Feeling the weight of the small suitcase in his good hand exacerbated the weakness of his left, making him feel vulnerable, but there was nothing he could do about that: he needed those photographs and documents he'd found at his parents' house after Christian had shot himself. There were answers in the past, he was sure of it.

As the streetlights flickered on, he walked alongside the commuters making their way back from the Underground to the safety of their homes.

Despite his inclination to avoid eye contact, it was hard not to stare: why were some of them wearing surgical masks? Was this some new terrorist threat? Maybe more Interventionists at work? He really needed to watch the news. At least he wasn't featuring on it quite so much these days, although with the corruption trials of his fellow ex-officers about to get under way, that was bound to change. He was glad the cases hadn't been thrown out of court after he went on the run, despite the best efforts of the defence teams. That was something. Claire May, Christian, Jessica and the poor kid they'd all thought was Luke, his nephew: they deserved justice.

Passers-by gave each other broad berths and suspicious glances, pulling their coats tight around their body. Whatever was going on, maybe a new bird flu outbreak, perhaps something more sinister, the mild panic it was causing was clearly visible.

Cass finally reached the front door to his haven and knocked four times in the agreed rhythm, then waited, his eyes level with the peephole.

The door opened and Mac grinned at him through the stream of smoke coming from the cigarette clamped between the big man's teeth. He peered up and down the street before locking up.

'You've got a visitor, son,' he said gruffly.

Chapter Two

By the time he'd followed the brisk PC down to the interview rooms, Dr Tim Hask was not only out of breath, but he'd managed to spill much of the foul substance that passed for coffee in Paddington Green nick all over his shirt and vast belly. At least that would save him having to drink it, he thought stoically.

'What's the rush?' he said. 'It's late – I was just heading home for the day. Is this about our missing friend?' Hask kept his tone light, but he was aware of both the tension and his own conflicting emotions regarding Cass Jones. A very large part of him hoped that the ex-DI hadn't been arrested, though he wasn't entirely sure why.

'No,' DI Charles Ramsey said in his transatlantic drawl, 'we've still got nothing on him.'

'Yet,' Armstrong added. 'We'll get him; I promise you that.'

Hask was sure that Armstrong was the only one of the three of them convinced of Cass Jones' guilt, and he was also sure that Armstrong resented Hask's and Ramsey's hesitance in the face of overwhelming evidence. Armstrong was clearly bitter about Jones, and Hask wondered if it was in part because he envied him. People stuck by Cass. There was no way to explain to the sergeant the kind of loyalty that Cass Jones inspired in people – he'd just have to figure that out for himself. Or not.

'So what is it?' Hask asked again. 'What's so important you need to drag me down here so urgently?'

Ramsey glanced at Armstrong before answering, 'It's this surge in Strain II cases. We think it's being spread intentionally.'

'The increase in infection is outside of the expected social groups as well as within – and it's been getting much worse over the past month.' Armstrong looked grim.

'It was bound to happen – it's human nature to be careless,' Hask said. 'What makes you think it's anything other than that?'

'The bosses have had a call from Charing Cross Hospital, someone on the bug wing. There're two things: firstly, whatever is infecting people is still Strain II, but it's hitting the patients harder and faster – they found that out when several sex workers developed symptoms just a week or so after they'd been pronounced clean at their regular check-ups. Until then, they had presumed these new cases had been infected for a while before they started showing.'

'You're saying someone's somehow mutated the bug?' Hask's stomach felt heavy. Strain II was dangerous enough without people messing around with it.

'Something's certainly given it some punch.'

'Like it needed it,' Armstrong muttered.

'Who knows about this?' Hask asked. The increase in infection rates had been all over the news in the past few days, but he hadn't seen anything about a mutation.

'Everyone important,' Ramsey said, 'and now us.'

'So we can presume that within twenty-four hours it'll be public knowledge – or at least rumour.' The profiler sipped what was left of his coffee. 'What was the second thing?'

'The ward sister said she'd heard something – a similar story, from three different patients, all talking about someone who gave them drugs. It sounded odd to me.'

'Junkie stories?' Hask sighed. It was almost impossible to get any useful information out of addicts – especially sick ones. Their perception was generally shot to hell.

'It's not just junkies, not any more. We've had a female patient brought over. Want to hear for yourself?'

Hask smiled. 'Lead on, Macduff.'

'I've lost everything.' Michaela Wheeler's eyes were red-rimmed, and dark shadows sagged beneath them.

'At least I didn't give it to my family.' Her voice was weary. 'That's one advantage of a stale marital sex life, I suppose.' Her breath hitched. 'But I did give it to my boss, and he gave it to *his* wife.' She looked up hopelessly. 'At least I won't have to live with that guilt for long.' She shook her head slightly. 'Most of the time it just seems surreal.'

Her hand was shaking as she sipped her tea. That mug would go straight into the bin when she was gone; these days no one would risk reusing a mug touched by someone with Strain II, even if the chances of catching the disease that way were so remote as to be practically impossible. The only good thing about Strain II was that it made the original HIV look almost harmless in comparison.

'How can you be sure that *he* didn't give it to *you*?' Hask asked gently.

'I only slept with him once,' she said. 'It was two weeks after his wife had given birth to their second child – and they were both healthy. Plus, we have regular checks at work, company policy. We'd been out for a drink after work. It was Hallowe'en, and he'd been asking if we should decorate the office, or maybe throw a party. You know, cheer people up a bit.' She chewed her bottom lip, and Hask couldn't stop himself hoping it wouldn't start bleeding.

Ramsey, sitting next to him, had his arms folded. Armstrong had stayed standing by the door. Their body language said everything about how people perceived Strain II victims. Hask let his arms rest on the table and leaned in slightly. This woman was now a pariah, but he at least would do his best not to make her feel like one.

'We ended up back at the office.' She smiled softly. 'It wasn't even all that good, that's the irony. I should have kept him in my fantasy.' Her eyes filled slightly, but she swallowed back the tears with a sniff. 'I'd never been unfaithful before. Not in ten years.'

'DI Ramsey tells me that you believe someone intentionally infected you?'

'Yes.' She coughed – a phlegmy, wet sound – and the room flinched. Michaela Wheeler either didn't notice or was past caring. 'That night – although I didn't really think about it until a nurse on the ward told me what some of the others had been saying.'

'So, a nurse prompted this memory?' Ramsey asked.

Hask knew what the DI was worried about: if they caught whoever was doing this, then her testimony could be ruled invalid. But the whole point was invalid, Hask wanted to say: this woman wasn't going to live long enough to get to trial, not even if they had the offender in custody right now.

'Do carry on,' he said kindly.

'We were standing outside so Bill, my boss, could smoke. Our drinks were on the windowsill. It was quite crowded, and I didn't really notice the man behind me until Bill went in to use the loo – then he came and stood beside me and clinked bottles. He was drinking Stella, like me, and he wished me happy Hallowe'en.' She frowned slightly, lost in the memory. 'I smiled at him, then we both drank. It was after that he said the funny thing – weird funny, not ha-ha.'

'After you drank?' Ramsey asked.

'Yes.'

'And what did he say?' Hask said. 'Exactly, if you can remember.'

'I can remember. I think I'll always remember. He said, "For this is the word of your God. Spread it." It was strange. He walked away after that and I was glad because it was creepy. Then Bill came back, and, well, you know . . . it went out of my head.'

'And you think he might have put something in your beer?' Ramsey was leaning forward now, his curiosity overcoming his fear.

'I'm sure he did. It would have been easy because my bottle was on the windowsill behind me. He was drinking the same beer.'

Hask could see Ramsey visualising the scene. Michaela Wheeler was clearly an intelligent woman, and there was no reason for her to lie.

'What did this man look like?' Hask's nerves tingled. This *was* shaping up to be interesting. He might have to forgive Ramsey after all.

'Respectable,' she said. 'More than respectable, actually. He was thin, but his hair was cut well. He was dressed smartly. He didn't look out of place. Until he spoke I'd have said he was like us, I guess: middle class, relatively successful, doing okay all things considered.'

'Can you give us more physical details?' Ramsey pressed her a little. 'Like how old he was? Skin colour?'

'He was white, early thirties, maybe. Thin, as I said, even

slightly gaunt. Chestnut hair with no grey in it. Short – with a side parting, I think. That's about it.'

'Was he wearing a suit?'

'He had a long overcoat on and just a sweater and shirt underneath, but with smart trousers. He looked like part of the office crowd, but someone doing well. Someone's boss—'

A coughing fit came out of nowhere and her eyes and nose streamed as she desperately tried to clear her lungs. Hask handed her his handkerchief, not that it would help her much. The WPC at the back of the small room looked as if she wanted to climb into the wall.

'I think we've got enough, don't you think?' Hask asked Ramsey.

'We'll get you back to Charing Cross now, Mrs Wheeler,' the DI said. 'Can you organise that, Armstrong?'

The woman recovering her breath looked like she might cry again.

Hask and Ramsey hung back in the corridor as the others left.

'Poor woman,' Hask said. 'She was just in the wrong place at the wrong time. Frightening.'

'That's what this man is banking on, don't you think?'

'Could be,' Hask agreed. 'I think I might take a trip up to the Strain II wing myself in the morning. I want to hear more of these stories before I start evaluating.'

'You sure you want to go up there?' Ramsey asked.

'People work there every day, Detective Inspector, and they don't catch anything. Hysteria is far more infectious than the bug.'

'Yeah,' Ramsey mused as they watched Michaela Wheeler haul herself up the stairs at the other end, oblivious to the

PC waiting for her to get round the corner before he started disinfecting the railing. 'But the bug is pretty damned infectious – and this version is twice as mean.'

Hask thought the American had a point, but there were some things you couldn't learn from hearing stories secondhand. Everyone's perceptions were different, and often what he needed was all in the nuance.

'Do you fancy a beer tomorrow night?' Hask asked.

'Sure,' Ramsey answered cheerfully, 'if you're not checked in to Charing Cross yourself by then.'

'Ha-bloody-ha.'

'Good. I'll give you a call later.'

They left the obvious subject of their pub meeting unsaid; it wasn't necessary. Whenever they were away from work their conversation invariably swung round to trying to figure out what happened to Cassius Jones, and where the hell he might be.

Chapter Three

'You look like a right poof with your hair like that,' Arthur – Artie to his mates – Mullins laughed. 'I wouldn't have recognised you.'

'Good to see you, too.' Cass sat down opposite the old London gangster and smiled. Mac brought in two glasses of brandy from the kitchen before disappearing again and the two men tapped their drinks together before swallowing.

'The boys tell me you've been out and about. Ready to fly the nest, then?'

'I've got things to do. You know how it is.'

'Too right I do.' Mullins was laughing again, a good earthy no-nonsense sound. 'Your life is nothing if not interesting, Jonesy. Fucked-up, maybe, but interesting. I'm getting a passport and driver's licence sorted for you. I'll take some pictures before I go. I'd tell you to make yourself look pretty, but you've already taken care of that. How's the shoulder?'

'Getting there – a way to go until I'm back fighting fit,' he admitted, wiggling the fingers of his left hand. Cass felt a little awkward now, as if the debt of gratitude he owed Artie had changed their relationship. Now he swallowed his pride and said, 'Thanks for everything you've done, Artie. I will pay you back for all this. When I'm sorted.'

'No problem – and technically, *I* didn't do nothing – I might've sent the boys after them, but I kept meself at a safe distance. Better all round, don't you think?'

Cass had no recollection of the events between falling, wounded, into the car with the tramp and the woman, and waking up in a makeshift sickbed in the flat before this one. From what he'd gathered talking to Mac, Artie hadn't been that impressed by the pair's interest in Cass Jones. He'd given them a car, yes – but he'd also had another two following them. No one knew the streets of London like Artie Mullins' men and it hadn't been long before they'd found themselves in a poor CCTV area, when they'd blocked the car in, stuck guns in the strangers' faces and taken Cass. What exactly had happened to the old violinist and the beautiful woman, no one – including Artie – appeared to know. The police hadn't found them; just the abandoned car.

'But why did you do it?' The question had been troubling Cass for as long as his thinking had been clear of his pain-killer fugue state.

'Dunno, really.' Artie Mullins sniffed. 'Call it instinct. Something about them wasn't right. If they was looking out for you, why come through me? Why not call you themselves to get you out of Paddington before they nicked your arse?' He pointed a thick finger at Cass. 'Cos you wouldn't trust 'em, that's why. And if you didn't trust them, then why should I?' He grinned. 'So I let them do the hard bit, and then took over. Figured if they were friends of yours you could find them when you were back on your feet.' His eyes met Cass'. 'They friends of yours?'

'No,' Cass said, then, 'well, maybe. But you were right to think I wouldn't trust them. I think they have their own agenda.' The girl's main interest was Luke, his nephew, abducted at birth – at least, that's what she'd told him on the phone. Cass was just her route to him. Why was his

18

long-lost nephew so important to all these people? The girl and the tramp had to be linked to the Network somehow, he knew that much: maybe not on the inside like Mr Bright, but connected all the same.

'But why did you do this *for me*?' he asked. 'We're technically on opposite sides of the fence. You don't owe me anything like this.'

'That's not how it works though, is it, Jonesy?' The old man leaned back on the armchair. 'Sometimes you've got to know when it's time to take a side. And right now, you're one man against the whole world. You've got no chance: you're so deep in the shit with the Old Bill you're making me look like an upstanding pillar of society.' He lit a cigarette and offered the pack to Cass. 'And more than that, son' – he held out his lighter – 'I don't think you killed those men. Someone is fucking with you, and I just don't think it's fair that they get to have all the cards.'

'You took a big risk, though.'

'The coppers gave me a tug – course they did; you used to collect from me. But what could they say? I didn't drive off with you bleeding in the back seat of my car, did I? They knew that. Plus, after all the shit with Bowman and the bonuses it didn't take much to convince them that you and me had had a severe falling-out. They were more concerned with finding the old man and the girl in the car. I've kept my head down since then. I wouldn't be here if I thought they were still on my case – or even putting too much time and money into finding you, for that matter. Two months is a long time in policing, I don't have to tell you that. They'll be busy managing the fall-out, running around with their arses hanging out.'

'Still – I don't really know what to say.' It was the truth; Cass had never been comfortable with emotional displays –

19

which hadn't helped any of his relationships – and owing anyone rankled. He couldn't help it.

'Don't say anything, just get this shit sorted and then you can pay me back. It'll be a good story to hear the end of, if nothing else. Now let's get these mugshots done. Got the best screever in the business waiting for them – two days and you can walk out of here a new person. All right with you?'

'All right with me, Artie.'

Chapter Four

As he'd moved between the beds on the ward Hask had started sweating behind his mask and inside his gloves. The temperature in this part of the hospital must have been set at somewhere near thirty, and with all the fat coating his bones he was starting to overheat. It wasn't a problem most of the patients shared: several were shivering, despite the medication that was no doubt intended to ease their fevers, and they were nearly all painfully thin. Those who were nearing the end of their run were sedated; little more than breathing cadavers waiting in a haze for their time to run out. He'd walked through the whole ward, spending time not just with those who were newly infected with stories to tell: he needed to try and view them as their killer had.

Once he'd signed the infection waiver form the ward sister had given him the names and bed numbers of those he needed and offered to come with him but he turned her down. She'd fetched him a cup of coffee, though, and squeezed his hand in a thank-you for what he and the police had done for poor Hannah West.

Perhaps that's what was giving him the unusual niggle in his gut, he decided as he waited for Graham Calf to muster enough energy to continue their conversation. The last time he'd been on this ward had been to see Hannah's body. She'd been a nurse on this ward, murdered by the serial killer who called himself 'the Man of Flies'. Being back here on the hunt for another murderer made him feel like they'd somehow come full circle. It also made him miss Cass Jones. Ramsey was good, but he didn't have the hard edge that Jones did, and sometimes that was what was needed. The world was a hard place, and callous eyes were often needed to see the truth of it. Cass Jones had those.

Graham Calf's eyes fluttered open. He was young – twenty-three, according to his medical chart – and he'd been in and out of drug programmes and hostels since he was sixteen. What had happened to Michaela Wheeler, a nice middle-class woman, had made people sit up and take notice. Graham Calf had probably never been noticed in his entire life.

Hask smiled gently and passed the boy – because he really wasn't much more than that – the plastic cup of water from the table. His skeletal arm was so pale it was almost blue.

'He was posh,' Graham Calf continued. He was speaking quietly, but his dry voice cut through the gentle hum and whirr of the machinery that filled the ward. 'Spoke well nice.'

'Were you concerned when he offered you free drugs?' Hask asked. 'That can't happen often.'

'He said it was something new – a smack upgrade. It was cheaper, too. He said if I liked it, then he'd be back round to do a deal.' His eyes wandered to a sad place somewhere in the distance. 'Seemed like a good idea at the time. I was cold and jumping.'

'And what was it he said to you that was unusual?'

'It was after I'd injected; was feeling warmer already. It was a good buzz.' He looked at Hask, who could see his understanding of the irony was clear. 'He stood up and watched me for a second, then pulled his gloves on – I remember wishing he'd given me them as well – and said, "This is the word of your God. Spread it."

'Those were his exact words?'

'Yeah. He said it, and then just walked away. I'd heard about a Jesus freak giving out gear – thought it was just a story, you know?' He smiled sadly. 'But it wasn't just gear he was giving out, was it?'

Ignoring the protocols, Hask squeezed the boy's hand. It was cold, as if his body had already started making preparations for the death that would soon be moving in.

'It wasn't your fault, son.'

Graham Calf didn't answer, but just closed his eyes. Within a minute his breathing had slowed and he was sleeping. Hask didn't bother waking him up – his story and description were the same; he had enough to form some kind of evaluation. He walked to the nurses' station and then turned to look at the patients. There was no hope in this ward. He was aware of the power of being healthy among so many who'd had health stripped from them. Was that what *he* felt, that power? Is that what drove this killer? Hask dismissed the thought: this was both more and less complex than that, depending on how you looked at it.

'How do you cope with working in this environment?' he asked the ward sister, who smiled up from her paperwork. He imagined a lot of the nurses working here were on some variety of anti-depressant. That, or they had the natures of angels. He'd only been on the ward an hour and he could feel the emotional strain dragging him down. 'How do *they* cope?' he added.

'Strangely, most of them aren't bitter – the junkies and homeless,' she said. 'That helps us, because they don't attack or lash out at us; they know we're trying to help. But it's terribly sad for them. I think they feel like it was their fate – they made their peace with it before it ever found them. Some people feel they have no value, I suppose.' Her eyes strayed to the far end of the ward, where some of the newer cases were separated by a curtain. 'It's worse for them. The bug is something that happens to other people in their world.'

'Not any more,' Hask said. 'I think you're going to find you have far more referrals like Mrs Wheeler.'

'Who would do such a thing, to infect people on purpose? So callously?'

It was strange to hear her use the word he had just thought of in conjunction with Cass Jones. Well, the ex-DI was a killer, that was a matter of record, but he wasn't like this one. They were different breeds entirely.

'I will never be surprised by the actions of men,' he said. 'Or women, for that matter.' He smiled. 'But sometimes those surprises can be pleasant. Don't forget that.'

He left her and made his own way out, dumping his gloves and mask in the bins at the door. He emerged from the hospital and, once outside its gates, sucked in the cold London air. It was good to be away from the quietly claustrophobic ward where he could practically *taste* death in the air. Here on the street, life and energy buzzed.

He watched the passers-by. Too many of them were smart men with neatly cut brown hair. The invisible attacker could be any one of them. A chill that had nothing to do with the crisp December morning settled in his spine. He found the idea of such a man stalking the streets and infecting strangers disconcerting. The media would whip the public up into hysteria when the story broke.

He sighed, his breath a stream of mist that reassured him of his continuing existence, and as he began to walk he tried to keep space between himself and the other pedestrians. God, he wished he were back in Sweden. London, for all the huge fees he was earning, was providing him with far more excitement than he'd ever desired.

Chapter Five

By lunchtime, Cass was walking through Oxford. When he'd told Mac he was going out for the day, he'd expected more of an argument from him and the rest of Artie Mullins' henchmen, but it looked like they were all happy to have the day off from babysitting him. Tomorrow he'd have his new identity; then he'd be free as a bird, so he figured they were seeing this as practice, maybe something like day release for long-term prisoners. It was one thing minding a bedridden patient who slept most of the day, but trying to tell a fully grown healthy alpha male what to do was too much like hard work, even if Mullins had given them their orders. Mac had put it succinctly just that morning when he'd growled, 'How am I supposed to keep you inside? Put another bullet in you? That would somewhat defeat the purpose, don't you think?'

Away from the capital, Cass felt the knots in his back start to loosen and he allowed himself to take in the skyline of the historic city. The freedom was strange: London was his home, and he loved it, but right now the city itself felt like his enemy: the mass of CCTV cameras, the heightened security since 26/09, meaning more police on the streets – not to mention the fact that just about every copper in London wanted to be the one to bring him in, the great DI Cass Jones, the whistle-blower, now wanted on two counts of murder. He couldn't blame them – he'd probably feel the same in their situation. At least the story of what he'd done undercover hadn't come out in the papers yet; that was one small mercy. He was quite sure he'd be portrayed as the devil incarnate if it did, but someone was making sure a tight lid was kept on that. He laughed at the irony: it was the only murder of the three he'd been fingered for that he'd actually committed.

He picked up an Oxford *A–Z* at a newsagent's and found his way to the address on the piece of paper Father Michael had given him the previous day. He'd been walking for at least an hour, and on top of the train and bus journey all the movement had left his shoulder throbbing. He felt exhausted. He hadn't done anything more than shuffle around a flat for the best part of two months and he was weak as a kitten. He didn't like it: if he was going to find Luke and take on Mr Bright and The Bank, he was going to need all his strength.

'Jesus,' he muttered as he took in the view. If the exterior of the house was anything to go by, then Father Michael's '*he may just be a crackpot*' evaluation of Dr Stuart Cornell was a massive understatement. The building itself was a pleasant enough terraced house with its own small front garden. Unlike those around it, however, there were no pot plants, or stretches of pleasantly coloured gravel tidily filling the gap between the street and the front door. The garden of Number 29 was a mass of waist-high weeds that had forced their way through the cracked paving slabs. At least they went some way to hiding the tyres and battered metal bins that littered the space. Beyond them, the bay window was an equally unprepossessing sight. The filthy paint was peeling off the rotting wood, and the glass was black on both sides, mud outside and what looked like layers of nicotine on the inside. The tattered net curtain was entirely redundant.

He didn't bother with the grime-coated bell – there wasn't a hope in hell it would work – but instead rapped loudly on the door. He left it a few moments and then rapped again, and this time he heard a shuffling on the other side, and the sound of paper being moved.

'If you're from the council, then you can go away. They came yesterday.'

The voice was well spoken, not the Fagin Cass had been expecting from the wrecked front of the house, but there was a tremble there that he recognised instantly: fear and paranoia. This was someone not used to talking to strangers – or talking much at all.

'I'm not from the council, Mr Cornell, I wanted to ask you—'

'*Dr* Cornell. I have a PhD. I'm a *doctor*. You can't keep coming round here. I have important work—' The fragile voice was becoming more agitated. Cass slowed his own speech right down as he leaned in closer. 'I'm just a visitor, Dr Cornell. I wanted to ask you some questions about someone.'

'This is a trick so you can get in and take my things away.'

'Honestly, I promise you, Dr Cornell, I'm not from the council.' The outside of the house was a good indicator of the state of the inside. He didn't envy whoever would eventually get in to clear out the clutter. This one was a hoarder. There was a need in the sharp edge of his voice that suggested someone desperate to make sense of things that they'd overthought. There were plenty like him among the lonely in London, people tucked away with nothing but piles of junk for company. Maybe he'd come a long way for nothing.

'Who do you want to talk about?' Dr Cornell asked plaintively. 'I don't know anyone around here. They don't talk to me.'

Cass was willing to bet the neighbours gave this blight on their pleasant landscape a wide berth. They might not speak to him face to face, but they'd sure as hell be on the phone to the council, the police, anyone who would listen, demanding they *get something done about him.*

'Alan Jones,' Cass said. Across the road a young woman pushing a pram along the pavement stared over at him. He kept his face turned towards the door. He didn't need any unwelcome attention.

'Hello?' There was silence on the other side of the door and Cass gritted his teeth in frustration. This negotiation was shaping up to take some time – time that Cass didn't want to spend standing out on a doorstep with passers-by watching his every move. The last thing he needed was for someone to call the police because the crazy old man at Number 29 was being bullied by some bastard who wouldn't leave him alone.

'Go away.' The aggressive edge was gone; Dr Cornell now sounded like a schoolkid, not sure if his friends were taking the piss or being serious.

Cass leaned in closer, his nostrils filling with the scents of rotting paint and damp wood. Being anonymous wasn't going to work with Dr Cornell. The man was too paranoid. 'I'm Alan and Evie Jones' son,' he said quietly.

'Their son's dead. I read it.' More shuffling on the other side. 'I read it in the papers. He's dead. All of his family.'

'I'm their other son. Now please let me in – I need your help.' He didn't want to think about what state his life had come to if he was begging an old recluse like Dr Cornell for help. He pressed his ear against the door and listened. If Dr Cornell was calling the police then he had about ten minutes to get away. This was a residential area, and his running wasn't up to much with his shoulder as damaged as it was – not that running would do him much good against a search helicopter. Basically, if Dr Cornell *was* ringing the police, then he was well and truly fucked. The only thing he could hope for was that Dr Cornell had a reputation for being a mad old time-waster and whoever took the call wouldn't pay him any attention.

The seconds ticked by. Finally there was a rasping screech and a bolt was pulled back on the other side, then keys were turned and chains were unhooked and, eventually, the door opened an inch. Cass stared into the suspicious faded blue eye that peered out.

'You'd better come in then,' Dr Cornell said after a long moment, and opened the door only just wide enough for Cass to get through, then slammed the door shut on the outside world and set to work resecuring his home. Cass looked down the corridor. The walls were lined with paper-stuffed carrier bags and piles of newspapers.

'I haven't sorted those yet.' Dr Cornell still had his back to Cass as he turned the last of the keys, so he must have expected a reaction.

Cass was surprised to find the lights were on and it was warm inside; somehow he was still paying his utility bills. The man's appearance was a surprise too; though his clothes were worn, they looked clean enough, and he was clean-shaven. How he managed it amidst all this mess, Cass couldn't figure out. Maybe the upstairs of the house was normal. He doubted it somehow.

'Come into my study.' The old man led him down the

corridor. 'You should be hiding. They'll all be looking for you, you know.'

Cass didn't answer. It didn't surprise him that Dr Cornell knew about his problems, not with this many newspapers filling the hallway.

'What are you looking for in all this?' he asked.

'Information.' Dr Cornell waved him into a room on the left and busied himself removing papers from a buried armchair before nodding Cass into it. As he started clearing a second for himself Cass looked at the towering piles of books and papers surrounding him: he could see natural history, geography, astronomy, astrology, religion, even the history of Christianity. Some were so old he couldn't distinguish the titles. There were folders, too, with handwritten labels: New York, Syria, the Middle East, Moscow, and the largest had London printed on a tatty sheet of paper and underlined several times in felt-tip pen. But it was at the wall opposite Cass found himself staring longest. It was covered in photographs and news-paper cuttings, pinned and Sellotaped and Blu-Tacked, with barely a scrap of wallpaper visible beneath the mass of paperwork.

Could that really be—? Cass stood up and took a closer look; it was definitely Mr Bright and Mr Solomon, together in one photograph. The two men were walking side by side across an airstrip. Both had hair slicked back in side partings and their suits had a baggy quality that belonged in the nineteen forties. They were tilting their heads towards each other and talking intently.

He scanned the rest of the clippings. They covered every-thing from the formation of The Bank to old reports of the Jack the Ripper slayings, an apparently random mix of political, business and criminal news. Surely Dr Cornell couldn't believe that the Network had been involved in all these things?

He looked back at the newspaper pictures and photographs. There were some of men he didn't recognise, but one of Mr Bright and another man had been taken in New York, perhaps in the sixties, and there was a very old copy of a photograph from around the start of the twentieth century, of Mr Bright and Mr Solomon standing on either side of a tall, broad, dark-haired man. Cass could see he was strikingly handsome, despite the grainy quality of the image and his ageing face. The three were laughing at the camera as if they had just been told the biggest joke. Cass frowned. Where were they?

'That was the opening of the London stock exchange in 1854. It had just been rebuilt,' Dr Cornell said, as if reading Cass' mind. 'The one in the middle – I've had no sightings of him for years, not much after the turn of the century.' He stood close enough that Cass could smell the mint on his breath. At least he brushed.

'He's the one, though: the key figure – the leader, if they have one. Although Castor Bright seems to have stepped into his shoes. It's hard to get photos now. I don't go out, not any more. And they're more careful.' Stuart Cornell's eye twitched and he turned away from the board. He picked up a bottle and found two glasses behind a stack of box-files and poured them both a drink.

'They want to take my papers. My evidence. They always say they're from the council, but I know better.' The old man tapped the side of his nose.

The glass looked clean enough and Cass figured he had enough antibiotics racing round his system to cope with any unwelcome bacteria. He *needed* the drink – he felt almost breathless. Here was someone else who knew about

31

Mr Bright and the strangeness that surrounded him. He took a long sip of the whisky. What would Dr Cornell have thought if he'd seen how Mr Solomon had died? Most likely that would have completely tipped him into madness ...

He looked closely at the old man. There was no glow in his eyes, not even a flicker of silver like he'd seen in Hayley Porter's mother's. Whatever the gold and silver lights meant, they were no part of Dr Cornell's life.

They want to take my papers. Cass was pretty sure he knew who the professor meant by *they*: the same *they* his dead brother Christian had been referring to in the note he left Cass: *THEY took Luke. They* was the Network. Whichever way life twisted and turned, it always came back to Mr Bright and the Network. He smiled grimly to himself. Looking at the mess here, in Dr Cornell's case, it might well be the council.

'Why were you so fascinated with my father?' he asked.

The professor sat in his chair beneath the pictures of the men who held both Cass and him in their thrall and sipped his drink. 'Why are you so fascinated by my fascination?'

The eyes were sharp. This was going to be trickier than Cass had first expected, when he'd arrived and seen the state of the place. Dr Stuart Cornell was not the nutjob he'd first imagined, nor was he totally delusional. And he was obviously capable of insightful thought. But he was para-noid – though Cass knew he had good reason to be – and what he didn't want to do was push the man over the edge.

'Was it because of his association with this man?' Cass pulled out one of his own pictures, the photograph of his parents with Castor Bright. 'The man you have all over your wall?' His photo had been taken in South Africa, before he was even born. Cass had found it in the envelope Christian had left for him at their parents' house. In the picture, the

three were standing under a sign that read THE
SOLOMON AND BRIGHT MINING CORPS.

Dr Cornell scrabbled for the picture, but Cass held it
firm. A slightly manic light had gone on in the man's eyes
and Cass doubted he would ever give the photo back if he
handed it over. He compromised, holding it close to the
professor's face and letting him study it before putting it
back in his pocket.

'Nothing is true,' Dr Cornell said finally, leaning back in
his chair. 'The world is on its head.'

'What do you know about Mr Bright and the Network?
Why are they so interested in my family?'

'They've really played you, haven't they?' Dr Cornell
laughed slightly. 'I've been watching.'

'But who are *they*?'

Dr Cornell raised his glass, then lowered it without drinking and got to his feet. He started pacing in the small cleared
area. The agitations were clearly returning.

'Things have changed. Since that one disappeared.' He
jabbed a finger at the image of the stranger between Mr
Bright and Mr Solomon on his wall. 'The whole world's
changed, can't you feel it? So many advances, and yet a sense
that it's all crumbling, don't you think?'

Cass shrugged slightly as Dr Cornell stared at him for a
response.

'I think they're starting to come unstuck. They've never
looked outside of themselves before – not like they did with
your father and mother.'

'And what about my father and mother?' He needed to
try and follow Dr Cornell's track.

'You're looking at the details.' Dr Cornell's head twitched
in a rapid shake. 'All wrong. You need to look at the forest,
not the trees.'

Cass wondered how a man who lived like this, who was obsessed with the details, could make a statement like that.

'The thing is, I don't really care about the forest – the bigger picture; whatever it is that has brought you to this.' Cass gestured at the mass of information that surrounded them. 'Mr Bright took something that belongs with me, and I want it back. And I want to fuck with him and his Bank a little along the way. What I want to know, and I think you can help me here, is why my family is so important to him? You were pretty much stalking my dad for a while, but I'm guessing he wasn't the real focus of your attention.' Cass spoke calmly and stared at Dr Cornell, trying to focus him.

It seemed to work.

'I don't know why *your* family exactly. Back then I had two other people researching with me. They're gone now.' The professor's face darkened. 'We knew they were looking for someone – someone special. They'd been looking for a long time, since that one in the middle disappeared from sight. Others had vanished before, but not like him. They became more active after that.' He jabbed a finger at Cass. 'I tried to warn your father, I really did. First of all in the Middle East when I was on a research trip, but they were starting to lure him in by then. I even went to South Africa, but I couldn't get near them, neither he nor your mother. Bright made sure of that.'

Dr Cornell perched on the arm of his chair. 'When he moved back to England and settled in Capel-le-Ferne, I knew he must have had some kind of falling-out with Mr Bright and his people. I thought then that maybe he'd join me in trying to get to the truth.' His jaw clenched. 'I needed someone like him, someone who'd been on the inside – who could maybe get back inside for me.' He let out a long, tense sigh. 'It didn't happen. He wouldn't even speak to me – just

34

called the police every time I was within a mile of him.'

His father had made a deal with Mr Bright – he had sacrificed his grandson Luke – for the freedom of his immediate family, so Cass wasn't at all surprised that Alan Jones had kept away from Dr Cornell. He would have been desperate not to upset the balance of the bargain he'd struck, and every time Dr Cornell showed up it would have reminded him of the terrible thing he'd promised to do. Cass' stomach churned with mixed emotions. Cass was of the opinion that Alan Jones had probably been a better person – or at least a more honest one – before he'd found religion and started forgiving everyone for everything. He wondered if his father ever realised that the only person he was really trying to forgive was himself.

'They destroyed me.' Dr Cornell's voice had dropped and now he was almost whispering. 'They got me discredited at the university, made me a laughing stock, leaking some of my research in dribs and drabs so it looked ridiculous. Everyone was saying that I was like David Icke, talking about crazy alien conspiracies, and by the time my paper was ready, no one would look at it.'

'Alien conspiracies?' Even with everything he had seen with Mr Bright and Mr Solomon, that was a claim too far. He almost smiled.

'Everything's perspective,' Dr Cornell muttered. '*Everything*. What you see depends on what you believe. It's all semantics. We live in a world built on a lie. You have to approach everything you see from that starting point. *Nothing is as it seems.*'

'What lie?'

'If you find the truth, then you will have the power to destroy them.'

'The truth about the Network? The Bank? What?' Cass'

head was starting to hurt. They were talking at cross-purposes. He'd hoped to get answers, but all the professor had been able to deliver were riddles.

'The Bank?' Dr Cornell's eyes were alight with a new fire. 'The Bank is nothing – it's a front, a useful tool, that's all. They have always had things like The Bank – perhaps not so global, but other institutions, just the same. But you can use it to dig into them, or *at* them, if you can get inside. Your brother was, wasn't he?'

Cass didn't like seeing Dr Cornell talking about Christian with that mad gleam in his eyes. Christian was better than the Dr Cornells of this world. He nodded anyway.

'Christian understood that everyone leaves a trace these days. Everything is recorded; everything is linked. The Network is Networked.' Dr Cornell giggled slightly at his own joke, but Cass thought of his brother's laptop, and the Redemption file he'd found hidden on it, containing all the information on his family and others . . . and the X accounts. He wouldn't share those with Dr Cornell, though: he was here to *get* information, not give it.

'You can cause a headache via The Bank,' Dr Cornell continued, 'but it's the *truth* you need. You need to find the truth and spread it right out across the world. Take us out of the darkness of their deceit.' Flecks of spit foamed at the corners of his mouth and his hands trembled as he gesticulated.

Cass was starting to feel claustrophobic in the over-warm house. 'But what *is* the truth?' he asked. 'What am I supposed to be looking for?'

'They don't age, have you noticed?' Dr Cornell was up on his feet and staring at the photos. The energy had dropped from his voice, leaving the air still, like a brief pause in a storm. 'Something's happening to them, and that's touching us all. Maybe they die, but they don't age – apart from that one in the middle. He'd started to age, just before he disappeared.'

Cass thought of his own meetings with Mr Bright and how he'd looked identical to the old photos taken with his parents. Dr Cornell had gathered pictures that were far older, and still the silver-haired man remained unchanged. The X accounts held information going back even further. Just how old *was* Mr Bright? The eyes twinkling back from so many images on the wall held on to their secrets.

'There are four sets of scrolls.' Dr Cornell turned suddenly. 'Hidden in four different locations important to them. These scrolls tell the real story of man's history – *our* history. Find the scrolls,' he said, 'and you've got the answers.'

'But where are they hidden? And what proof do you have that they even exist?' Cass finished his drink. The problem with talking to obsessives like Dr Cornell was that they built fantasies out of the facts they gathered. That there was a conspiracy at work, Cass was in no doubt, but all this stuff about stories and scrolls? Maybe it was craziness and maybe not, but it was hard to tell the difference. As interesting as this hunt might turn out to be, Cass' main interest was finding Luke. Everything else was secondary.

'Who are you, anyway?' Dr Cornell frowned as the paranoia borne out of his obsession took control. 'You haven't shown me anything to prove you're Alan Jones' son.'

'I can't. I don't have anything,' Cass said. 'I'm– I'm on the run. You know that. Remember?'

'I want you to leave.' Meanness glinted like shards of broken glass in the professor's eyes. 'You're not with the council – maybe you're with *them*. I want you to leave now.'

Cass' nerves tightened and he stood up. Dr Cornell was

afraid – it was clear that was where the sudden aggression was coming from – but Cass had a healthy respect for the violence the unbalanced and scared could do. He was in no physical condition for fighting a sane old man, let alone this one. And Dr Cornell wasn't small.

'I'm going.' He held his hands up in supplication. 'But can I come back? I'd like to talk to you some more about all this.' Somewhere in the middle of this junk he was sure there would be something of use against Mr Bright.

'You're not from the council.' Dr Cornell leaned in closer. 'What are you doing here?'

'I never said I was, Dr Cornell. I'm Alan Jones' son.'

'Get out of my house!' The words flew at Cass' face in a spray of spit.

Cass didn't wait any longer but headed straight for the front door, He half-expected Dr Cornell to stab him in the back with a letter-opener while he negotiated the locks and bolts, but the old man stayed in his study, muttering to himself.

Finally back outside, surveying the mess of the front garden, Cass paused to light a cigarette. From the other side of the front door came the sounds of the strange old professor resecuring his property. Cass blew a long stream of smoke out into the cold air and let his thoughts settle. He might not have got the answers he'd hoped for, but the meeting had certainly raised some interesting questions. It had also helped formulate his growing plan. One thing was for certain, he was going to need some help.

Chapter Six

'I thought DI Ramsey was just here for the Jones case?' Sergeant Toby Armstrong closed the door of the small conference room behind him. 'No offence, sir.' The sergeant nodded the brief apology at the American who was already seated, and then looked back at DCI Heddings, at the head of the table. Hask watched the game play out: it was clear that Armstrong didn't entirely trust Ramsey, and Hask couldn't blame him for that. Charles Ramsey hadn't been exactly over-committed to Cass Jones' guilt, despite the impressive array of evidence Armstrong had gathered.

In some ways, Hask felt sorry for the young DS. He was finding out that doing the right thing didn't always win you friends or gratitude. There were plenty among Heddings' superiors who would have been happy to see Cass Jones go – but with early retirement, not like this. Where there had been a mess of corruption that was at least slightly balanced by a few straight coppers, it now looked like the force was filled with drug-dealers, bung-takers and murderers, all playing out their vendettas against each other. There might not have been any choice but to follow up on Armstrong's information, but there were plenty who wished the young DS had just kept his nose out of everyone else's business. So Armstrong had done his job, and now he was getting kicked in the teeth for it. It was no wonder that he clearly hated Cass even more for that. Maybe when he got older he'd see that he and Cass were perhaps not so different.

'This isn't just a Paddington case.' DCI Heddings waved Armstrong towards a seat. 'Whatever information the excellent – and *very* expensive – doctor here can give us will be going out to all the stations across the city.'

Hask knew it was more than that. Both Heddings and the Chief Superintendent liked having Ramsey around. Those from outside were apparently more trustworthy than those from within.

'Let's get started then, shall we?' Hask smiled.

Heddings turned the digital recorder on. 'Whenever you're ready.'

'Let's get the basics out of the way. We already have the description, from those infected by our man: he's a white male, slim, average height – no more than five feet eleven. Mid-thirties. Brown hair, well cut, and well dressed.'

'We've got an e-fit being done now,' Ramsey said. 'It should be ready to go out with your analysis. That description does cover quite a chunk of the population though, so I'm not holding out much hope for it bringing a suspect in.'

'When it's done get it over to Michaela Wheeler and the other witnesses at Charing Cross Hospital,' Heddings said. 'We want it as exact as possible. Perhaps seeing the likeness will prompt the memory of a more distinguishing feature like a mole or something.' He nodded at Hask to continue.

'His approach to murder is interesting. He's clearly a serial killer – he *has* murdered Michaela Wheeler and the other victims – but unlike other serial killers he's left them alive. He doesn't have a need to *watch* their decline. For most serial murderers, seeing the victim suffer is a key part of the process. It's where they get their satisfaction – we know that some will keep their victims locked up alive for several days before finally disposing of them. This one has no such inclination that we know of. Nor does he take any mementos, and that is also unusual. Most killers like to have something belonging to their victims, in order to relive the event when they're alone. There's also no evidence of sexual motivation for his actions. Most serials will get some form of sexual gratification from what they do.'

'So what does that tell us?' Ramsey asked.

'He's a cold person: he lacks passion. I would say he was capable, but detached. I'd hazard a guess that he has a job with plenty of responsibility but isn't well liked in his workplace. He's ruthlessly efficient, though – let's not forget the secondary victims. He sees those as his, too, and he's never even met them, or apparently felt the need to.'

'Secondary victims?' Armstrong frowned.

'Those people his victims have infected: the family of Wheeler's lover, for example. Every person anyone he's infected has slept with, or shared a needle with, and then the people *they've* slept with, etc., etc. Don't you see? The secondary victims are the *point* of what he's doing.'

'How?'

'Think about what he says to them. "This is the word of your God. Spread it." Every one of the victims we know about says he used those words. It's as if he's using these primaries as disciples; he's sending them out to kill for him. However, the original word of God was supposed to spread love. This one spreads death.'

'Does he think he's God? Superiority complex?' Ramsey leaned forward.

'He definitely has a superiority complex; his disregard for the lives of others shows that, especially given how clinically he's killing them. But he doesn't say he *is* God; he says, "This is the word of *your* God", not "this is *my* word".' Hask paced

41

in front of the table as his mind focused on the unknown man. 'Of course, he could mean himself as God and it's just his phrasing that's ambiguous. Or he could be passing a comment on the very nature of God and his relationship with man. Perhaps he feels that this death – and let's not forget the fear that comes with it; I'll be coming back to that – is exactly what God really wants for us.'

'So he's religious?'

'Ah, don't be too hasty: there's no denying the religious connotations here – he started off moving around the sick and vulnerable, giving them what they thought they wanted, so he's certainly set himself up as a Jesus-style figure. But I can't help feeling that there's something very tongue-in-cheek about it all. If he ever *had* religion, I think it was long ago. These acts aren't borne out of an anger at God, either. If he had anger, then by its very nature that would imply a belief. I can't help but feel that it's more like the whole thing is entertaining him.'

'Spreading the bug throughout the population is *entertaining* him? Jesus.' Ramsey looked up. 'No pun intended.'

'Do you remember the Man of Flies killer? How he left "Nothing is Sacred" written on the victims?'

'Of course.'

'He was sending a message: he wanted someone to figure out what he meant. He was making a point. This one is different. I get the feeling this is a private joke solely for him. In his head he's parodying a serial killer for his own amusement.' He paused. 'Of course that still makes him a serial killer; it's just that his motivations are very different from the normal. I doubt he sees himself a serial killer – that would be beneath him.'

'So he started off infecting the junkies and homeless,'

Heddings said, 'but why move on to people like Michaela Wheeler?'

'There's one thing we have to keep in mind here. I think we can presume he himself is infected with the bug.'

'So he's angry with these people? He blames them or their ilk for infecting him?'

'He's not acting out of obvious anger; there's no vicious-ness in what he does. He doesn't *hurt* people and then infect them. There's clearly a deep-seated bitterness, but he probably isn't even aware of it; I doubt he spends a lot of time analysing his negative emotions. This is a hugely arrogant man, one who is used to being in control. Thanks to the bug, his life is now completely *out* of his control. By spreading the disease, he is gaining some form of control back – if not over his own remaining life, over the lives of others.'

'We need to check any new diagnoses of Strain II over the past – let's say six months.' Ramsey looked at the sergeant. 'Somewhere there's a doctor or hospital managing his symp-toms. And if he's as middle class as his appearance suggests, then there won't be too many fitting his bill. I know the numbers have gone up dramatically in the past month or so, but if the spread was started by him then he'll have been diagnosed well before that.'

'Exactly,' Hask said. 'And as for why he's moved up into a different society grouping – I think he wants to be noticed. All serial killers do, and though he might not think of himself as one, we know better. I don't think he cares about *your* reactions to him, but he definitely cares about society's. Perhaps he started out with his: "This is the word of your God. Spread it," message as a joke to himself, but as time has passed he's either come to believe it, or come to realise its potency. Or both.'

'At least if he's infected, then there's a time limit on the damage the bastard can do,' Heddings said. 'He's got to get too sick for this soon, surely?'

'Yes, the upside is that he'll die. The downside, unfortunately, is that the sicker he becomes, the more he's going to want to spread the disease. What's been a relative hobby for him could become something far more driven. The damage he could do if we don't find him is quite terrifying.' He took a long breath. 'And that brings me to my final point. This isn't just about spreading the disease – maybe it was to start with, but not any more, not since he began infecting people like Michaela Wheeler. This is about spreading the *fear*.' He looked at the Detective Chief Inspector. 'I presume you know you can't contain any of this? If the nurses at Charing Cross know, and this profile is going to go out to all the stations, then I give it forty-eight hours tops before the papers are running the story. There's already the start of a panic over the increase in cases – I've seen people in masks like in the early bird flu days – and if this gets out the population will become hysterical. It certainly won't be pretty.'

'It has crossed my mind.' Heddings looked tired at the thought of what was to come.

'To sum up: you're looking for a male who fits the physical description. He's probably single, and will have recently quit a relatively high-powered job. I say "quit" because the big companies are becoming increasingly like the police – they test their employees regularly, every month or every other month. So he was either diagnosed by his workplace, or privately, but either way he will have had to quit. My bet is that he was diagnosed privately – he's strikes me as a man too much in control to allow his employers to know something like that about him first. He would rather resign of his own free will. He doesn't have many friends. Perhaps he once had some religious affiliations, but not for some time. He's far more interested in his own power than that of any higher authority. He's not a drug user. He will have been infected sexually, but not through a typical relationship; I would expect from a sex worker.'

'Don't you think that's odd, though?' Armstrong asked. 'I mean, if he's so controlled, then why the hell didn't he wear a condom?'

'The same question has been bothering me, and I don't have a clear answer. If I had to put money on it, I'd say his sexual preferences were for those underage – and I mean *very* underage. I think the purity would attract him, as well as the sense of power it would give him. Perhaps he didn't think he needed protection with a child.'

'Get on those diagnoses too.' Armstrong was already writing as Ramsey spoke out loud. 'There can't be that many new cases among children.'

'This man sounds more charming by the second.' Heddings had aged in the course of the briefing. 'I'll speak to the boss, but I expect we'll be organising a press conference for tomorrow morning. It's best this comes from us than via a leaked source.'

'It's going to be chaos out there,' Hask said softly.

No one disagreed.

Chapter Seven

'I don't see why you're insisting on showing this again.' Mr Bright sipped his coffee. 'We saw it two months ago.' He kept his tone light and his gaze steady as the TV screen replayed the images.

'Perhaps if we keep showing you,' Mr Craven sneered, 'then you'll actually start to believe what you're seeing instead of just ignoring it and hoping it will go away.'

Mr Bright smiled. Mr Craven did not look well. It was no secret that the Dying had found him, and though Mr Bright always felt the loss of one of their number, he wondered if he'd grieve at all for Mr Craven. There had always been something decidedly unpleasant about him. Solomon had never liked him; said he was too similar in nature to *him*. He didn't have *his* strength of course, but the cruelty for cruelty's sake was definitely there. Still, the Dying was the Dying, and despite his exterior cool, Mr Craven would be feeling the fear. No wonder he was so absorbed by the people in the film.

The fear, Mr Bright had discovered, was proving dangerous. In recent weeks he'd felt his grip starting to loosen slightly. There were far too many murmurs of dissent making their way back to him. The cohorts weren't meeting regularly; it was becoming an 'each to their own' situation, and perhaps the only thing unifying them was the growing belief that Mr Bright was no longer up to the job. The loss of Mr Bellew had not helped. He had been a general back in the old days, and many had followed because he had encouraged them.

Mr Bright had tried to keep a lid on the true story of Mr Bellew's fall, but the rumours were rife and many were now staring at him with visions of *coup* in their eyes. He looked again at Mr Craven's pale, thin cheeks. Thus far they'd avoided the promotion of a new fourth to the Inner Council, but when Mr Craven went, new members would be unavoidable, and the First Cohort was not currently over-flowing with friendly faces. He wondered how any of them had the arrogance to think they could do any better than he could.

His delicate coffee cup still in his hand, Mr Bright let his gaze drift back up to the screen. There he was, Detective Inspector Cassius Jones, tumbling into the back of the car that had screeched to a halt at the end of the road by the building site. The door flew open and he was pulled inside. It was the same CCTV footage that the police had studied, but they wouldn't have seen what Mr Bright was seeing and what had disturbed the others so much. The Brightness – the *Glow* – it poured across the screen from the driver's seat, and when the door opened for Jones to get in, more gold streamed out.

'We know it's an emissary,' Mr Bright said. 'There were already rumours of one. I don't see why you are so fixated on this as if it were some kind of surprise.'

'Come, come.' Mr Dublin smiled gently. 'It's not that simple, is it, Mr Bright? There has never been an emissary here before – they have been rumours only, the stuff of myths and legends.' He sat down, careful not to crease his linen suit. 'And I know as well as you do that most of those rumours were started in one or other of your offices to keep us all toeing the line. I always respected that.'

He flicked a finger in the direction of the still image. 'But this? This is not a creation of your mind. This really is an emissary. And if an emissary is here, then perhaps *he* isn't far behind.'

'I understand your concerns, Mr Dublin.' Mr Bright maintained the twinkle in his eyes despite his exhaustion. Why did they think they needed to tell him what to do? He had always been the thinker; he was always ahead. He was the Architect.

'Of course we need to find out what the emissary wants,' he said. 'Clearly they are not here to speak with us, or they would have come directly. Perhaps *he* is just curious to see how we have got along in all this time. Maybe *he's* having a moment of boredom. The emissary may well leave without ever contacting us.' He carefully put his saucer down on the desk. 'I am, of course, doing all I can to locate them, but as you can imagine, that is not the easiest task.'

'Why would they save Cassius Jones? Why would the emissary even know who he is?' Mr Dublin's voice was as soft and languid as ever, but Mr Bright was not fooled by it. He had the bit between his teeth, and he wasn't going to let go simply because of some reassuring words.

'Perhaps it's something to do with the elusive child?' Mr Dublin finished.

'Perhaps,' Mr Bright said. There was no point in denying the possibility.

'And what did you do with the child, Mr Bright?' Mr Dublin asked. 'His existence used to be a matter of record, at least for the Inner Cohort. What made you decide to hide him away? Or did he die?' Mr Dublin leaned forward. 'I don't wish to be challenging. I haven't always agreed

48

with you, but I have always respected our order. However, I cannot help but wonder at the wisdom of having the location and condition of the boy known only by you.' He paused. 'He may boost morale if you could perhaps show him, at least to us. Explain his importance.'

'That isn't possible at this moment in time.' Mr Bright had known that this was coming. He could understand them resenting his secrets, but he had promised the First before he slept that he would do what was necessary, and that did not include sharing their plans with the cohorts. Plus, he was tired of the weight of their expectations. Currently the child was merely a rumour; to make him more than that at this stage could be foolish. If he unveiled his plans and they didn't work, then the child would become another nail in his coffin.

'I don't care about the child,' Mr Craven snapped. Mr Bright was sure there were flecks of blood in the spray of spit that flew out with the words. 'You're missing the point.'

'And that is?' Mr Dublin asked. Small lines pinched at his naturally smooth face. Mr Dublin was clearly no more fond of Mr Craven than Mr Bright was.

'The emissary is *here*. If the emissary can get *here*, then why can't we find the Walkways to get back? What is going wrong with the Experiment? If we can find the emissary, then maybe we can find a way home.'

'This is home,' Mr Bright said.

'No.' Mr Craven shook his head vehemently, '*This* was a mistake. We should never have fled.'

'You were young. I think perhaps your memory of events is no longer clear.'

'With all due respect' – Mr Craven's face fell somewhat short of a smile – 'you and I are in very different positions. And I am not alone, as you know. The Dying is coming to all of us – even you, Mr Bright, one day. You won't be so keen to stay here then.' He let out a long breath and the stink made Mr Bright grimace.

'I think mad Mr Solomon was right.' The fight had gone from Mr Craven's voice and now he spoke as if only to himself. 'This whole place is dying. Mr DeVore says the Interventionists are barely projecting any more. The data stream is a jumble of darkness and infrequent nonsense images.'

'Don't be so dramatic,' Mr Dublin cut in before Mr Bright could. 'We know that the Interventionists are having their own problems. They've been changing since they arrived – this could be another phase for them.'

Mr Craven snorted. 'The only difference between the Interventionists and us is that they *want* to be dying. If I have to die, I don't want to do it here, not like this. Not so *small*.'

'Please.' Mr Bright raised his hands. 'This is getting us nowhere. We're all agreed we need to find the emissary; that must be our priority.' He flashed a look at Mr Craven. 'And just because the emissary has *got* here, it doesn't mean she knows the way back.'

The phone on the desk rang and Mr Bright stared at both Mr Dublin and Mr Craven for a second before answering. Whatever the call was, at least it had ended the difficult conversation.

He listened to the excited speaker and then smiled. 'Excellent,' he said. 'We'll be there shortly.' He put the receiver down and allowed for a moment's dramatic pause.

'Well, gentlemen.' His eyes twinkled and golden *Glow* sparkled triumphantly at the edges. 'It appears that the First has woken.'

Chapter Eight

They were in the pub by half-five, but night had fallen so heavily that by the time they were on their second drinks it could have been midnight. Each time the door pushed open to let red-faced and runny-nosed customers in or out a blast of icy air swirled around the tables, so dry it hinted at snow. It was a perfect nearly Christmas evening.

Hask stared down at his vodka and tonic. He'd made a half-hearted effort at drinking, but his stomach wasn't really in it. Beside him, Ramsey's pint was barely touched.

'This time tomorrow,' the American policeman spoke quietly, 'this place will be empty. Don't you think?'

'Probably. Worse than that, they'll all be at home wondering about who they spoke to or slept with last night or last week.'

'The test centres will be flooded. I guess it'll at least give the government some real idea of the spread of Strain II through the population.'

'You think?' Hask leaned back in his seat and folded his hands across his vast belly. 'I'm not so sure. Most people don't actually *want* to know. How many tests did you have before the bug came along? When it was just plain old less-complicated HIV?'

Ramsey didn't answer.

'I never had one either.' Hask smiled softly. 'But if I said

I'd always played safe, that would be a lie. I just *hoped* I was fine, and thought that those things tended to happen to *other* people. Poorer people.' He sighed. 'This man is trying to level the playing field.'

Groups of people laughed and joked around them, filled with the optimism that comes with the approaching end to a year and the start of a fresh one. In some ways, Hask envied their ignorance – at least for this evening.

'Sometimes I get the feeling that the world is on the brink. There's a strange atmosphere everywhere, haven't you noticed?' Ramsey picked up his pint and took two long swallows from it.

'This is London. There's a different atmosphere every ten minutes, depending where you are,' Hask said.

'Not like this: it's in the air. It's as if I'm half-seeing something from the corner of my eye – something big that we're all missing. But then it's gone, and I'm not sure if I'm just going slightly mad.' The American's face was taut and his eyes dark.

'Are you okay?' Hask watched him carefully. 'Maybe you need a couple of days off. You've been overloaded of late, and it's about to get worse.'

'It's okay, doc.' Ramsey laughed gently. 'I'm not going crazy. It's just a weird feeling of unease inside me – like I should know something, but I don't. Whatever it is, I'll figure it out.'

'Maybe it's the Cass Jones issue.'

'Yeah, that's definitely playing on my mind.'

'I wonder where the hell he is.'

'He's nothing if not resourceful.' Ramsey grinned. 'Maybe he's in the south of France sitting out on the deck of a boat somewhere.'

'Not with his bank accounts all frozen.' Hask sipped his

vodka. He paused. 'That always struck me as odd.'

'What?'

'Cass isn't stupid: surely if he were going to go on some murderous spree, he'd have put some money somewhere, in case of this situation? It's not as if he's anywhere near broke. Why didn't he shift a hundred grand somewhere we couldn't stop him getting to it.'

'There's a lot that I don't understand.' Ramsey leaned in, focused now. 'Did you see all the info Perry Jordan had gathered for him? He definitely believes there was something suspicious about what happened to his brother's kid, and looking at everything, I don't blame him.'

'But do you think he killed those two men? Bradley and Powell?' It was the key question, the one the two men had avoided asking of each other since the case exploded. All the evidence pointed to Cass, that was indisputable, and maybe in the early days that had blinded them both to their gut instincts, but now that the dust was settling, Tim Hask knew what he believed: Cass Jones may have killed in the past, but he wasn't a *murderer*. Cass Jones was an honest man, despite all his efforts to be otherwise. The question was, did DI Ramsey feel the same?

'I don't think I know,' Ramsey said. 'I know it looks like it, but for some reason my head just won't accept it. After everything that happened with Bowman and his wife, it just seems wrong that he would do something like this.'

'I agree.' Hask was surprised by the relieved thumping in his chest. 'Maybe we should take a quiet look into it. Revisit the evidence.'

'Maybe.'

'Adam Bradley was pulled in over the Man of Flies case. Perhaps we should take a look at that interview. What do you think?'

'Can't hurt.'

Hask smiled. They may not be able to do anything about the hysteria that would grab the country after the next day's press conference, but they might be able to help out one friend.

It was warm in the private room at the top of Senate House, but none of the three men who were standing by the hospital bed removed their overcoats. The nurse checked the machinery attached by fed wires to the old man before leaving and quietly closing the door.

For a long moment, no one spoke. They stared at the figure bathed in the pale yellow light from above. No *Glow* came from the watery eyes that darted, panicking, around the room. His mouth moved madly as he tried to speak, and spit dribbled from his toothless gums and down the wrinkles in his ancient cheeks. He had looked old when he had been sleeping, but now that his face was twitching and awake, every year of his existence was engraved in the sagging skin of his neck and the hollows of his cheeks. His hair wisped like fragile clouds across the sky of his liver-spotted skull.

'Wha — Wha— I don't—' The words finally came like wet farts from his mouth, before they were overwhelmed by his keening. Tears ran from his eyes into the snot leaking from his nose. None of the three men wiped his face.

'Where is his *Glow*?' Mr Dublin finally muttered. The old man's eyes flicked towards him, still pleading for an answer to a question he couldn't articulate. He looked lost, confused – as if he didn't even know who he was any more. Mr Dublin's mouth twitched in disgust. 'Why does he have no *Glow*?' he repeated.

'Is this what we have come to?' Mr Craven trembled. 'The First is a drooling, gibbering idiot?'

In response, the old man began to cry quietly, parts of words lost in the snotty mess of his face.

'Let's not be hasty,' Mr Bright said. 'He's only just awakened. He make take time to recover.'

'You're a fool, Mr Bright.' Mr Craven spat the words out. His hands were trembling as he pointed a finger at the silver-haired man. 'You *promised* us – you said the First would wake and all would be restored to its former glory. *We* would be restored to our former glory.' He looked down at the figure in the bed. 'And this is what you deliver us.'

'The First with no *Glow*.' Mr Dublin spoke softly. 'How can that be? What does this mean for the rest of us?'

'It means we're all dying,' Mr Craven snapped. 'Not just me and the others, but you too one day. This whole crumbling kingdom: we're decaying, and there lies your proof. The glorious First – our leader, the shining one. What would the rest say if they saw him now? We should finish him off. Give him some of his dignity back.'

'I think perhaps,' Mr Bright retained his calm, 'it's best we keep the news of his awakening to ourselves for now. Give us time to evaluate the situation.'

'Give you time to come up with a way to explain yourself, you mean.'

'I don't need to explain myself, Mr Craven,' Mr Bright said. 'Don't forget who I am.'

'We'll keep it quiet for now,' Mr Dublin cut in, 'but not for long. And I must warn you, Mr Bright' – he carefully moved his fine blond hair out of his eyes – 'that between this and the Dying, many of our number are going to want to find a way home. Rightly or wrongly, they will blame you for the decay around us.'

'Thank you for your concern,' Mr Bright said. 'Now I think I'd like a few minutes alone with the First.'

He saw the look that flashed between the two men before they turned towards the door. There was an alliance forming there – Mr Dublin didn't like Mr Craven, that was clear, but that wouldn't stop them discussing this, and plotting how the cohorts should move forward. It was exactly as Mr Bright had expected. There was danger there, for sure, but he wasn't prepared to show his full hand yet – not until he was absolutely certain that all had gone according to plan. And anyway, Mr Dublin would be a fool to ally with Mr Craven; the latter would hedge his bets. The two would want to approach things differently, and they'd realise that soon enough. They could cause him problems, that was certain, but they would never work together, not like he and Solomon and the First had done, and alone they could never take him on.

When the door had clicked shut he pulled his gloves off and laid them on the side-table before taking a tissue from the box and carefully wiping the old man's face. The crying got worse as he touched him. Mr Bright let his hand rest for a moment on the hot, dry forehead.

'Try not to be afraid,' he said, giving the thing in the bed a kind smile. 'I will look after you – I will put you somewhere safe.'

Fresh tears sprang into the old eyes, and Mr Bright's heart squeezed slightly with pity and more than a little guilt. If only the other realised the burdens he'd had to bear for them – for *all* of them. He wasn't a monster, but he'd done monstrous things on their behalf.

He squeezed the old man's hand and felt it weakly pull away. He wondered if he should get the nurse to sedate the creature in the bed, but decided against it. A return to an unconscious state might have disastrous consequences. He would wait and see for now. He stepped back and smiled. It had been a long wait, but he was quietly confident that the plan they'd formed when the First had started ailing was all coming together. His heart thumped in anticipation, an excitement he hadn't felt in many long years. It was like a return to his youth, to *before*, when they had all been so bold.

He left the room, and there was a spring in his step that hadn't been there before. He had phone calls to make. By the time he'd reached the ground floor of Senate House, the old man's tears were forgotten.

For the first time in weeks she felt like music. She stared out of the grimy window of the small attic apartment at the world below. She still felt its energy and excitement, but her superior confidence had faded. Artie Mullins had done what she'd expected and taken Cass Jones from them, and at the time she'd been pleased: she could keep track of him without having to answer his questions – and the one thing she'd learned about them was that they *always* had questions – and then find him again when the time was right. That was before they'd started weakening.

Over the past fortnight or so, these strange days and nights all blurring into one, she'd found she lacked the energy to play. She hadn't extended beyond herself. She'd stayed *small*. Sometimes, in the quiet of the night, while her old friend muttered in his fevered sleep, she felt as if this hectic, harsh world was consuming her. The possibility that they might not be able to get back hadn't crossed their minds – not even just theirs; she was just the emissary, after all, and he was her companion – but *his* mind. Or perhaps it was just a risk he had been prepared to take. If they didn't return, perhaps that was information enough.

Frost covered the glass on the outside like a network of dead veins. There was so much hidden beauty here that sometimes it astounded her. She let out a long breath and watched the condensation form. She felt its damp heat on her face and ignored the sweet scent of rot it carried with it. She had become used to that now, as she had to the flecks of blood that appeared between her paling gums. But perhaps, she decided, as she turned away from the glass and headed over to the bed in the corner, all was not lost. Events were finally moving forward.

She sat on the edge of the bed and pushed a loose strand of her red hair from her face before leaning forward to kiss her companion's cheek. His face burned. When his eyes opened there was still some humour there, even though he was no longer able to play his violin, not even on his very best days. She wasn't sure which was drier, her lips or his cheek. She squeezed his hand.

'Have you found the way home, Gabbi?' he asked. He had been the one to try when he'd first sickened; he would go back and report and she would stay and wait to answer the so-faint call that had brought them all this way. He hadn't gone, though. The Walkways were lost in the Chaos, and that had almost sucked him in. She had tried after that, with more urgency as his efforts added to his weakening state and she could see her old friend crumbling away, but there was no way out. They had found their way here, but there was no way back. Someone had locked the exit door. Perhaps that was about to change.

'Not yet, but I think we will be home by Christmas.' She smiled. He almost managed a laugh at that play on all the television shows that they had watched on the small machine that came with the flat.

'He's awake.' She squeezed his hand again and felt sudden life flood his system with the excitement of her news. She'd felt it herself. 'He called to me – it was so loud and clear it woke me. He knows we're here; he's been listening. He knows we're sick.'

Her companion, still looking like the tramp he had so recently played, pulled himself up into a sitting position against his sweaty pillow.

'He's really awake?' he asked.

She nodded. 'I understand it all now – why the boy is so important.'

'Do we go to him now?' His eyes were wide, as if he'd never expected the news to come. 'It's been such a long time.'

'He's not ready yet. He'll tell us when and where.'

'And then we can go home?'

'And then we can go home.' She smiled as she spoke, but her heart twinged. She *hoped* they could go home. 'I feel stronger already though,' she added. 'Don't you?'

'Play me some music,' he said after they'd sat for a moment in silence. 'There should always be music.'

And so she did.

He moves through the bitter night, his feet pounding against the pavement, thumping out his rage with every stride. His anger makes him stronger than he's been in a long time and he fights the urge to become everything that he is; to shake off this tiny, frail body. But he can't afford the wasted energy; he'd only have to pay the price later. These things have become a consideration.

He pauses on the Embankment and looks out at the other side of the city carved off by the midnight river. Lights twinkle merrily, and further ahead another bridge is lit defiantly against the night. It is beautiful, and the thought feeds his bitterness. He prefers the bitterness to the fear; the fear makes him feel even weaker than his decaying body. The fear makes him feel like one of them, and that he will not abide.

He turns his back on the water and faces the biting wind. His anger at the futility of their situation was fading. He would recover himself and start planning – tomorrow. He wouldn't give up – he never had. But for tonight, he would let his power be felt in other ways. It was time to spread his word. For the first time that evening, he is smiling.

Cass was in the dream again. It wasn't a room, as such; it was a space somewhere *between*: a place where people became trapped. Cass was pressed against the pale wall, held back by a pressure he didn't understand, and in front of him his dead brother and dead father stood facing each other. His father was burning, the fire engulfing him from head to feet, his thin hair waving upright in the orange and red flames as if he were under water. Cass could see him; his skin sizzled slightly, but it stayed pale, and his mouth hung open, as if trying to produce words that wouldn't come. He didn't look at Cass but stared directly at Christian.

His younger brother was wearing the dark trousers and pale blue shirt he'd been wearing the night he died. His tie was loosened. His shiny black brogues had spots of blood on them. He stood a few feet away from their burning father, the heat lifting his blond fringe as if he were standing in a breeze. Tears ran in streams down his pale face and evaporated on his cheeks. A drop of blood fell from the arm by his side and landed on his shoe. The sound made Cass' eardrums ache.

Between his father and his brother, a Rastafarian teenager sat cross-legged, holding a baby. The teenager had no face, but he was staring at Cass from somewhere within the dried bloody mess under his hair. He cradled the baby carefully.

Cass tried to take a step forward, but something pulled him back and he gasped as cold fingers pinched his skin. It wasn't a wall behind him at all; it was the dead, and they were tugging at him. Hands came up through the floor and pulled him down until he was lying on his back. He called to Christian and his father to help him, but they didn't move. He didn't exist to them. He wasn't there.

Cold bodies swarmed over him and he knew who they were; he recognised their touch. Kate, Claire, Jessica, the poor boy they had thought was Luke, the people Solomon had killed, the student suicides, the doctors, the Jackson and Miller boys. There were so many, and they all blamed him.

He tried to scream, but fingers crammed into his mouth and tugged at his tongue. They were all over him now, pulling his clothes away, eager to tear at his flesh. He caught flashes of hair and angry eyes amidst the rotting skin. For a moment, the ceiling above flashed into view: twinkling eyes within a ruddy face framed with silver hair stared down at him. Cass almost laughed in his terror. Mr Bright was looking down at them all, overseeing the game, as always.

The man lying on the ceiling winked. As he did so, the baby, out of sight, began to cry.

And the dead swarmed.

Chapter Nine

It was a strange farewell. After two months under his supervision, Cass still didn't feel he knew Mac any better than he had on day one, and he figured maybe that was how he liked it. If Cass got nicked, all he could say about the big, bald man was that, despite the nickname, he wasn't Scottish.

They'd got up early, and Mac and a younger man Cass didn't know had driven him to leafy Crouch Hill. Mac pulled the car over on the corner of a wide boulevard.

'First left. Number forty-five. He's expecting you.' Mac got out with Cass and gave him a nod and a wink and an envelope with what looked like at least a couple of grand in cash wedged inside.

'From Mr Mullins. To get you started.'

Cass took it. He was in no position to be proud – the day for pride was long gone as far as Artie Mullins was concerned. He owed the man, and he owed him big. Between Mullins and Father Michael, Cass felt slightly over-whelmed. Both had helped him, and it was more than just giving him money, or a place to stay: more importantly, both believed in his innocence. The dichotomy between the two men's natures wasn't lost on him. He didn't deserve such faith from either of them. Cass'd always felt he existed in the grey area, but recently he couldn't help but think that the grey was getting darker, and whatever goodness he'd once had inside him was getting swallowed up until all the goodness in his life had gone and he was just left with vengeance. Perhaps that would change when he had Luke back. Perhaps that was why finding the boy had become so important to him. Luke was his last hope for redemption.

Redemption is the key. His brother's last words echoed in his head, and the meaning in them still rang true.

He nodded goodbye to Mac and waited on the kerb until the car had disappeared before starting to walk, a small holdall of clothes over his good shoulder and carrying the battered suitcase that Father Michael had brought him in his right hand. He thought of the big house in Muswell Hill, not so far from here, that had been his home for so long, and the new place in St John's Wood, and all the money that he'd accumulated in the bank. None of it mattered any more; he was reduced to what he was carrying – and within an hour he'd have a whole new identity too. Maybe he should have felt more like a phoenix, but he didn't. He picked up his pace and headed for Number 45.

In the movies, forgers worked out of tiny backroom offices. They were generally skinny, nervy types who looked like they'd been bullied in school. If this one was anything to go by, that stereotype was well out of date.

'Before you ask,' the man smiled as he led Cass into the large open-plan kitchen, 'this isn't my house.' He hadn't introduced himself and neither had Cass. Given the nature of the man's business, current names were irrelevant.

'It belongs to an overseas corporation, rented through a variety of holding companies.' He gave a wide, friendly smile over his shoulder. 'Should you find yourself in an unfortunate situation with the police, sending them here will do you no favours. They won't find anything.'

'I understand your concern,' Cass said, 'but if the police

catch me, then I don't think giving them a forger – however good you are – would do me much good.'

'No, you're probably right.' He poured two coffees from the filter jug on the side and slid over a jug of cream and a pot of sugar. 'Help yourself.'

Cass did, watching the man warily. He was older than Cass, mid- to late forties, but his face was chubbier, and smooth. He had the look of a man who had had an easy life; he could pass easily for someone involved in any number of respectable professions; Cass would've put money on him having a membership to some exclusive golf club some-where in the suburbs. Mind you, he still might. It just went to show that you could never judge a book by its cover.

'Feel free to smoke.'

Cass did, and the forger pulled an ashtray from a cup-board before taking a large brown envelope from one of the kitchen drawers. He lit a cigarette for himself and inhaled deeply before tipping the contents out between them. Watching him, Cass wondered how much of this man's exterior was a construct. He smoked like an expert, and held the butt between his thumb and forefinger. There was no hint of East End in his smooth voice, but Cass thought there must have been at some point. This forger had created a forgery of himself.

'I'm pleased with these – some of my best work, I think. Of course, the passport itself is kosher, which helps. Don't ask how, but it is. Take a look. It's yours now.'

Cass picked up the passport and flicked to the back. The man was right – to his untrained eye it looked exactly like his real passport, sitting back in his bedroom drawer in St John's Wood. He looked at the name typed next to the photo Artie Mullins had taken only days before and his heart thumped. *Charles Silver.*

'Who picked the name?'

Charles. *Charlie.* The last time he'd had a false identity he'd been Charlie Sutton. His stomach lurched slightly as the years tumbled away, bringing that time and this together, folding his existence so the two moments touched. *It was just a name.* A long stream of smoke escaped through his gritted teeth.

'It's not a matter of picking the name.' He looked up. 'It's about which identity fits. You have a problem with the name?'

Cass shook his head. 'I can live with it.' According to his new passport and driving licence he was also forty-one. He could live with that too. He hadn't planned on having a big fortieth birthday, so bypassing it altogether was probably a good thing. He was also a business analyst, whatever that was.

'Thanks for these.' Cass tucked the driving licence into his wallet and zipped the passport into the inside pocket of his jacket.

'Mr Mullins is always a pleasure to work with. Pass on my regards if you see him.'

Cass nodded, but didn't speak; who knew when he'd be seeing Artie again?

He finished his cigarette and drained the rest of his coffee before getting to his feet.

'Do you want me to call you a minicab?'

'No,' Cass said, 'thanks. I'll walk.' Walk to where was a different question. The first thing he needed to do was find somewhere to stay: a bedsit or cheap motel, from where he could plan on how to get Luke back.

'Well then, goodbye and good luck, Mr Silver.'

Cass shook the smooth hand and headed back to Crouch End. He'd walk up to Highgate and jump on the tube there.

65

Letting his head fall forward and his shoulders slump – any cameras he passed would have a harder job getting a clear image of him – he started to walk.

He had walked barely ten paces when the doors of a parked car ahead flew open and four men climbed out. Cass barely registered the visible gun within one man's overcoat before the cloth was over his mouth and the nauseatingly sweet smell of chloroform overwhelmed him. He saw the boot of the car being opened. He was out cold by the time it shut over him.

Chapter Ten

Mat Blackmore had been getting edgier as the trial drew closer, and he hadn't exactly started from a place of calm. Sometimes, despite the months that had passed, he still found it hard to believe that this whole shitstorm had come down on them at all. Gary Bowman had promised him it was all fine, that they wouldn't get caught – and then everything went to shit, with the two boys getting killed, and the Christian Jones family murder – it was a mess, a bloody mess, and he was stuck right in the middle of it.

He rocked slightly on the side of his narrow cell bed and rubbed his face. His eyes were gritty from lack of sleep. He hadn't had one good night in months – so much for the old adage about the guilty sleeping like babies; it sure as fuck wasn't true in his case. But then, it wasn't so much his guilt keeping him awake – that saved itself for his dreams. It was the fear that left him staring wide-eyed into the shadows of his cell until the early hours of the morning.

There was plenty for him to be afraid of. He'd sold out just about everyone he could – Gary Bowman, other Paddington coppers, Macintyre's contacts, anyone he could think of – to try and get his charges reduced. He was staring at the death penalty, his lawyers had been clear about that from the outset, and he needed to do whatever he could to get that down to life.

His stomach felt greasy as it tied itself in a fresh knot, as it did a thousand times a day, as the memory of Claire May's face as she tumbled downwards assaulted him. He could see shock and realisation fighting with the dread in her wide eyes. Those eyes were with him, everywhere. Sometimes, in his dreams, time had rolled back and she was alive and well and they were naked together in bed. In those dreams he could feel the warm, wet inside of her, and smell her skin. For a moment it was wonderful, and then her limbs would become cold and stiff and he look down to find himself fucking her dead and broken body.

Most days he just wanted to cry, and today was no exception. How could it be, that after everything that had happened, *he* was the only one facing a first-degree murder charge? If he didn't feel so sick he'd almost laugh. Bowman must be laughing at him, that was for sure – after all, Bowman's lawyers had been quick to point out that their client hadn't *actually* killed anyone. He couldn't be held responsible for Macintyre's actions, or Blackmore's. Bowman might be facing a long life behind bars, but at least he didn't have the gallows hanging over him.

Sweat pricked on Mat's palms. His brain was in such a state of frenzy most of the time that he felt he was going slightly mad. Maybe if he went fully mad that wouldn't be so bad – they couldn't execute a mad man, could they? He almost giggled. They must all have been mad, to get so carried away, and now every time he went out on recreation or to the library he could feel eyes on him – not only was he a bent copper, he was also a grass. No one gave a shit that he'd grassed Bowman, but the underworld contacts he'd given up? They all had friends on the inside. Someone would get him one of these days; he knew that much.

'Brief's here.' The cell door opened and Blackmore jumped slightly as his reverie was broken. A mix of anticipation and dread washed over him. He hadn't been expecting a visit – what had developed? Everyone – all the accused, from Bowman downwards – hoped for the same thing. With Cass Jones discredited, no one wanted to drag these trials out. There were more plea-bargains being offered; maybe at last one had been thrown his way. He got up and followed the whistling warder out into the main prison corridor, moving meekly, like a lamb. There was no strut left in his stride and his trousers hung loose on his hips from where his fear had burned off his weight.

The door closed behind him. He was surprised to see a suited stranger on the other side of the desk. The man was twenty years younger than Blackmore's normal brief, and he was wearing the kind of suit he himself had spent a lot of his ill-gotten gains on: designer, tailored, and very expensive. Maybe the law did pay better in the end.

The well-dressed stranger held out his hand.

'I'm sorry, Mr Johnson is off sick today. He wanted to come, but he doesn't trust himself to be more than ten feet from a toilet at the moment, if you catch my drift. My name's Anthony Ware.'

Mat gingerly shook his hand. The man had pronounced his name with a soft 'th', like the Americans and those educated at Oxbridge did. A year ago such a man wouldn't have intimidated Mat Blackmore, but a year ago was a different lifetime. He sat down without saying a word.

Ware remained standing. 'I've been working on your case behind the scenes, so I'm fully up to date with the situation. Two weeks until the big day then?' He grinned again and Mat just nodded dumbly.

'Well, I come with good news. We finally have an agreement that the courts will not seek the death penalty for you. The prosecution have accepted that the murder of Miss May wasn't premeditated and you acted in panic, making it virtually a crime of passion. Normally, you know how it is, this wouldn't be enough to get you off the hook, but with all the co-operation you have already provided, and with your agreement to be a witness for the prosecution in regards to Gary Bowman, leniency has prevailed.'

Blackmore hadn't listened to anything beyond Ware's second sentence. His heart was thumping loudly in his ears, and his relief was so profound he almost didn't recognise the emotion. His skin tingled and he wanted to laugh. He wasn't going to die. Thank fuck! Thank fuckity fuck for that! No more dark dreams of being strapped onto a table and injected; no more imaginings of that terrible day. Claire May and her ghost could go fuck themselves.

It was only when the lawyer tapped him on the arm that he looked up and remembered that someone else was there. The grin on his face was so wide that Ware must have thought he looked like a gibbering idiot, but he didn't care. No death sentence. That was all that mattered.

'Happy Birthday, Mat.' Ware pulled something out of his briefcase. An iced chocolate cupcake.

Mat Blackmore laughed aloud this time. He was thirty today, and in all the panic it had been only a passing thought that morning: he was thirty, and that milestone might be the last birthday he would ever have. Not any more though. Life imprisonment loomed ahead of him, but who knew what changes lay ahead? There were always appeals; life could become twenty, or even ten years. People had served a lot less for murder in the past.

As he grabbed the cupcake and took a bite he felt a little

of the old Mat Blackmore return: the one who swaggered when he walked. The one who always had one eye on the game and the girls. He chewed and swallowed and laughed with Ware until the cake and the weak prison tea was all gone. He walked taller on his way back to the remand wing.

By the time Mat Blackmore was writhing in agony and crying for his mother in the prison hospital and the doctors were rushing around like blue-arsed flies wondering how the hell this could have happened, the man who had called himself Anthony Ware, with a soft 'th', was long gone, disappeared into London, the smart suit and briefcase abandoned with all his false paperwork. Johnson had been sick, but he hadn't sent anyone to visit Blackmore in his stead. There had been no visit planned, because there was nothing new to report. The prosecution hadn't offered any plea bargain with regard to the death penalty.

As it turned out, by four p.m., when the sheet was being pulled over Blackmore's face, the whole issue of leniency was quite redundant.

Chapter Eleven

In the basement of the Centre for National Security, two floors lower than most of Commander David Fletcher's colleagues were allowed and one floor beyond where most thought the building actually finished, the head of the Anti-Terror Division stood back and watched as the team of scientists and data analysts huddled over the various monitors and whispered quietly among themselves. Fletcher wasn't sure they actually needed to whisper – hospitals, libraries and churches: these were the only places that people needed to lower their voices, and this place was none of those. Perhaps it was simply that the whole nature of the project was to eavesdrop, and on some subconscious level people thought their presence might be detected if they spoke too loudly.

Or maybe he was just tired, and overthinking things. Fletcher didn't pretend to understand how this department worked – and he didn't really care, as long as he was presented with all relevant information in a timely fashion. Satellites, both stationary and mobile, watched the world and all their information (from those the UK owned, at any rate) was fed back and sifted through these computers. Everyone was watching everyone these days. Near-Earth space was full of junk, and they were all running around like headless chickens trying to keep track of it, although, hopefully, not for much longer.

In the far corner of the room, a muscular man studied a bank of screens before scurrying over to one station and whispering into an ear. He was tanned, despite having worked all his adult life in facilities like this one. He looked like an athlete rather than a number cruncher, but his personality veered towards the autistic. Fletcher felt unsettled just being around him, though the two had never even had a face-to-face conversation. People that clever were unnerving. There was something fundamentally wrong with genius, he'd decided long ago. It wasn't natural.

The door opened behind him and Arnold James, the Defence Secretary, came in holding a mug of coffee. His visit was low-key, and, thus far at least, appeared to have gone unnoticed. The new Prime Minister, Lucius Dawson, was eager to know immediately if the project had worked, but he also needed to make sure that the satellite's launch wasn't considered anything unusual – to the rest of the world it should look like nothing more than an ordinary defence upgrade.

'All well?' James' eyes always looked unhappy, regardless of whether he was smiling or angry. Fletcher wondered if it was fall-out from all the political back-stabbing of the past few months. McDonnell had been sent packing to the back benches after her party's revolution, but at least they still had a grip on the country, even if it wasn't as firm as it should be.

'Launched perfectly from South Korea,' Fletcher said. 'It should be in position to activate in the next thirty minutes or so. *Then* we'll see. Our super-scientist doesn't appear concerned, so I'll take that as a good sign.'

They both looked over at the dark-haired foreigner who was studying the array of large screens on the wall.

'Who is he?' Fletcher asked. 'What's his history?'

'Classified, I'm afraid.'

'Even from me?' Fletcher almost smiled. 'Christ, now he really *does* scare me.'

'What I can tell you is that he's a number genius, codes, programming, astro-physics, you name it. There's no one else who comes close – not even *nearly* close. He's worked at all the top space facilities, but it's hard to pin down where he started, even for us. He was involved with the Gaia deep space telescope production and launch. He still monitors it, in his spare time, as it were. Our new baby, SkyCall 1, was virtually designed by him alone. I'm not sure the rest of his team even understands it. He uses them like monkeys, telling them exactly what to do, but they can't keep up. Not in here.' Arnold tapped the side of his head. 'Still, if it does everything he claims, then who cares? It'll be up there for a hundred years before it starts to decay.'

'And of course, if it doesn't,' Fletcher mused, 'then we may well have brought Armageddon down on our heads.'

'You need to have more faith.' Arnold James' mouth smiled, even if his sad eyes didn't.

'People that clever disturb me.'

'Don't worry, he'll be back in Harwell by the morning. That's his current base, though I don't really understand why he wants to be researching there. He must be worth a fortune – he could probably buy the government out of here if he wanted to.'

Fletcher turned his back on the quiet hubbub and led the politician back out into the corridor and upstairs to the less oppressive atmosphere of his private offices. Nothing would be happening in the next half an hour or so, and he hated standing around feeling redundant.

74

His assistant brought them coffee and he sipped his as James stared out of the large windows.

'Anything else I need to report on when I go back?'

'No more than the usual,' Fletcher said. 'We always have a variety of threats coming in, but none that we think rate any particular attention. Still too many to lower the alert level, obviously.'

'Obviously.' There was a pause. 'This spread of the bug...'

Fletcher should his head. 'No, no takers on that. As far as we can tell, this is a lone crazy, and unless he's politically affiliated, that makes him not my problem.'

'Still, they tell me that the virus attacks far more quickly in these victims. You don't think that's odd?'

'It's a virus – by its very nature, it mutates. We know that from the emergence of Strain II itself. The labs tell me they can't find any evidence to suggest it's manmade.'

'I'm not sure whether that should reassure us or alarm us,' the Defence Secretary said, his sadness creeping from his eyes and into his soft smile.

Fletcher changed the subject and they talked inanely about politics and sport and things that could change with the breeze and not really affect the workings of the world, while watching the minutes tick away until someone came to tell them whether SkyCall 1 was going to be everything it had promised. He thought about the scientists down below: they might be clever, but he and the man standing next to him: they were the big-picture thinkers. They were decision-makers. And they were the ones who had to know how to live with the consequences of those decisions. The number crunchers uncovered the information, but it was people like Fletcher who had to decide how to act on it. They decided who lived and who died, and they had to carry that.

Eventually the knock came, and the man in the white

coat who stood there had to shuffle from foot to foot to contain his bubbling excitement. 'She's up and the virus is sent,' he said. 'And she's working.'

Fletcher's heart picked up – not entirely from excitement – and he hoped that the satellite that was now spying on everyone else's satellites really had been registered through enough companies to hide the trail. Because if any other nation realised that all their information was being routed through the small, barely noticeable addition to the space junk, then the UK was going to be truly fucked.

Chapter Twelve

Mr Dublin's London home, situated in the heart of the South Bank, was an ocean of sleek white and chrome, a vast open-plan arrangement that looked endless. Everything from the shutters to the front door operated smoothly and silently at the press of a button; even the furnishings reflected the innate calm that their owner liked to present to the world.

Mr Dublin's main home and responsibilities lay in the Far East, and he had always favoured natives of those areas when selecting his servants. His London home was no exception. The man who had welcomed Mr Craven with a curt nod and then disappeared was of that origin, and it was clear from Mr Dublin's home and appearance – always dressed in cool, pale linens – that there was something about the supposed Zen of that continent that appealed to him.

Mr Craven found it all a touch affected, as if Mr Dublin's style choices revealed a sense of spiritual superiority, if such a thing even existed. He peered out of the bank of tall windows that presented a breathtaking view of the river and the city beyond. He smiled a little. Mr Dublin wasn't so different from the rest of them. They all chose to live as close to the sky as possible.

He sighed into the silence. Hopefully, this meeting wouldn't take long. He was tired and he needed to sleep.

His bones ached. He didn't have energy to spare, and he had very little inclination to spend time among the healthy of his kind. Over the past few days he'd started to *feel* this illness that had no place in his body. Until then, he'd been impressed with his control over his own fear, but as the pains in his chest grew worse, and the fevers that came suddenly upon him left him weak and sweaty, he realised that all he'd been feeling before was denial. The fear had come with the exhaustion. He could understand how Mr Bellew, now just a poor, gibbering fool, had gathered so much support among the dying for his attempted coup. Any hope would do.

He turned away from the window and his eye caught on a pale vase, an Eastern antique – hundreds of years old, and priceless, no doubt. He had a feeling it would be sitting on that shelf long after he was gone. His gut twisted with a now-familiar blend of tired rage and fear. He badly wanted to smash it.

Soft footsteps tapped down the large spiral staircase and the expressionless servant gestured. Mr Craven followed him up and when they reached the top the man disappeared into a side-room, leaving him outside the closed door of Mr Dublin's office. Mr Craven took a deep breath. He found, to his dismay, that he needed one after the climb. When his hands and legs were steady, he opened the door without bothering to knock.

Mr Dublin was alone, which came as something of a surprise. Mr Craven had expected to see Mr Bright with him. The discovery of the First to be a drooling idiot had certainly and surely sealed his fate, but Mr Craven had expected Mr Dublin, always cool and precise by nature, to be slower in withdrawing his support. If Mr Bright wasn't here, then perhaps the purpose of this meeting might be to plot his removal and form a new Inner Cohort.

He almost smiled at Mr Dublin, but the newspaper that slammed down onto the round table between them wiped the expression from his face. He stared at the headline: ANGEL OF DEATH STALKS LONDON. Next to it was a computer-generated image that clearly showed his own features.

'I don't think they've done me justice,' he said, drily. 'I'm far more handsome in the flesh, wouldn't you say?'

'So you admit that this is you?'

'Does it matter?' He stared at Mr Dublin, with his healthy skin and blond hair. Why did he care?

'Of *course* it matters! Just as it mattered when Mr Solomon was killing them.'

'But Mr Solomon was insane.' He smiled.

'And this isn't?' Mr Dublin pointed a well-manicured finger at the paper.

'I suppose it's just a matter of perspective. Aren't you going to offer me a coffee? Or are you worried you might catch something?'

'You find this amusing.' Mr Dublin's voice was still cool as an Alpine stream, but his pale eyes were flints.

'I find that it makes me feel better.' The words were surprisingly honest. 'And yes, I suppose it does amuse me. The irony of it all.'

'This is the word of your *God*?'

'Oh, they mention that, do they?' Mr Craven's smile was brittle as he looked down at the paper. 'You took the time to read it. I feel flattered.'

'This isn't funny, Mr Craven.'

'No, it certainly isn't. I'm dying. *They're* all dying, and they always have been. If that isn't the cruel word of their God, then what is?'

'Everything is unstable enough without this – the situation with the First, the emissary being here, the problems finding the Walkways. All of our unsettled feelings are affecting the world, don't you see? We *can't* add to it. We need to be restoring calm and order.'

'What I'm doing doesn't affect that. A little fear doesn't hurt them.'

'Fear has never brought out the best in anyone.' Mr Dublin leaned forward, his hands on the table. 'It clearly hasn't brought out the best in you – although I've never been entirely sure that your best was good enough.'

'Don't lecture me on fear, Mr Dublin. And I've never cared for your high-horse attitude. Even in the old days you were all about the greater good. Let me remind you, this wasn't about the greater good. It was about power and freedom.'

'For you, perhaps.' Mr Dublin let out a small, disgusted snort. 'We have always turned a blind eye to your cruel hobbies. We all have our weaknesses. But this is too much. You've broken the boundaries. I won't punish you – you're dying – and from the look and smell of you, I'd say quite quickly. But I'm removing you from the Inner Council.'

'What?' The bark of laughter burst from him. '*You* won't punish me? And who are you suddenly? The great Mr Bright? Does he even know about this?'

'Of course.' Mr Dublin smiled. 'Mr Bright had other business to attend to and so asked me to do this. I may be many things, Mr Craven, but I am not a fool.'

'But he must be if he doesn't see the changes coming.' His blood boiled with rage. How *dare* they cut him out like this? How *dare* Mr Bright dismiss him?

'Whatever changes there may or may not be coming are no longer your affair. You've become a liability. I can't stop you infecting them, not without compromising my own values. Go and live out whatever time you have left. I shall need you to return to us all Inner Cohort possessions.' Mr Dublin nodded at Mr Craven's neck. 'Starting with that.'

As Mr Craven undid the top buttons of his shirt, his smile was genuine. His neck was bare. 'I seem to have forgotten to bring it.' He wasn't a fool either. 'I'm presuming you're about to freeze all my accounts. I remember how this worked with Mr Solomon. As soon as I've withdrawn what I consider a reasonable amount, I'll make sure everything gets back to you.'

'Make sure that you do.'

'You needn't worry, Mr Dublin.' Mr Craven swallowed his rage, hiding it deep within. 'I'm still one of us. My loyalties have always been with us.'

'I'm sorry it's come to this.'

Mr Craven thought he probably was, and that truly made him a fool. If it wasn't for the Dying, it would be Mr Craven kicking Mr Dublin from the Inner Cohort, and he and Mr Bright would be strapped into the Experiment. Mr Dublin had had a lucky escape.

'So am I, Mr Dublin. So am I.'

By the time he was back out on the street, cut loose from everything he had always known, Mr Craven's rage was calming slightly. Mr Dublin was no match for Mr Bright, and neither of them, old as they were, would be a match for him were he healthy. Did they really think he was stupid? He'd known this was coming. This care they had for *them* and what *they* thought was laughable. The Network should never have hidden in the shadows; they should have ruled as the gods they were. He managed a bitter smile and thought of the small item he'd left under that Zen desk of Mr Dublin's. Whatever that one was planning, at least he'd hear about it first.

Chapter Thirteen

T he first thing Cass did when he came round was to throw up, and given the small confines of the boot, that wasn't the best fun in the world. His head still felt woozy and his stomach roiled with every bump in the road. After ten minutes the stench of the vomit mixed in with the other smells of petrol and cheap carpet fibres made him pretty sure he was going to be sick again. He shifted himself as far back as the space would allow and lifted his head, trying to get whatever tiny amounts of fresh air were seeping in through the gaps.

He didn't bang or shout; there was no point. All that would do was alert whoever had grabbed him that he was awake and angry, and if they stopped at all it would just be to knock him out again, and he could live without that. Instead, he tried to ignore the pain in his cramped shoulder and wondered who the fuck was behind this. He ruled out the police: if they'd caught him, they'd have been screaming it from the rooftops – and they wouldn't have made it look so easy. It would have been the full team of armed officers, and there would have been a camera around catching it all for the news. Plus, they'd have nicked the forger too.

The forger. That smug bastard. It had to be him who was behind the set-up. It was all too tidy. The car hit another bump and his teeth rattled as his stomach lurched. He swallowed hard. Who had he been set up *for*, though? Someone in the forger's line of work couldn't get away with crossing the likes of Artie Mullins and still have his kneecaps, let alone a career.

Could it be Fletcher? He was certainly curious about Cass after Hayley Porter died while covering his escape, and he had no real idea how the ATD operated. It didn't feel like their style, though; he thought they'd be more likely to sling him in the back of an unmarked van than the boot of a car.

Maybe all the bent coppers he'd inadvertently brought down had clubbed together to find him and put him in a ditch somewhere. They certainly had enough underworld connections. That wasn't a pleasant thought. The final option, and the one that he had the most ambivalent feelings about, was that this was the work of Mr Bright. He had a feeling that man didn't have a typical modus operandi; he probably used whatever methods he felt were required in differing situations. Having seen the pictures in Dr Cornell's house, he knew for sure that Mr Bright'd been around long enough to try them all. The one conclusion Cass did reach was that none of the options were good. All things considered, he wasn't the most popular man in London.

When they finally hauled him out of the car, he saw only flashes of burly arms before his mouth was taped up and a bag tugged down over his head, plunging him back into darkness before his eyes had even adjusted. Gruff voices swore about the vomit, and then they dragged him away. He didn't think for a second that he had a chance of breaking away. His whole body ached from being stuck in the boot, and his shoulder was on fire. Whatever was happening, he was just going to have to go with it for now.

Over the next few hours, he wondered if maybe he should have at least tried. The situation had gone from bad to worse: after being hauled from the car he'd been dragged somewhere, then tied to a chair. Someone had thrown a bucket of icy-cold water over him and by the time he'd recovered from the shock, the voices were gone and he was pretty sure he was alone – though for how long, he had no idea. It was hard to keep track of time in the pitch-black, and with every inch of your body aching from the freezing cold. He was in a garage or a warehouse, he was pretty sure about that. The men's feet had echoed slightly and the ground had felt rough through his shoes as they'd pulled him along. And even before they'd soaked him, the air had felt unheated.

His toes and fingers grew numb and he drifted in and out of something close to sleep before the men came back. The first punch came out of the blue. He was so surprised that he almost didn't feel it as his head whipped sideways. The second fist went straight to his stomach and he felt that one all too much, and as he desperately tried to suck in air through his nose, he thought he might pass out all over again. By the sixth or seventh punch, he wished he would. He couldn't see a thing, so there was no way he could even attempt to protect himself, not even to roll his head with each blow, when he didn't know when they were coming. It was a world of darkness and pain, and he was lost in it.

He's been expecting them to beat him up ever since they'd tied him into the chair, so that came as no surprise. But he'd been expecting a point to it: questions needing answers; information wanted. At the very least he thought that someone would want to hear him scream or cry or whatever. But thus far, there seemed to be no purpose to this, and if this wasn't about information, then he was seriously fucked. Could this be Bowman's contacts? Were they just going to beat the crap out of him until he was dead?

Eventually the punches stopped. Cass' head rolled forward, but snapped straight up again when one of the bastards threw another bucket of cold water over him. He screamed behind the gaffer tape long after they'd closed the door and left him alone. This time he did drift off into blissful unconsciousness ... but just as he did so, a thought tried to get his attention: they'd stayed away from his shoulder. Why would they have done that? Surely if they wanted to hurt him properly, then that would be the way to do it? It wouldn't stop them keeping him alive as long as they wanted, but it would have put him in agony ... Always questions, he mused as the darkness took him. Why the fuck was his life so full of questions?

He must have been out cold when they came back, and everything happened so quickly that he didn't know *who* he was, let alone *where* he was as the lights went on, the bag was pulled off his head and someone tore the tape from his mouth, leaving his face stinging. He gasped in lungfuls of cold air, his heart racing so hard that his eyes burned in the corners. For a few moments, as the golden warmth from his eyes turned inwards, his body felt no pain at all, as if he had healed, or become something bigger and better than he had been. With renewed vigour he tugged at the ropes binding his hands and feet until the chair tilted sharply, threatening to capsize.

'You always were an angry bastard. Just calm the fuck down; you're not going anywhere.'

Cass froze with the first word and whatever glow he'd been producing vanished instantly, letting every ache and pain flood back into his bruised and battered body. It couldn't be – it couldn't *possibly* be him. He forced his blurry eyes open despite the bruises, squinting against the light. He had to *see* . . .

An old man stood in an open doorway between the vast tiled garage and what must be the rest of the house. He wore a cashmere sweater and casual trousers, and an expensive watch glinted at his wrist. Those were just frills, though. What Cass saw, what couldn't be changed by money or circumstance, was the man's battered nose, broken four times by the time he was seventeen. Cass could remember him laughing when he told that story. He stared, aware that as he panted for breath a long line of spit was dribbling from the corner of his mouth and hanging off his chin. He no longer knew how he felt. Afraid, probably. Shocked, definitely.

'Your shoulder's healing fast. You're lucky. Mine took the best part of a year. I was a lot older than you are, though. But still. You heal fast.'

Cass sat and stared like a dumb idiot as inside his head memories that he'd spent a decade fighting came at him like juggernauts, each one hitting him with more power than the earlier punches.

You've got to look up, Charlie.

Well, what are you waiting for, Charlie?

Run, Charlie! Run, Charlie!

And always, always, those dark terrified eyes and the barrel of a gun. He could almost feel how his hands had been sweating. Time was folding in on itself. He was back where he started. Wheels within wheels.

'Your face, however, is a right fucking mess.' The voice was still all grit and growl but there was a touch of respectability in it that hadn't been there before. Cass wasn't the only one who had changed over the past ten years. 'The boys did a good job on you.' The old man didn't move but nodded at the two heavies on either side of Cass, who stepped forward and began to untie him.

'But you deserved it. You lied to me. You betrayed me. I needed to get that off my chest. You've come off lightly, all things considered. The boys'll take you to get showered and cleaned up now.' He paused and stared for a second, and Cass knew it wasn't only him who was being assaulted by the memories.

'And then you and me, Charlie,' Brian Freeman said, 'we need to talk.'

Even from the limited amount Cass could see, he knew the house was big. More than big. Brian Freeman, one-time Birmingham gangland boss, now lived in one of those modern mansions TV stars always inhabited in their endless reality TV shows. The en-suite bathroom Cass was shown to was bigger than the double bedroom of his own flat. Freeman had been doing well for himself when Cass – or Charlie, as he was then – had known him, but he hadn't lived anywhere like this.

The shower was powerful and the heat a godsend to his frozen, aching body, and he could have stayed under it all day, but Cass forced himself to keep it short. He had too many questions that needed answering – not least of which was how did a man who should have been behind bars come to be living in such an openly opulent house? If this was Freeman's house, of course: he didn't think they'd driven him that far – definitely not as far as Birmingham – so he must still be somewhere in the London area. So what was Brian Freeman doing here?

Fresh clothes were laid out on the bed – a good enough fit – and there was also a glass of water and a packet of co-codamol. Cass almost smiled. They beat him up, then give him something to ease the pain. Brian Freeman always had been on the unusual side. As he followed the silent henchmen back downstairs, he was surprised by a sudden pang of guilt, for once not because of the poor kid he'd shot, but because of his betrayal of Brian Freeman all those years ago.

The young man Cass Jones had once been had liked Brian Freeman, even if he was just a job. The old man had been a father figure to him: a tough character Cass could relate to, so different from his own born-again ever-forgiving dad – and yet for all his softness, it was Cass' own father who'd betrayed them all by giving Luke away. As far as Cass was concerned, Brian Freeman's soul was a lot cleaner than Alan Jones' had ever been. Good and bad were only really grey, as far as he could tell. It was only the holier-than-thou police bosses who didn't see that, or didn't want to see it.

In the lounge, Brian Freeman had already poured them both brandy. They sat on leather sofas facing each other, studying each other, and for a moment neither spoke. Brian Freeman looked better in his seventies than he had in his sixties, Cass concluded. He'd lost weight and his face was still a craggy mess of old broken bones, but it was tanned and healthy. His eyes were just as hard as they'd ever been. Nothing had changed too much in there.

'Not a boy any more, are you, Charlie?' Freeman took a sip of his drink. 'Or should I call you Cass?'

'It's my name.'

'Cass it is, then. What are you now, nearly forty? It's showing on you. Those wrinkles don't look fresh to me.'

'If you know anything about my life, then you know I've earned them.' Cass took a mouthful of brandy and it burned the cuts in his lip. 'How did you find me?'

'Wasn't difficult. You weren't dead, that was clear, so eventually you were going to have to resurface, and you could hardly move around under your real name. There're only so many quality forgers in London, so I made it clear it would be worth their while in lots of ways to let me know when you showed up.'

'I'm still surprised. The man who was looking after me isn't normally messed with.'

'Mullins? I've made some phone calls, taken care of him.'

Cass' bruised face must have managed some kind of expression of alarm because Freeman barked out a short laugh. 'Don't worry, he's not dead – I just squared it with him. Explained a few things.'

'I didn't hear that you were out,' Cass said. 'I'd have thought someone would have told me.'

'Some people are very good at keeping things quiet, Cass. You should know that. I was out after two years, as it happens.'

'How?' After the initial shock, Cass had a feeling he knew the answer. What was it Mr Bright had alluded to back in the Covent Garden church all those months ago? He'd somehow protected Cass from Freeman?

'It was part of my deal, not sending anyone after you: out in two. I couldn't stay in my old manor, of course.' He spread his hands wide. 'But the world is a big place. And I had plenty of money and investments. That was the other part of the deal.'

'By the looks of things it's all paid off.'

'You could say that. I've been playing the markets. Got some good insider info here and there, made myself some respectable money.' He grinned and nodded over at the thugs standing at a polite distance from their conversation. 'I've always kept my hand in the old business, here and there, but I've been a bit more discreet. I quite like my new-found respectability.' He picked up his glass and tilted it at

Cass. 'But don't make any mistake: for a long time I wanted to fucking kill you – and I don't mean just fucking *kill* you; I wanted to rip your skin off strip by strip and then let the boys break every bone in your body. But you were lucky: what I wanted more was to spend my life free and with a few quid in my pocket.' He sniffed. 'It still sticks in my throat though. Guess that's why I've always kept an eye on you.'

'Seems like everyone's always had an eye on me. It must get crowded for all of you in those shadows.'

'Still a cocky sod, then.'

'It's part of my charm.'

'There were people out there with an eye on you long before I added myself to the list. Guess I just couldn't stop wondering why men like Bright and Solomon would be interested in a fucked-up copper like you.'

Hearing the names spoken aloud felt like yet another blow to Cass' solar plexus. *Bright and Solomon.* Even though Mr Bright had alluded to paying Brian Freeman off in some way or another, Cass hadn't expected the old gangster to know his nemesis' name. Nor that of the serial killer who called himself the Man of Flies, and who had died in a blaze of supernatural light.

'What do you know about Mr Bright and Mr Solomon?' He glanced over to one of Freeman's men. 'And where are my cigarettes?'

'Interesting pair, weren't they?' Freeman smiled. 'I reckon Bright would have been happy just to have had me and the boys done in and have that be the end of it – that's the feeling I got when he first came to see me. I was strapped up in the hospital and high on all kinds of painkillers, but I still knew he had to be someone fucking powerful to get past the armed guards.'

His crumpled pack of cigarettes, a lighter and an

expensive crystal ashtray appeared on the coffee table, and Cass lit one. Freeman didn't complain, but neither did he have one himself. Cass had never taken the old man for a quitter, but in this instance he must have been wrong.

'Bright did all the talking and Solomon – I didn't know his name then – he just stood in the background.'

'And they offered you a deal you couldn't refuse just to leave me alone?'

'Something like that.' Freeman's eyes darkened. 'Of course I'm no mug, and I wanted to check them out. Sent a couple of the lads to follow them around, that kind of thing. They never came home, and at that point I realised that I didn't actually have a choice.' He paused. 'I've got cleverer about looking into them; I've learned the ways of subtlety since then.'

'How did you get to know who Solomon was?'

'Strange one, Solomon.' He leaned back against the sofa, his drink in hand. 'I quite liked him, as it goes, back then, anyway. There was something almost spiritual about him. Maybe it was just that he had those kind of looks that you can't help liking. He was a handsome bastard – and you know I'm no poof – but he was. He drew people to him like a movie star or something.'

Cass thought of all the women Mr Solomon had left dead across London. They would have known exactly what Brian Freeman was talking about. He remembered the story of Solomon killing the kittens in the animal sanctuary – cruelty and kindness all rolled into one.

'But sometimes he had this air of melancholy about him. I should have seen that as a sign there was something fucking up his head, but I didn't. I was too busy adjusting to my new life.'

'But how do you know so much about him?' The

combination of booze, painkillers and nicotine was giving Cass a steady buzz despite the throbbing pains in most of his body.

'After I moved down here he came to check on me a few times. He would stay for hours, just talking. Sometimes we talked about you – you hurt me, Charlie, there's no denying that – and sometimes we just talked about life, and how it took you in all kinds of directions you weren't expecting. I *liked* talking to him. He had no blokey bullshit. I used to think that he was visiting me on that Mr Bright's instructions, but now I don't think Bright even knew. I think he was just getting information. I think he was planning ahead, even back then.'

'What do you mean?' Cass leaned forward. *Wheels within wheels.* Mr Solomon had used the phrase, and the truth of it had replayed in his head more with every passing week. How many people's lives had the Network toyed with – and why? What was the point of it all?

'I told him about my family during those talks. Looking back, I can't understand why, but like I said, there was something about him. It was like he *understood* you. I figure that by the end of it, what he didn't know from whatever files Bright had on me, I'd told him myself.'

'I still don't get what you mean? *How* was he planning ahead?'

'There's something you haven't asked me yet, Cass, and it surprises me. You were always pretty sharp.'

'It's been a long day.'

'You haven't asked me, *why now*? Why I'm coming for you a decade after you fucked me over?'

'Well, until a couple of moments ago,' Cass stubbed the cigarette out, 'I was presuming that Mr Bright had paid you to find me for him. It's the only reason I can think of why you'd have grabbed me and I'd still be alive and not halfway to the bottom of the Thames with concrete boots on.'

'What, like that poor fucker the police claimed was Charlie Sutton? That would be fucking ironic, don't you think?'

Cass felt the sting: another black mark on his soul – the unknown John Doe who had been buried in his place to bring the whole sorry undercover mess to an end. He wondered if a woman somewhere still looked out of the window at nights with tired, sad eyes, wishing for her boy to come home, or at least for someone to tell her what had happened to him. He knew it was that, not knowing, that was the killer, even after all hope was gone.

'Yeah, like him.' He didn't let his guilt show. He'd become an expert at that over the years – and no way was he going to let Brian Freeman take the moral high ground here: it was Brian who had told him to shoot the kid. Brian Freeman's soul was far from stain-free.

'Well, you're barking up the wrong tree – quite the opposite, in fact. Things have changed. Mr Bright may have forgotten about me, but I'm coming after him. All bets are off.'

'Why?' It was a curveball, and Cass wasn't sure whether to trust it.

Freeman poured more brandy before continuing, 'Do you remember a dead girl called Carla Rae?'

Cass almost visibly recoiled. What would Freeman know about Carla Rae? 'Of course I do – she was one of the Man of Flies' – Solomon's – victims. The first crime scene I went to when I took the case over from Bowman. What about her?'

'She was my half-sister's granddaughter.'

For a second Cass didn't speak. His brain was trying hard to get to grips with everything beneath the haze of pain and drugs. 'But that can't be right – it would have come up on the system. Someone would have spotted any link with you, especially because of me.' He couldn't even remember Carla Rae's file mentioning Birmingham.

'They wouldn't have known, son: that's my point. My old man never put his name to our Maggie's birth certificate – my mum would've had his balls if he did – but we all *knew* Maggie was his. He'd been knocking off her mum for years. Me and Maggie were close because we came along within two months of each other. We went to school together, played together, and although I never called her my sister because my mum would have gone mental, I still knew it. I was godfather to her Jenny, Carla's mum. They'd all gone to London by the time Carla came along, but I still sent Jenny some money every now and then. That is, until you turned up and I ended up banged up and with Bright and Solomon reorganising my life.'

'So what's the point?' Cass was struggling to keep up. Hearing how someone else's life had been woven so closely with his own with him having no knowledge was a head-fuck. He could remember staring down at Carla Rae's dead body, looking at the words *Nothing is sacred* scrawled across her naked chest. How would he have felt then, if he'd realised she was related to Freeman?

'The point is: I told Solomon about Maggie and her family. Bright wouldn't have known – you and the police wouldn't have known – but Solomon did. And he killed her.'

'But why?'

'To bring you and me back together – hedging his bets, maybe. He knew that I'd follow the case, and he knew you'd be on it. Maybe he knew you had more trouble coming your way, and if so, then he was fucking right, wasn't he? Maybe he knew if he went that far, then I'd want to go after his mate Bright and find out what the fuck all this was about. Solomon was a crazy, and you know better than I do whatever was driving him to kill all those people, but I know that he chose Carla because I told him about her, and because his mate Bright wouldn't know about her. I think all his visits to check on me and chat with me were to get to a name – a name he could use in whatever fucking game they're playing with you.'

Cass sat back, numb.

'Now the thing is,' Freeman continued, 'I'm no hot-headed pup, and Carla was blood, but she was also a virtual stranger, so I wasn't going to do anything rash. But my interest was flagged. I had people – proper people, not the lads like last time – try and dig into our Mr Bright and Mr Solomon, and all they brought me back were questions, no answers.'

'Welcome to my world,' Cass muttered.

'I've even got people working at The Bank's headquarters, and that wasn't easy, I can tell you. But they've been coming up with nothing. And then all the shit with you kicked off. I'd seen about your brother and his family, and I knew he'd worked at The Bank, but then it came back on Bowman and Macintyre. It was when you went on the run with two murders stuck on you that I knew there was more.'

'How?' Cass' mouth was dry. All this time Freeman had been watching him.

'You ain't no murderer, whether you're Charlie or Cass or fucking Shirley. I saw you blow someone's brains out once, and I know what it did to you – don't think I don't. You ain't no killer, not like that.' Freeman leaned forward and rested his arms on his knees. 'Someone's playing with you, and we both know who that is. I've been through that little suitcase of yours and there are some interesting photos in there.'

'If you're looking for answers about who Bright and Solomon are, then I don't have them. I want to find them, though, and I want to bring that bastard Bright and all his people down if I can.'

'And that's what seems strange to me. As far as I can see he's done his best to protect you over the years,' Freeman said softly. 'So what the fuck has he done to piss you off so badly?'

Cass stared at Freeman. It would be easy to tell him everything – he *wanted* to – but this could all be some elaborate fuck-up devised by Bright and the Network. The only man he'd trusted was Artie Mullins, and in the end even he had given in to Freeman.

'How can I trust you?'

'Ha!' Freeman snorted. 'Coming from you I find that rich. But as it happens, I thought you might need a token gesture of my sincerity.' The old man's eyes were smiling. 'So I took it upon myself to do you a little favour.

'I recorded this from the news earlier.' He turned the large TV on. Mat Blackmore's photo filled the corner behind the newsreader.

'Detective Sergeant Mat Blackmore, who was awaiting trial on a charge of murder and several counts of police corruption, died earlier today of what is believed to be strychnine poisoning. Mr Blackmore had received a visit from a man claiming to be from his solicitor's office to discuss the impending trial. The man, as yet unidentified, is believed to have given Mr Blackmore a birthday cake, which contained the poison, before leaving the prison. Mr Blackmore's solicitors, Watson, Harvey and Rogers, have told police the visitor was not affiliated with their company in any way, and they are demanding an inquiry into how he gained access to a high-security prisoner with false paper-work.'

Cass watched, dumbfounded, until Brian Freeman turned it off again.

'You killed Blackmore?'

'I thought you'd rather him than the other bastard.' Freeman grinned. 'This one killed that girl you worked with.'

For a moment, Cass couldn't speak. Freeman knew him well, even after all these years. Bowman might have been the ringleader, and the one who had been fucking his wife, but Blackmore had killed poor Claire May. Yeah, he'd rather the young sergeant was dead. And now Bowman would be sweating, believing someone would be coming for him next.

He looked up at Brian Freeman. 'Mr Bright's got some-thing of mine that I want back,' he said.

'What?'

'My nephew.'

It was Freeman's turn to be silent for a moment. 'Tell me everything,' he said eventually.

And Cass did.

Chapter Fourteen

Mr Bright dismissed the car that had been waiting for him outside the small private nursing home tucked away in the heart of London. Despite the freezing cold, he wanted to walk in the midst of the noise and life of the city for a while and clear his thinking. He pushed his leather-gloved hands deep into the pockets of his overcoat as he strolled casually among those who hurried and scurried to their destinations. Newspaper hawkers tried to push the latest issue into his hands – the headlines screamed of an Angel of Death walking among them – but he ignored them. There was nothing he could read in the paper that he didn't already know.

First Mr Solomon, and now Mr Craven: both so different in character, and yet both chosen to make a point by killing *them*. He was tired of it. He had no feelings for Mr Craven; unlike Mr Solomon, Mr Craven's message and purpose was crude and bitter and selfish. Mr Dublin could deal with it while they all waited for Mr Craven to hurry up and die.

Here and there he saw people with medical masks over their faces, their eyes scared, and he felt a vague disgust. They reminded him of those among his own who whined about the Dying that had come among them and how they feared it. The fear was pointless: the Dying would either come for each of them or it wouldn't. He was proud that most in this city were more like him – they shopped and drank and ate and loved and kept their fear quiet. Sometimes their unknowing strength left him in awe. They refused to give up. They were like a vermin on the face of the planet, but vermin were survivors. There was nothing crumbling about this world, despite what the cohorts might think. It was changing, perhaps, going through a dark time, but it wouldn't crumble. *They* wouldn't allow it.

The air was so cold that his nose had numbed and the dryness in his lungs made him want to cough. He had hoped the fresh air would clear away the niggling doubts, but if anything it made them sharper.

He should be feeling pleased. Thus far, everything was going according to the plan they had hatched all those years ago, when the First's body had started to wither. It had been daring and dangerous but they had thrown themselves into it in the way they had that rebellion so long ago: with complete and utter belief in themselves, knowing that they could not fail. And they hadn't ... but still, there was undeniably something wrong. He knew it.

The First was still weak and bedridden, but his mind was clear. It had been good to talk to his old friend again after so long. He rarely admitted it, but since Mr Solomon had gone and he spent his days merely fulfilling his duty he had found less joy in his existence. It was good to talk to the First; it was almost like the old days. He had wanted to announce to the others that he was rising once again, but the First had shaken his head: *no, not yet.* That had surprised him; it wasn't like their leader to hide away. He had always been so gregarious and flamboyant. Perhaps he was waiting until he was fully restored and adapted.

He paused and bought some roasted chestnuts from a street vendor, enjoying the warmth of the small packet through his gloves. He should be less suspicious. He had spent so long having to manage everything alone that maybe he had learned to see problems where there weren't any – though he had had good cause to be alert after first Mr Solomon's behaviour and then Mr Bellew's recent traitorous performance with the Interventionists – not to mention Mr Craven, of course. His disquiet, however, refused to die.

Something had been *wrong*. The First's easy smile had been slightly too wide as he'd squeezed Mr Bright's hand. The reaction to the news of the emissary had been *off* – Mr Bright couldn't put his finger on it, but he was practised in watching responses, and the First was out of practice at hiding them. And why had he casually thrown in that question about Jarrod Pretorius? The name had come as a bolt out of the blue and it was Mr Bright who'd had to cover his reactions then. Sometimes during the last millennia he'd even managed to convince himself that he'd forgotten Pretorius completely.

His hands warmer, he threw the uneaten chestnuts into a bin. The First had not asked about the Jones family. Perhaps he felt that they were no longer relevant – and perhaps he would be right. Mr Bright was surprised by his own reaction to that thought. He had watched the bloodlines for so many years, long before he'd ever brought Alan and Evelyn together, and he'd felt a little private pride as they produced their children, enjoying the wilful human moments of all concerned. There had been disappointments – Alan Jones had been weak, after all that – but he found he was glad that the deal had been struck and it wasn't Cassius who had been given up.

At the time, the wait for the extra years to pass had been mildly frustrating, and he'd become irritated by Mr Solomon's fondness for both Cassius and Christian, which had moved beyond the simple interest in the blood ties to something else – something deeper. Now, after so much time spent managing Cassius, he found he perhaps had more than a little fondness for the man himself. But fond or not, he was not oblivious to Cass' nature: wherever he was, Mr Bright knew Cass Jones would still be coming after them. He was sure of that. Blood was truly thicker than water.

And that might not prove to be such a terrible thing, after all.

He picked his pace up slightly. Cass Jones was still the wild card. The First's behaviour had been strange, and that might be expected, given everything he had been through, but Mr Bright still needed to plan around it. Cass Jones might well have a part to play in that too – Cass Jones and his bloodline were still important, and the others would be stupid not to realise that.

His mobile phone vibrated and he checked the caller before holding it to his ear. 'Mr Dublin?'

'Mr Bright.'

'You've taken care of Mr Craven?'

'In a manner of speaking. He still has some items to return, but he's gone. I don't think he has long left.' Mr Dublin's gentle voice always had a touch of the maudlin about it and today was no exception.

'That's good.'

'I never thought I'd wish death on one of our own.'

'Then don't,' Mr Bright said prosaically. 'Your wishing of it or not will bear very little relevance to the outcome. I believe that is already quite certain.' He didn't have time for this endless sadness over the things that could not be helped. Their world was changing and they with it. Mr Dublin had never liked getting his hands dirty, but he was no different to the rest of them under the surface. 'Was there a purpose to this call?'

'The Experiment,' Mr Dublin said. If he had been offended by Mr Bright's tone, then it wasn't reflected in his own. The words were still soft and precise.

'What about the Experiment?' Despite the rash of suicides and the investigation that had followed, all blame had landed squarely on the shoulders of the unfortunate Dr Shearman – who, wisely, had opted to stay silent regarding his knowledge of the missing Jones child, and who would reap the benefit of that when his case finally got to court. But the search for the Walkways continued, more quietly, perhaps, and with less carefully selected test subjects, but it continued all the same. They couldn't afford not to, even if the results were still a dismal failure so far.

'I'd like to be more involved.'

'Are you saying you want to try for the Walkways yourself?' Mr Bright allowed himself a small laugh of good humour.

'Of course not.' Mr Dublin did not join in his mirth. 'I would like to take a greater part in it – perhaps oversee the facility for a while. Especially given the . . . disappointing nature of the First's recovery. And you are, of course, always so busy.'

Mr Bright almost smiled. They always come in friendship when they plan to stab you in the back. It had ever been thus. *They* were the same.

'Thank you, Mr Dublin,' he said smoothly. 'That would be a great help.'

He ended the call. Wheels within wheels, as Mr Solomon would have said. Wheels within wheels.

*

Mr Dublin slipped the phone back into his pocket and smiled softly. 'We have the Experiment.'

'Good,' Mr Escobar grunted. Mr Dublin was sure that he could smell the hot grime and corruption of South America on the swarthy newest member of the Inner Cohort. He was Mr Bellew's replacement. Although he was rougher in appearance, there was something similar about the two. Mr Escobar didn't have the inner strength or intelligence of Mr Bellew – he had led them in battle all that time ago, while Mr Escobar, bloodthirsty as he was, had been far behind in the ranks – but he was a warrior. And like Mr Bellew, he had changed his allegiances.

It was interesting, Mr Dublin thought, to watch the warriors among them. They had always been the most loyal back then, but once the revolt had come and they had been persuaded to side with the First, it was as if something inside had broken. Perhaps once a traitor, the potential was always there.

'Does he suspect anything?'

'I'm not sure,' Mr Dublin said. 'With him it's hard to tell.'

'We should move against him – before he makes moves to attack us.'

'Not yet.' Mr Dublin sipped his coffee. And sometimes warriors were like children; they certainly never understand the complexities of politics. 'Let him find the emissary. Right now, he won't be looking to fight – he'll be looking to consolidate. He's not a fool. He knows he's in danger.'

'What about the First?'

'He's moved him.' Mr Dublin was annoyed about that. The old man in the bed was a gibbering fool, so why had Mr Bright decided to hide him away? Perhaps he didn't want the others to see him – that would make sense. But it didn't actually matter; Mr Dublin had filmed the visit after the First's awakening and when he was ready to make his move against Mr Bright, he would send it to all of the cohorts. Mr Bright would be finished. He hoped there would be no bloodshed. Deception had never been part of his nature, and even though he knew he was doing what was best for them all, he had not rested well since his decision to go against Mr Bright.

'I thought we were going to use him for the Experiment?' Mr Escobar's eyes were dark knots of wood and his skin was leather. Mr Dublin tried to remember what he had looked like before he became small. Fierceness was all his memory could muster.

'We were, but on reflection, I doubt he would be of any use. He has no *Glow* – none that we could see anyway.' He shivered slightly and saw Mr Escobar's frown deepen. It was an unsettling thought for all of them.

'So what are we to do? Sit and twiddle our thumbs?'

'No.' Mr Dublin slid a thin file across the table. 'I think we might try this man in the Experiment.'

Mr Escobar opened the folder and looked at the photograph. 'Who is he?'

'He's Mr Bright's pet project. He's the bloodline.'

'So the rumours of the boy were true.' Mr Escobar looked up sharply.

'Mr Bright still has the boy – I don't know where. In fact we don't even know if the boy is alive. The records are unclear.'

'And this man?'

'His name is Cassius Jones. He's out there somewhere. We need to find him before anyone else does.'

'And how do we do that?'

'We wait and we watch. He's a fighter. You'd probably

quite like him. He'll be coming after Mr Bright.' He paused. 'He'll be coming after all of us.'

'And you think he can find the Walkways?'

Mr Dublin gazed out over London. Everyone wanted certainties. His sympathy for Mr Bright was growing. How had he managed everything for so long after the First started sleeping? Yes, he'd had Mr Solomon for a while, but he too had changed, and a long time before his madness came. How those glorious three, the shining lights who led them all the way here, had fallen. It made him ache inside. Perhaps they were fighting a losing battle – perhaps they always had been. He had never thought the day would come when he wanted to go home, but now with the Dying, the First's degradation and no doubt imminent demise, and the rage and rot that was filling the world they'd been so proud of, he ached for the heat of home. He ached to be truly himself. He was tired of being small.

'I think so,' he said. 'He's of the bloodline. If an emissary has found the way here but we can't go back, then the only logical conclusion is that someone has locked the Walkways *outwards*. *He* must have done it to keep us out, so perhaps if it is His own blood trying to get through *He* will open them – *He* will know.'

'*He* always knew everything.' For the first time, Mr Dublin heard nervousness in Mr Escobar's gruff voice.

Yes, and there was the downside of home: *He* was there.

'Well, let's deal with *Him* if and when we have to.'

Mr Dublin smiled. He needed to lift this mood before Mr Escobar left. He pulled open a desk drawer. 'I have something for you.' He held out the item hanging on a slim chain. He had taken it from around the neck of the wrecked Mr Bellew. 'Wear it well. It's our history.' He smiled. 'Welcome to the Inner Cohort.'

Chapter Fifteen

Dr Cornell hadn't slept in two nights, not since Alan Jones' boy had visited. Even when his brain was at its feverish worst, he knew that was too long for a man of his age to go without rest – it was too long for a man of any age. That level of tiredness allowed the shadows to creep in at the edges of his mind; the demon paranoia he knew was always *somewhere* back there now had full rein with his friends fear and doubt.

During the long hours he'd reordered piles of paper to try and keep his mind clear. At some point he'd cried a little. Not for the first time he wondered if they'd put something in his water to keep him just the wrong side of confused – a touch of LSD? No, it wouldn't be anything so basic. He couldn't begin to imagine the kind of drugs *they* must have at their disposal.

He had dozed in his office chair for an hour or so at some point between the grip of the dark night and dawn, and awakened with a jolt – the kind that made you feel like you'd been somewhere other than in your body. That disturbed him; the idea that he could have left his body and all his amassed information, both completely unprotected. And what if he'd left his body and couldn't get back in? What then?

He sipped his coffee and looked down at his gnarled,

ageing hand. He didn't recognise it as his own. Time passed so quickly. For a blissful moment, the demons fell silent and he was aware of his own inadequacies. He was in a battle for his sanity, he knew that. In his clearer moments, he wondered if perhaps he was experiencing the onset of dementia. So many years spent living in fear, trying to get to the bottom of what might possibly be the world's biggest secret – no, *was* the world's biggest secret – had taken their toll. His mind had been pushed to the limits even before natural wear and tear set in, and the shame of being decried as a lunatic had gone some way towards turning him into one in truth.

The knots on the back of his hand were like those in his mind: calcified. Damaged. He looked again at the stacks of paper around him. Alan Jones' son had been here – Cassius, the eldest, the man on the run. He rubbed his tired eyes. Or had it been him at all? Had it been one of *them*? How would he ever learn to tell the difference? Perhaps it had been Cassius Jones, but maybe he was working *with* them. Maybe the whole murder charge was part of some elaborate plan not yet revealed. He sighed. It was exhausting trying to work out all the possibilities. He looked for links in everything, because *they* were everywhere, controlling everything. At some point over the years, he'd lost the ability to believe in any random turn of events. Perhaps that was his madness.

He stared at the mass of papers and documents that surrounded him. Somewhere in those piles there were answers, and yet every step forward raised more questions. He had been on this quest so long that he'd forgotten more questions than he'd ever had answers, though the basic queries still remained, haunting him: *who, why, how*? And how much longer? The only two things he knew for certain were that they weren't like us, and they'd been here for ever.

The *who* and the *why* were responsible for starting his sanity cracking, he knew that. He was slipping through the gaps. He just needed to find the answers, then make people believe. He needed there to be a point to all these years spent hoarding. He thought he might cry again.

A sudden bang on the front door made him drop his coffee cup, spilling the lukewarm drink all over his trousers.

'Dr Cornell?' It was a rough voice, demanding. He moved cautiously into the hallway and stared at the door with dread.

'If you're from the council,' he started, happy to hear indignation rather than fear, 'then you can't come in. You have no right—'

A crash came from behind him and he turned, startled. At the other end of the corridor, a booted foot could be seen as it kicked the back door open. Dr Cornell mewled slightly. It had finally happened: *they* had come for him. He looked back at the front door. He couldn't get out that way – even if there weren't men on the other side it would take him too long to undo all the bolts and locks. Why hadn't he taken the same measures with the back door? What had they done, climbed over the back wall? The gate was long gone, he'd bricked that up years ago. His stomach turned to water. A heavy figure came towards him, cutting through the stream of sunshine from the back.

'You can't be in here, this is private prop—' He didn't get to finish the sentence as a thick arm wrapped around his thin neck and covered his mouth.

'It's like a fucking a junkyard out there.' A second man walked towards him through the kitchen, pouring liquid from a small bottle onto a piece of cloth. He didn't look at Dr Cornell but at the brute who was holding him so firmly. 'I told you to wait for me. Here.' He handed over the cloth.

Dr Cornell's heart was racing so fast he thought it would burst. His mind was pure white panic as a hand pressed the cloth against his mouth. He tried not to breathe, he really did, but still the world started to blacken at the edges and his head swam.

In front of him, the man in the black leather coat put the bottle back in his pocket and peered into the study.

'Fuck me,' he muttered. 'We're going to need a bigger van.'

Chapter Sixteen

'I brought doughnuts.' Hask closed the door of the small conference room behind him and smiled. 'Cliché, I know, but also very tasty and marginally less messy on a suit than an almond croissant first thing in the morning.'

He was glad they'd found a space away from the hubbub. Ramsey and Armstrong both had dark rings around their eyes and neither was standing as tall as normal. He couldn't blame them for their tiredness. The news of Blackmore's poisoning had broken two days ago, and there were plenty of accusations, spoken and otherwise, flying around. If it hadn't been Bowman or one of his criminal associates who had organised the murder, then perhaps it had been the police, protecting themselves. That wasn't something the public would have a problem believing, not after everything that had happened in recent months, and it was an accusation that Paddington Green Police Station really didn't need.

'I could do without being the lead in this case,' Charles Ramsey grumbled. 'There's enough shit going on here as it is – and now the pressure's back on to find Jones. As if I'm some kind of magician.'

'Maybe they think Paddington has something to prove,' Armstrong said.

'Yeah, and they surely do,' Ramsey agreed, 'but why pick on the clean officers to do it?'

It was good to see that even if they weren't exactly bonding, Armstrong and Ramsey were on the same side.

'No, it's my fault,' Hask said cheerfully. 'They need me on it, and I told the Commissioner that I wanted to work with you rather than start afresh with new people. Plus they're already paying me to consult on the elusive Mr Jones' case, so I suppose they think they might keep the bill down if I don't have to factor in travel time between stations. You can thank me later.' He smiled, and then rubbed his hands together before pulling a doughnut out of the box. 'So, what have we got?'

Armstrong stared at him for a moment and then sighed. 'We've been through all the cases of Strain II diagnosed in the past six months. There's no one coming up who fits our man's description, not from the corporations that insist on it, the hospitals, the private clinics, or even those Portakabin testing centres that turn up in the estates. And since it's illegal to do anonymous testing now, I don't know where else we can check. I've got some people going back another six months – maybe we'll find him there.'

'You can have them look,' Hask washed down his dough-nut with coffee, 'and it's worth doing just so you look like you're ticking all the boxes, but I doubt you'll come up with anything. This spate of attacks – how long has it been going on, do you think?'

'Michaela Wheeler said she was infected at the end of October,' Ramsey said. 'But he was working with the junkies and homeless before then. Let's say the beginning of October as a ballpark date.'

'So two to three months. He should be well within your original six-month range for diagnosis. This man is arro-gant. And he's bitter. He would have started "spreading God's word", or *his* word, or both if he sees himself as the

111

not-so-good Lord, pretty soon after he learned of his own illness. He can call it what he wants, but this is a case of *I'm going down and you're all coming with me.* That kind of thinking kicks in fast – it's a knee-jerk reaction. If he'd been choosing particular targets, people he had personal grudges against, for example, then I might say different, but I'd put my money on this man getting to work quickly. Despite his apparent cool, he's very, very angry, even if he's conned himself into believing that he's above that.'

'So you're saying he knows he's got the bug but he hasn't been diagnosed?' Ramsey frowned.

'He's a smart,' Hask reached for a second doughnut, 'and apparently sophisticated man. He definitely has an ego. Perhaps he self-diagnosed.'

'I don't buy it.' Ramsey shook his head. 'The early symptoms could be down to any number of diseases – after all, no one dies from AIDS; you die from something else that your body can't fight. I don't care who this guy is, he'd have got himself checked out. Surely the bigger the ego, the less likely he'd think it would be that he would have something terrible like Strain II?'

'Good point.' Ramsey was smart, Hask thought. 'But he didn't get checked here. Could he have done it out of the country?'

'There is another way he could have known – something else I've been checking out.'

Hask and Ramsey both looked over at the young sergeant.

'What if someone he knew got diagnosed as infected? Someone he'd slept with but he'd thought to be clean?'

Hask slowly nodded. 'That's possible. And if he'd started getting symptoms, then he'd know what it was. I wonder if he's privately wealthy? It's a tall ask, but you might want to check with those corporations that do the bug tests, find out whether they've had any high-ranking staff member suddenly quit with no warning.' He smiled at the sergeant. 'Good reasoning on the diagnosis, but I'm not sure how much it helps us.'

'You might be wrong there.' Armstrong shuffled through a stack of papers in a thick file. He glanced up. 'I had another comparison done. Thank fuck we've got city-wide co-operation because this would have taken bloody months otherwise. A grimmer one.'

'Go on,' Ramsey said.

'I got a list of all the Strain II deaths in the past six months and then cross-referenced it with the diagnoses. We know that the bug he's infecting people with is somehow far more aggressive – not a mutation, according to the doctors, but somehow more virulent. Don't ask me to explain the science – in fact, don't ask *them* to explain the science, because they don't know how it works either – but that seems to be the case, even if it isn't killing our man quite as fast.'

'Stick to the point, Armstrong,' Ramsey said. 'My brain is too tired for tangents.'

'Sorry. My point is this: anyone infected by him, before he started doing it wilfully or since, has a much shorter life expectancy than a normal Strain II case. With normal Strain II, you have maybe a year, or eighteen months if you're in good heath, right? But these new cases are deteriorating fast, and on a daily basis. Even Michaela Wheeler, who was both young and healthy, isn't expected to last beyond January.'

'I take it you've found something?' Hask asked.

'Yeah.' Armstrong pulled a photo out of the file. 'I think I might have done. But you're not going to like it.' He placed the picture in the middle of the table where both Ramsey and Hask could see it. Pale blond hair falling over a slightly chubby, cherubic face.

'He's just a kid,' Ramsey said, not quite hiding the fear in voice.

'Joey Brannigan. Eight years old. He died of Strain II two weeks ago.'

'Jesus.'

'Carry on,' Hask said. His mind was ticking over, already a step ahead. 'I'm presuming this story gets worse?'

'Yep. Joey Brannigan's a care-home kid; he was taken by Social Services when he was five after running away from an abusive family home. He showed early signs of TB, but other than that he was clean. He was fostered when he was six, but got put back into the system seven months ago when the foster mother got pregnant. He was put into a private care home in Lambeth. Social Services tested him on the way in: his lungs were weak, a result of that early TB, but he had put on weight and other than that was looking healthy. When he suddenly fell very ill in October they gave him a routine Hep-and-TB test and bang, there it was: Strain II.'

'How?' Ramsey asked.

'At first the care home manager tried to claim that his previous test must have been misread, or mixed up with someone else's, but Social Services weren't having any of that. Apparently they'd had concerns about the welfare of the children in the—'

'—Happy Smiles Care Home?' Ramsey broke in. 'Caroline Hurke's place?'

'That's the one.'

'Have I missed something?' Hask asked.

'You must have,' Ramsey said. 'It was all over the news: she was arrested a month ago and charged with supplying

114

minors. She ran a small home for difficult children in the state's care.'

'Yeah,' Armstrong said, 'the alarm bells started ringing because the children all became *too* manageable: turned out they were terrified – being abused, and kept mildly sedated to stop them kicking up about it. Little Joe's test results finally made Social Services sit up and take notice, and once they started looking more closely they discovered all the kids showed physical evidence of sexual abuse.' He swallowed, hard. 'They were all under ten.'

There was a momentary silence while they all considered this.

Then Ramsey said quietly, 'I don't remember reading about a Strain II case.'

'Lambeth Social Services have kept it quiet, at least so far. They figured things were bad enough without the public getting hold of that as well. So far they've managed to keep it out of the papers, but when Hurke's case goes to trial next year it *will* come out. They got a statement from Joey Brannigan before he died.'

'And how does this piece of shit account for poor Joey Brannigan's Strain II infection?' Ramsey asked.

'Interestingly, she hasn't. She's given up other clients, but not the one who requested Joey. Prosecution have stopped pushing – they've got more than enough to convict her – and Brannigan's family don't care. You know how it is, sir—' Armstrong looked at Ramsey a little apologetically. 'You never get the whole lot of them if there's a paedophile ring. Time and resources are too thin.'

'I think we should pay Ms Hurke a visit,' DI Ramsey growled, his eyes still on the photograph.

'I've already primed Holloway.'

'People in her situation stay silent out of fear.' Hask looked thoughtfully at the photo. 'We have to make sure she's more afraid of us than she is of whoever killed Joey Brannigan. That shouldn't be too hard; I should imagine that she's feeling isolated and paranoid by now.'

He grinned and took another doughnut from the bag for the journey. Waste not, want not. At least it was finally beginning to feel like they were getting somewhere.

Caroline Hurke had a face that matched her personality: deeply unpleasant. She was an overly thin woman in her fifties, and hard lines pulled down her mouth, leaving her with a permanent sour frown – not that she'd had much inclination to smile recently. Her eyes looked bitter too; Hask could see clearly exactly how Caroline Hurke felt about her current situation: *she* was the victim here; she was the one left to carry the can when all she'd done was facilitate – she'd never touched the brats herself . . . There was an angry whine of *it's not fair* coming clearly from her. It was all there in the expression. Hask decided he didn't like her very much at all.

'I have nothing to say about that. I don't remember.' She leaned back in the chair and folder her arms defiantly.

'Of course you remember.' Ramsey smiled. 'And you will tell us.'

'No, I won't.' She looked like some awful parody of a sulking teenager being told off by a headmaster. 'I didn't tell them, and I won't tell you.'

'If Joey's dead, then maybe he is too.'

'He's not dead.' She smiled, but under it was a death mask of terror. 'You know that and I know that. We get the papers in here too, you know. I'm only on remand, remember?'

Hask felt the tension crackling between them. She'd recognised the e-fit: so she really had procured children for the man they were hunting.

'Remand's a funny thing, isn't it?' Armstrong hadn't sat down. Now he leaned against the wall next to the table. 'It's like you're a prisoner and yet not – it's amazing how slack security can get in remand . . .'

'What do you mean?' Hurke flashed a glance at him.

Armstrong didn't answer, but he nodded at the female prison guard standing by the door. She looked at Ramsey, who also nodded, and then she left the room. She didn't look at her prisoner once.

Hurke squirmed round in her chair. 'Where's she going? She should stay in here, shouldn't she?' Her eyes narrowed. 'Don't play games with me. I know the law.'

'Do you think anyone actually cares? On the side of the law, that is?' Ramsey smiled.

'What do you mean?'

'He means, you thick bitch' – Hask leaned forward – 'that the prosecution have got everything they need to convict you and your clients – physical evidence, phone records, statements from the children – so why do they need you? You're not important.'

Her pupils widened slightly. He'd hit a nerve.

'In fact, you're just an embarrassment to the system,' he finished.

'They *need* me,' she said forcefully.

'*No one* needs you,' Armstrong said with conviction.

'You do – you want to know about *him*.'

'That's true,' Ramsey agreed, 'we do want to know about him, and we know no one cares about you. That's an interesting combination, don't you think?'

Caroline Hurke paled slightly. Hask wondered how she'd looked at the height of her respectability, with her hair and make-up done, wearing something soft and feminine rather than her baggy jeans and sweater. It was hard to picture.

'Where's the guard gone?' There was a nervous rasp in her voice now.

'I think you have rather bigger worries than whether the guard is taking a piss or having a cup of tea.' Armstrong still hadn't moved. 'Do you know what station we're from?'

'Does it matter?' Hurke kept up her sullen tone.

'Oh, I think it does. We're from Paddington Green. Most of our lot got nicked not so long ago. Some of us got away with it.' Armstrong smiled.

'Bullshit.' Hurke said, though she didn't sound convinced, despite her strong language.

'You get the papers in here, remember? So you must have read about our young sergeant?' Ramsey took over. 'The one who got poisoned? On remand?'

'Are you trying to tell me that you did that?' Hurke's chair shifted an inch, scraping on the cheap lino.

Hask smiled inwardly; her face might still be all arrogant rebellion, but they had her on the back foot.

'I'm not saying anything. I'm just pointing out that he was on remand and now he's dead.'

'And,' Armstrong cut in, 'he was in isolation for most of the time – harder to get at.'

'Are you threatening to kill me?' Her eyes widened slightly and then she snorted a bitter laugh. 'Going to get someone to stab me in the shower? I think you'll notice less of that happens these days, ever since you brought the death penalty back.' She grinned triumphantly. 'I have learned some things in my time here, you know; you can't fool me with a trick like that.'

'It's no game, I assure you. And we were not thinking anything nearly as complicated as a stabbing in the shower would be required.' Ramsey smiled. 'There was a *point* to be made with young Sergeant Blackmore; people needed to *know* he'd been taken out. With you it would be different.'

A wave of confused anxiety crossed Caroline Hurke's lined face. They nearly had her.

'Let me break this down for you,' Hask said. He pulled the padded envelope from his pocket. 'I brought a visual aid – just so there are no misunderstandings.' He tugged the evidence bag out of the envelope and placed it on the table between them. Hurke stared at the syringe inside.

'Before you ask, yes, it is infected.' He waited until she looked up at him. 'This is a prison – don't tell me you haven't learned how rife drug usage is in a place like this? How hard would it be to knock into you with a needle? One tiny prick, and that's you taken care of. Maybe they'll even spare you a bit of smack in there too, get you high before you die. To all the world you'll look like one more prisoner-turned-junkie who'd got unlucky.' He kept his voice slow and steady, letting every word sink in. 'You don't think there'll be plenty in here who would do that one little thing for the right price? Women who have children?' He leaned forward. '*Guards* who have children? You don't think people will actually care if you come to some awful end, do you? I think you'll find most folks would see it as natural justice.'

Hurke's mouth moved as if she was trying to spit out words of denial, but it was clear she couldn't find any.

'It would be easy,' Hask finished. 'And believe me, I wouldn't lose a minute's sleep over it – why should I? You're not losing any sleep over the people out there getting infected because you won't open your mouth, are you?'

'I'm no killer,' Ramsey added, 'but I think I'd almost enjoy reading about you dying slowly of the bug.'

'He'll kill me,' she whispered, 'if I tell. You don't understand.'

'I hate to break this to you,' Armstrong snorted, 'but your

options aren't great here. At least if you tell us what we want to know, we can put you in solitary – that'll keep you safe. And wherever he is, he's sick – he's moved onto other things. I doubt he even remembers who you are.'

'I may not be a killer,' Ramsey grinned, 'but I'm a very good liar. And here's the thing, Ms Hurke: if you *don't* co-operate with us, then I'll just say you have anyway. I'll announce it to the media, and I'll do it loudly – it's not like they'd be expecting us to actually give up any details, is it? Then if you were unfortunate enough to find yourself infected with this rather virulent strain of the bug, no one will blame us, no matter what you might try to say, because everyone will be certain it's all the fault of this Angel of Death, as they've so poetically dubbed him.'

She stared at them for a long time, and then her shoulders slumped. 'I'd never done anything like this until I met him – you know, with the kids. I'd never even thought about it, not even when the bills were mounting and the government were cutting how much they were paying for each child ...'

'You're all heart,' Armstrong muttered, and Hask and Ramsey both flashed him a sharp look; now she was starting to open up they didn't need him needling her.

'It's not something I'd even have thought of.' She frowned a little as if remembering a previous version of herself, someone so long gone she was hardly recognisable. 'I *liked* the children, even the ones who could be little shits. I've been running foster and care homes for years. I started with Jake, and then when that broke up' – the frown turned into a slight sneer and Hask was pretty sure that there'd been a third party who'd taken Hurke's husband away – 'I carried on by myself.'

'So what happened?' Ramsey asked, trying to sound sympathetic.

'Things started getting really difficult, about a year ago – personally, that is. I had some credit card debts that I was struggling to pay after I'd gone a bit mad on retail therapy when Jake left. It was stupid, really; I didn't even *like* the stuff I bought. Anyway, I started cutting corners at the home and used the extra money to meet my payments, but even that wasn't enough. I defaulted on the mortgage twice.' She looked up, and the hard mask had slipped a little; now she looked like a scared woman who knew she'd fucked up. 'You know that horrible feeling, when you realise you're sinking and you've slipped so far back that you're only just stopping new leaks rather than solving the problem?'

Hask nodded. There was a whole lot of it around; sometimes it felt like the whole world was trying just to keep its head above the waterline. Too many people – governments, corporations and citizens alike – had spent too much, and no one had any money in the banks to back it up. The whole house of cards had started to topple.

'Then a man came to visit me – he told me he knew about my financial situation, and that he could help.'

'Was that our man?' Ramsey asked.

'No, not him, not yet. I only saw *him* once – and once was enough. This man was called Draper. I was in my study – my flat was the top floor of the home, and he rang that doorbell, not the home. I don't have a first name for him. He was in his forties, I suppose. Brown hair. He was average build – he looked ordinary but smart. I thought he was from Alliance & Lloyd, my mortgage company, and when he said he wasn't I told him to go away – I presumed he was a loan shark; there's plenty of them around, but tempting as a quick fix was, I knew it wasn't going to help me. At that point I was waiting to see if Jake would lend me some money to tide me over – we'd been married for fifteen years and

I thought that counted for something. As it turned out, he couldn't help me: apparently *she* was pregnant and they needed all their money for the baby.'

Her face twisted sourly as she spoke and Hask was struck once again by her bitterness. Was she typical of the population in general? Were they all blaming each other for their ills?

'The Social doesn't provide that much for each kid, and even though I'd squeezed another couple in, there was only so much I could skim from the top. I started ignoring the credit cards completely and tried to get the mortgage together, but I didn't have anywhere near enough – I was at rock bottom. People say that a lot, don't they? *I've hit rock bottom.* But when you do, you really know it. I was numb, couldn't focus at all. I was thinking of just burning the place down, kids and all, and walking away.' Her eyes filled up. 'How terrible is that?'

Hask realised that something had cracked in Caroline Hurke back then, and it had never repaired itself. He wondered if she had any idea of the enormity of what she'd done since then?

'That was when Draper came back, and this time I let him in. I don't even know why – I think he just looked so calm, he looked like he could make my mess go away.' She gave a wry smile. 'I suppose in his own way he did.'

Armstrong had slipped out of the room, no doubt to get someone checking on the name Draper, but Hurke hadn't noticed; she was lost in her memories. Despite their desperate need for the information, Hask hoped they weren't doing her too much more damage. The heavy-handed bad-cop/worse-cop game to get her to talk had been his idea, and it had worked, but now that he was watching her crumble he found himself almost regretting it. The bitterness she wore was like a shell; inside, she was so damaged – she'd obviously had a breakdown, whether she knew it or not.

Oblivious to Hask's thoughts, she went on, 'He told me he was there on behalf of his employer, a very wealthy man, who wanted to enter into a business arrangement with me.'

Ramsey flashed at look at Hask: so their man did have private money.

'He told me what that *arrangement* would be, about the boys, and he sounded as if he was offering to come and clean my carpets or buy jam from me. As if it was *normal*.'

'Just boys?' Ramsey asked.

'Yes, just boys – for him, anyway.' She sniffed. 'I told him no, of course. I was shocked – *disgusted*. And children are *people*, aren't they? What if they *told*? People always talk, don't they? I couldn't do it; even when he said he knew about my fiddling the books I said no. I'm *not* a monster.' For the first time, Hask saw terror in her eyes – not because of this mysterious man who'd made her do these things, but for what she had become: she *was* a monster.

'I was angry, and I told him I'd report him to the police.' She took a deep breath. 'He wasn't fazed by my reaction, but he made a call on his mobile and asked if I'd give his employer ten minutes of my time. By that point I just wanted Draper to go – I didn't know who he was and I was starting to get scared; his boss might be some Russian gangster. The children were due back from school about then and I knew I'd have to get back downstairs and help the staff.' She half laughed. 'I was *worried* about the children.'

'And?' Ramsey had moved forward on his seat, impatient to hear the rest. 'So what happened?'

'Draper said that he would give me a thousand pounds just to hear his boss out. He promised me that I'd be quite safe, and that if I still wanted nothing to do with them after the meeting, then they would leave and I'd never hear from them again. I said yes – I didn't think I had much of a choice, to be honest. So I called the office and made some excuse about a migraine, and then Draper and I waited in silence until his phone rang again, and he went downstairs to get his boss. He wasn't what I'd expected – he was slimmer, and younger, maybe mid-thirties. I don't know why, but I'd been imagining a much older man. Anyway, he looked like the man in the paper – well, *when* he did anyway.'

'Have you seen him since then? You said you only saw him the once?' Hask frowned.

'He talked to me,' Hurke said, caught up in the memory. 'He made it all sound so reasonable – so *normal*. He talked about history, and cultures, and nature, until my head was spinning and I didn't know what to think any more.' She paused. 'And then, when I asked him how he could know all these things' – her breath hitched, a small gasp – 'he showed me what he really was.' Her eyes went wide and she looked upwards towards the ceiling. 'He *changed*, right in front of my eyes. One minute he was a man in an expensive suit, and the next he was … He was *gone*; he'd become something else, something beautiful and terrible – a *god*. He was all light and claws and sharp edges and in all the brightness that held me I could hear the awful beating of wings. They were like my heartbeat.'

'I don't understand,' Ramsey said. 'What do you mean, he *changed*?'

'You *wouldn't* understand,' Hurke said. 'You didn't *see* him.' She let out a long sigh. 'After that, there was no way I could refuse. I couldn't refuse *him*.' Tears started running down her face. 'He made it sound normal. He made me think it was okay. How could I refuse him?'

*

They left her there, crying bitter tears over her own memories, and headed back out into the crisp December air. Hask found the cold bite a welcome relief.

'No one warned us she was fucking mad,' Armstrong said.

'To be fair,' Hask shrugged, 'I didn't realise until about halfway in.'

'Anything on this Draper, Armstrong?' Ramsey asked.

'Not yet. Shame she couldn't give us a first name.'

'How did he know to target her? How did he know about her financial situation?'

'Draper's certainly valuable, but I don't think we should see him as any more than a puppet.' The cold was losing its allure and Hask was pleased to get into the relative warmth of the car. 'Anything he's done has been under instruction; it's his employer who does all the thinking.' He leaned back against the leather. 'Interesting how she refers to our man as a god – not only *refers* to, but actually had some kind of hallucination that allowed her to see him as one.'

'*This is the word of your God*,' Ramsey muttered.

'Exactly.'

Armstrong's phone rang and he flipped it open. 'Yes?' There was a long pause and Hask leaned forward in his seat, but he couldn't make out any of what the speaker at the other end was saying.

'Thanks.' Armstrong looked at Ramsey. 'Draper's dead. He's on the Strain II list.'

'When?'

'Last week.'

'Shit.' Ramsey thumped the steering wheel.

'I guess,' Hask looked out at the grey city, 'he outlived his usefulness. Or perhaps this mysterious employer simply didn't want his servant outliving him.'

Chapter Seventeen

Cass waited for the fresh coffee to bubble through the expensive machine. It was only eight in the morning but he'd already showered, and he felt more refreshed and awake than he had done in months. In the two days since Brian Freeman had grabbed him, Cass had continued to heal surprising quickly. Although there were still dark smudges of purple and black bruising under his eyes, the swelling on his face from the beating had gone down almost overnight. Freeman had laughed at his men – both Steves, and therefore known by their surnames, Wharton and Osborne – for having lost their battering skills, but Cass knew it was more than that. It wasn't just his face. His shoulder felt better too. The constant ache had been replaced with an itch on the inside, as if all the damaged flesh was finally knitting itself back together. The first time he sat up in the morning had been agony, every inch of flesh and bone from his ribs to his neck screaming at him, but the past two mornings that unspeakable pain had been replaced by a dull throb that had passed within ten minutes.

He remembered the surge of heat he'd felt when they pulled the bag off his head in the garage. It had burned outwards and inwards, feeling like adrenalin and cocaine mixed together and then souped-up with something to give them an extra kick. His eyes had *glowed*; there was no other way he could describe the feeling.

The boys see the Glow! His mother's long-ago words scribbled on the back of an old photograph echoed in his head. Was that what was responsible for this sudden improvement in his health, the glow that he was finding harder and harder to deny? Or was it just optimism: that not only did he have a plan, but it was actually moving forward, and, even better, he was no longer alone in his fight to find Luke, even if Brian Freeman did have his own agenda? Cass liked to think it was the latter. To acknowledge the Glow, especially to accept that it existed inside him, would be to admit that he and Mr Bright were linked by something stronger than circumstance or conspiracy, and he wasn't ready for that, no matter what evidence to the contrary presented itself.

The dreams had also let him go, for now at least, and he'd had two solid nights' sleep. That surprised him even more than his speedy recovery. Maybe it was all just too much to grasp – Mr Bright and Mr Solomon's manipulation of Freeman and then Mr Solomon's murder of Carla Rae. The Man of Flies had definitely had the last laugh over Mr Bright with that one, using people as pawns in their personal battle.

Cass poured a mug of coffee; the rich, nutty blend was a far cry from the muck they served in the machines in Paddington Green nick – and took it over to the patio doors. Good coffee and a cigarette: there was no better way to start any day. The wind was bitterly cold, but he didn't mind; it helped his thinking.

Carla Rae's pathetic naked corpse drifted to the front of his mind. Did Mr Bright and his Network have any respect for people's lives at all? It didn't look like it. So why had Mr Bright taken Luke? What had been so important about him – or was it what he represented? The Jones family?

What had been so *right* about them compared with the other families who had had voided files in the Redemption directory he'd found on his brother's laptop? What was in their blood, the Glow? It was all about the Glow; he knew that much, so what was so *special* about it? An unwelcome memory stung him: those wide, terrified eyes looking down the barrel of that gun, and the single thought: *he has no glow.*

When they'd met in that half-built block, Cass had shouted at the ageless man for setting him up, and Mr Bright had shouted back, '*I set you free.*' That had been his answer – but free from what – and to *do* what? Memories of that day burned as hot as the air was cold. Cass pulled in a long, rebellious lungful of smoke. What had they done to Abigail Porter, the PM's bodyguard who'd bought him time to get away? Something had happened to her eyes; he'd seen the universe in them, he was sure of that – although he'd left that detail out when he'd told Freeman his story. He didn't need the old man to think he'd gone batshit-crazy over the past ten years.

'Time to go.'

Cass jumped; he had been so lost in his own thoughts he hadn't noticed Wharton appearing behind him. He flicked the butt out onto the perfect lawn as his heart picked up pace. The game was on.

If Cass had thought about the location for the meet with Freeman and the hacker, he didn't think a crematorium would ever have featured in his list of possibilities.

'You're kidding me,' he muttered as the car pulled through the gates and right up to the small chapel door.

'Where else in London can several cars with tinted glass all arrive within minutes of each other and not arouse suspicion?' Wharton grinned proudly. 'Other than that other home of all great criminals, Downing Street, of course.'

'You may have a point.' Cass grinned as he stepped out and followed Wharton inside. There was a service taking place, but the two men slipped in through a side-door and climbed the narrow stairs to the offices above where Osborne was waiting. He nodded to his colleague, and Wharton opened the door. 'In you go then, son,' he said.

Cass did as he was told. The room was sparsely furnished with basic office chairs and a desk with a computer on it. The window had been pulled open slightly and a thin man in jeans and a Ripcurl sweater was sitting close to it, smoking. Cass looked at the ashtray, which was already half full.

'If you can't smoke in a crematorium, where can you smoke?' he said with a smile.

The hacker smiled back. He was older than Cass had expected, early forties perhaps, his hair still full, but already grey. He leaned back in his chair, looking relaxed, that ease that comes only with being incredibly good at what you do, and having the money to prove it.

Cass looked from him to Brian Freeman and once again decided that the phrase 'crime doesn't pay' was utter bull-shit.

'Cass Jones, meet Dijan Maric, just arrived from Romania. Dijan Maric, meet Cassius Jones.' Freeman smiled.

'Good to meet you,' Maric said. His voice was all light-and-sunny California.

'Likewise,' Cass said. 'Romania?'

'My home from home – it's great for anything computer-related. I figured I'd better use a name that matched. It's not my original.' He grinned. 'But then I hear that you haven't always been known as Cass, either.'

'Ain't that the truth, Charlie?' Freeman laughed.

'Sometimes a different name is necessary.' Cass took the spare chair, and the three men sat huddled like gossiping women.

'That I can understand,' Maric agreed. 'Now, I haven't as yet agreed to undertake this work for you. First, I need to hear exactly what you want, get to know you a little, and then I'll decide. I get a lot of offers and I take very few of them. I need to know if we're on the same page, as it were – think of this as a kind of first date.'

'It a bloody expensive first date,' Freeman growled. 'It cost enough to get you over here. I'm really hoping you'll put out.'

'Nice metaphor,' Maric said; 'I'll add it to my spiel for the next client. Yes, this meeting is costly, but I value my freedom and travel is always risky. I'm wanted in four different European countries, and the US still have ants in their pants over that little incident with the defence network back in '95. They have no sense of humour.'

'I'm not without a few governmental and police problems either, trust me,' Cass said. 'And speaking of trust, how can we be sure we can trust you with any information we give you?'

'We are both men who could spend the rest of our lives behind bars – if we're lucky enough to keep our lives – if we get caught. Trust is implicit, wouldn't you say?'

Cass had to agree. 'Okay, well, fire away. What do you want to know?'

'You mentioned The Bank.' Maric looked at Freeman. 'I have to tell you now, if this is a straightforward bank robbery I'm not interested. You know my reservations about this sort of job: I don't want to make my money by making the little people poorer. They've been fucked over enough by all our governments, wouldn't you say?'

'It's true, the little people get fucked all the time, but they tend to survive,' Cass said. 'But you can put your mind at ease: we're not after The Bank per se. Just one man. And there is money – a lot of it – but it's not coming from ordinary people's accounts.'

'I should say that we have two agendas here,' Freeman cut in, 'but we both want to fuck with the same man.'

'Go on.' Maric lit another cigarette. 'Is this man someone I've heard of? One of the founders of The Bank?'

'Yes, he is, but he's not one of the men you're thinking of. He's no public figure.' Cass leaned forward. 'My brother Christian worked for The Bank. He was headhunted. And then he was killed. After his death I went through his laptop, and I found all the usual stuff – but I found something I hadn't been expecting: evidence of a second system running secretly underneath The Bank's own network. Christian had copied over a folder of various files. I tried to copy them externally, but I couldn't. What I need is access to the information in those files – as well as the information I need, there were also details of twenty bank accounts – identified only by an X and a number, one to twenty. There are vast amounts of money in them – I'm talking *billions*, not millions. You can take your paycheck from them, if you can get in and get it out safely.'

'The getting in, well, we'll see about, but the getting money out and hidden? That I'm an expert on.' Maric grinned from behind a cloud of smoke.

'There are transaction records going back a couple of hundred years, but the opening balances were huge,' Cass continued. 'Somewhere there'll be paper records – there have to be.'

'And this money is nothing to do with The Bank?'

'There were some transfers between the two, but no – this is old money. This is *hidden* money.'

'Interesting: the more hidden it is, the less noise people can make if it's stolen.'

'True, but be warned, these people won't take the theft lightly.'

'No one ever does – and I'm not so stupid; I'll skim it, make it look like the money has been lost. You say there are billions there? I could take five million and it would be months before any notices. How much do you want from there?'

'We don't want that money,' Cass said. 'I want the information in that directory.'

'What kind of information is it?'

'Personal. This man we're after, his name is Castor Bright. You could say he has an unhealthy interest in my family. He's taken my nephew and I want him back. I am quite sure that there'll be a file somewhere in that sub-system that will help me find him. Mr Bright is a meticulous man: he's an analyst, a planner. My nephew can't have just vanished into thin air. There will be a record somewhere of the money Mr Bright has spent to acquire Luke, I'm sure of it. Everything is an investment, a project; people are a game to him.'

'He sounds interesting. I almost like him—'

The hacker's words threw Cass for a moment. The idea that Mr Bright might be in some way likeable had never crossed his mind.

'—but that's irrelevant,' Maric finished. 'If I agree to the job and get into the system, then that information is yours to do what you want with. You say this sub-system is separate from The Bank's?'

'Yes, it even looked different. It wasn't Windows-based for a start – at least, it wasn't on the copy that Christian had made.'

'And these twenty accounts, the X ones – do you know whose money it is?'

'It's a group called the Network, they're the people really in charge of The Bank – and most of the world's governments too, I wouldn't be surprised – and Mr Bright appears to be in charge of them. I don't know *who* they are, but I do know they are *very* powerful, and they've been around for a long time – too long. It sounds crazy, I know, but it's the truth.'

'So some shadowy conspiracy is behind the world's largest financial organisation, and the man who runs it has taken your nephew?'

'And set me up for murder. Twice.'

Maric let out a low whistle. 'This is unbelievable.'

'I don't pay out fifty K just to get someone to my beautiful city on the basis of a fantasy,' Freeman said.

'I didn't say I didn't believe it, just that it was unbelievable.' Maric grinned, the sparkle in his eyes dropping ten years from his age. 'I'm tempted to take the job just to find out.'

'I also want to drag this Mr Bright out into the open,' Cass said. 'People know about him, but only at the highest level, and no one will touch him. We want to knock him off his guard – make people lose their faith in him.'

'In other words,' Brian Freeman's face cracked into a smile that added rather than subtracted years from his craggy face, 'we want to fuck him over a bit. This is the second part of what we want from you. In order to draw attention to him, we need to do something public, and that's going to have to involve The Bank. I've already got people working there.'

'What kind of thing were you thinking?'

'Stock dumping, shares fixing – things I can make a few quid at while we're doing it, obviously. I'm not like Cass here – I have absolutely no objection to getting richer out of this. To be honest, this fella has fucked with my life too; whatever I get back I feel I've earned.'

'I've already said I'm not touching ordinary people's money—'

'You won't be. We'll hit the big corporations, make some dodgy investments – arms and terrorist organisations, that sort of thing.'

'There was a list of companies in that sub-folder,' Cass cut in, 'we'll start with those. They must be Network businesses, so that will turn his own against him too.'

'There will be ordinary people among the shareholders, though,' Maric said thoughtfully. 'I'm an information thief; this isn't my normal thing. Hurting governments is one thing – people are different.'

'The way I see it' – Cass took a cigarette from the hacker's packet – 'is that this group, the Network, they won't want the economy becoming any more damaged or unstable than it already is, because that would damage their power base. Whatever damage we do, they'll rectify with money from the X accounts.'

'We just want to make some waves around this Mr Bright,' Freeman said. 'And I'd like to make some money.'

'And it will also work as a distraction while I'm looking for Luke. Mr Bright likes to have things under control; he'll be going crazy while you're fucking with him from the inside.'

There was a long moment of silence, and then Maric nodded slowly. 'This might be even better than the defence system breach. I've never had a buzz like that since, and that was a long time ago.'

'Do you think you can do it?' Cass asked.

'The Bank tried to hire me, you know. They offered me a lot of money. I turned it down, of course – twice. And then I had to change my identity and go into hiding for a year or more because they pointed several unfriendly government agencies in my direction. They told me that if I took the job, then my history would be cleared and I'd be taken off the wanted list – *every* wanted list.' His voice was soft and thoughtful. 'That's power, huh? I didn't entirely believe it at the time, but I think maybe I do now. The point is, they wanted me in, not out, and I take that as a clue that if anyone can get into their systems, then it's me.' He looked at Freeman. 'You have someone placed in-house?'

The old man nodded.

'And they can bring their laptop home without suspicion? And remote access?'

'Yes. She's working nights there on an international project. She's been bringing her laptop home every day.'

'Good. That will give me a chance to look around The Bank's systems, get a feel for it. When we do it, it'll help to know as much as I can about this man you're so interested in. Systems tend to reflect their owners, so knowing him will help me decide the best way to break his security.'

'Not a problem,' Cass said. 'I can talk you through what I know.'

The hacker smiled. 'Okay gentlemen, consider me hired.'

'Then I'll arrange for someone to collect you tomorrow at twelve,' Freeman said.

'Tomorrow it is.'

The three men grinned, and then Freeman slapped his rough hand down on Cass' thigh.

'Time for us to get back. I've got a surprise arriving for you.'

'What kind of surprise?' Cass felt a vague unease. He hadn't quite accepted that he and the old gangster were on the same team now; it was that same unease that made sure he'd locked his bedroom door, just in case Brian decided it was time to pay him back for that long-ago betrayal.

'Trust me, son,' the old man said with a wink, 'you'll like it. It's something I thought might help us with our little venture.'

'Let's go then.' Cass got to his feet. He was on this ride with Brian Freeman now, so there was no point trying to second-guess when the ride might fall apart.

'See you tomorrow, then,' Maric said with a smile.

'See you tomorrow,' Cass said as he opened the door. He hoped he would.

Chapter Eighteen

Her bones felt brittle, as if they would snap with even the slightest move, but she smiled as she squeezed the old man's hand. His skin was so dry that sore cracks had appeared across his palms. He wanted to be home. She wanted to be home. They didn't belong here.

'Have you heard more?' he asked. His voice was barely more than a whisper. 'Do we have to go and find him?'

She shook her head. Her hair had dulled to somewhere nearly brown, and a strand fell across her eyes. She tucked it behind one ear. 'No, not yet. We wait for now.'

'Does he talk to you often now that he's awake? Can you hear him clearly?'

'Yes,' she said, softly. 'Every day he sounds stronger. He's so grateful that we heard him from so far away, that we made this long journey. When we are home we will be very well rewarded.'

'To be home will be a good enough prize for me.'

'True. For me too.'

His eyes were watering and she wiped his cheeks. 'But what stories we will have to tell – we have *seen* it in a way no others ever will.'

'He does think we will get home then?' The old man's tone was uncertain. She had never heard that in him before, not in all their years together. It was hard, this place –

magical, but hard. She looked out of the window at the grey sky and the lights coming from the tall building around them in this heart of the city. In many ways it was glorious, breathtaking and brilliant, and there was so much more of it to see – so many wonders. She let out a small, sad sigh. No wonder *he* wanted to destroy it.

'Yes. He knows why we can't find the Walkways. We need to find someone.'

'Who?' He pushed himself up from the pillows slightly.

'Jarrod Pretorius.'

There was a long pause. There had been a long pause in her own head after the First had spoken the name to her in the space between bodies and places. It was a name she hadn't thought about in a long time. Her heart had ached in a way she'd almost forgotten.

'Why him?'

'He's why we can't get home.' She was glad to hear her own voice was still light and musical.

'Where is he?' The old man looked thoughtful.

'He doesn't know. He just says that we need to find him.'

'He doesn't *know*?'

'He's been sleeping a long time.'

'Not that long – he called out to us when he started sleeping, that's what he said.'

She watched the old man carefully. She had never heard such suspicion in his voice.

'Maybe he hadn't kept track of Pretorius.' Her voice softened slightly. 'He was never really like them.'

'He was never really like any of us.'

'True.'

They sat quietly together. In the silence he was as lost in the memories as she was.

'It was all a long time ago, wasn't it?' he asked after a while.

'Yes, it was.'

'They've done all this in that time. That's quite something.'

The silence lingered as the day darkened outside.

'One thing bothers me,' the old man said eventually, his voice stronger than it had been.

'Go on.' She had a vague idea what was coming. The thought had occurred to her, and if she knew anyone at all after this very long existence, it was this old man – this old spirit.

'The First must have known it would be you and me who came if he managed to call for us. Who else would be sent?'

'That's true.'

'We were close,' he said. 'He put me in his legends here. It made me smile to see.' He smiled at her. 'He put you in too.'

'He was still fond of us – even then, after everything – just as we are all still fond of him. He was the First. He *is* the First.'

'So why didn't he tell us before we came? Why didn't he say he didn't know how to get home?'

'He used a lot of energy calling. It weakened him dangerously.' She wasn't answering the question, even if what she said was truthful. 'He was desperate, perhaps.'

'We would still have come.' The old man smiled. '*He* would always have sent us, and we would have come willingly, you and I.' A frown wrinkled between his eyes. 'So why didn't he tell us we might not be able to get back?'

The silence settled between them again, a more honest silence, perhaps, as they mulled over the nature of their place in the hierarchy. In the end, she sighed and smiled before shrugging a slim shoulder. 'Like father, like son, my old friend. Like father, like son.'

Mr Craven was exhausted. What he'd done was stupid, but he couldn't help himself. He couldn't help *becoming*, not in that instant of rage, though it had cost him dearly. He could feel it in every inch of his thin body, in the racking pain in his watery lungs. He had stolen from his own *time* – how much? Days, months? Time had never mattered before. From where he was sitting against the wall he could see the bloody mess on the bed. Time didn't matter for that boy any more. He let out a small, wet laugh. There was one person he had outlived.

He dragged himself to his feet and went through to the second room, ignoring the tangled sheets and the various plates that littered the floor. Housekeeping could take care of them when he was gone – although he doubted the untidiness would be the first thing that grabbed their attention. Hotel staff saw plenty of strange comings and goings in their most expensive suites over the years – that was the whole point of paying all that money, after all – but he defied any of them to have experienced anything like the gift he was leaving behind.

He glanced over his shoulder at the remains of the boy. He might well have overstepped the mark somewhat there. The understatement almost made him giggle again, and, not for the first time, he wondered idly if he was losing his mind. That probably didn't matter either, he concluded, not with the way time was slipping away from him.

He sat down in the desk chair and pulled the thick hotel robe tighter around his body. The heating was on full, but the chill in his bones was unshakeable. He ignored it, and put the tiny earphones in before replaying the recording. It didn't surprise him that Mr Dublin hadn't thought to sweep for bugs after his visit; Mr Dublin would have considered such a thing too *low*, without the honour their kind had always had. That's why Mr Dublin would never be as good a leader as Mr Bright. Mr Bright had always known that they were capable of *low*. He'd always recognised the similarities between their kind and *them* – that's why they'd all left together, the rejects and the rebels, united.

When he'd heard the relevant parts, he switched the device off again, returning the room to silence. He stared out of the window at the dark sky. What was it? Four, five o'clock? Night already, and another day gone. He pushed the fear far down into his belly, though it didn't feel far enough.

So, Mr Dublin was looking for Cassius Jones to try in the Experiment. He expected to feel more of a flurry of excitement about that, but each time he'd listened to the recording, all he could think was that even if they were successful, it would be too late for him. Would Mr Dublin even care? Even if they got home there would be scapegoats required, and it didn't take a genius to figure out that he would probably be among them. Would he even be able to get home? Perhaps the sick – *the dying* – wouldn't make it?

So many questions, and none of them had comforting answers. The only thing that he did know – that he was becoming increasingly unable to *avoid* knowing as the days passed – was that in all likelihood he would die in this godforsaken – *literally* – place, a shadow of his former self. And he would die sooner rather than later. The bitterness threatened to overwhelm him and he chewed hard on his thin bottom lip. His mouth tasted of metal. His gums were bleeding again.

Cassius Jones. The bloodline. He thought of the dribbling First. Would he rather that fate for himself than death? It surprised him to find the answer was yes: anything was better than death. That's what the smug and untouched like Mr Dublin and Mr Bright would never understand, not until it came for them.

Cassius Jones, however, was a wild card – and more than that, he was a *missing* wild card, and Mr Dublin was right, he would no doubt want to come after the Network. Cassius Jones had a score to settle with Mr Bright, and at some point, when he was recovered and ready, he would come out into the open. Mr Dublin would be waiting for him, as would Mr Bright, no doubt.

So perhaps it was time to bring ex-Detective Inspector Cassius Jones up to speed – finish what Mr Solomon had started, but be somewhat less ambiguous about it. He didn't have the time available for the fun to be found in watching people trying to unlock riddles; he wasn't sure Cass Jones did either.

He turned away from the window and sighed. This place was a dump; it was time to gather his belongings and move to another hotel. He wondered if he should shower first. Probably, given the blood that had dried on his skin after he'd become small again. It wouldn't do to draw too much attention to himself. He walked through the bedroom and paused at the en-suite door to look back at the child on the bed. Without his skin, which was now tangled up some-where in the mess of sheets on the floor, the boy looked even smaller. The bedside lamp was broken, he noticed, as was the mirror on the wall. He might have lost the ability to fuck, as he'd discovered moments before the mayhem ensued, but he certainly hadn't lost his natural skills. It had felt good to be *himself*, to do what only *he* could do. He still had his sharpness, and he would savour the memory, if only the experience hadn't cost him so much. Not quite as much as it had cost the boy, he reflected, but still too much.

The shower was hot on his aching shoulders. The thought that Mr Dublin might find the way home after he was gone was almost too much to bear. He would enlighten Cassius Jones. But before that, he thought, rubbing apple-scented shampoo into his thinning hair, he would spread his word and find a new hotel for the night.

Chapter Nineteen

Hask wasn't entirely sure why he'd closed the office door before bringing up Adam Bradley's interview file, but he had. He and Ramsey were entirely within their rights to look at any evidence that might lead them to Cass Jones – that was, after all what the Force was paying him for, at least partly, and finding Cass Jones was definitely Charles Ramsey's primary case – but he couldn't help but feel sneaky about it. Ramsey clearly felt the same – neither of them had mentioned to Armstrong that while he was briefing Heddings on what they'd learned from Hurke, they'd be going over old interview tapes. Probably because they both knew what the answer would be – *what for?*

And therein lay the crux of the matter: the overstretched officers of what was currently London's most scrutinised police station had already decided that Cass Jones was guilty of murder, twice over. And they had also decided those murders had been as a result of his paranoid delusion that someone had stolen his nephew at birth, rather than the child going missing due to yet another fuck-up in the long history of NHS fuck-ups.

As far as Armstrong and the rest of the station were concerned, Cass had paid for Adam Bradley's help, and then killed him when he was no longer useful. Three men were dead – two by Jones' hand, allegedly, and one paid for by him. Cass Jones had run; on top of all the other evidence against him, only fools would think that the DI could be anything other than guilty after the way he'd fled into hiding. So that must make him and Ramsey both fools, because they couldn't believe that even in the aftermath of so much personal loss, a man like Cassius Jones could turn psychotic himself. It might be the *easiest* thing to believe, but that didn't make it the truth. In fact, in Hask's long experience, the easiest thing to believe was often a far cry from the truth.

They'd started listening to the interview to try and get some sense of the interaction between Jones and Bradley, to see if there was any hint in Jones that he found the boy in any way interesting or remarkable. What they'd found was something completely different.

'How could we have forgotten Mr Bright?' Ramsey muttered.

'I *shouldn't* have forgotten. I was *there* at this interview.' Hask leaned over the desk, his vast stomach resting slightly on the surface. 'Play that middle bit again. And then see if we can get Cass' report on the Solomon call. I can't remember it exactly.'

'Me neither.' Ramsey dragged the mouse back along the timeline a minute. 'Too many dead since then.' He clicked play and Adam Bradley spoke once again from beyond the grave. Hask could almost hear him sweating through the clicks and swallows between his sentences.

'*So he was there waiting for me when I got back. He opened his bag – his briefcase – and took out some things. There was this big envelope. It had a typed label on it already: Detective Inspector Cass Jones – that's you, I guess.*'

There was a small pause, and in his mind's eye Hask

could see the boy looking to Jones for confirmation before continuing,

'*I was sitting in the armchair, sorting out my shit, and he put it on the arm of the chair and then chucked a pair of gloves on my lap. Nice leather ones, expensive, I reckon. He said I was to deliver his envelope to Paddington nick, right after he'd gone, and to make sure I wore the gloves when I did it, and to bin them after. And not to give my name.*'

'*Did he give you his?*' Cass' voice.

'*Yeah, he did, as it goes. He gave me the hundred quid, and I thought he was leaving so I shot meself up. But he didn't go; he was peering out through the curtains and going on and on about how everything was planned and there were no coincidences. He kept saying everything happened for a reason, and asking if I believed that. I wasn't really listening, I'd got the dosh and I just wanted him to go. He gave me the creeps. When the smack hit me I said something like, "Who are you, anyway?" He smiled that creepy smile again and said, "My name is Mr Bright." It was a real smug smile, as if I'd done just what he'd expected.*'

'*Mr Bright? No first name?*'

'*I don't think he's the sort of bloke that uses one. I don't remember much after that. I zoned out a bit, and when I came to he was gone. I went down to my mum's place for a while and when I was a bit straighter I brought the envelope here.*'

'He was going on and on about how everything was planned and there were no coincidences,' Hask said softly.

'So,' Ramsey leaned back in the chair, 'junkie Adam Bradley meets Mr Bright, who tells him to bring Cass this video of the killings. They meet in a flat where later the Man of Flies, Solomon, kills Carla Rae. We're pretty sure that Bright wanted Bradley to be identified, which can only mean

146

that Mr Bright wanted Cass to know his name. Am I getting this right?'

'You're getting it exactly as well as Jones and I did at the time.' Hask had pulled a piece of paper from the printer and was scribbling on a spider diagram with the words Mr Bright in the middle. He'd seen eyebrows raise at his schoolboy approach to thinking things through, but it worked for him. He'd so far jotted down the given description, as well as the phrase 'no coincidences'. He added another word. *Solomon?*

Keys clicked fast and then Ramsey said, 'Got it.'

'Solomon mentioned Mr Bright to Cass when he called him,' Hask said. 'I know he did. I remember wondering if maybe Solomon and Bright were perhaps the same person, and then deciding against it.'

'I remember. And then Cass told us that DCI Morgan had made it clear that the Bright line of enquiry was a no-go and not to give it any more manpower.'

Hask scanned the screen. 'There.' He pointed.

The words were there in black and white; he read, '"Cass Jones claimed he asked the caller if he was Mr Bright, and then Solomon answered, "He'd love that. He looks for me, I watch him."' Ramsey scrolled down further. '"Solomon went on to give his sympathy to Cass over Christian's death and say that it was nothing to do with him."'

'Look.' Hask pointed at the screen. 'He refers to Cass and Christian as *family*.' He added the word to the scribblings on his sheet of paper.

'Yeah,' Ramsey said, 'and he also says "it wasn't us". When talking about Christian's death. Not just him: *us*.'

'How did we ignore this?'

'We were told to – and there was a lot of shit going on.'

'Well, we might have done as we were told,' Hask tapped

his pen thoughtfully against the sheet of paper, 'but I wonder if Cass Jones did.'

The door opened without warning.

'I've got a team trying to find out as much as they can about Draper, but I doubt we'll have much to go on before the morning.' Armstrong closed the door behind him and came up to the desk. 'You may as well go home, Dr Hask.' He paused, and Hask realised too late that his jottings were far too large to go ignored by a policeman with as sharp an eye as the young sergeant had proved to have.

'What's this?' Armstrong picked it up and frowned, and the profiler couldn't help feeling like he'd been caught with his hand in the cookie jar.

'We were looking at the Bradley/Jones interview from the Man of Flies case,' Ramsey said, looking up. If he was feeling caught out, he wasn't showing it. 'We thought it might bring up something – some kind of hint that Jones might revisit Bradley later.'

'What it did bring up, however, is Mr Bright.'

'Who?'

'Before your time. His name came up in the Man of Flies investigation twice, and we were told to leave it alone.'

'And?'

'Read through the files for yourself. This Mr Bright character manipulated Adam Bradley and was instrumental in getting information to Jones about two separate murder cases. When Solomon rang Jones at his parents' house, it was clear that he knew Mr Bright.'

'You can't count that transcript,' Armstrong cut in sharply. 'It's all just Jones' word. There's no recording. He could have made it all up, for all we know.'

'What?' Hask snorted. 'Why would he do that? Because he *might* go on a killing spree in six months' time after his wife and sergeant are both killed – events that haven't even happened yet? You're saying Cass Jones fed in the name Mr Bright to the record of a conversation in the unlikely event that should he go on the run at any time in the future *someone* might decide to go through old records?'

'There's no need to be facetious,' Armstrong growled. 'The transcript is unreliable. That's a fact.'

'Aren't you in the slightest bit curious about the Mr Bright character?' Hask asked. 'Even if just to understand why we were put off trying to find out more about him?'

'I don't see his relevance. Not to Jones' case.' Armstrong's face had coloured slightly; whatever goodwill they'd worked up while investigating the so-called Angel of Death was gone. 'Jones was a murdering bastard. He brought the station down and then added shame to it. I'm sick of people defending him. And investigating this Mr Bright isn't going to change Jones' guilt.'

'Well, it's not as if we're overloaded with leads.' Ramsey's voice was light despite Armstrong's clear aggression. 'This Mr Bright character has shown that he's capable of manipulating situations – who's to say he didn't manipulate Cass Jones?'

'You're suggesting this Mr Bright set Jones up?' Armstrong half laughed. 'That's *ridiculous*. Set up for murder once, we can believe. Twice? You're having a laugh.'

'Unless of course,' Hask looked down at his piece of paper, 'that's exactly the reaction he knew we'd have.'

'Jones would think so too. That would go some way to maybe explaining why he ran.' Ramsey stared at Armstrong. 'It's worth looking into.'

'You can't seriously believe that Cass Jones is innocent?' Armstrong paced in a circle, his hands on his hips. 'After *everything*? All the secrets? His research into the victims, thinking they had something to do with his missing nephew? It's classic paranoid behaviour – you even said that yourself, Hask!'

'And if his behaviour is exactly as you would define it, then yes, it is,' Hask said. He couldn't deny it. The surface analysis was exactly that; Armstrong was right to feel certain that Cass was guilty.

'We just need to make sure that everything is exactly as it appears.' Ramsey stood up. 'And as I'm in charge of the Jones investigation, I want to be sure for myself. I thought he was a good man – troubled, maybe, but pretty tough. So I'm going to play this my way and try and keep an open mind for now.' He stared at the sergeant. 'Innocent until proven guilty, remember?'

'You're both as crazy as he is.' Armstrong spat the words out and then stared at them both for a moment as if he were seeing them for the first time. 'You're clutching at straws – and wasting police time.'

'Your opinion is noted, sergeant,' Ramsey said and then gestured at the door.

Armstrong took the hint, closing the door hard behind him.

'Well, that went well,' Hask said.

'The arrogance of youth.' Ramsey leaned back in his chair. 'He's a good policeman, though. And to be fair, he's probably right. But in the meantime, I think it's time we paid a visit to Perry Jordan. See what he can tell us.'

Night had fallen, bringing a freezing chill with it. Hask felt the ice in the air stinging his face on the short walk between the car and the apartment block. If Perry Jordan's expression was anything to go by, they'd brought the cold in with them. He'd started his professional career as a policeman, but it looked like he'd definitely lost any residual affection he might once have had for his first employers – except for maybe Cass Jones. Jordan had been politely compliant throughout the investigation thus far – he wasn't a fool – but he hadn't offered up anything extra, not even with pressure coming from Commander Fletcher and the ATD. Perry Jordan was loyal to Cass Jones; that much was clear.

An open beer bottle sat on the coffee table next to an empty one and the ashtray was half-full. Hask checked his watch. It was only just gone six; Jordan had started early. He looked at the computer desk in the corner; he could make out a small pile of bills half-hidden underneath a newspaper. Jordan must have tried to cover them up before letting the police in, but the red payment slips were visible. So business must have dried up since the police investigation and careless talk in the papers about Jordan being an accessory. Two months probably wasn't long enough for that kind of muck to be washed off.

'You lot might think all he's the son of the devil,' Jordan picked up his beer, 'but Cass Jones was – *is* – my friend. He would never have told me anything that could damage me. You know everything I know.'

'I don't believe that for a second.' Between Ramsey's height and Hask's physical bulk they filled the small room. Hask wished that the investigator would just ask them to sit down; that would at least make it feel less like they were squaring up for a fight.

'Put it this way.' Jordan's mouth twisted in a slight smile. 'You know everything that you need to know. Everything that I'm obliged by law to tell you.'

'Did he ever ask you to find out anything about a Mr Bright?' Hask asked.

'Who?' Perry Jordan broke his stare with Ramsey and looked at Hask. 'Who's he?'

'His name came up in the both the Man of Flies case and the Miller and Jackson shootings.' They needed Perry Jordan on side and giving him the standard police *we're not at liberty to share that information* responses wasn't going to get them anywhere. 'He met Adam Bradley in the flat where Carla Rae was later killed and sent him to Paddington Green with the DVD of the shootings.'

'What?' Perry Jordan was visibly shocked. He took a small unconscious step back. Whatever aggression had been bouncing between the three men had, for now at least, slipped away.

'We also believe he knew the Man of Flies killer, Solomon,' Ramsey said.

'He sounds like quite a character.'

'Did Cass Jones ask you to do any traces on him? Get any personal information?'

'No.' Jordan shook his head. 'Why would he? Surely your lot would have done all that.'

'That line of inquiry was closed down early on,' Hask said.

'Closed down?' The PI sat down on the arm of the sofa.

'There was a lot going on. Mr Bright was deemed irrelevant.'

Perry Jordan looked from Ramsey to Hask, his expression thoughtful. Hask could almost hear his brain ticking over. There was a quirky cockney charm about the ex-policeman, but it was deceptive. Jordan was no fly-by-night kid any more. He was earning his wrinkles.

'So why are you asking about him now?' he asked.

There was a moment of silence. Hask understood Ramsey's reluctance to share their thinking with someone who was a key witness in the case against Cass. It could damage them, and Ramsey was old school: there was police business and there was civilian business. Perry Jordan might have been the former once, but he was now very much the latter. If it were down to him, Hask thought, he'd be straight with the PI, but this was Ramsey's case, and he'd already probably overstepped the mark by giving so much information on Mr Bright already.

'I'm just trying to explore all the avenues while I can,' Ramsey said eventually. 'This man, like Solomon, had a clear interest in Cass. Jones was set up once – we just want to be sure that he wasn't set up again.'

'I can't help you. He never asked me about a Mr Bright.'

'Well, thank you anyway,' Hask said. He looked over at Ramsey. Staying here and pressurising the man wasn't going to get them anywhere. Frustrating as it was, if Perry Jordan had any more information for them, they were going to have to wait for him to give it up in his own time.

'We'll let ourselves out then,' Ramsey said and led the way towards the front door. Hask followed. They were halfway there when the PI spoke.

'You know, it's only paranoia if it's not real.'

They stopped and turned, staying where they were in the corridor. Jordan was still in the sitting room, still perched on the side of his sofa.

'What do you mean?' Ramsey asked.

'Luke – the missing nephew? I did all that research for Jones. You want my opinion? Someone did swap that baby intentionally. I don't know why, but they did. And the dead men knew something about it – which means someone wanted that secret to stay hidden.'

'We've already worked through that possibility,' Ramsey

said softly. 'Some kind of baby-smuggling ring, maybe. Cass lost it and killed them.'

'The thing is,' Perry Jordan continued, 'I don't believe it was Cass who killed them – and not because I think he's a *good* man – I'm not convinced that he is – but because he never came after me.' He sipped his beer. 'I'm the nail in the coffin for his evidence trail. Why didn't he come here and kill me? Or at least take my notebooks and papers? It doesn't make sense.'

'You're his friend,' Ramsey said.

'Yes, I am, but cold-hearted paranoid psychotic killers tend not to have friends. Or if they do, they tend not to care that much about the friend's survival compared with their own. If Cass *was* everything he's been painted to be, I'd be dead by now.'

'I'll bear that in mind.' Ramsey smiled softly, and turned back to the door. Hask stood where he was for a moment. Perry Jordan was right. Why hadn't he even considered that when he was making his own evaluation? He knew the answer, of course: too much work and not enough man-hours. There was only so much *good* thinking someone could do before needing a break, and there had been very little rest over the past nine months or so. His bank balance was healthy, the rest of him less so.

'Evidence is a funny thing, isn't it?' Perry Jordan hadn't moved. 'Sometimes there's so much of it, and so many cases, that you can't see the trees for the wood.'

'What do you mean?' Hask asked.

'Those student suicides? Cass' final investigation before all this madness started?'

'What about them?' He had Ramsey's full attention now.

'Cass got the result at the same time you were about to try and take him down for murder. The ATD were over at

154

the station, and everything was manic, am I right?'

'What about it?'

'I'm willing to bet that after all the dust settled, no one thought to ask what Cass was doing at that private facility in the first place. The place where Dr Shearman, the man you've got banged up for causing them, worked.'

Hask felt like he'd been slapped in the face. A *doctor*. Of course! His heart started pounding as the penny dropped. '*You* gave him the address? He asked you to find Shearman as part of the search for his missing nephew?'

'No flies on you.' Perry Jordan smiled. 'I probably don't need to spell it out to you, but I will anyway: maybe Shearman's someone you should talk to. He's probably had enough time in a cell to be think about his future.'

'Thank you,' Hask said with a big smile.

'You're welcome, Doctor.'

'Why the hell didn't you tell us this before?' Ramsey said.

Perry Jordan ignored the DI's obvious anger and looked at Hask. 'That's simple – nobody asked me. Shearman wasn't dead.'

Chapter Twenty

C ass Jones hadn't expected the surprise Freeman had in store for him to be a human one.

Dr Cornell had settled surprisingly well into the annex flat above the double garage. Cass wasn't sure if Brian Freeman was keeping him mildly sedated, but he'd been relatively calm for the short time Cass had been with him. Perhaps now that his biggest fear – that of having his life's work taken from his home – had actually happened, the old professor had found some peace at last.

Osborne had brought him in strapped into a wheelchair, just this side of conscious. It had taken them more than half an hour to unload the van full of papers and junk they'd brought from Dr Cornell's Oxford home.

Even in an area as exclusive as this one, where houses were hidden behind high gates and walls, the activity was noticeable, so Freeman had made a point of telling a passing neighbour that Dr Cornell was his brother, moving in until his dementia got bad enough that he'd need to go into a home. Something about that amused Cass. They were a strange trio to be united in their fascination with Mr Bright and his Network: an ageing gangster, an ex-copper on the run and now a half-crazy academic. The Network would be trembling in their boots, he was sure.

When Dr Cornell had recovered from the chloroform or

whatever Osborne had used to knock him out, Brian Freeman took him in a cup of tea. Cass stood in the doorway and watched as the old gangster spoke softly to the frightened man, sitting on the bed and steadying the cup. Cass couldn't make out the words, but the tone was softer and kinder than he'd have thought Freeman capable of. Even all those years ago, when Cass had been Charlie and Freeman had started to love him like a son, he hadn't heard that gentleness.

Dr Cornell's wide eyes had darted from Freeman to Cass and back again as the old man spoke, and then after a few minutes he'd started to sip his tea. Cass left them to it. His shoulder was aching, and to himself at least he admitted that found something about Dr Cornell disturbing. Whatever happened with Mr Bright and the hunt for Luke, Cass knew that bullets aside, men like he and Freeman would survive. They might add to their mental and physical scars, but they'd most likely live. Even if he didn't find Luke – or if he found that Luke, like the boy he'd been swapped with all those years ago, was now dead, he knew he'd survive it.

For Dr Cornell, it would be different: he was fragile, and he'd been alone in his belief of this conspiracy for so many years that it had driven him half-mad. Now here they were, he and Freeman, telling the professor that it was okay, that they were on his side and they believed everything he did. Maybe in essence all that was true, but in reality they were using the old man for his information, and then they would do with it exactly what they wanted, regardless of how it might break Dr Cornell. They weren't good people, he and Freeman, and part of him hoped Dr Cornell would figure that out and protect himself.

He left the two men talking and went in search of a sandwich and some painkillers. The old man's frantic madness made him tired and uneasy.

The house was quiet for the rest of the evening. Cass stayed in his own room, dozing for a while when the pills kicked in before waking and taking a long shower. A TV was on somewhere in one of the rooms, but Cass felt no urge to see what was going on in the world; someone would let him know if there was anything relevant to him. It would be the same old doom and gloom; Alison McDonnell, her career wrecked after the London bombings and the Lucy Porter fiasco, was in the process of being replaced as Prime Minister by her own Home Secretary while the rest of London was scaremongering about the bug. None of it felt like a world he inhabited any more. Where did he live exactly? Had he himself become one of the ghosts that had haunted him for so long?

At about half-twelve he went to find a drink to soothe his melancholy. Soft light poured through a half-open doorway on the ground floor, and inside, Brian Freeman was sitting in an old armchair and sifting through yellowing bits of paper pulled from the mountains of boxes around him. He was so absorbed that he didn't even realise that Cass was there. The sight reminded him of Dr Cornell. Cass sipped his brandy, then murmured, 'Don't spend too much time reading that shit. You don't want to end up like the mad professor.'

'No chance of that, son.' Freeman looked up and smiled. The reading glasses he wore looked out of place on his broken face. 'Just trying to get all this in some kind of order – an order than makes sense, anyway. He's got stuff going back years, from all over the fucking world.'

'So I noticed.'

'Want to give me a hand?'

Cass thought about it. There would be lots of information in those boxes that would fascinate him – times, events and places that could have lines of connection drawn across them, and that could all be linked, if looked at with Dr Cornell's eyes, to the Network. The frightening thing was that Dr Cornell was probably right: Cass had seen the X accounts, he'd met Mr Bright and he'd *seen* what had happened to Mr Solomon when he died. In many ways, that was all he needed to know for now. The rest could wait until Luke was found.

'I don't think so,' he said. 'I want to keep my head clear.'

Freeman nodded and returned his attention to sorting the piles.

'I still don't understand why you're so interested in all this. I mean, I understand your grief for your niece, but—'

'It ain't grief, Charlie – Cass – whoever you are,' Freeman said. 'I just don't like being fucked with. *You* should know that.' Light from the table lamp reflected on the surface of his lenses, creating something that was almost a mockery of the golden glow that Cass couldn't hide from, and his expression was lost.

'It's where you and me are the same, isn't it?' Freeman added. 'Fuck with us and you're in trouble.'

'Ain't it the truth.' Cass half-smiled. He turned to leave.

'You still look up?'

The question threw Cass slightly and he looked back at the gangster. After a moment, he said gruffly, 'Yeah— Yes, I do.'

'Good.' There was warmth in Freeman's voice. 'At least I drummed something into that thick skull of yours. Now fuck off to bed and get some sleep. Busy day tomorrow.'

Sleep didn't come; instead, Cass lay in the buzz of silence and stared at the ceiling, wondering about how the world turned. He could never have imagined a time when he'd see Brian Freeman again that didn't involve one or the other of them becoming dead very quickly. Yet here they were and, despite all the fall-out his undercover work in Freeman's world had brought to his life, Cass could feel the echoes of his old affection for the man. It wasn't the same, of course – they had both changed too much for that – but it was still there.

When he blinked he saw brown eyes at the end of a gun barrel. This time, along with the fear, there was sadness and disappointment in their endless liquid darkness. Not for the first time Cass wondered if Freeman hadn't made him a murderer; perhaps it had always been there. How many other officers would have done what he'd done?

It was a question he'd asked himself hundreds of times over the years, and the conclusion he always reached was that even had he chosen differently, it wouldn't have made any difference: someone else would have shot the kid, there was no doubt about that, and once they'd shot the kid, Freeman would have wondered why someone with Charlie's supposed credentials hadn't pulled the trigger himself. The kid was dead either way, and the officer more than likely.

Cass had done the only thing he could to ensure his own survival. In the cold darkness of night, he saw that clearly; what kept him awake was whether survival was always the right thing. For the first time since he'd arrived at Brian Freeman's house, Cass felt the ghosts drawing closer, finding their places in the corners of his room and round the sides of the furniture, only their clawing hands visible. He knew more of the dead than the living, and one day they'd realise that and drag him down as one of their own.

The house was warm, but he shivered as he sat up, feeling claustrophobic. He itched to get out in the freezing air, just for a walk, to clear his head of his demons and focus on tomorrow. So much now lay in Maric's hands: getting into those systems was the route to finding Luke – he was sure of it. Carrying his shoes with him he crept silently through the sleeping house. He found a set of house keys in the kitchen drawer and slipped them in his pocket. The light in the downstairs room was still on, and when he peered in he saw Brian Freeman snoring softly, his head tilted backwards. Papers had fallen from his lap to the floor and Cass fought the urge to replace them. He carefully pulled the door closed. Slipping his shoes on, he left the house.

'You've got to look up, Charlie.'

At three o'clock in the morning the city was eerily quiet. Cass asked the black cab to wait for him, and the driver was amenable. Even though it was December and the office party season had kicked in, the night shift were simply cruising the deserted streets. London hadn't regained its footing after the bombings and with this new bug scare people clearly preferred keeping to the relative safety of their own homes to celebrate the festive cheer.

Cass closed the door behind him. As he turned the corner the chug of the engine was still audible. There was something comforting about it, he thought, as he stared at the impressive building. Most of its windows were still alight. Of course he had come here to focus his thinking: The Bank's headquarters, the old MI6 building. Where else was there for him to go? Somewhere inside there, Freeman's mole was studiously working away, and someone else's computer and photos and files would be in his dead brother's office, as if Christian had never existed.

His breath came out in a mist, and he added to it by lighting a cigarette. His fingers numbed quickly outside of his coat pocket, but he didn't care. The hot smoke was good. Was Mr Bright in there now? he wondered. His eyes scanned the building for that elusive extra floor. Which was it? The apartment had been high up, he knew that. Mr Bright was the kind of man who liked to survey the world, keep an eye on all the pieces in the game. *There are no coincidences. Wheels within wheels.* Mr Bright and Mr Solomon, and a world of mysteries in between that somehow had the Jones family, and Luke especially, at the heart of it. Luke: the faceless boy; the relative who was a stranger.

He sniffed hard, his nose starting to run. Right now all his drive was focused on finding the boy, but what did he really intend to do when he found him – raise him? A cop on the run and an orphaned kid – surely that was just the premise for a bad Hollywood movie; no way it could work in the real world. Why was he doing any of this? He wasn't father material, that was obvious; maybe that just wasn't in their blood. There was very little that was good about the Jones family. His father had given away his grandson to protect his own freedom, and Cass had shot a teenager in cold blood. He flicked the glowing cigarette onto the slick, dark pavement and shoved his hands back into his coat. The last thought wasn't entirely correct.

He looked up at the sleek lines of metal and steel, glowing in the night: it looked like some kind of heavenly citadel, bringing hope to a battered world. Ghosts whispered to Cass from its shadows. Christian Jones had been a good man – the white sheep of their particular flock. Cass may not have spent much time figuring that out while his younger brother was still alive, but he knew it now, and that was why he was going to find the boy. For his dead little brother, who had asked him to. What came after would figure itself out. He owed Christian – for Jessica, at the very least. He turned his back on the building that had come to represent his nemesis and walked back towards the purring taxi. He could live with a murder on his conscience, but he couldn't live with ignoring Christian's last request. And besides, Mr Bright had it coming.

Chapter Twenty-One

DeVore was tired. It had reached the stage where he constantly felt slightly sick and his eyes grated against their lids when he closed them. For a while he wondered if maybe the Dying had found him – he'd started to expect it; after all, it had claimed those far greater than himself. But after running tests on himself the truth became apparent: he was simply exhausted. He hadn't rested properly in the months since the Interventionists Bellew had taken had chosen to die. Since then, the rest, housed in their pods, had become listless, vacant. He expected *stillness* from them – it had been a long time since they had physically moved; their Reflections explored the world for them – but this apathy was something new. Most of the screens around the room had been blank for more than a month, and those who were projecting were just throwing up random images that made no sense; they hinted at madness. This awful quiet had stolen his sleep.

He poured a coffee from the jug beside his desk in the outer chamber. It was the middle of the night and he didn't *need* to be here; the technicians in the thought chamber would come and get him if there were any significant changes or projections. He should be relaxing upstairs, in his sprawling living quarters high up in the building – better than that, he should be asleep. He sipped the hot liquid, enjoying its strong bitterness. Well, if he couldn't sleep, then he might as well have something to help him stay awake. Once he'd drunk it, he'd go in and see them, soothe them.

A realisation had dawned on him during the past difficult months: strange as the Interventionists were, he was fond of them. He had been here such a long time that they had become family to him. Mr Bright might be *the* Architect, but DeVore had his own smaller triumph – he had built the House of Intervention.

When the women had started this phase of their transformation, only he had taken the time to recognise their potential; only he had had the foresight to harness it, to develop the methods to interpret their thoughts. For a while the place had felt as much like a prison as a castle, so far away from everything, but after a while he'd realised it was his *achievement.*

Until he'd had the House, he'd thought himself lacking compared with the others. He'd been barely a Fourth Cohort, swept along with the revolt, rather than being an active part of it. He wasn't stupid: he'd known how Mr Bellew and Mr Craven and others had mocked him in the old days. And Mr Bright and Mr Solomon had barely known of his existence until he'd discovered the Interventionists. But then he'd been given a place in the First Cohort and met the First himself. He had become someone important – maybe not be as glorious as those who had led them here, but he had *achieved* something, and that was more than many.

Now, however, that achievement was crumbling. He'd been in the House for so long, hidden in the heart of the cold mountains so far away from the machinations of the rest of the world, that it had become his safe place, and like the Interventionists themselves, he only now travelled when summoned. Would he soon be left with nothing but living ghosts for company? Or were the Interventionists finally preparing for the next stage of whatever strange path they had been on since they arrived here?

He didn't want them to leave him: he loved them, and on some level he thought they might love him too.

He jumped slightly when the intercom buzzed on his desk.

'You need to come to the thought chamber now, sir.' The urgency in the young man's voice – Stoldt, was it? – was unmistakable. 'They're projecting. *All of them.*'

DeVore's heart leapt and he put the cup down on the desk so hard that coffee slopped over the side, but he didn't even notice.

The room was filled with a high-pitched keening that made his ears ache so much he thought they might bleed. The sound was coming from the fat bodies of the Interventionists lying rigid in their pods, their black eyes staring directly upwards, even though their mottled mouths weren't moving. DeVore had barely glanced at them; his attention was focused on the vast screens.

For a moment he couldn't speak, so glorious was the sight, and so terrible. It had been a long time since he'd seen anything like it: the beauty of so many of his kind in their honest form, huge, *Glowing* – perfect. The skies were filled with them.

'This can't be right,' he said at last. 'Is this from their memory, do you think? The war?' The Interventionists hadn't projected backwards before, but that didn't mean they weren't capable of it.

'No,' the man beside him said. There was a slight tremble in his voice that DeVore hadn't noticed before. Was that fear? 'I thought that at first. But then— Well, wait and see. There's more.'

DeVore watched as they came from the sky in all their furious glory. Behind them the trumpeters, silent on screen, heralded the warriors with music he knew would deafen the humans below. The scene was magnificent and terrifying and awe-inspiring. There were so many of them he could scarcely comprehend it, not after all this time. His eyes widened. This was only the beginning; *He* would not be far behind. As the army marched, the blue sky was lost in gold and silver so bright that DeVore flinched. It would blind those below – *them* – their eyes would burn in flames.

'But this can't be right,' he whispered as the Earth came into view and he saw the ashes of the destroyed cities, people wandering crying through the wreckage of their civilisation. They were blind and deaf, and doomed. There were two kinds of dead lying broken amidst the rubble; they had fled together and they had died together. Above them the sky danced in a blaze of victory.

The sun vanished and the husk of the Earth was left for ever in the midnight darkness of space. For a moment neither man spoke. Eventually, the cycle of images started again, as if on a loop.

'Look,' the technician breathed. 'Look at them.'

DeVore tore his eyes from the horror playing out in front of him and looked down into the nearest pod. Tears were streaming from the dark eyes, sliding down the unhealthily fat cheeks and into the matted hair.

'They're crying,' he whispered. 'All of them.'

DeVore looked back at the screen. He needed to speak to Mr Bright; it looked like the Dying was now the least of their worries.

'Keep monitoring them,' he said, turning his back on the

doctor who was still looking at the weeping Interventionists. 'And get a full team in here now. If anything in that sequence changes, I want to know. The slightest thing.'

'Mr DeVore.' The doctor looked up, and DeVore stopped. They never called him by name, it was always 'sir'.

'What is it?'

'They're all projecting it – all of them.'

'I'm not blind. What's your point?'

'They normally each show different possible futures, don't they? When information is requested—?'

'This information wasn't requested,' DeVore snapped.

'I know that, but if they're all projecting the same images . . . Does it mean that this is the only possible future?'

A fearful silence hung between them for a long second.

'Don't be a fool,' DeVore said. 'Nothing in the future is decided.'

His decisive tone did nothing to slow his own heartbeat as he walked quickly back to his office. The sound of that awful keening echoed in his ears, and black spots danced across his eyes. Whatever the outcome, *He* was coming, that much was for sure. His hand was sweating when he picked up the phone.

Mr Bright was glad to find his palms were still dry when he replaced the receiver after DeVore's call. He left his office behind and stepped back out into the main living room. Most of the room was in darkness, with only a pale blue glow coming through the large windows from outside, where so much life refused to let the city ever be truly dark.

He glanced back for a moment at the closed study door next to his own. The name plaque still read MR SOLOMON, despite his repeated promises to himself that he would remove it. For a moment he considered sitting behind his old friend's desk, but decided against it; the memory of that light, brilliant smile would make him melancholy, and there was no time for sentiment now. He could not afford to be weak.

He walked across and stood by the window, which stretched from the floor to the high ceilings, and stared out at everything and nothing. DeVore would send him the projections, but he didn't need to see them – he didn't *want* to see them. If *He* was coming, then all of this would be destroyed. There would be no mercy.

He sighed and forced his mind away from the possible – the *likely* – coming destruction of all that he had built. Right now there were other things that demanded his attention. There were always puzzles and deceits with their kind, and as they had passed that trait on to *them*, nothing was ever straightforward. Ergo, he concluded, as the clock ticked around to 3.15 a.m., there would be nothing straightforward about this projection either. If *He* was coming in the manner the Interventionists declared, then why was there an emissary among them? Why send a communicator? *He* was too arrogant to think they might have developed ways to fight against a multitude of their own, even if they had such a capability that wouldn't also result in a destroyed Earth.

The answer was obvious: it was about the First. *He* would save the First, of course – and *He* might even save Mr Bright himself, purely to drag him back home and humiliate him for all eternity before finally destroying him. No, that was an outcome that would never happen. Mr Bright had built this place and he would stay with it. It was his home now. Perhaps *He* had sent the emissary to find the First before the attack – that was likely. But if that was the case, then why had the First not mentioned it? The emissary would be calling out in the old ways – was the First simply too weak to hear it?

His mind lingered on the old man and the boy. Despite how successful everything had been, something still disturbed him. He thought for a bit, and decided it was that conversation with the First, and his mention of Jarrod Pretorius, and his strangely exaggerated surprise at the mention of the emissary. As his frustration grew, Mr Bright felt himself *Glow* slightly and his senses heightened. The clock ticked too loudly; his heart beat too fast. A black cab chugged somewhere in the quiet street below.

He turned away from the window and reluctantly let the *Glow* go. The world dimmed again, darkening like his thoughts. What was his old friend playing at? *Betrayal?* He couldn't believe it – he wouldn't believe it, not after everything they had done together. But still DeVore's final words wouldn't leave him: how could an invented myth come true?

It's the Rapture, he'd said. *It's coming.*

Climbing the stairs, Mr Bright was surprised to find himself thinking of Cassius Jones. The wild card. He lay down, shut his eyes and tried to sleep. *He* might be coming, but there were still moves in this game to be played out. And Mr Bright had learned to play the game well.

Chapter Twenty-Two

It was a clear, bright December morning, but there was no hint of that inside Dr Richard Shearman's house. All the curtains were drawn, and the narrow beams of light that managed to creep through the cracks illuminated hundreds of dust motes, hanging in the air. Hask sat on the sofa and Ramsey joined him. There were sweat patches under Shearman's arms, and he fiddled with his hands – he was surprisingly nervous for a man who'd already been charged.

Hask smiled at him.

He didn't smile back. 'What do you want?' Shearman glanced over to the covered windows and then back again. He'd ushered them inside the house very quickly, and he clearly wasn't happy about the visit. Did he think he was being watched?

'You could be more polite,' Ramsey said. 'At least you're not on remand in prison – trust me, this is better.'

'That had nothing to do with you,' Shearman snapped. 'Everyone knows I'm no risk – the judge was quite clear on that. I'm as gutted as everyone else that those kids killed themselves weeks after leaving my facility; all I did was try to help cure them of their phobias. All you've got is some discrepancies with cash payments and records, and I've got nothing more to add to my version of events.' He spat out the well-rehearsed speech, and then stared at them defiantly.

There was something rather childish about it, Hask decided. Dr Shearman was not a strong man.

'Tell us about Mr Bright,' Hask asked quietly.

'I don't know anyone by that name,' he snapped, but the doctor's physical reaction told a different story: he'd recoiled as if punched.

Hask fought the urge to look over at Ramsey. On their way over he and the DI had agreed that to get any truth out of Shearman, usable or not, they were going to have to hit him hard and fast, take him off guard. He wasn't sure either of them had expected their ploy to work quite so quickly. Dr Shearman definitely knew a Mr Bright, as evinced by the man's wide eyes and growing sweat patches.

'Why would DI Cass Jones have been so interested in you?' Ramsey took up the baton and Shearman's head whipped round to him.

He swallowed, and started, 'What do you mean? He was in charge of the suicides investigation—'

'But it wasn't through *that* investigation that he found you, was it?' Ramsey smiled, and leaned forward, as if inviting a confidence. 'He found *you* through a private investigator he'd hired to track his missing nephew. The link to the suicides was just a bonus, I believe.'

Shearman's reaction was more contained this time – he was definitely on his guard now – but it was still there: the dilation of the pupils; the half-second drop of his mouth as he struggled to find something to say. They were just small tics, but they were as clear as day to the profiler.

'I don't know what you're talking about,' he said at last.

'Ah, but your face tells a different story,' Hask said.

'Why aren't you out looking for Jones, anyway?' Shearman snapped. 'Why are you here bothering me? He's a murderer, I'm not. I've never been in a day's trouble in my life until this ... this *situation* happened. I've got a good mind to call my lawyer and tell him you're harassing me—'

Ramsey laughed, cutting the rant off. 'I think you'll find one pre-trial visit doesn't count as harassment.' His smile dropped. 'But yes, you do make a valid point: Cassius Jones is wanted for the direct murder of two people and the organised murder of another. Two of those people he killed because he believed they had something to do with the missing baby. Just like he thinks you did.'

'I don't know what you're talking about.' Shearman had paled further.

'Oh, but you do. Jones might have gone off the rails quite dramatically, but he was always a good copper, and he must have had a reason to have been looking for you that day. I've been wondering what he said to you in the interview room – he didn't record it, and there must have been a reason for that.'

'I've done nothing wrong,' Shearman muttered. The fight was gone from his voice and he was withdrawing into himself.

'Looking at you, I find myself confused,' Hask said softly. Shearman looked over at him and he continued, 'We spent some time last night going through your files. I saw your initial mugshots – I must say, you look quite different now. You've lost a lot of weight. Your pallor and the bags under your eyes would suggest you haven't been sleeping very much at all. Your clothes are now too big for you, but I note you haven't been shopping to replace them. So you're not going out, but at the same time your house isn't exactly spotless, if you don't mind me pointing this out. I could go on, but that's already more than enough to tell me that you're feeling either fear and paranoia or guilt – and there's a good chance it's all three. And if you haven't done anything to feel guilty about, as you keep repeating, then I have to wonder what – or *who* – it is that you're so afraid of?'

'Prison.' There had been a whisper of hesitation before the word.

'No, I'm not buying that: your lawyers are all over the fact that those students killed themselves weeks after leaving your facility, and despite the links between them, there is only circumstantial evidence to prove that your phobia therapy had anything to do with their actions. It's clear they took their own lives, and without any definite proof, the court will have a hard time convicting you. You'll probably get two or three years, tops, in one of our more polite prisons. So for a man who could have been facing the death penalty, or at least life imprisonment, that's going to feel like a walk in the park. You're far from broke, and even if you never work again, you'll survive that period and get out to a comfortable existence and before long all this will be forgotten.' Hask had kept his voice low and pleasant. 'None of that warrants this level of fear. If you tell us what's frightening you so much, then we might be able to help you.'

It was Shearman's turn to snort out an unpleasant hiccough of a laugh. '*You* can't protect me – Jones told me as much.'

'You're afraid Cass Jones is going to come after you?' Ramsey asked.

'Not him.'

There was a long pause.

'Mr Bright?' Hask said.

Shearman's eyes glistened as they watered. He wasn't going to cry, but he was close. *Trapped*, that was the word Hask would use: the man looked trapped.

'I'm not saying anything.'

'We can't help you if you don't tell us.'

Shearman stared at Ramsey as if weighing something up and for a moment, Hask thought he was actually going to break down and finally start talking, but then he squared his shoulders and stood up. 'I'd like you to leave now,' he said, 'or I will call my lawyer.' The moment was over.

'And?'

They'd driven further down the road before stopping so that Ramsey could call Perry Jordan and get the information they required. Ramsey flipped the phone shut.

'The Bank are the ultimate funding behind Flush 5, who own Shearman's facility. But he says you wouldn't find that out easily; there's a whole network of companies dividing the two. He said Jones warned him off digging around The Bank too deeply but there was plenty about it that made him want to. Doesn't surprise me, though. Damned institutions. You can't trust any of them.'

Hask stared ahead, his stomach rumbling. 'So let's get this straight. We can presume from Shearman's reaction that he knows this mystery Mr Bright. Adam Bradley knew him. If we believe Cass' account of the phone conversation – and we've got no reason not to – then Solomon, the Man of Flies, knew him pretty well too. Solomon worked at The Bank, right?'

'Yes. And so did Christian Jones – he was headhunted in 2010, so he must have been damned good at his job.'

'Maybe we shouldn't read too much into everything coming back to The Bank. After all, The Bank has its fingers in all the world's pies these days.'

'There's more,' Ramsey said, turning the car's engine back on. 'I've still got all Jones' emails on my system – I had to wade through them all when he disappeared. I went through them again last night, just out of curiosity. I did a search on The Bank and on Mr Bright.'

'And?' Hask looked over at the soft-voiced American DI.

'I was waiting to see whether Shearman knew our man or not before I said anything, but during the Man of Flies investigation Cass Jones got Claire May to email The Bank to see if they had a Mr Castor Bright on their employment records. This was just before the Bright line of inquiry was pulled.'

'Did she get an answer?'

'Yes. They said they didn't have anyone of that name in their employment.'

'Bugger.' Hask sighed. His stomach rumbled again. Thinking always made him hungry – although, to be fair, most things made him hungry. Life was short and bitter enough without denying yourself the pleasure of food. 'But still, interesting that Cass thought he might work there.'

'Something struck me when you asked Shearman about Bright. Something about that request Jones gave Claire May.'

'Go on.' Now he was curious; what had he missed?

'He asked her to find out about a Mr Castor Bright.' He looked over at Hask, but the profiler stared back blankly.

'Don't you get it?' Ramsey continued. 'How the hell did Cass know the man's first name? Adam Bradley didn't mention it.'

Hask's hunger was momentarily forgotten. *Castor* Bright. Unusual name – but Ramsey was right, how had Cass found it? 'Solomon's phone call?'

'No, can't be: he asked May to check before the call had taken place.'

'And we know Perry Jordan didn't do any checks for him. So Cass found something out by himself, away from the investigation.' He looked out at London as it sped past his window. In the car time felt as if it were standing still.

'So,' he said softly, 'Mr Bright had a film of the boys being shot and gave it to Cass. He knew Solomon, who wanted Cass on the Flies case. He knew Dr Shearman, who Cass believes had something to do with his nephew being swapped.' He paused. 'He's like a puppet-master, wouldn't you say? Pulling Cass' strings – playing with him? Maybe he killed those men and made it look like Cass had.'

'But why? Who the hell is he?' Ramsey asked.

'That, my dear Detective Inspector, is what we need to find out.' Hask grinned. 'Let's go and see the DCI. What we've got may be circumstantial, but there's plenty of it. And it's nearly lunchtime. We can grab something lovely to eat on the way. I'm on expenses. Let's use them.'

Chapter Twenty-Three

One thing Cass had learned on the Force was that the recession was good at making criminals out of ordinary people. There were no taxes to be paid on illegal earnings, and as the world had sunk into debt, so the basic tax rate had risen. Diana Jacobs, Brian Freeman's inside woman at The Bank, lived in a rented apartment in Islington. It was relatively spacious and nicely done up, but nothing too flash – quite like the woman herself, who was somewhere in her twenties, somewhere in the ordinary range, and no one you would overly notice in a crowd. There was nothing about her or her home that might draw any unwarranted attention from her employer.

Cass imagined that she was being paid well by Freeman, but she was bright enough to show no signs of any extra wealth. No doubt there was a separate bank account somewhere that was filling up nicely for Miss Jacobs.

Freeman had arranged for another flat to be available for them within the same apartment block, where they could meet and do what was needed without occasioning any noticeable change to Diana's daily routine. Cass was impressed with Freeman's excessive caution and attention to detail – but then, he was the only person other than Cass himself who understood how Mr Bright worked. Underestimating him could be fatal. Cass had done it himself and now he was on the run for murders he hadn't committed.

Mr Bright's eyes were everywhere.

The owner of this second flat had been persuaded to leave his keys behind while he enjoyed a two-week holiday. Cass doubted he'd taken much persuading: a paid trip, some cash in hand, and more as a bonus when he got back, no names, no pack drill: easy.

'There you go.' Diana Jacobs handed round the mugs of coffee and Cass took one. Maric gestured and she put his down on the table. He had her laptop open.

'What time do you normally get up?' he asked.

'About now. Why?' Diana said.

'Would you normally log into work first thing?'

'Yes.' She smiled. 'There's no such thing as time off at The Bank. If you're awake, you're working, and if you're asleep you should be dreaming about it.' She looked over at Brian Freeman. 'I'm very much looking forward to handing in my notice and disappearing off into the sunset.' She dropped the old man a wink, and in that split second as her eyes lit up and she grinned impishly, Cass realised that he'd been wrong, there was something very special about her. She'd worked hard to make herself seem quite ordinary.

'Good.' Maric's eyes were focused on the machine. 'We don't want them to find anything suspicious about you when all this shit hits the fan.' He typed in her username and password. 'Let's have a look at you,' he muttered, 'see what you're made of.'

'If it's all right with you lot,' Diana said, 'I'm going back to bed. Wake me when there's something interesting to tell me.' She turned and headed off in the direction of one of the other rooms. There was something sultry in her stride, and Cass would have put money on that not being the walk she used in the corridors of The Bank. It could, of course, be that it had just been a very long time since he'd had sex. He didn't think so, though. Diana Jacobs was a woman of layers.

The hacker lit up a cigarette and held it between his teeth as his fingers whizzed over the keys. He was totally absorbed in his exploration of the computer. Cass lit one of his own and headed into the kitchen. It felt strange just sitting and watching someone working; although Maric wasn't showing any signs of it bothering him, Cass wouldn't have liked it if their roles had been reversed. And this wasn't going to be a quick job, anyone could see that. At least these past two months had taught him a little patience. He was getting better at biding his time.

Freeman followed him out.

'I hope he's good,' Cass said, leaning against the sink.

'Good? He'd bloody better be. He's costing a fucking fortune.' Freeman leaned against one of the kitchen cabinets. 'Let's hope he's finding one too.'

An hour or so later Maric shut down the laptop and closed the lid.

'And?' Freeman asked.

Cass felt his heart racing slightly. It all came down to Maric: if he couldn't get into the systems, finding Luke was going to be a lot harder, impossible, even. And now that Cass was out and about there was always a risk the police would find him, and if they did, it was game over. He had no illusions about that.

'There's no sign of your Mr Bright or the second network, not that this laptop can find, but that comes as no surprise. He'll be in there somewhere.' Maric's whole demeanour had changed now that he was working. Yesterday's laid-back surfer dude was completely gone; today the slim man virtually crackled with energy. 'Everyone who has any kind of standing in the world today has an email address. Your Mr Bright will have one, hidden away somewhere, and I can almost guarantee that he'll use the same password for accessing the missing system.'

'You don't know this man,' Cass said.

'No, but if his email address isn't available on the staff network, then only a select few will have it – so why would he bother with a new password for a system that is just as secret? But it doesn't matter – we'll find it, one way or another, and then we'll have some fun with it. But first I have to find the second network.'

'How?' Freeman asked.

'This is a very complex system, just like I imagine your Mr Bright is a very complex man. The thing is, the more complex the problem, the simpler the approach should be to solving it. We could spend a lot of time unpicking this computer and get nowhere trying to break through the defences; all we'd do is draw attention to ourselves, and then our sleeping beauty would be in trouble and we'd be out in the cold.'

'So,' Cass said, 'what's this simple approach then?'

Maric smiled. 'I'm going to need access to the telephone exchange, a van, a uniform and some identification.' He clapped his hands together. 'Let's make some trouble!'

'I just don't see the point!' Armstrong said, not for the first time. 'It'll be a complete waste of money – everything in this case points to Jones; we all know that. The knife used in Powell's murder was from his flat, his fingerprints were at that crime scene and he *ran*. He's *still* running. Why do you suddenly want to waste time and money on a wild goose chase?'

'It has to be said,' DCI Heddings leaned back in his chair, 'Sergeant Armstrong has a point.'

'About the money?' Ramsey asked.

'No need for sarcasm, Detective Inspector. You're starting to sound uncomfortably like DI Jones, and you can see from his record that never did him any good.' He looked over at Hask, who was keeping himself as much out of the way as a man of his bulk could. This fight wasn't his; at the end of the day he was simply a hired consultant. 'You agree with Ramsey on this, Doctor?' Heddings finished.

'Yes, I do, sir.' So he was gong to be drawn into the fight after all. 'It's certainly worth exploring. If you go back to my original report you'll see that I was never convinced that Cassius Jones could be this kind of impetuous killer. This new evidence – circumstantial though it may be – does cloud the initial conviction that Jones was responsible.'

'Of course he's going to say that,' Armstrong muttered. 'He's a Jones crony. They both are.'

'Enough, sergeant!' Heddings snapped. 'We pay Dr Hask enough of our budget for his professional opinions, so let me at least do him the courtesy of hearing what that is.'

'There's something else,' Ramsey said, trying to calm the room. 'We know that Jones spent time in the interview room with Shearman – if he was so intent on killing all these doctors, then why didn't he kill Shearman when he had the opportunity? It doesn't add up.'

'Maybe he didn't have a weapon with him, 'Armstrong said. 'Or he didn't get whatever information he wanted from him so wanted to keep him alive. Just because he didn't kill Shearman it doesn't make him innocent.'

Heddings looked down again at the report Hask and Ramsey had compiled. He sighed. 'Who closed down the initial inquiry into this Bright character? I can't help but agree that it's strange – he's not a bloody Member of Parliament or anything, is he?'

'Not as far as we know. Chief Inspector Morgan must have done it – or been told to by someone higher up – that's something you could help with finding out, sir.'

'Why the hell would I want to do that?' Heddings leaned on his desk. 'This is all a big enough mess as it is without suddenly chasing ghosts. If we start saying this might be a set-up the press will be all over us for trying to protect our own.'

'Then don't tell them,' Hask said. 'Cass Jones is old news; the public are far more concerned by the Angel of Death walking among them.'

'And you *have* to let us check this out.' Ramsey leaned forward, his hands on Heddings' desk. 'Because the one thing all of us in this room have in common is that we're clean, yes? We're honest coppers in a station that currently doesn't have a reputation for that. If you don't let us follow this lead simply because there might be fall-out, then you're as bent as Bowman in my book.'

'You just don't want to believe that Jones is guilty,' Armstrong said.

'That may be true,' Ramsey said. 'I like Cass, I admit it. But if he's guilty, I can promise you I won't fight against the death penalty for him. Just let me prove whether he is or not, so if that is the eventual outcome, we can all sleep in our beds at night knowing he truly deserved it.' He stared at the young sergeant, and Hask was struck by how strong the DI looked in that moment. There was something about him that reminded Hask of Cass, but he couldn't put his finger on it – something in the eyes, perhaps. 'Because, believe it or not, I like you too, Sergeant Armstrong,' Ramsey continued, 'and I don't want the death of an innocent man to be on your conscience if Jones gets executed and then five years later we figure out we were wrong. Can you get that through your pig-headed skull?'

'You've all changed your tune,' Armstrong grumbled.

The phone on Heddings' desk started ringing, but the DCI ignored it.

'Does that matter?' Ramsey said. 'Dammit, that's the point of our job, isn't it? We all have to have that ability, to change the way we think about something if the evidence points that way – until we find the truth.'

Hask frowned. Something was happening on the other side of the glass window. Police officers were getting out of their seats and he could hear someone out of sight shouting, 'Hey, you can't just come storming through here – you have to sign in!'

'I think you should answer that phone,' he said. Armstrong and Ramsey were still sniping at each other, horns locked, but he'd zoned them out. Who could cause so much ruckus in a police station?

The answer came through the door before his brain could reach for it. Heddings' phone stopped ringing and the two policemen finally stopped arguing.

'Sorry, sir,' an out-of-breath constable said as he stumbled into the doorway. 'He wouldn't stop.'

'That's all right.' Heddings' voice was tight. 'Shut the door on your way out.'

There was a moment of silence before David Fletcher, head of the ATD, slapped a large photograph onto the DCI's desk. 'Thought you might like to see this.'

The grainy enhanced image had clearly been taken at night, but the man at the centre was still recognisable as Cass Jones. His hair was longer and he'd lost weight, but it was definitely the missing DI. He was staring up at something, cigarette in hand.

'Where did you get this?' Armstrong asked.

'It was taken outside The Bank at 3.15 this morning. Most of the security cameras in that area belong to The Bank, but we still have one or two left over from the days when it was the MI6 building.'

'He was outside *The Bank*?' Hask asked. 'In the middle of the night?'

'Did he go in?' Ramsey said.

'No, as far as we can tell, he just stood there for about ten minutes, looking at the building, and then he left.'

'You don't happen to know where he went, do you?' Heddings asked.

'No, we lost him.'

'He was looking at The Bank,' Hask said softly.

'Well, his brother used to work there,' Fletcher said.

'No.' Hask shook his head. 'If he was having a moment of grief, then he'd have gone to Christian's old house. Grief leads people to treasure personal, not professional, things. He'd have been taking less of a risk as well. This ... this is something else.'

'Mr Bright,' Ramsey said quietly.

'Who?' Fletcher frowned.

Hask smiled at the DI. 'Cass Jones was looking for his nemesis.'

Chapter Twenty-Four

It was past one o'clock in the morning when the telephone company van parked up outside The Bank. A man stepped out and walked, head down, towards the building, a large computer bag over his shoulder.

He smiled as he spoke to the smart young woman behind the reception desk and slid over his identification card. She studied it thoroughly before politely returning both it and his smile. *One moment.* He nodded. He stayed by the counter as she spoke softly into her headset before smiling efficiently at him again. *The administrator will be down shortly.* The administrator. From his place at the counter he'd seen the name on her screen as she'd looked up the extension: *Stephen Bestwick.*

He waited. Bestwick appeared, looking as expected: middle-aged, suit, tie, slightly harried – the look acquired by network administrators across the world. The only difference was Mr Bestwick's suit was more expensive, bespoke, even, and his shoes were Italian, handmade. He in turn looked at the telephone engineer: thick workman's boots with traces of muck on them from too much time outside. A uniform that was clean but not overly new. A watch that was hardy rather than expensive. He explained that he needed access to the servers – there were some looping issues; they could cause data damage or transfer speed issues, at worse data loss entirely. Stephen Bestwick listened as he led the engineer into the building. He would need to call and check this work was authorised, of course – company procedure. The engineer nodded himself. *Of course.*

Although it was one o'clock in the morning, the building was still busy, though the staff worked quietly, as if unwilling to break the sanctity of the peaceful night. Their feet tapped out a steady rhythm as the administrator led the way to the lift and took them down. He wasn't surprised; the cool of the basement levels were the best places to keep secrets, and that's exactly what computer systems housed: flirtatious emails, financial wrong-doings; everything was backed up and locked away. Emptying the trash can on a personal computer rarely deleted any file's entire existence, and certainly not in a place like this. Everything was stored in case it was needed later.

Beside him, the administrator had dialled through to the engineer's supervisor. In the silence the ring tone was loud. The engineer imagined the connection changing direction as he'd programmed it to do at the exchange earlier that evening; he visualised it like a streak of light, racing towards Brian Freeman and Cass Jones. It was Jones who answered, and now his voice was lighter and he spoke with the rising inflection the world had come to expect from any phone-drone, whether based in Mumbai or Glasgow. After a few moments the administrator appeared satisfied. He ended the call.

The lift stopped gently; no thud of arrival here. The Bank was a smooth operator in every way. For the first time since embarking on this project, the engineer allowed his heart to flutter with excitement and his mouth almost watered at the prospect of exploring – of *breaking* – the systems in front of him. He followed the administrator, forcing himself to slouch instead of tapping his foot impatiently while he unlocked the door ahead.

The air inside was cool, and the hum that surrounded them was like the whisper of a calling lover. His skin tingled. He put his case down and then put his hands on his hips for a second and let out a long breath of air, as if disappointed to be presented with so many banks of servers. He opened the case and started pulling out the usual equipment, all company labelled. He glanced at his watch. *I hoped I'd be getting home early tonight. Not going to happen is it?* He shrugged and smiled again. The administrator looked at the heavy drop-safe laptop in the bag and the flask and sandwich box and then at the engineer before chewing his bottom lip. Is it going to take long? The engineer had been expecting the question; the one thing guarantee-able in this world was a lack of patience. *An hour? Maybe more? Hopefully less.*

There was a longer pause and then Stephen Bestwick pulled a business card from his top pocket and handed it over. *Call me when you're done and I'll come and let you out.*

He waited a full five minutes after Bestwick had left before pulling the chunky laptop from his case, unclipping the false bottom beneath the keyboard and removing the far sleeker model beneath. He tipped out the seven number-labelled datasticks from the empty flask, opened a port, accessed the network and entered the administrator's user-name, using the same formula as for Diana Jacobs, with a full stop between first and surname. He slotted the datastick marked '1' into the side and ran the sophisticated dictionary attack stored on it. Within minutes, he had the admin-istrator's password.

He sat back for a moment and smiled. For the next hour and a half, he was lost.

So, everything's okay now? The lift was as smooth on its way up as it had been on the way down. *No issues?* The engineer reassured the administrator – while yawning – that The Bank's system had not been affected by the problems with the lines. Some other businesses in the area had not been so lucky, however; if The Bank had any external offices or servers in the area then they might find they have problems in the morning. But hopefully all would be sorted by then. The team was working around the clock.

He kept his head down as he walked to the van – *not hiding, just tired* – as the cameras tracked his every move, even though by the time anyone thought to double-check his identity all hell would already have broken loose. All the information Cass Jones required was stored on the laptop, and the servers were a ticking time bomb of chaos. All in all, it had been good night's work.

He thought of Stephen Bestwick, heading back up to his desk, the engineer no doubt already forgotten. His world was about to collapse. Still, most clouds had a silver lining, and within a month, just when he'd be at his lowest ebb, the by-then very much fired network administrator would receive a letter from an overseas bank which would, he was sure, restore Mr Bestwick's previous good humour. There were far better ways for Mr Bestwick and his lovely wife Carole – The Bank's personnel records were comprehensive – to spend their remaining years than as slaves to The Bank. Sitting on a boat in the Caribbean, for one.

The engine throbbed loudly as he pulled the van back out onto the street. He had customers waiting.

It was past four in the morning when Maric had knocked gently on the door of the flat. The van and uniform had been left in a car park, as arranged, and he was once again dressed in his expensive battered jeans and surfer-style top. The solid workman's watch had been replaced by his own Jaeger-LeCoultre and his Converse boots had not one fleck of mud on them. For a moment he'd stood there, looking at them both, and then, after Cass had wondered if perhaps time had stopped and left him in this limbo, Maric grinned. Cass was so relieved that his eyes burned and, for him at least, the corridor filled with gold that evaporated the December cold from the communal space. He was astounded the others didn't experience it, but looking at how Freeman had shivered as he ushered the hacker in, the brightness had clearly evaded them. Cass had turned his back on it. *There is no glow* was no longer a mantra he could truthfully repeat to himself, but he wasn't yet ready to make it his friend.

After the initial celebrations were done, Cass left Brian Freeman and Maric sipping their champagne and went into one of the bedrooms and opened the slim laptop. Sweat prickled in the creases of his fingers and his heart pounded. He should have been tired, but adrenalin had been pumping through his veins since Maric had left, and right at that moment there wasn't even a twinge of an ache in his shoulder.

As the various copied folders filled the home screen he lit a cigarette, ignoring how dry his mouth was. Brian Freeman's throaty laugh carried easily into the room, but he barely heard it. There was simply him and the computer. He clicked on the first copied file: details of the X accounts. He closed it down; fascinating as they might be, those weren't what he was looking for. Once he'd found what he needed, Freeman and Dr Cornell could pore over them to their heart's content, but right now any curiosity over the Network's cashflow had to take a back seat.

He searched impatiently through the files. He wouldn't have much time to act once he'd found where Bright was keeping Luke. He had no doubt the boy would be moved as a defensive measure as soon as whatever magic Maric had worked on the systems took hold. He probably had twenty-four hours, maybe thirty-six.

He lit a fresh cigarette from the butt of the first before stubbing it out in a saucer. The bedroom would stink by the time the owner got back. Hopefully Freeman's cash would make up for it.

He found the folder called POTENTIALS and went straight to the fifteenth file: the Jones file. When he'd first looked through it all those months ago at his dead parents' home, under the watchful eye of his dead brother's ghost, there had been some strange medical records in there. At the time he hadn't understood why Luke had had so many medical tests, or why there was a note referring to 'secondary' medical records held within The Bank's employee folders.

Now he understood: those 'secondary' records referred to the boy he'd thought of as his nephew for all these years, the poor cuckoo in the Jones' nest. These hidden records were for the stolen baby: the *real* Luke.

He read them over and over until his eyes blurred, but there was nothing that gave him any clue to the boy's location. All he could see was a series of dates, and tests with names he didn't understand. He closed the folder down and gritted his teeth. There had to be *something*. He tapped the tracking pad, refusing to let his frustration get the better of him. He couldn't afford to miss *anything* . . .

Just when he was about to hurl the computer across the room in frustration, he saw something, in a secondary folder labelled SUNDRIES, located within a folder that appeared to detail household payments. He almost smiled. Mr Bright was a clever fucker, he'd give him that; even Cass, who had been *looking*, had almost missed it.

He stared at the list. The first set of outgoings was called FEES, and at first he thought they were a load of shit lawyers' costs – then he looked at the dates. The payments had been made over several years, at three points in each in one; the beginnings of September and January and mid-April. The last few payments were for thirteen thousand pounds. He stared at the figures until he could see them in his mind's eye: FEES. *School fees.*

Luke might be only eight years old, but he wasn't with Mr Bright, so someone had to be looking after him, and now he thought about it, he was quite sure that someone in Mr Bright's position would have chosen the finest in-dependent infant school. No doubt the child boarded as well. *So what did he do in the holidays*, Cass wondered, *stay behind?* He didn't imagine there would be many other children who lived in the school. It would be a lonely life for a small boy – maybe there weren't any other children at all.

His heart ached for the faceless child given away by his own grandfather. He sat back slightly and rolled his injured shoulder. How long had he been hunched over the com-puter? The lights were still on in the rest of the flat, but the laughter had died down and he was working in silence. He felt like he'd just woken up. *School fees*, hidden in among staff payments and laundry bills – why? The answer was whispered in his brother's voice: *He doesn't want the others to know.*

Cass stared at the computer. If he looked anywhere else he'd see Christian's highly polished brogues, complete with drops of crimson blood. Those last few months must have been terrible for Christian as he slowly became convinced that his son wasn't his own. That was an example of how different they were: Cass wouldn't have been able to live with that; he'd have *had* to go looking, no matter what the consequences. And that was why Christian had charged him with this task from beyond the grave, of course: because he knew Cass would keep going, no matter who got hurt. He wondered if that was why Christian's ghost had dis-appeared – *he* could rest in peace now; it was Cass who could no longer sleep.

He focused on the numbers again. The termly payments stopped almost eighteen months ago, replaced by a monthly payment of just over three thousand pounds. He frowned. Even if Luke had moved from an infant school to a junior school, surely the fees would still be paid termly? He copied down the account number and then started to work back through the other files, trying to match it with anything that might give him some more information. He itched to speak to Perry Jordan – he had friends who could get access to some of The Bank's accounts – but that path was definitely closed; if he called Perry, the investigator would *have* to call Ramsey, whether he wanted to or not.

He got to his feet and stretched out his cramped legs, relieved to see no evidence of Christian anywhere. His bladder ached and he was halfway to the toilet when his stupidity struck him: there was someone in The Bank who could help him – Brian Freeman's mole, Diana Jacobs.

Cass was half-expecting to find Maric and the old gang-ster asleep in their chairs, but when he walked into the quiet lounge he found the two men hunched over a second laptop. Freeman was copying something down in his uneven scrawl – he might have the brain of an Oxbridge scholar, but his education had been left in the gutter, and he had the handwriting to prove it. Cass waited until he'd finished the current note – looked like a list of companies. That came as no surprise: Freeman intended to make a killing out of this, as untraceably as possible. *Leave no trace.* That was their motto. He wondered if somewhere along the line they'd all become ghosts: him, Brian Freeman, Mr Bright. It was just that no one had bothered to tell them.

'You found what you're looking for?' Freeman glanced up over the glasses perched so incongruously on his crooked nose.

'Nearly,' Cass said. 'I need details of a bank account. I'm pretty sure the company will be Bank-owned – Bright would want control. I wondered if Diana Jacobs would be able to get it for me?'

There was a pause, and Cass understood why: they'd gone to great lengths not to ripple the surface, and now here was Cass, wanting to drop an anvil into that quiet pool.

'She can do that,' Maric answered, 'if she logs in with this username and password.' He scribbled something down and handed it to Cass. 'I created a new user. The Bank has an imaginary employee.'

'Won't it be traceable to her computer?'

'No.' Maric grinned. 'Not unless they get someone as good as me to dig around. And there isn't anyone as good as me.'

Freeman called the young lawyer, and while they waited for her to call back, Cass paced the flat, leaving a trail of smoke in his wake. He guessed this must be how most people felt waiting for a bug test after having unprotected sex. His stomach churned greasily and his skin tingled. If this account number led nowhere, then he was fucked. Not only would he have let his little brother down, but Mr Bright would have beaten him.

Maric watched him thoughtfully, his casual demeanor the complete opposite of Cass' nervous electricity.

'You have to learn to care less, Jones,' he said eventually. 'And you have to remember that there are many ways to skin a cat. If you don't find the boy this time, there will be other times.'

Cass paused in his pacing. Maric was older than him, and had no doubt led a more interesting life, but it was all lived within systems and behind screens. He played with people from a distance. Cass' life was blood and earth and guilt. It was *real*.

'Time for me may well be limited,' he said after a bit. '*Free* time, that is.'

Maric smiled. 'This is true for both of us. Makes the time more fun though, doesn't it?'

Cass almost laughed; maybe they weren't that different after all. Knowing the game could be over at any moment certainly made him feel more alive.

Brian Freeman's phone rang in the other room and Cass' heart stopped. This was it. He stared at Maric and the hacker winked.

'Let's go and see if Fate is on your side.'

'I don't believe in Fate,' Cass said automatically. As he followed the slim man along the corridor, he wondered if that was still strictly true.

'There,' Freeman said after he ended the call, 'that's who the account belongs to. It's a medical facility, and not Flush5 either. She couldn't go deeply enough through the layers to see who the final owner was, but my money would be on our Mr Bright.'

'What kind of medical facility?' Cass frowned as he looked at the address. The name of the place, *Calthorpe House*, didn't give much away. What had all those medical tests revealed? Was there something seriously wrong with his nephew?

'Guess that's up to you to find out.' Freeman got to his feet. 'I'll let you have Wharton and Osborne. They're good blokes, and they like you.' He gave a tired laugh. 'Fuck knows why. You must still have some of that old Charlie Sutton charm. But first we need to get back to the house and get some sleep.' He held up the small, sleek laptop. 'And I can keep this?'

'It's yours,' Maric smiled. 'You paid for it.'

'It's been a pleasure doing business with you, son.'

'Likewise.' The hacker followed them to the door. Night had somehow disappeared into morning and now the building was alive with the sounds of water rushing through pipes as showers woke the residents up, and doors slamming as they answered the siren call of the office. For a while it had felt like they were the only people alive in the block, and thinking of how these people had all been asleep throughout the activity of the night made Cass wonder again at how little anyone understood of the world around them. What had Dr Cornell said? *Nothing is real. The world is on its head.* How right was the old man going to turn out to be?

'Good luck, gentlemen.' Maric opened the door. 'And goodbye.'

Chapter Twenty-Five

The two days since DeVore's panicked phone call had passed relatively quietly. At first Mr Bright wondered if DeVore's nerves would get the better of him and make him call Mr Dublin or one of the others, but it appeared not. Perhaps the rumours of his own current moment of instability hadn't reached the House of Intervention yet.

That was quite likely, of course, since Mr Bellew's clumsy attempts at a coup had failed and the House of Intervention had gone back to its normal place in the world; keeping watch over the inhabitants, letting Mr Bright know if anything too untoward appeared in the data stream. Outside of the Inner Cohort's annual reviews it was a forgotten place, and he doubted that Mr Dublin had remembered DeVore yet, or got around to explaining what he believed to be a shift in the powerbase.

That thought gave him some sense of comfort. Mr Dublin was good – Mr Bright quite respected him – but he had a long way to go to reach the top of this game they all played. Perhaps Mr Dublin was too pure for the machinations required in the First's absence; he certainly lacked fire. It had always been Mr Rasnic of the pair who *Glowed* the brightest.

He fought back disappointment as he stared down at the reports that had slowly trickled back to him. He'd hoped to have found the emissary by now, but there was still no trace. And it was highly unlikely an emissary would have been sent here alone, not after all this time – so where could they be hiding? He'd expected to hear something of them by now. After all, he knew how long it had taken those who'd travelled to learn to hide what they truly were, how to fight the urge to *become* and *be*. Surely the emissary would not have such restraint?

He drummed his fingers on the desk, his neatly clipped nails tapping like cockroaches on tiles. He always prided himself on maintaining his calm, and for the first time he knew that was slipping. He focused his mind; he was still the Architect. He might not have led them here, but this was *his* place. It was born of all their flavours and personalities, the First's most of all, but *he* understood the way it worked better than anyone. So if there was no trace of the emissary there were two possible reasons: the first, the emissary had gone, and that he discounted; logic dictated that if they couldn't find the Walkways back, then neither could the emissary. After all, they had created the Walkways, not *him*, so they had the advantage in that regard.

The others might be in awe of an emissary, but he wasn't. They were only servants, after all, *messengers*. He hadn't been able to see much beyond the brilliant *Glow* in the CCTV footage of the car, but he had a good idea who the emissary was – *he* would have picked someone close to the First, and Mr Bright's memory was still good when it came to those who had chosen their side and stayed behind. It didn't do anything to ease his nervousness, though. If *he'*d sent them here, then *he* was prepared to lose them, two whom *he* had always claimed to love. Everyone was expendable: that was a lesson they had all learned quickly. It would appear that hadn't changed.

Mr Bright brought his mind back to the present. It was, after all, all there was.

If the emissary couldn't get home, and there was no evidence of any unexplained *becoming*, then there really was only one explanation: the emissary and companion didn't want to bring any attention to themselves, so this was no great heralding of war. Whatever the emissary's message was, it wasn't to be delivered to the entirety of the cohorts – so who was it for? It had to be the First, the only one *he* would have any interest in among those who had left. Was it a warning of the impending attack?

His mobile phone started ringing, but he ignored it. He wanted to think. Why would *he* warn the First? Did *he* hope that after all this time the First would come back to the fold? His mobile paused, and then started again with its insistent pealing. The First wouldn't turn his back and flee, leaving them all to the fate the Interventionists were projecting. Surely they would fight all over again if they had to, even if it meant their own destruction – *surely*?

The phone on his desk joined his mobile, both now demanding his attention, out of time and tone with each other and making thinking impossible, but still he ignored them. It was only when the intercom started buzzing too that his stomach chilled. *What now?* He went for the intercom first.

An hour and a half later, all thoughts of the emissary had been pushed to the back of his mind; that could wait. He had a far more immediate problem: The Bank was in turmoil; its companies in disarray as their shares were being dumped unexpectedly on the stock market. CEOs were scrambling to reassure the public and various governments that there were no problems, and desperately trying to buy their own stock back before others did – mainly unsuccessfully. This had apparently been going on for some hours and only now was anyone coming to him about it? He was seething.

'Who's doing this?' he snapped into the phone, immediately annoyed at revealing his irritation in his voice. He hadn't wanted the conference call with The Bank's founders; he had not liked being told he *had* to have it. 'And why was I not told *immediately*?'

There was a long pause, no one wanting to say anything, until eventually the British billionaire broke the silence. 'Um . . . *you're* doing this, apparently. All of the companies and corporations affected are from those owned by you and your own private cabal, whoever they are. Staff received email orders – from *you* – telling them to sell a certain amount of stock, none in amounts that would raise alarm, but as a whole . . . well, here we are.'

'*My* email?' Mr Bright had control of his voice again, but his brain was racing. 'Only a handful of people have that – the instructions cannot possibly have come from me.'

'Not your direct email – we know your obsessional desire for privacy – but there is no doubt they came from you: the instructions came from the email addresses you have set up for each of the companies affected.'

'That's why we hadn't spoken to you,' the American computer geek cut in. 'It wasn't until the bigger picture became clear that we realised that something was going wrong.'

'This needs to be stopped,' the Englishman said. 'The Bank was formed to create stability – that's why we agreed to partner with you despite how little you share with us. You must deal with this immediately.'

'I will take care of it.' Mr Bright's smooth voice displayed none of his inner rage, though his eyes burned and he felt himself on the brink of *becoming*. To be spoken to like this by Mr Dublin, that would have been bad enough – but these little people? No matter how right they were, it was *beyond* acceptable. For the first time he felt as if his power really might be wrested from him. Mr Dublin would hear about this soon, that much was certain, and then it would be all over for him. He needed to contain this – whatever *this* was – and fast.

He ended the conversation and breathed deeply until the burst of *Glow* had faded.

His immediate thought was this was Mr Dublin, or perhaps the errant Mr Craven, following in the footsteps of Mr Bellew and trying to take him down by proving that he was losing control. But even if that were the case, they would have needed someone to have broken into The Bank's system to find a way to access his hidden email addresses and passwords. No one knew those. Within the cohorts they had always trusted each other, at least until relatively recently, and no one had even asked for access to his systems. Until the First started sleeping and the Dying came among them they had been happy for him and the First Cohort to take care of things – it wasn't as if anyone was lacking for anything they wanted. For a very, very long time they had all been contented.

Not any more, he thought; now they were all obsessed with the Dying and the idea that their world was crumbling and taking them all with it. So let them panic. They'd always needed a strong leader, and as soon as the First was ready to face them, they'd realise that nothing was over. This world was hardier than they gave it credit. He hit the intercom button. 'Get all the network administrators in. I want to know how we were hacked and who allowed it to happen. I want images of every person who's been in and out – staff as well as visitors – checked. Access every database worldwide for people capable of doing this. I want to know who it is, and who hired them.'

Perhaps the trail wouldn't lead directly back to one of the Inner Cohort, but it would go far enough for him to find out who had done this. He didn't wait for the answer but pressed a small button on his desk, and the concealed computer console rose. First he needed to send out instructions to buy back the stock, regardless of cost, and then he had to change all his email settings. He would also need to transfer money from his X account to make sure everything was stabilised.

He quietly cursed Mr Dublin or Mr Craven for their actions; this had to be their doing. To try and take him down was one thing, but to add more uncertainty to the short lives of those who existed in ignorance of their heritage lacked vision. He expected more from those who had known greatness. He logged into the sub-network and moved expertly through the files until he came to the overview of the X-section accounts. As he went to click on X1, his own sector's finances, he froze. For a second, he couldn't react at all. Each column was in flux, figures moving in and out of them too fast for even his eyes to keep track of.

His heart pounded and a cold sweat burst into life in the palms of his normally dry hands. Surely not even Mr Craven would do this? Creating havoc out *there* was one thing – but this was *Network* business.

He clenched his teeth and allowed himself to burn slightly to ease the moment of panic.

When his breathing was steady once again, he looked at the columns and set up a new command to register the totals. He needed to see how much they were losing. The command ran and he looked at the figure it produced, he frowned slightly, his initial panic replaced by thoughtfulness. The balance remained the same, despite the constant changes in the numbers in each of the columns. So the money was moving between the accounts, but not out of them.

He opened a second page and retrieved the stored balances. Only twenty-five million pounds of the billions the Network held were missing, gone over the past forty-eight hours. He went back to the screen where the figures were changing several times within each blink of an eye. So why this trickery if it wasn't to drain the accounts? His fingernails tapped the desk once more. It was all smoke and mirrors, he decided, allowing himself a tight smile, a way of stopping him tracking *how* the twenty-five million had gone and to *where*, for now at least.

He ignored the huge sense of relief; admitting he was relieved would also be an admittance that he'd been afraid. Whoever was playing with him was cleverer than he'd given them credit for: they'd created enough of a mess to cause him trouble, but not enough that the trouble couldn't be put right. This was just part of the game, not the end move, and he was an expert when it came to games. He started resetting his passwords.

The phone on the desk rang again, and this time he answered it straight away. It wasn't Mr Dublin, and he was glad. If he could manage it he needed some time before speaking to that one.

'Sir?' The voice at the other end was nervous, and Mr Bright was pleased. News of Asher Red's rather unpleasant termination of employment had spread through the small group of those aware of who really controlled the machinations of The Bank. It was all rumour, of course, not actual facts, but a little fear could go a long way. Asher Red had failed to serve his purpose in many ways, but at least with his ending he'd managed to find a way to please Mr Bright. It was good that at least someone out there was still nervous of his reaction to their news.

'Yes?'

'We've been going through the external and reception camera footage—'

'Have you got the hacker?' The problem with fear was that it invariably prevented people from getting to the point quickly, and he was in no mood for hesitancy.

'Not yet, sir, but one of the night network administrators said that there was a visit from a telephone engineer on his shift two nights ago. The engineer needed access to the systems. The administrator called and checked with the company and it was all legit so he let him in.'

'Did he stay with him?'

'No; he was sorting out some problems on the third floor at the time – Japan's markets were open and he was under pressure to get them sorted. He said he left the engineer to it and then let him out when he was finished.'

'Fire him. And get a picture of the engineer and run it. He's the man we're looking for. Let me know when you have a match.'

'There's another thing.'

The phone had been halfway to the cradle, but he grabbed it back. 'What?'

'We did find something else in the footage. I'm sending it to you now.' He paused. 'It's that policeman. It was filmed the night before we were hacked.'

Mr Bright put down the phone and waited for the file to arrive. He clicked on it and there he was, Cassius Jones. He looked different – thinner. His hair was longer. Both changes suited him; he looked more reminiscent of his heritage, of what was so strong in his blood. On the screen Cass Jones smoked into the cold night, and Mr Bright found himself smiling. So Cassius Jones turns up to simply stare at The Bank, and shortly afterwards all hell breaks loose around them. Coincidence? Mr Bright didn't believe in coincidences. So this wasn't the work of Mr Dublin and Mr Craven after all: this was Cassius Jones, bringing a war to his table – but who else? Who was standing with him? He couldn't be acting alone.

He felt his mood lifting slightly: a new game with DI Cass Jones. Of all the Jones family, he was the one who had turned out to be the least disappointing. He had something of the rebel in him. Mr Bright poured himself a brandy. He supposed that was a matter of blood too.

Chapter Twenty-Six

'I've dreamed it,' the old man said. He was sitting on the side of the bed. He hadn't got as far as leaving the safety of their small apartment yet, but since she'd told him of the First's waking, she was pleased to see his spirits had definitely lifted. Each day he was eating more, and now he insisted on getting up and walking around their rooms. Whatever doubts he'd had about his old long-lost friend seemed to have passed; now he wanted to be well when he saw the First again. It made her own tired heart lift, helped her to ignore the truth, that the red in her hair was fading and that she too was getting weaker. She hoped the First called for them soon. She was conserving what energy she had for that.

'I've dreamed *him* coming here.' He looked at her with a vague wonder in his thin, sagging face. His mouth hung open, revealing just two teeth remaining. They shone like stars in the vast gaps of darkness around them. She was surprised he wasn't lisping.

'What do you see in your dream?' She sat alongside him.

'A great battle,' the old man said softly, his eyes drifting to some faraway place, 'the trumpeters filling the sky – *this* sky – with perfect music. I'm leading them, just as I always do.'

'Then it must truly be perfect music.' She smiled at him.

The music in his dream *was* beautiful and terrible; she knew that because she'd had the dream herself.

'*He* has no mercy. This world is destroyed.' The old man spoke in bursts, as if reliving the images. 'This is the final battle of this great war, setting brother against brother.'

'Except this time, the rebels don't stand a chance, do they?' she said. 'They're out of practice. They die in the dust and the darkness.'

He looked at her, his watery eyes wide. 'You've seen it too?'

She shrugged her delicate shoulders. 'I've dreamed it, just like you have.'

'Then it must be what shall come to pass.' His voice was agitated, filled with a rising excitement. 'It means that we find a way home!'

She smiled, glad that he was happy. She would have to go soon, taking her aching body out into the cold to continue her search for Jarrod Pretorius, and she never liked to leave him when he was maudlin. So far, her search had been fruitless; she had found nothing using the search engines of the local library computers – nothing of any use, at any rate. But it was unlikely he had kept his own name ... She knew that at some point she was going to have to look for him in the ways that belonged to her other body, but right now she didn't have the energy – and she needed to be careful. She was in no condition to draw unwanted attention to herself.

The old man got up and started his exercises, shuffling his thin body around the flat. She picked up her coffee and went through their small sitting room to the window – it had the best view, and she liked to look out over the uneven lines of the tops of the buildings, some old and some new and all full of life and activity. Lights flickered in houses and flats, and on the pavements below people scurried here, there and everywhere. She allowed herself to get lost in it all for a few minutes. They had so much energy, so much life – and though there was little *Glow*, and at first she'd found that hard to bear, she'd adjusted. She was learning to understand *them* – the rejects – and how ferociously they burned during their short lives. They fought until the last.

A brass band had stopped in the middle of the street and now it burst into loud song. She tilted her head to catch the words, watching as people shook buckets at passers-by and thanked them for their small donations and wished them a very merry Christmas. *In the bleak midwinter, frosty wind made moan. Earth was hard as iron, water like a stone.* The music and words worked together, and although it was a coarse sound compared to that made by the trumpeters of home, it had its own honest beauty. She thought for a moment that perhaps *he* had judged them too harshly all that time ago. Perhaps when he *saw* . . .

She stopped that thought: *he* wouldn't see, not when his mind had already been made up. This would always be treachery to him, and forgiveness wasn't in his nature.

She felt the warmth of the old man at her back. The music had drawn him to the window too, and for a few minutes they stood together and stared out at this fascinating world. Reflections of themselves that they didn't recognise stared back like ghosts trapped in the glass. She looked past them as the sun cut shadows through the rooftops and onto the street below.

'Why do I feel sad at the thought of its destruction?' he asked eventually. Her reflection smiled back at him. She didn't answer, choosing silence to do it for her. The sadness – and she felt it too – was neither here nor there; what must be done must be done; it was *His* will. At least the two of them had *seen* it in all its glory.

Mr Craven had given up spreading his word, not because he'd had an epiphany regarding the terrible wrongness of his actions and was now plagued with guilt. If anything his feelings on the matter were quite the opposite; if he could, he would love to infect every single one of them. He had started to hate them for their continued ability to survive. As for his own kind, in his fevered dreams he'd imagined them all suffering like he did as he rose, glorious, above them and returned home. Any joy to be found in the dream was always shattered on waking, when he found himself back in his ever-more-obviously-failing little body.

He had given up spreading his word because he could no longer move among people unnoticed. The sickness had taken hold and now it was beating him quickly. His clothes hung too loosely on his wasted frame, and he'd had to make extra notches in his belt. He had tried to order new clothes – in smaller sizes, so he could try to look halfway respectable – but the tailors of Savile Row had closed their doors on him, muttering distastefully. He'd considered fighting his way through the Christmas shoppers swamping the cheap retail outlets that filled the city, but everywhere he went people squeezed themselves out of his way, backing into over-crowded aisles and scurrying out into the streets to avoid sharing the same air that he breathed. No one recognised him as the 'Angel of Death' – not the one in the newspapers, anyway – but they all saw death's mark upon him, and the disease that was destroying him.

He'd soon given up: new clothes would no longer have disguised the ravages of the bug, though at least he would have been spared the indignity of seeing it each time he dressed. Not that he had much intention of getting undressed again. His five-star hotel had asked him to leave the previous evening, after he'd been racked with a terrible, bloody cough just as the room-service waiter was serving his dinner. He'd seen the terror in the young man's face, and had smiled at him through his stained teeth, despite the agony ripping through his body as his lungs fought for air.

Surprisingly, the waiter hadn't hung around for a tip, and five minutes later the manager had rung Mr Craven. He understood the gentleman was sick and had taken the liberty of calling an ambulance for him. There would be no charge for the room, naturally, but if sir could collect his things together . . . ?

Mr Craven had listened in silence, and then he had walked out past the untouched tray of food. He hadn't been hungry anyway.

But he was surprisingly hungry now, despite the ulcers that had sprung up all over his gums and throat at some point in the night. He'd ended up in a filthy little bed and breakfast up by King's Cross which rented out rooms not only by the hour, but by subdivisions of that. He'd paid extra so they could buy new sheets and get the room deep-cleaned once he'd left. He was so exhausted he hadn't even tried to argue. The springs in the ancient mattress had dug into his emaciated body and he'd managed no more than a few hours of fitful sleep, waking well before dawn. He was no longer running out of time, he'd decided: time had run out. His hour glass was empty. Every watery breath told him that any successful scheme to get home would come too late for him.

He'd cried a bit after that, tears that were bitter and full of rage and self-pity. He should have stayed; he should never have rebelled. He could have quietly risen through the ranks at home instead of letting his ambition and impatience get the better of him.

When daylight broke he left the noisome little room and wandered the freezing streets, pausing to buy hot coffee now and then. He wasn't the only one up so early, and he watched as people hurried about their business, collars turned up against the cold, hats pulled low over frozen ears, some with those ridiculous dust masks on. He kept walking despite his exhaustion. He had this terrible feeling that if he stopped moving he would die, right there on the spot. His breath was icy, but his skin burned with fever and sweat prickled in the gap between his shirt collar and his scrawny neck. He was so used to the thing hanging around his neck that he'd never noticed its weight before; now it felt like a millstone – or an albatross. It was time to give it up. It was time to speak to Cassius Jones.

He had admitted defeat. He found he was crying again.

Chapter Twenty-Seven

Sergeant Armstrong was a professional, so he hadn't been openly rude to Dr Hask, or at all insubordinate to Detective Inspector Ramsey – he was too clever for that – but it didn't take anyone with even half of Tim Hask's copious qualifications to know that the young police officer was seriously pissed off.

After Fletcher had produced the photograph of Cass, DCI Heddings had spoken to Neil Morgan, Cass' old DCI, to find out why the Mr Bright line of inquiry had been shut down. Morgan told him it had come from the top: all questions in that direction were to desist immediately, and if they didn't, then heads would roll, starting with Morgan's own.

Hask had been surprised that Ian Heddings had been so candid with them, but the exchange had clearly piqued his own interest. He might be stuck behind a desk these days, but he was obviously still a detective at heart. The public emphasis was still on finding Cassius Jones and bringing him in, but Heddings had quietly told Ramsey that if they wanted to make some discreet inquiries regarding this elusive Mr Bright, then to go ahead – but they were to be subtle, careful, no careering around like bulls in a china shop, making a mess that he'd have to clear up.

That hadn't gone down at all well with young Armstrong,

and since then he'd concentrated on the Angel of Death case, searching through Draper's history to see if he could find any link to the man he'd been procuring children for. *Allegedly.* Despite the tense atmosphere when they were all in the incident room together, Hask thought it might just work out. Armstrong was a sharp cookie, and if anyone could find the Angel of Death it was as likely to be him as many of the older and more experienced coppers on the case. He was already out chasing up some lead he'd found. It'd been a good move, giving him something to do where he could actively make a difference. It was making the sergeant even more tenacious than usual.

Finally Hask found the small meeting room Ramsey had summoned him to and he let himself in. Ramsey wasn't alone. David Fletcher was standing next to the round table.

'To what do we owe this pleasant surprise?' Hask asked, beaming at the head of the ATD. 'Have you got some more information for us?'

'Finding Cassius Jones has just become part of my remit too,' Fletcher said quietly. 'I'm not going to interfere with what you're doing, but I need to make sure you keep me in the loop.' He looked tired. 'Trust me, I've got quite enough work of my own at the moment; I'm happy to let you run the show. If you need any of my men at any time, just let me know. The only rule is: you don't hold anything back.'

'So why are you so keen to find him?' Ramsey asked. 'Is this to do with Abigail Porter's death?'

'No – the shares fiasco that's apparently taking down some of The Bank's most stable subsidiary companies?'

'Yes, I caught something about it,' Ramsey said, 'but to be honest, I didn't pay it much attention – I don't deal much in stocks and shares myself.'

'Well,' Fletcher said, 'you should have done. A hacker's

caused untold damage – God only knows the true extent of what they've done. I guess only time will tell. But right now the country – if not the whole world – depends on The Bank to maintain whatever minuscule amount of confidence there might be in the idea of economic recovery, so hacking into its systems and causing chaos is considered an act of terrorism.'

'And what's this got to do with our investigation?' Hask asked, beginning to put the pieces together.

'The Bank was hacked approximately twenty-four hours after Cassius Jones was caught on camera standing in the street staring at the building.'

'You think *Cass* hacked The Bank?' Ramsey was incredulous. '*Why?*'

'I have no idea – I was hoping you could tell me. But the proximity of the two events is too much to be coincidence.'

'I agree,' Hask said. 'Jones isn't stupid, and in the main he's not hot-headed, and he certainly wouldn't risk being caught for no reason. Something drew him to The Bank that night. The tape shows him doing nothing but standing and smoking and staring at the place, for fifteen minutes or more, so my guess is that he was there to clear his thinking somehow. He must see The Bank as the root of his problems – a puzzle, maybe.' He looked at Fletcher. 'Let's just presume for a moment that Jones is innocent. Someone has maliciously kidnapped his nephew, and murdered anyone who could lead to the boy, and then set him up for those same murders.'

'But Jones ran,' Fletcher started.

'Tut, tut.' Hask smiled. 'I expect better thinking than that from you. It's a common misconception that only the guilty run from justice and it's just not true. Lots of innocent people run – people who are afraid, people who think they have no chance of being believed – they run just as much as the guilty. And I think I'd have run if I were Jones, guilty or innocent.' Hask was enjoying himself. The police might get a thrill from the actual chase, but his buzz came from digging into people's minds. Getting paid so much for it was just a bonus.

'Okay, so for the moment I'm presuming he's innocent. What next?'

'Cass must think that The Bank – or someone inside it – is at the root of his problems. It's the only thing that makes sense.'

'But why the financial mess? Is he sending a message? Maybe a "fuck you" signal?' Ramsey asked.

'Maybe,' Hask said, 'or maybe the financial stuff is just a smokescreen to hide his real intention. If I know Cass Jones, the only thing he actually wants is information. Right now everyone at The Bank will be so busy trying to stabilise their problems that they won't be looking to see what files were accessed or copied – if such a thing is even traceable. I'm an expert on the human computer' – he tapped the side of his head – 'not the mechanical ones. And there's something positive in all this: if Cass got what he was looking for, then he's going to surface, and for more than just a middle-of-the-night think.

'And the sooner he surfaces, the sooner we can catch him and figure out what the hell is going on.'

'Why would anyone want to take Jones' nephew and then go to such lengths to stop anyone finding him? And why The Bank?' Fletcher didn't look convinced. 'It all sounds too much like a crazy conspiracy theory.'

'Maybe it is,' Hask said. He looked at Ramsey, who gestured at him to continue. 'This Mr Bright—'

'—Mr *Castor* Bright,' Ramsey cut in.

'—the man Cass was told *not* to investigate during the Man of Flies investigation? We think he didn't stop.'

'We need *you*,' Ramsey leaned forward, 'to find out what you can about him for us. On the quiet. If you make too much noise—'

'—*any* noise,' Hask added.

'—you'll find all manner of shit will come down on your head,' Ramsey finished. 'Jones got his sergeant to do a simple employment enquiry for that name at The Bank, and the headshed immediately put the kybosh on it. He's a massive no-go area.'

'If he's traceable, my people will dig him out. No one can stay that well hidden these days, trust me. It's not just a carbon footprint we have now, it's an electronic one too; everyone leaves a trace.' The commander stared at them both. 'You find Cass Jones and I'll find your Mr Bright. Deal?'

'Deal.' Ramsey grinned. Fletcher didn't return the smile. From where Hask was standing the man didn't look as if he had the energy. He couldn't help but wonder what drove anyone to do the job Fletcher did. There couldn't be much glory in it, and he was certain that the pay cheque wouldn't be anywhere near as rewarding as his own. People were strange, he concluded as they said their polite goodbyes. Strange and fascinating.

'Back to the office, sir?'

David Fletcher nodded and rested his head against the leather seat as they left Paddington Green Police Station behind. The driver was one of the very few perks of his job, but Fletcher normally preferred to drive himself. It normally concentrated his thinking; you couldn't drift while you were driving. Over the past few days, however, *all* he'd wanted to do in between one interminable meeting and the next was to drift off into a haze of jumbled thoughts. He was definitely too damned tired for driving.

Until the launch, his main concern – that being something of an understatement – had been SkyCall 1, that the project's true purpose would be detected and bring Armageddon, both political and quite likely otherwise, down upon them all. He found that he rather missed that fear; if it happened now, it would be someone else's problem. As it was, they'd hugely underestimated the sheer volume of information that now needed to be sifted and sorted and examined and made into some kind of sense.

The geeks working under the supervision of the virtually autistic South African liaising from Harwell were trying to process the information into some kind of filing system, but there was so much visual data that it was making it tricky. They'd pulled in more staff from MI6, but still there were nowhere near enough people – and that was without the constant calls from Arnold James demanding updates on the movements of the Chinese and Koreans and just about every other nation on the planet with any kind of nuclear capability. The one thing he had discovered was that constantly spying on others could make you paranoid … Meaning could be read into everything if you tried hard enough, and most meanings could very easily be misinterpreted.

He wondered, not for the first time, if perhaps they'd created a monster. It wouldn't be the satellite that gave away what they were doing; it would be the paranoid behaviour of the nation's politicians. He never thought he'd find himself thinking it but he was fast coming to the conclusion that people – *countries* – should be allowed their secrets. He thought of the old saying, repeated by politicians endlessly to justify their spying, *Knowledge in the wrong hands is dangerous.* It always made him smile. If there was one thing he'd learned through the years, it was that too much knowledge in *any* hands was dangerous.

Maybe the rest of them would catch up when the world was reduced to burned-out remains. Probably not though. The politicians would be holed up in the bunkers that would also serve as their coffins, consoling each other with the thought that they had had *no choice.* It was all bollocks, of course. There was always a choice, even if no human being was ever able to make the right one.

SkyCall 1 was supposed to *create* security, but Fletcher believed it would have the opposite effect: they'd be looking for plots behind every message, and nothing would be seen in context. It would be WikiLeaks a million times over, but this time only one small nation would be getting the information. He sighed and closed his eyes as the car moved slowly through the London traffic, letting his mind drift until it came to rest on Cass Jones and this mysterious Mr Bright. It wasn't a name he'd come across before. He'd put out some discreet feelers when he got back to the office – if nothing else, it would delay his return to the underground level he'd started to think of as hell.

Chapter Twenty-Eight

Toby Armstrong sat in the window of the grotty pub on the corner of Denman Street and nursed a pint he had no intention of drinking. The bitter cold outside had been creeping in through the cracks and gaps in the old building all night and even though the landlord had put the heating on when he opened up an hour ago it hadn't yet dispelled the chill. Armstrong didn't mind; the cold was helping to cool down his bubbling anger. At least he'd got out of the office and away from the fucking *Free the Paddington One! Save Cass Jones!* crusade. He smiled sharply at his own humour, but it was laced with a dark bitterness.

That he liked the DI and the profiler somehow made it all worse. Why couldn't they see that Cass Jones was as guilty as sin? Surely the evidence spoke for itself? It wasn't as if he even blamed Jones for cracking up – the man had been through enough to warrant it and more – but crack he had, and if the others couldn't see it, then he'd just have to prove it to them himself. Jones was a liability and he, Toby Armstrong, was going to bring him in. Jones wasn't good for people – he'd shot a *kid*, for God's sake. Why the fuck did people – *sensible* people, *intelligent* people – still care about him?

He sipped the beer absently as he stared at the doorway to Moneypenny's – Arthur 'Artie' Mullins' girly club and central office. If anyone knew where Jones was, it would be Mullins. They'd watched him for weeks after Jones' disappearance, but there'd been nothing the slightest bit suspicious in his movements and eventually the surveillance had been called off. Too expensive. Armstrong had never believed for a second that Mullins knew nothing; he and Jones had a relationship that went beyond Cass collecting illegal bonuses from him. He'd seen it in Mullins' eyes when he'd interviewed him. Now that Cass had come out into the open and Mullins thought the heat was off, maybe they'd get careless – and if they did, Armstrong intended to be there to catch them out.

Mullins had arrived at the nightclub half an hour previously, and Armstrong figured he'd watch the place until he left, see who came and went, then he'd follow Mullins himself. He intended to be the old man's second until he found Cass Jones.

He felt a slight twinge of guilt about misleading his colleagues on the Angel of Death case – they thought he was going through David Draper's life, chasing down leads, and he intended to keep letting them think that. He was a good detective and he'd find enough on Draper in his spare time to avoid drawing suspicion on himself.

The parallels between his own actions and Cass' during the investigation into the teenage suicides didn't pass him by – but what he was doing was *different*. Cass had been sneaking off to satisfy his own paranoid delusions and murder people; *he* was trying to track down a killer. As it was, there had been no reported sighting of the Angel of Death for a few days now. Perhaps that one had finally had the good grace to lie down and die himself.

Piccadilly Circus was always a hub of activity, but none of the passers-by buzzed at the door to the club. He sipped his beer again. It wasn't that early, and one pint wouldn't kill him; it might even help calm him down. He wondered for about the tenth time since leaving the station whether he should have mentioned to Ramsey that David Draper was paid by a company that appeared to be wholly owned by The Bank. PC Spate was trying to get more information on it now; that was the reason he gave himself for keeping it quiet – nothing to do with not wanting to feed this new obsession.

What did it matter anyway? Just because the Man of Flies had been an employee of The Bank, it didn't mean that the Angel of Death was too – Draper could have been doing his work for the Angel of Death as a hobby, an act of love, perhaps. He'd died of the same strain of bug that the killer was spreading so it wasn't a huge leap to think that perhaps they had been lovers, despite Hask's profile of their killer as a paedophile.

He took a larger gulp. That would sound more plausible if he'd been able to find some hint of what Draper actually *did* for the money he was paid. The company he was allegedly employed by was some sort of offshore holding company. Draper himself appeared to have no university degree, nor any specialist qualifications. In fact, the man was something of a ghost.

Armstrong turned his thoughts away from Draper. He hadn't done *anything* wrong by not telling Ramsey. That case wasn't connected to anything they were interested in. Maybe he'd tell them when he next checked in, let them tie themselves in knots trying to join all the dots while he got on with finding Cass Jones. He gripped the glass harder. When he looked down, he was surprised to see more than half the pint was gone.

*

A thirty-foot drive separated the building from the road, the kind of distance that didn't imply secrecy, but at the same time meant anyone peering between the iron bars of the electronic gates would never be able to see anything going on behind the sparkling windows. Osborne had done a stroll-by, and there were two security cameras attached to the gates and a card-entry system by the discreet brass sign on the gatepost that read Calthorpe House, *Residential Home.*

Their black Range Rover was parked a little way down the leafy suburban road, and Cass had quite a good view of the place. The three-storey red-brick house looked like an old folks' home. The drive went right up to the front door, and although there were some trees and plants near the gates, close to the house it was all gravel. The layout would give those inside a clear view of any comings and goings. The high wall surrounded the other three sides of the property, and if there was any sort of lawn and gardens for the residents to enjoy, they were at the back, hidden away from prying eyes.

It was gone midday, and Cass had been sitting there since dawn. He wanted to crash in and grab his nephew, but this wasn't something he could rush, and anyway, he doubted Osborne and Wharton would let him – that was probably why they'd been sent with him. He liked them both, even if they didn't say much, but he also had a healthy respect for their cold-bloodedness. He was conscious he might have become like them all those years ago, had he really *been* Charlie Sutton – and if he'd been on the other side of the law when he pulled that trigger.

'This is a nice little location,' Osborne said. 'Clever.' He didn't look at Cass but kept his eyes on the building. A woman pushed a pram past the gates, desperately trying to keep the large dog she was also walking under control.

'Bedford Park – that's where anyone walking down here will be headed. Like that bird.' He gestured at the woman as she disappeared out of sight. 'I bet no one gives a shit about what goes on here.'

'Plus, this is Chiswick,' Wharton added from the back seat. 'They're all too posh to ask. As long as it looks pretty, isn't run by the council, and no one makes too much noise they don't care. I bet they just check how much it costs to check in. If they're high enough, then all's good.' He let out a small snort of a laugh. 'Fucking middle-class muppets. Could be a bunch of psychos in there for all they know.'

'Watch what you're saying, mate.' Osborne turned round in his seat and glared at his colleague. 'His boy's in there.'

'Oh, sorry, Jonesy – didn't mean your nephew's a nutter.' Wharton leaned forward and slapped Cass hard on the shoulder.

'Jesus!' The sudden pain was like an electric shock and his knitting muscles screamed.

'For fuck's sake, Wharton,' Osborne said. 'The man was shot.' He laughed and turned back to face the front.

'No problem,' Cass wheezed, trying to catch his breath back. 'It distracted me from my numb arse.'

Wharton joined in Osborne's short burst of laughter. 'You're all right, Cass. I'll give you that.'

'Hang on, here we go again,' Osborne muttered. 'Is this our guy?'

The laughter stopped and they all sat up, alert and completely focused, as the gates swung open. There'd been a flurry of activity at seven that morning when the night and day staff had swapped over, but since then there'd been one car at eight – clearly another staff member, as they swiped an entry card to open the gates – and two more cars had arrived an hour previously. Both drivers had spoken into the intercom, so Cass presumed they were visitors, relatives, perhaps. Unlike those who had come and gone first thing in the morning the arms appearing from the car windows had not been wearing white; those pale sleeves had been virtually the only things visible in the morning darkness.

Wharton was the only one who'd been able to see any of the drivers. Since six a.m. he'd positioned himself in the shadows a little along from Calthorpe House. He was dressed in jogging gear and as he stretched against the wall he was able to grab a glimpse of each of the people going in and out.

'No, not him,' Wharton mumbled, 'wrong car. That's one of those that only just went in. Look – own clothes.'

He was right. The middle-aged couple inside the sleek Mercedes were sitting in silence as they pulled away. Whatever they'd seen inside hadn't cheered them up.

'Our guy drives a Saab,' Wharton said. 'I don't think he's going to be coming out until the end of the day. What do you reckon? Eight-hour shift? Or twelve?'

'They came in when the others left, so my money's on twelve. We'll be sitting here till seven.'

'I can wait,' Cass said. He hoped they had enough time. How long would it be before Mr Bright showed up here? He stared at the building. He'd get Luke out, one way or another – even if they had to get the guns out of the boot and blast their way in. The Network had kept the Jones boy for long enough.

Toby Armstrong was just returning from the bar with his second pint when he froze, his glass forgotten in his hand. A few moments more and he would have missed it completely. He leaned forward so that his nose was almost touching the window, his eyes wide. A man stood on the step of Moneypenny's and glanced around him. Armstrong's mouth dropped open slightly.

That *couldn't* be – it didn't make sense. He slowly put his drink down and focused as his heart thumped fast and his face tingled. Was that really him? The face was thinner, and he looked more diminutive than the sergeant had expected.

The man pulled open the door and went inside. Armstrong stared after him as his head spun. He wasn't sure what he'd been expecting from this stakeout, but a collision of cases wasn't one of them. *The door is open.* The thought struck him suddenly: the man hadn't touched the intercom button, at least as far as Armstrong had seen, which must mean that the door was unlocked. He pulled his mobile phone out of his pocket and rang through to the station. He needed back-up.

The call made, he went out onto the cold street, his hands clenching in his pockets. His breath came out in impatient bursts of steam as two minutes ticked by with no sound of approaching sirens. They'd told him to wait – he *should* wait; that was the professional thing to do. But his gut was screaming out for him to take action. Moneypenny's was a confined space – the man would be easier to detain inside if he made a run for it; out here, he could get lost in the masses of Christmas shoppers. He bit down on his lip. Still no sirens.

'Fuck it,' he muttered, and crossed the road.

'Is that you, mate?' Artie Mullins looked up from his desk when he heard the door above bang closed and footsteps coming down into the basement bar. 'I'm in the office.' He looked at his watch. 'You're early! That makes a fucking nice change. Wasn't expecting you for at least thirty—' His words drained away as the slight figure stepped into the windowless room. Even from six feet away, Artie could smell the sickness emanating from him. His mouth dried. The man was thinner, and his head of hair wasn't as full as it was in the pictures that filled every red-top and a fair few of the broadsheets, but it was definitely him: the Angel of Death.

'You won't mind if I don't shake your hand?' he said. He stayed in his seat and although he kept his eyes on his unwelcome visitor, he mentally went through his options should the man lunge at him. Physically, he had the advantage, but one wrong move that resulted in a drop of saliva or blood in the wrong place and he would be getting measured for his coffin. And that wasn't the way he saw the rest of his life panning out, thank you very much.

'Very droll,' the man said. 'You must be Arthur Mullins.' He smiled. His teeth looked far too large for his receding gums to manage. 'I presume you know who I am?'

'By reputation.' Artie was glad his voice was steady despite the healthy burst of fear he was feeling. 'But I'd prefer a name.'

'You can call me Mr Craven.'

'All right then, Mr Craven.' Artie leaned forward slightly, resting his hands on his knees. It was a relaxed pose, but chosen carefully. Mr Craven had his own hands in his coat pockets, and fuck only knew what he was holding in them. If he came at him, Artie would take him out at the ankles. The man would fall and his hands would go down to protect himself, that was human instinct, and close as this man obviously was to death, the old gangster would bet he wasn't quite ready to give up on what was left of his life. 'So, Mr Craven, what the fuck are you doing in my club? You didn't wander in here by accident, did you?'

Craven smiled again, an uncomfortable mix of bitterness

and superiority: this was a bloke who was used to having people do *exactly* what he told them, and with no questions asked. Artie should have felt some sense of kindred spirit, but his gut told him that he was miles apart from this dying man. This man was *cruel,* he could see that in his yellowing eyes. There was no honour there. Artie Mullins wouldn't have liked this man when he was healthy; he sure as fuck didn't like him now he was dying – and even more dangerous.

'No, Mr Mullins, I did not.' He swayed slightly, then straightened himself, but his eyes didn't waver; they stayed fixed on Artie. 'And you have nothing to fear. The kind of word I wish you to spread for me is entirely lacking in metaphor.' He let out a laugh that sounded almost girlish.

Artie kept the grimace of revulsion off his face. Mr Craven might say he had nothing to fear, but people like him changed their minds fast.

'I wish to speak to Cass Jones,' Mr Craven said.

'What?' The completely unexpected demand knocked him off guard and he sank back in his chair. 'What the hell have you got to do with Cass Jones?'

'You can give him this as a token of my goodwill.' Mr Craven pulled his left hand free of his pocket and took something from around his neck. It was a small silver datastick attached to a delicate chain. He held it up and it sparkled in the light. Then he slowly leaned forward and placed it on the desk. Artie was pleased that Craven was at least a little wary of him too.

'Why would I put you and Jones in touch?' Artie didn't touch the datastick; taking it would amount to a deal being made, and they were far from that. For one thing he wasn't even sure that he and Cass were on speaking terms any more – not after he'd handed him over to Freeman. Still, the worst Cass'd got there was a bit of a kicking, and even he'd put his hands up and say he'd deserved that. Yeah, Artie reasoned in that split second of thought, he could get this man to Cass. But right now, he had no inclination to do so. Craven stank of all manner of bad. 'What makes you think I even know where he is?'

An icy draught crept into the office. He was sure he'd heard the door close upstairs, but the sick man must have left it ajar. Artie didn't mind. The cool air was a welcome break from the sick man's stench.

'We do not have time for these games,' Mr Craven said. 'I certainly don't. I think you know far more than you share, Mr Mullins, and I am fine with that, of course. I have no problem with secrets – that is the very reason I wish to speak to Jones: in order to share some with him.'

'What kind of secrets?'

There was a quiet thud on the stairs and Artie felt the hairs on the back of his neck rise. Craven had closed the door properly, but now someone else had come in, and it couldn't be Mac, because he wouldn't be coming down so cautiously.

'The only ones that really matter,' Mr Craven said, his smile stretching. 'Just tell him I have all the answers, and I wish to share them with him.'

'Why would you do that?'

Mr Craven hadn't moved, nor was he giving any indication that he'd heard anyone coming slowly down the stairs, and for a second or two Artie wondered if he'd imagined the noise. For now he would keep the sick man talking while he figured out exactly how to play this.

'I'm dying,' Mr Craven said, 'and I don't intend to go quietly. What's that old adage? If I'm going down they're all coming with me? It's something like that.' He gasped for breath suddenly, and the unhealthy sound made Artie flinch. 'Cass Jones is angry enough to do what I can't.'

'I really don't know what you're going on about.'

'To be fair,' Mr Craven said, 'you don't need to. Mr Jones will. But here's one thing you will understand.' A shadow fell across the doorway and Artie did his best not to look at it. Whoever was hovering out there couldn't be any worse than his current visitor.

'I know that he has been set up for those murders,' Mr Craven continued, 'and I know by whom, as I am sure he does. What is clear from his current actions, however, is that he has neither proof nor witnesses. If he agrees to meet me, I will give him both.'

'Like I said,' Artie said, raising his voice slightly, 'I don't know where Cass Jones is, and after all the problems with the bonuses, he's no friend of mine.'

'Nobody move.'

Mr Craven's head whipped sideways, and the condescending laugh about to spill from his lips stopped short before it made a sound.

Artie looked up. 'I'm not normally pleased to see you lot,' he said, surprised at how much relief was buzzing through his veins. He might well have got in touch with Jones; it would have been up to Cass whether he wanted to meet the bloke or not. But he *really* didn't want to be breathing the same air as the bug-infected man any longer. 'I'll make an exception today.'

The young man took a small step forward and Artie saw the gun in his hand. So did Craven. The danger wasn't over yet; this could still play out a million ways. He stayed in his seat. Something would kick off, and if he didn't get an opportunity to leg it up the stairs and out on the street first, he'd decide on his own course of action then. There were times when just getting the fuck out of somewhere was the best solution.

'What's going on here?' The policeman – Artie couldn't remember his name, but he'd seen him often enough since Cass did his runner – spoke calmly, but he was obviously nervous, judging by the way his Adam's apple was bobbing up and down.

'Just a little private business,' Mr Craven said. 'Why don't you run along and leave us to it?'

'He's looking for Cass Jones,' Artie said.

'So I heard.'

Artie felt another small wave of relief. If the copper had heard that, then he'd have heard Artie saying he didn't know where Cass was – and why would he lie to a man carrying the modern plague and who'd proved he wasn't shy about sharing it?

'I am telling you to leave.' Mr Craven hadn't even looked in Artie's direction since the copper had arrived, and his initial surprise had been replaced by something much more malign. 'It will be better for everyone if you do.' His voice was icy. 'Especially you.'

'I'm arresting you on the charge of multiple murder.' The policeman might have been holding the gun, but he was getting more nervous with every second. Artie didn't blame him: it was very obvious Mr Craven was a dangerous man – and verging on the insane, if he wasn't mistaken.

'Well, you do have the gun,' Mr Craven said idly, 'so I suppose it's game over. I've had a good run at things, though, wouldn't you say?'

Too many things happened in an instant. The first was Mr Craven's tone of voice, simply lulling the policeman into thinking he'd won. The second, the door upstairs thumping loudly against the wall as it was flung open and heavy feet tromping down the stairs towards them.

'*Armstrong? Armstrong, are you down there?*'

Armstrong. Sergeant Toby Armstrong: that was his name. Cold air washed into the small room, and a smile crossed the copper's face. He'd thought he'd won. Artie's heart was racing and his mouth started to open, to warn the youngster not to let his guard down, the fat lady wasn't singing yet, but Mr Craven let out a yowl and suddenly the world was filled with light—

Artie raised an arm to protect his eyes from the brightness and for a moment Toby Armstrong was just a black outline, frozen in the doorway, and then he vanished, swallowed up in glimpses of claws and searing white sharpness, and the awful, loud beating of wings. Artie closed his eyes against the blinding light and pressed his hands into his ears. Were they bleeding? He was sure they were bleeding. His eyes and his ears were going to burst. A scream built in his chest—

—and then it all stopped. The light was gone so suddenly that Artie thought they had been plummeted into darkness. The pain in his eyes dulled to a throbbing ache. His ears hummed, but slowly, somewhere above that sound, he could make out voices. They were shouting. Someone touched his arm and he jumped and pulled away.

At last he managed to blink away the dark stars that danced at the edge of his vision and found that the office was filled with police. He frowned. What was going on? What had just happened—?

'Nobody touch him! Get an ambulance crew down here, double quick! Make sure they've got all the gear!'

From between two officers' legs, he could see a pair of expensive leather shoes. Mr Craven's, he assumed. Artie got to his feet, shaking off the man beside him.

'I haven't done anything wrong,' he muttered, taking a shaky step forward, trying to see what was going on.

Mr Craven was sitting on the floor, leaning against the wall. His head lolled to one side, and Artie couldn't figure out if he was trying to laugh or cry, or perhaps both. What was clear was that Craven was a whole load closer to being dead than he had been when he arrived. It couldn't be possible, but he'd lost weight in the last few seconds, and his skin, pale before, was now a sickly yellow. He coughed, and the small gathering flinched away as one.

'Nobody touch me either,' a voice said. The tone was all wrong: it was flat, lifeless. Artie turned to see Armstrong pressing himself against the wall next to the desk. The young man was trembling as he tugged down his collar. Crimson bloomed on his neck. 'I think he bit me.'

No one said anything after that.

It was only hours later, when they finally let him leave the station and he was back in the club sipping a very large brandy and letting the buzz of life from the girls and the punters around him calm his nerves, did he think about the datastick. He went down to the office and looked at it, lying exactly where Mr Craven had left it. He picked it up. It was heavier than he expected. What was it made of, pure silver?

He turned it over in his hands, and then slipped it into his pocket. He hadn't mentioned it to the police – it wasn't their business – and why would he want to muddy the water with extra information when his account of the events of that afternoon had been corroborated by that poor bastard Armstrong, before they whisked him off to hospital brimming over with platitudes that no fucker actually believed.

Aside from that, he thought as he sank heavily into his office chair, his own curiosity had been piqued. What kind

of secrets could Mr Craven have for Cass Jones? He remembered the conversation he'd had with Cass in this very room,
after Christian had died. They'd talked about The Bank;
more that than, Cass had asked him about Mr Bright, the
man who was everywhere and nowhere. A name all the
firms were a little afraid of.

He sighed and lit a cigarette, then leaned back and flicked
the switch for the powerful air-conditioner to kick in and
kill the smell. Compared to the other laws he broke on a
regular basis, smoking in a venue open to the public was
the least of them, but he knew only too well they'd get you
on the little things if they couldn't get you on the big ones.

Maybe he'd said too much to Cass about Bright – maybe
it was his fault Cass had got himself into all this mess in the
first place. But Cass never had been very good at knowing
when to turn and look the other way, had he? Artie rubbed
his face. It had been a fucking long day. He'd leave Mac to
sort the club for the night and go home and get a good
night's rest, if only he could switch off his brain. Every time
he closed his eyes he saw Armstrong's wide eyes and dead
expression as he pulled down his collar.

Fucking kids, he thought. What did the sergeant think he
was doing, coming down here to arrest a serial killer on his
own when he knew back-up was on the way? Young men:
they all thought they were immortal. His heart ached a little
bit, and he wasn't sure if it was for the policeman who'd just
become the latest of the Angel of Death's victims, or for
himself, or for the fact that however much they all chose to
ignore it, the truth was that all their days were numbered.
Maybe that was why he was drinking his brandy so fast. He
was going fucking soft, that was for sure. Old fucking age
was kicking in.

He pulled the datastick out of his pocket and stared at it

again. *Secrets,* that's what Craven had said: *the only ones that really matter.* He drained his brandy and got to his feet. He'd let things die down and then get the stick to Cass. Stubbing the cigarette out half-smoked, he told himself that it was simply to satisfy his own curiosity, but he knew that was only half the truth.

Artie Mullins had an old dog's instincts and he'd learned to trust them. He might not have Brian Freeman's clout, but he was happy with his place in the order of things and he'd stayed where he was for so long by trusting his gut. It was telling him now that Cass Jones was at the heart of this game, whatever it was. *Everyone* was interested in the DI: the nick, that strange woman and old man who had come and warned him about Cass' imminent arrest, Mr Craven, everyone – he must have the luck of the devil, to still be free of them all.

And Artie now knew his own place in the game. He was the link, and Craven's arrival this afternoon made it pretty plain that everyone else with an eye on events knew that too. Maybe it was time he took himself on a bit of a holiday.

He'd give things a day or two to settle down, then he'd get the datastick to Cass. Between now and then, he decided as he flicked off the light switch and happily turned his back on the room that still stank of Craven, he'd spend some time booking a nice long break for him and the missus. Somewhere warm. And somewhere a long fucking way away.

Chapter Twenty-Nine

W harton had been right: the Saab didn't leave Calthorpe House until ten past seven, moving off in the
sudden flurry of activity that accompanied shift changes.
They'd followed at a safe distance until the man reached his
home, a few miles west in Isleworth, and then Cass stood
back and let the Steves do what they did best – and they
were good, he'd give them that.

By the time Cass had parked the Range Rover further up
the road from the nondescript semi-detached house and
walked back they'd got inside the man's house and had him
sitting quietly on a chair, with only one small bruise coming
up on his cheek. He looked terrified.

'You're right,' Osborne said, looking from the man in the
chair to Cass. 'He's not a bad match at all.'

'Told you,' Wharton said with a nod, 'it's good enough.
Jones might have to trim a bit off his poncey barnet, but it's
still close. Right, I'm going to find the kitchen and make a
cup of tea. I'm gasping.'

'And call Jimmy. We're going to need him here later to
keep an eye on our host.' Osborne looked over at Cass. 'So?
What do you reckon?'

Cass came in to take a closer look. Wharton had chosen
well: the man was about his age and much the same height,
build and colouring. If he kept his head down, then he

might just get away with it. 'I think it's doable.' He looked at the man, trembling in the chair. 'What's your name?'

'Martin Cromer. Dr Martin Cromer. What—?' He licked his lips and steadied his nerves before asking, 'What do you want from me?'

'Don't look so afraid,' Cass said. 'We just want the next few hours of your life.' He smiled. 'And some information.' He lit a cigarette, waited for Wharton to return with the drinks, and then started asking the questions.

At half-past four in the morning, when Dr Cromer had told them that most of the nurses and staff would be relaxing in the staffroom before doing the final drug rounds at six, Cass stopped the Saab outside Calthorpe House. He slid Cromer's card into the slot and the tiny light changed from red to green and buzzed before the gates slowly swung open. He drove round to the side of the house and pulled into the third bay on the left. That was the space Cromer claimed he always used. Cass didn't doubt him. He didn't think the doctor had it in him to lie; he'd been far too scared. Once he'd started talking he'd almost given them too much information.

Cass doubted Cromer was part of any sort of conspiracy; he was just an ordinary man, and if he wasn't so focused on Luke, Cass might even have felt a bit sorry for him. But no harm was going to come to him – just one night of being scared senseless, and all men could live through that.

The weather had turned bitter during the night, frost was thick on the windscreens of the cars around him. His nose started to run, and he wiped it on the doctor's coat sleeve as he headed towards the main entrance. There were security cameras on both the side and the front of the building, and Cass kept his stride short, mimicking

Cromer's own walk as demonstrated to them earlier that evening. At the door he placed his ID card in the slot, and then when through the main door, he paused at the second scanner and made sure the logo on the breast pocket of his white coat was right in front of the light. *Dr Cromer: 04.38* read in the small screen above. That was why all the staff arrived already in uniform: the secondary security measure had been installed quite recently, according to Dr Cromer, and Cass knew exactly who'd come up with that unusual idea, probably at about the time Mr Bright'd stopped paying school fees for Luke and started paying medical expenses here instead.

Cass' heart thumped. This was it. He turned and headed to the right, forcing himself to keep his pace steady. Behind the reception desk a woman glanced up for a moment before returning to her magazine. Cass said a silent prayer to the joys of modern technology. He'd passed both electronic checks, so what did she care? It might not be so easy on the way out, but he'd cross that bridge when he came to it. Away from the main entrance, the corridors were less homely, the carpet gave way to lino and the air became tinged with the faint smell of Dettol. His feet broke the silence with every step.

I want to know where the boy is kept.
The boy?
Yes. He's eight . . . no, nine. He's nine now.
I don't know any boy. The patients are mainly young adults, up to early twenties.
Not this one. He's been there about two years. Think.
Widening eyes: the penny drops. You mean the boy on the lower level? The coma boy . . .
Coma?

Well, he's in and out of some kind of trance-like state. They say it's psychosomatic. I don't treat him.

But you could get into his room?

Of course. I'm a doctor.

Does he get visitors?

I don't know – maybe occasionally. No family. I think his grandfather brought him in.

Grandfather. Cass had almost laughed at that. No, he'd wanted to say, his grandfather is the dead man who gave him away; this man? He's something else. A nurse appeared around the corner ahead and Cass' heart nearly stopped, but the woman barely nodded at Cass as they passed. Luck was on his side, thus far at least. In his head, Cromer's nervous voice talked him through the directions: *follow the corridor round. There's a small staircase that comes off at the middle once you're round the corner. It only goes down. Take it.*

Cass did.

The air cooled as he headed below ground level and although the stairwell and corridor that followed were well lit, there was a sense of abandonment about the place. His footsteps sounded louder and the homely atmosphere of the entrance that had faded further in had now disappeared completely in this small area. There were only three doors, and if Cromer was to be believed, then Luke was behind the furthest: the one by the wall. Cass' mouth dried and his heart thumped. This wasn't fear of getting caught; everyone else in the building was forgotten. This was the sheer antici-pation of reaching his goal. He felt a pang of grief for the small dead boy whom he had loved as a nephew, and mixed with this was guilt from being glad that the boy that Chris-tian and Jessica had raised as their own had died instead of the boy he was about to meet. His *real* nephew.

Hairs prickled on the back of his neck as he approached the door and he glanced backwards, fully expecting to see Christian's ghost standing there, but the corridor was empty and he found he was disappointed. This was Christian's moment: the fulfilment of his wishes from beyond the grave. For once the two brothers could have stood side by side and made up for all the time they'd missed out on. After all the betrayals, Cass was finally putting something right. He hadn't realised how much he'd hoped that Christian would somehow *know* that.

The door was metal, like a prison door, but painted white, and there was a sliding window in the middle. Cass slid his card into the expectant slot and it beeped and the door clicked and whirred. His hands suddenly clammy, Cass gripped the handle and turned. The door opened.

He'd expected the boy to be asleep, but instead he was sitting slightly up in the bed. He stared at Cass with wide blue eyes – *just like Christian's* – and his mouth dropped open slightly.

'I wasn't making any noise,' he whispered.

For a second, Cass was confused, and then he remembered the white coat he was wearing, with the Calthorpe House logo emblazoned on the pocket. He closed the door quietly behind him. His skin tingled with nerves. He didn't know how efficient the staff here were, but the system would show that he had just come into the boy's room, and they might send a nurse down to find out why. He needed to move fast – preferably without panicking the child. Wharton and Osborne had suggested chloroform, in their brutally practical way, and Cass had refused. Now he wondered if he might have been a bit hasty. Still, the thin boy in the bed didn't look too healthy, and even if he'd brought some of the drug with him, he probably wouldn't have used it.

'It's okay, you're not in trouble.' He smiled and sat on the edge of the bed. The boy had Christian's eyes and features, but his hair was dark like Cass', and his heart ached just looking at him. He looked so thin in his pyjamas, and his skin was so pale that blue veins were visible here and there on his neck. Had he even seen the sun in the time he'd been at Calthorpe House? This room, hidden below ground, didn't have a single window. He gritted his teeth as he fought a rising wave of hate for Mr Bright. The bastard was going to pay for this if it took him the rest of his life to track him down.

The boy was still staring politely at him, stroking the blankets that lay crumpled around his crossed legs.

'What's your name?' Cass asked.

'Luke,' the boy answered.

The word stabbed at his heart. So Bright had given him the same name that Christian had chosen – why? His own private little joke?

'So, Luke,' he said, keeping his tone light, 'do you like it here?'

Luke didn't answer, but kept staring at Cass with his wide, sombre eyes. He was afraid. Cass didn't blame him.

'Can I tell you a secret?' Cass asked.

Luke nodded.

'I'm not really a doctor.'

The child's eyes widened slightly.

'I borrowed this coat from a real doctor because I wanted to find you.' Fuck it, he thought. Sometimes, honesty was the only policy. He had a feeling kids were pretty good at sniffing liars out. Maybe that's why he and Kate had always avoided having any. 'I'm your uncle and I've been looking for you for a long time.' Still Luke didn't speak. 'The thing is,' Cass continued, 'I was wondering if maybe you'd like to leave? It's nearly Christmas. We could spend it together. Get some toys. Roast a turkey. All that stuff.' He wished he'd planned this speech out better. 'But the thing is, we have to go now if we're going to go. People will come looking soon.'

'I'm not really sick,' Luke suddenly blurted out. 'They made me take tests. They made me think I was sick, but I don't think I am.'

'Who?'

'The people,' he said, 'and my guardian. And they keep making me sleep. I'm not tired but they keep making me sleep.'

Behind his smile, Cass' blood was boiling.

'Do you want to leave?' he asked again, gently.

The boy nodded.

'Then come on.' Cass grinned and Luke grinned back: Christian's smile, open and honest, and Cass' heart broke for his little brother all over again.

'I don't have any clothes,' Luke whispered.

'Pyjamas will do for now. Just put your slippers on.'

Luke did as he was told, and watching him wheeze and wobble as got to his feet, Cass wondered what the hell they'd been doing to him. Or maybe he *was* sick? If he was, Cass would get him the best doctors – they'd go to Switzerland or somewhere. He took the dressing gown from the end of the bed.

'Put that on too. It's cold outside.' He opened the door and peered out. The corridor was empty.

'Ready?'

Luke nodded. His eyes were sparkling. Cass reached back and took his hand. It was small and warm and it hung on tightly. Cass squeezed back. *I got him for you, Christian*, he thought as he led the boy back to the stairs. *Can you forgive me now, little brother?* There was no answer; no shoes splashed with blood were waiting in the corridor. The gun tucked into the back of his trousers felt cold against his sweating skin. They weren't out yet, but they would be, even if he had to shoot everyone who stood in their way.

Behind him Luke was panting slightly even though they'd only been moving for a few moments. Cass wasn't surprised; even if he wasn't ill, the boy had been confined to one small room for more than a year, and he doubted he'd had much in the way of exercise.

He gripped the small palm tighter.

'You okay?' he whispered.

Luke was leaning against the wall with his eyes shut. Beads of sweat gathered along his hairline and his face had paled. After a second, he nodded.

'We're going to go out through the kitchen, okay?' Cass said. 'But we have to go near the reception area. If I tell you to run, do you think you'll be able to?'

Luke nodded again. His eyes were determined, even if his body was telling a different story.

They moved forward, as quickly and as quietly as they could. Cass fought the urge to hunch over and run: if they bumped into an orderly, he wanted to be looking as much like a doctor who was meant to be there as possible – if only to take the other person off guard for a vital moment or two. His heart sped up as they neared the large carpeted central reception area, the building's main thoroughfare.

There was a large staircase behind the desk, leading up to the second and third floors, and about ten feet from the end of the corridor was another, leading down to the laundry rooms – and if Cromer's directions were to be trusted, it also led to the old servants' staircase that would bring them

241

back up to the ground floor and the kitchen at the other end of it without having to walk past the receptionist or the staff room. If all went according to plan, they shouldn't meet anyone: the kitchen staff weren't due in for at least an hour, and the back door would be locked only with the swipe card system. From there they could go round and through the side-gate that opened from the garden into the car park.

The only unknown, and he couldn't blame Cromer for this, was whether his swipe card would work on the kitchen entrance. Cromer had never used it – it was for the kitchen and cleaning staff, and they had different-coloured cards to the medical and office admin personnel. If it didn't work, Cass had already decided that he'd break out; with any luck they'd be in the car and through the gates before anyone realised what was going on. Hopefully.

He peered across at the reception desk. The middle-aged woman behind it had her head down over some paperwork. The ten feet or so to the stairs beside her looked like miles; she'd only have to catch a glimpse of something in the corner of her eye and they'd be rumbled. And Luke's heavy breathing was bound to draw attention to them.

Cass took a deep breath. They had no choice. He took a step forward, but Luke pulled him back.

'Wait,' he whispered. He was staring intently at the receptionist, sweat shining on his face. The woman had picked up her bag from beneath the desk and now she stood up and smoothed her skirt down before disappearing along the other corridor. Where was she going? The toilet? Right now? Cass could barely believe their luck. This time when he tugged at Luke's hand, there was no resistance. He moved quickly to the door and waved his coat badge in front of the sensor and without waiting for it to register his name and the time he yanked the door open. Outside, he slid his card into the slot again, to verify that it actually was Dr Cromer leaving the building and not just someone in his coat, then he swept Luke up into his arms and jogged round to the car. He no longer cared about keeping up the pretence; he just wanted to get Luke away.

The boy was light – even lighter than Cass had expected – and he could feel his bones even through the dressing gown and pyjamas. He hugged him tight against the cold air and then slid him into the passenger seat of the Saab.

Five minutes later and the gates were closing behind them. Further up the street, the Range Rover headlights came on. Cass waved as he passed the two Steves, who pulled onto the road and followed him back to Cromer's house, where Jimmy – another thickset and fearsome gentleman – was looking after the doctor. He turned the heating up full in the car and looked over at the small boy dozing beside him. He looked exhausted. Cass smiled, and for once there was some proper joy in the expression, as well as a healthy amount of satisfied revenge. *Fuck you, Mr Castor Bright*, he thought. *Fuck you.*

He didn't go back inside Cromer's house, but carefully transferred the sleeping boy from the Saab to the Range Rover while Osborne returned the medical coat and card and gave Jimmy instructions to stay with the doctor until six forty-five, or his phone started ringing with news of the missing boy, whichever came later. That would give them plenty of time.

Wharton and Osborne were in the front. Cass got in the back with Luke and draped his coat over the boy.

'So, where to next, guv'nor?' Osborne asked quietly.

'Head to the M25,' Cass answered. Their reunion needed

to be brief, just for a little while, until he was certain Mr Bright wouldn't come after them, and that meant going back and working with Freeman and the crazy professor to find something he could use as leverage. And if they found that they couldn't bring Mr Bright down, then he was damned well going to make sure that at least he and Luke had their freedom, to make their own choices. Until then, he needed to keep Luke somewhere safe. Somewhere he hoped no one would think of looking.

'Kent,' he said. 'We're going to Kent.'

Chapter Thirty

It had been a long night, even by Mr Bright's standards, but it was starting to look as if they might at last have everything under control. He poured himself a fresh coffee and added thick cream and a teaspoon of sugar. It was that kind of morning. Later he'd want pastries, and perhaps a full breakfast, but for now the blend of bitter and sweet hot liquid would do.

He felt mildly satisfied, even though many in the building around him felt as if they were still on the brink of catastrophe. Someone out there had made a killing on selling back the stock, and at some point in the future he had every intention of finding out who that was, but for now he was just pleased that he had managed to stabilise the situation. The virus in the X accounts was still running, making the numbers move too rapidly to follow, but that would stop, and when it did, he'd make sure that the money he'd used to buy back the stock came from his account.

Ultimately, very little harm had been done, just a little confidence shaken, and confidence could always be recovered. All that was required was for The Bank to make some big announcements in the next week or two – large investments of some kind in something useful to the national and global good, and they'd be back to being the saviours of the world again. Give the population a big exhibition of smoke and mirrors, and they would feel perfectly safe again, and completely forget that one precarious moment when they caught a glimpse behind the curtain and realised that everything was dependent on The Bank's stability; there was nothing else left.

He sipped his coffee and his mind drifted to Mr DeVore. The world might very well find that a few stocks and shares crashing was the least of their worries. The clock ticked closer to seven a.m. and outside midnight blue stained the blackness of space. He thought of Mr Rasnic and Mr Bellew and the others who had left parts of themselves out there screaming in the Chaos. Would *he* even pause at that sound on his way here? Somehow, Mr Bright doubted it.

The phone started to ring and he turned away from the window. That day hadn't come yet; he had this one to get through first. He picked up the phone.

The words at the other end came in such a garbled rush that at first he couldn't make any sense of them.

'Say that again – but slowly,' he said when the caller at last paused for breath. Mr Bright listened carefully, then put the phone down without saying a word. His brain whirred and his skin tingled. The boy was gone. Cassius Jones had taken the boy. And now, suddenly, the purpose behind the hacking was glaringly obvious: Jones had been looking for his nephew, and the policeman – the *detective* – had found him, somewhere in Castor Bright's own records.

In the midst of his irritation he felt a small rush of pride. Cassius Jones had what his father and brother had lacked: he had cold steel in his core. He was driven by rage rather than love and he was too proud to bow to anyone, and that made Mr Bright smile. Luke had been given up by Alan Jones, but it was his eldest son who carried the traits of their bloodline strongest in that special family.

So, Cass had the boy. That confused and disturbed him. There was a secret game being played here, and every day more pieces came to light, and with each one he was forced closer to admitting that there might be substance in his doubts. He had expected the boy to be safe at Calthorpe House – he certainly hadn't expected him to leave. He gritted his teeth. This would not be a good time for Mr Dublin to start asking exactly what he'd been doing with the child. He'd – *they'd* – planned a big reveal. Someone had changed that plan without telling him. And if it wasn't him – and it wasn't – there was only one other person it could be.

The phone cut through his thinking.

'What?' he snapped into the receiver.

'Mr Bright.' As soon as he heard the soft voice at the other end he regretted answering it with such obvious irritation.

'Mr Dublin,' he said. 'What can I do for you?'

'We'd like you to come to Senate House. I need your help clarifying a few points on the subject of the recent unfortunate events at The Bank.'

'Why don't you just ask me over the phone? I'm sure I have all the information here, and as you can appreciate, it's been quite a long night.' What was Mr Dublin's game? Was this the move? Was he going to try and take the Inner Council? Mr Bright had no intention of walking into a den of snarling dogs.

'I'm afraid we need you here. Some things are best discussed face to face, don't you think?' Mr Dublin's voice remained cool, and Mr Bright could almost see him, dressed as ever in a linen suit, despite the cold, as if he carried the heat from home inside him.

'I don't think—' Mr Bright began, and then a light above the lift caught his eye, flashing red. Someone was coming

247

up. Someone *unauthorised*. His words of refusal died in his throat.

'Of course,' he said pleasantly. 'Let's get this misunderstanding cleared up, shall we? And then we can all get back to doing what we do best.'

The phone clicked off at the other end without a farewell. Mr Bright almost smiled as he took his long woollen overcoat from the stand and carefully put it on. It would appear that Mr Dublin had won this round – but one round was far from the match.

When the doors slid open he stepped immediately inside. Mr Escobar looked surprised, but what had he been expecting? Mr Bright running? Mr Escobar was a good warrior, but he wasn't a thinker; he was a pale imitation of the lost Mr Bellew.

'Shall we go?' Mr Bright asked pleasantly, and started the lift on its way back down. He smiled at the other beside Mr Escobar. He didn't know his name, but from his clearly nervous look, Mr Bright presumed he was from the Second Cohort rather than the First; all of this was rather out of his league. Mr Bright smiled at him and his mouth twitched in an awkward smile and his face flushed slightly. That's what Mr Dublin and his new council had forgotten: he was still the Architect. He still commanded reverence from the lower cohorts – even those like this one, who had been sent to help bring him down.

No, he decided, as he walked confidently between his two guards towards the waiting car in the basement of the building, the game wasn't over yet.

They'd stopped first at a twenty-four-hour supermarket and picked up some clothes for Luke, who'd changed quietly in the back seat of the Range Rover before immediately falling asleep again. They stopped a second time, as the morning slowly broke, at a motorway service station. Cass woke Luke and watched as he devoured a huge fried breakfast and several slices of toast. He didn't say much, and his eyes lingered wide on Osborne and Wharton every now and then, but he seemed happy enough. Cass was relieved to see him eat so much. If he was sick then it wasn't affecting his appetite.

After rather half-heartedly managing a piece of toast himself, Cass left the boy with Wharton and went outside with Osborne for a cigarette. There was only one entrance to the small café and they stood in front of it, where there was also a clear view of the car park. They could see Luke and Wharton sitting on the other side of the glass behind them.

They smoked in silence for a while, punctuating it only with the occasional sniff brought on by the freezing cold.

'He seems to be taking it in his stride all right, doesn't he?' Osborne said eventually.

'Yeah.' Cass looked over. 'I guess it hasn't settled in yet.'

'Suppose you're right.' Osborne looked past Cass and through the window to where the boy was drinking a large glass of milk. 'I just thought he'd have more questions, that's all.'

His face was thoughtful and Cass felt suddenly defensive. 'He's just tired. It was only a couple of hours ago that I dragged him out of bed. I'm sure he'll make up for it soon.'

They smoked some more, quiet once again, but Cass watched as Osborne's hooded eyes kept glancing at Luke.

'He must have really hated it in there, that's all I'm saying.' Osborne ignored the provided outdoor ashtray and threw his butt on the ground. 'Most kids would be shit-scared at a stranger turning up and taking them away from somewhere they've been for ages.'

'I'm not a stranger. I'm his uncle.'

'He don't *know* that though.' He met Cass' gaze. 'I'm not saying anything really. It's just odd, that's all.'

On the way back to the car, Cass put one arm round his small nephew. 'You know, if there's anything you want to ask me, just go ahead. I know all this might seem a bit scary right now, especially those two' – and he nodded at the two heavies who were walking slightly ahead – 'but they're here to look after you. Think of them as your guard dogs.'

Luke smiled, but he didn't look up.

'It'll all settle down soon, I promise. And then I'll be able to tell you about your real family, and you can tell me all about the people who have looked after you up until now.' Cass looked down at the dark head, feeling slightly disappointed at the lack of reaction. Luke seemed distracted, and he wished the boy would share whatever he was thinking so Cass could reassure him. He guessed that would come in time. Luke would have a few quiet days coming up where he could get his head round this. He'd be safe and well looked after.

Back in the car, Luke fell asleep again and Cass idly stroked his head, lying in Cass' lap. What would Christian make of this quiet boy of his? What had Mr Bright done to him to make him so meek?

Father Michael was up and waiting for them, and once they were inside the warmth of his home, Cass was surprised to see how moved he was by Luke.

'This is Christian's boy?' He smiled. 'Doesn't he look like him?' He looked up at Cass. 'He looks like both of you.'

Cass shrugged, never comfortable with conversation that veered towards emotional territory. 'Are you sure you're okay with this?' he asked. 'I should only be a few days.' It sounded like the truth because he hoped it would be.

'Of course.' Father Michael smiled and finally released Luke from the close hug. He looked down at the boy. 'Now why don't you and one of your friends go into the kitchen; you might find some hot chocolate and marshmallows in there.'

Cass envied Father Michael's light touch with the boy compared to his own awkwardness. He would improve over time – if they had the time, of course. That was yet to be decided.

'Come on, mate.' Osborne led Luke further into the warm cottage and it was only when they'd disappeared that the remaining three men let their smiles fall.

'I didn't have anywhere else to take him,' Cass said.

'If you had taken him anywhere else I wouldn't have forgiven you,' Father Michael said. 'And I'll look after him for as long as you need, you know that. It will be a pleasure.' His face darkened. 'But are you sure you wouldn't be better off just taking him and getting out of the country?'

'Go somewhere no one will ever find me?' Cass smiled gently. 'And where is that? There isn't anywhere that Bright can't get to me if he tries hard enough. I need to find some kind of end to this thing.'

'He won't give in easily.'

'And neither will I.' Cass hesitated. He had no idea what was coming next; he was hoping that Brian Freeman and Dr Cornell would have found something they could use against Mr Bright, but the tricky part was going to be staying alive and staying free. Bright had played with Cass up until now, but taking Luke might push him to try and dispose of Cass altogether, by killing him or by getting him nicked – either way would mean the end of Cass' life.

'Look,' he continued, 'if I don't make it back for whatever reason—'

'Don't talk like that,' Father Michael cut in.

'No, but—'

'Luke can stay here for as long as he needs to. I'll look after him for you. You can trust that.' He smiled softly, sagging cracks lining his face. 'I'll protect him with my life.' He must have seen Cass' eyes lingering on his wrinkles. 'I may be old on the outside, Cassius Jones, but I'm still fiery on the inside. I'll look after your boy. I'll look after him for Alan's sake as well as your own.'

Cass flinched at the mention of his father.

'Don't think too harshly of him, Cass,' Father Michael said. 'He was doing what he had to, to protect you and Christian. It was all he *could* do.'

Without commenting, Cass gently slapped the priest on the arm and smiled. 'I'd better be going. Osborne and Wharton will stay with you. They won't get in your way.'

'The more the merrier. It'll be nice to have company.'

At the door, the priest pulled Cass into a sudden embrace. Caught unawares, Cass found himself hugging Father Michael back. He was thin underneath his sweater, but then Cass wondered how changed the priest found him. He wasn't blind to the changes that the past year had wrought on his own physical appearance.

'You will come back, Cass,' Father Michael said. 'Of all the possibilities in this strange situation, that is the one I have the most faith in.'

For a moment Cass wished he had just taken Luke and fled the country. This frail old man didn't deserve to suddenly be in so much danger.

'It's okay, Cass.' Father Michael smiled. 'This is okay. Now go and do what you need to do. And take care.'

Cass nodded. He didn't believe in the priest's god, the same god his father had found, and he never would do, but he envied the peace it appeared to have brought them. There was a quiet acceptance about Father Michael, even with all this sudden activity in his house. He didn't have Cass' rage. Still, Cass thought, as the door closed behind him and he was once again alone, it was his rage that kept him going.

The Range Rover was still warm and the village was quiet, lights just beginning to flicker on as he passed. He envied the small lives within. People oblivious to The Bank and the Glow and Mr Bright. This was where his parents had sought refuge from all of that, although clearly they had never quite been able to let it go.

The boys see the Glow! His mother's handwriting was etched behind his eyes and he slowed the car as he passed his parents' locked-up house. The dark windows stared back sullenly, giving nothing away, and there was no sign of the police who had ransacked the building in the first days after he was shot. As he drove away, he didn't glance back. Whatever emotional attachment he had to the place had started dying when he'd learned about his father's deal with Mr Bright, and knowing that Armstrong and his colleagues had trampled through, turning over every inch of the place, had pretty well finished it off.

His childhood home had been built on lies and his father's faith was simply an escape, a crutch to help him cope with the choices he'd made. All that time Cass had felt guilty for not being good enough, and as it turned out, he was just doing what came naturally: like father, like first-born son. At least he didn't run from his choices.

He left the sleepy village behind and headed back to the city. There'd been enough running. Now it was time for action. His eyes burned and heat flooded his body, energising him.

There is a Glow, he thought, bastardising the phrase that

had been his mantra for so long, *and I intend to use it.* He left the radio off and enjoyed the silence as he drove.

Mr Dublin was waiting in a large conference room in the medical wing at the top of Senate House. It was through a door and up a small flight of stairs from the lift. Mr Bright was mildly surprised. He hadn't even been aware that the room existed. Mr Dublin had clearly been exploring rather than overseeing. It was quiet, away from the screams of the homeless unfortunates being put through the Experiment. But then, if the gathering in the room was anything to go by, Mr Dublin had been keeping himself very busy indeed. As well as the newly promoted Mr Escobar there were at least fifteen members of the First Cohort lining the walls of the room.

Mr Bright paused in the doorway and smiled slightly as he took in the faces. On either side of Mr Dublin, standing at the head of the table in the centre of the room, were Mr Dakin and Mr Ede. Mr Dakin was almost salivating, although given his bulk that could just have been his natural greed, and Mr Ede's sharp eyes flicked nervously from Mr Dublin to Mr Bright and back again. So: it was these two whom Mr Dublin intended to add to his Inner Cohort along with Mr Escobar. As choices went, they weren't bad. They'd managed their sections well enough. However, this coup was not the way to form a new Inner Cohort. He understood only too well that Mr Dublin had clearly wanted to make this a democratic decision. That was apparent in the sheer volume of their kind here to witness his downfall. He felt almost sorry: Mr Dublin would be destroyed by his own honesty.

If Mr Bright had been in his opponent's shoes he would have dispatched himself somehow, and then claimed to the others that the Dying had come for him. They would have believed it because they *wanted* to believe it; it would have obviated them from guilt. As it was, should Mr Dublin fail to deliver, they would all look back with rose-tinted glasses – as so many were currently doing about home – and they would turn on Mr Dublin. There were some things, however, that you just couldn't teach.

'Thank you for coming,' Mr Dublin said.

'Thank you for sending a car,' Mr Bright said. 'And with such charming company.' The warm twinkle in his eyes cooled. 'I presume this isn't a social meeting? And if not, then why are we not meeting in the privacy of the Inner Cohort Chamber? This' – he gestured at the room – 'is unacceptable.'

'*This*' – and Mr Dublin copied Mr Bright's gesture – 'is necessary.' He looked ephemeral, with his fine ash-blond hair and pale skin. 'We felt this was a decision that needed to be agreed on by more than the Inner Cohort. Please take a seat.'

Mr Bright remained standing. 'You will find that most decisions are best taken *only* by the Inner Cohort. The world runs better that way.' He didn't see the point of explaining the guilt mentality; Mr Dublin could fall or stand on his own. 'I would just like it to be noted that I find this location insulting. There are some tasks, Mr Dublin, *especially* the unpleasant ones, that should always be given the respect they deserve.' Feet shuffled around the room. 'We should be in the Chamber, not here. And this should just be you and me.' Embarrassment settled like an invisible shroud over the room. Their aggression was still there, and he wouldn't be able to change them from their current path, but he was pleased to have unnerved them.

Mr Dublin smiled slightly. 'That was *your* way, Mr Bright:

the old way. Sadly, and mainly because of your own recent failings, we do not have the time for such niceties.' His slim frame stood tall and his naturally soft voice was clear and strong. 'Over the past few days it has become clear that you are struggling to maintain your position. This "problem" with The Bank is a clear indicator of that. You may well have stabilised the situation, but that does not excuse the fact that not only The Bank's accounts were hacked, but the X accounts too.' He paused. 'You must be aware that this is unacceptable.'

'Whoever did that got what they came for. And no one will be able to get into our systems again.' Mr Bright once more felt a shiver of irritation at having to defend himself. 'You must know that's been taken care of – as you appear to be so aware of all my movements.'

'That is not our concern, Mr Bright,' Mr Dublin continued. 'What concerns us is that none of this attention would have come our way were it not for you. We are getting reports of people asking questions about you, far more than normal – between that and these problems with The Bank there is a general feeling that even *they* are concerned: you have become a liability to the balance between us and *them*.'

Mr Bright burst into merry laughter. 'Oh, Mr Dublin, you have so much to learn.' He looked around the room. Most wouldn't even meet his eyes, and to his left, the young one who had come to collect him with Mr Escobar dropped his head. His face was red. Not all of them were convinced, he was sure of that, but they wouldn't turn against Mr Dublin yet.

'So? What now?' he asked pleasantly. 'Am I about to find out that it's my turn to try for the Walkways?'

'You've moved the First. We want to know where he is. We also wish to know the location of the boy. The bloodline.'

'Ah.' Mr Bright remained focused on Mr Dublin. 'Well, I'm not sure I'm prepared to share that information just yet.'

'This is no time for playing games, Mr Bright.'

'That's where I must respectfully point out that you are wrong, Mr Dublin. All of this is a game – a serious one, perhaps, but still just a game.' He looked down at his manicured fingernails and then up again. 'And I don't feel ready to give up my pieces just yet.'

'I don't want this to get unpleasant, Mr Bright.'

'Oh, but it already is.' Mr Bright reached up and loosened his tie so that he could reach the item that hung around his neck. 'Let's not pretend otherwise, shall we?' He pulled the thin chain free and over his head before sliding it across the table. Mr Dublin caught it at the other end.

'Now,' Mr Bright continued while redoing his tie, 'I think the dirty work has been done for the day. I have no intention of giving you the information you require, so you'd better get on with doing whatever it is you intend to do to me that you think might change my mind.' He tugged his cuffs down slightly and his polished cufflinks glinted.

'As you wish,' Mr Dublin said. 'Mr Escobar? Mr Vine? Lock our guest up for now, please. We'll give him some time to rethink his position. He's served us well. It would be a shame for that to change now.'

Mr Dublin waited until Mr Escobar had returned, leaving Mr Vine standing outside the secure cell, and then dismissed the rest of the gathering apart from Mr Dakin and Mr Ede. For a moment they stood in silence, before Mr Dakin finally pulled out a chair and slumped into it.

'What a morning,' he sighed.

'Momentous,' Mr Escobar added.

'I shall hold onto this' – Mr Dublin slipped the chain

around his neck and let it fall against the other under his loose linen shirt – 'until we have recovered Mr Craven's. I wouldn't wish to insult either of you by picking one over the other to carry a quarter until we are back in possession of all four.'

Mr Dakin and Mr Ede both nodded curtly. Neither argued and Mr Dublin was relieved. They were just pleased to be part of the Inner Cohort, and they had accepted that Mr Escobar was going to be the primary among them. They could wait a little while longer before they got their own trappings.

'You've seen the news, I take it?' Mr Escobar asked.

'Yes, and that brings me to our first point of business.' He was pleased to get away from the subject of Mr Bright. He'd expected to feel more relief now that the Architect was locked up, but the greasy sense of guilt in the pit of his stomach wouldn't leave. This was not a treachery he had chosen; it had been unavoidable. The last time he had rebelled, it had been against a despot, and he'd been proud to fight. This was altogether cloudier water in which he'd swum. Still, it had needed to be done, and the world would settle.

'Mr Craven has finally been caught. He's still alive, but only just. We'll have his quarter returned to us once it's in the police evidence lockers, just as Mr Solomon's was.'

'He has brought shame on us,' Mr Dakin said. 'He deserves his unpleasant death.'

'A little respect.' Mr Dublin flashed a glare at the fat figure sitting alongside him. 'This Dying could come for any of us and who knows how we each would react if it did?' Hearing himself, he wondered at his sudden defence of Mr Craven. He had never liked him; he was cruel and selfish. But he was familiar, and Mr Dublin understood how to play him, just as he was sure Mr Bright had. Now there were new characters to negotiate, and he was all that was left of the original Inner Cohort. Unlike Mr Bellew, Mr Dublin had not sought this position out of any great love of power himself. Mr Bright had to be removed from office for the greater good.

'As it is, this may work to our advantage,' he said. 'Mr Craven infected a policeman during his arrest – a Sergeant Armstrong, the last man to work with our elusive wild card, Detective Inspector Cassius Jones.'

'What was Mr Craven doing with him?' Mr Ede asked. Between Mr Dakin and Mr Ede, Mr Dublin preferred the latter. The slim dark-haired man was always impeccably dressed, and although quiet by nature, when he did speak, his words were always well thought out.

'I presume that he was trying to find Jones, just as we are.'

'But why?'

'Maybe he wanted to bring him to us as a gift – to regain our trust and be allowed to try for the Walkways.'

Mr Ede shrugged slightly as if he thought that was an unlikely possibility but was too polite to say so. 'Perhaps.'

'*Why* he was with Armstrong is, however, irrelevant now. What *is* important is that this might be our opportunity to find Jones. I want the hospital – the Strain II ward especially – watched. If he turns up there then I want him here, do you understand?'

'I'll take care of it,' Mr Escobar said.

'Good.' Mr Dublin poured himself a coffee. He turned to Mr Dakin. 'And can I leave the extraction of the whereabouts of the First in your capable hands?' Mr Dakin had been the natural successor to Mr Craven in many ways. He had an unpleasant cruel streak, just as the other had. But sometimes these things were necessary. Mr Dublin had never had much of a stomach for inflicting pain, but sometimes pain was the only option.

Chapter Thirty-One

The atmosphere in Paddington Green Police Station had been grim since the Angel of Death's capture the previous afternoon, and when Dr Hask opened the door of Ramsey's office, he found the DI staring out at a dark grey sky that belonged somewhere in the late afternoon, not ten-thirty in the morning. It was oppressive, doom-laden – just like the mood pervading the building. Hask said nothing but closed the door behind him and waited until Ramsey turned round. One look at the dark circles under his eyes and Hask felt his own heart sinking.

'News from the hospital not good?' he asked.

Ramsey shook his head. 'He's infected. He's sick already.' He slumped into his chair. 'The doctors don't know what kind of mutation has occurred, but it looks like our unknown killer infects people at whatever stage his own disease is at. The good news for the rest of the world is that it's unlikely to be an actual new strain of the bug, but what it means for us is that Armstrong is very ill indeed.'

'Jesus.'

'Why didn't he just wait for back-up?'

'The curse of youth is invariably stupidity,' Hask said, 'with a hefty dash of bravery and impatience.' He perched his heavy frame on the edge of the desk. 'You know all the reasons; you probably did something like this yourself in your time. Most people get away with making those less-than-wise choices, but every now and then the luck runs out. It was Armstrong's decision to go in without back-up and neither you nor he can relive that moment.'

Ramsey looked up. 'People pay you good money for this kind of cheerful talk? Because if they do, you should know this isn't making me feel much better.'

'I'm not being paid for *this*.' Hask smiled. 'This is just me and you – no bullshit, no cuddles, just the plain truth.'

'Yeah, well it may be the truth, but it sucks.' Ramsey let out a long sigh.

'Have you heard anything from Fletcher?' Hask felt lousy about Armstrong too, but what he'd said was true: there was nothing they could do for him. They could, however, keep on with their own work, which had also been affected by the previous day's events.

'Yes.' Ramsey sat up straight. 'He said he's tried a few routes to get information on this Castor Bright and he's drawing a blank.'

'He's got nothing at all?'

'No, that's not quite right: what he's getting are doors shutting on him. High-level doors. This Bright fellow exists, but no one wants to talk about him. At all.' He frowned. 'Weird, huh? Who *is* this man? And if he's that élite then what's he doing interested in someone like Cass Jones?'

'Isn't it strange how everything is weaving together?' Hask said. 'I just wish I knew why. What's the piece of this puzzle that we're missing? Armstrong goes and loiters outside Mullins' club hoping to find something to lead him to Jones and along comes our Angel of Death, *also* looking for Cass Jones. He calls himself Mr Craven, right?'

Ramsey nodded.

'Ring a bell?' Hask continued. 'Mr Bright, Mr Craven?

Who introduces themselves as mister any more? It's very old-fashioned.'

'You think Bright and this Craven know each other?'

'Bright knew the Man of Flies, so why not?'

'And why would he be looking for Jones?' Ramsey mused. 'According to Mullins he wanted to talk to Cass – he didn't say anything about giving himself up, or feeling any death-bed remorse for his actions. He wanted to *talk* to Cass: so does he know something he wants Cass to know?'

'That must be the case. And if he knows this Mr Bright, then perhaps the information he has is about him – or Cass' missing nephew?'

'Do you ever get the feeling that we're way out of our depth here?' Ramsey asked. 'My brain is too tired for all this.'

'Perhaps we are – but everything comes back to Mr Bright and Cass Jones, doesn't it?' He smiled. 'The good news is that your boss wants me to go and speak to our Angel of Death before he shuffles off this mortal coil. I'm heading over to the hospital now.'

'I'll come with you.' Ramsey hauled himself to his feet. 'I'll go and see Armstrong. His family are up there too – they're devastated, course.' He stared out at the grey day as he pulled on his coat. 'It would have been easier for them if the bastard had just been shot – easier for all of us.'

'Especially Armstrong,' Hask added. Neither of them spoke after that.

After twice veering into the middle of the road, Cass had pulled into a lay-by to rest his eyes for five minutes. He didn't think he'd sleep; the combination of adrenalin and fear of being caught should have been enough to keep him this side of consciousness, but as it turned out, it was half past ten when he woke, cold, aching and confused to find himself behind the steering wheel. His shoulder screamed, waking him up fully, and he turned and peered out of the window. He'd been out cold for more than two hours – no dreams, no ghosts, just the sleep of the dead. The once-quiet road was now a stream of traffic.

He lit a cigarette for breakfast and turned the engine on to warm the car. The radio came alive and he flicked away from the music to a news station before grabbing a couple of painkillers from the dashboard and then leaning back in the leather seat and letting his shoulder ease down to a gentle throb. He smiled slightly as he listened to the news-caster talking about the various City companies still righting themselves after being rocked by share troubles. *'Details are still emerging as to the cause of the momentary loss of confidence in some of the most stable companies on the stock market today,'* she said, and Cass shut his eyes for a moment. Dijan Maric would be smiling, and so would Brian Freeman who, hidden behind a convoluted network, had just made himself a small fortune on the back of the confusion.

'The officer who was attacked yesterday while capturing the serial killer known in the press as the "Angel of Death" has been named as Sergeant Toby Armstrong, twenty-six, of Paddington Green Police Station. His commanding officer, Detective Chief Inspector Ian Heddings, has commended his officer's bravery. He has confirmed that Sergeant Armstrong has been admitted to hospital, and his condition has been described as "serious". The police have not yet confirmed the condition of the suspect – who has been identified only by the name "Craven" – who has also been admitted to hospital. The arrest took place at Moneypenny's, a nightclub in London's Piccadilly Circus.

'The police have confirmed that club owner Mr Arthur Mullins was also present at the time. Mr Mullins, sixty-two,

owns a string of businesses across London. He served three years in prison in the 1990s for extortion, but he has always strenuously denied rumoured links with several underworld organisations. Police have confirmed that Mr Mullins has not been charged, nor is he being considered a person of interest in this case.

'Members of the Opposition are calling for an inquiry into how one officer came to be acting alone when facing a suspect described as "armed and extremely dangerous". A police source claims Sergeant Armstrong had called for back-up, but moved in before it arrived.'

Cass sat bolt upright and stared at the radio. Despite the heat blasting from the vents, his skin was icy. *Armstrong?* What the fuck had the stupid fucker done now? The newsreader had said 'attacked', not 'injured'. He was suddenly very wide awake – too awake. If Armstrong had been attacked and was now in hospital, then he'd been infected. Cold prickled his scalp and rippled in a wave of goosebumps over the rest of his skin. The killer had been arrested at Artie's club – what was he doing there? He tapped the steering wheel thoughtfully. Brian Freeman would be waiting for him, but he might have to wait a bit longer. It looked like he needed to see Armstrong before he did anything else. For one thing, the sergeant must have been watching Artie's place in a bid to try and find Cass, and although he was innocent – of the crimes Armstrong wanted him for at any rate – he felt an ache of guilt that Armstrong was now suffering because of that.

And if this 'Craven' had been at Artie's place, then perhaps the same conclusion might well be drawn. There was no way Freeman would sanction Cass taking a trip to the hospital – there was likely to be a massive police presence there – but Cass was done taking orders. Getting back to Freeman and

Dr Cornell could wait; he needed to find out what the Angel of Death had wanted with him and he couldn't call Artie to find out. The police would be all over his phones, even if they'd been convinced up until now that he had no idea where Cass Jones was. The Angel of Death and the Man of Flies: both serial killers, both perhaps interested in Cass Jones – and both, perhaps, linked to Mr Bright? Or was he seeing a pattern in coincidences that did not exist?

He threw his stub out of the window and pulled onto the road. There was only one way to find out.

There were only two hospitals in London with dedicated Strain II wards, and only one – the same hospital the late Dr Gibbs worked for – was still NHS. It was overcrowded and underfunded, and would hardly be good PR. No, Charing Cross Hospital was where Cass would place his money: that same ward where Mr Solomon had left the body of Hannah West. The dead moved in small circles, it seemed: wheels within wheels.

Arthur 'Artie' Mullins had used public transport and taken a circuitous route to get to Brian Freeman's place. Not that he thought anyone was on his tail; there'd been no one on him on the way back from the club the previous day, and the street outside his house was clear of suspicious vehicles. Either the police truly believed that he didn't know where Cass was, or they thought he wouldn't be so stupid as to try and see him immediately after something like this. Either way worked for Mullins.

As it turned out, Jones wasn't at home, just Brian Freeman and some old academic, surrounded by papers and files and open computers. Their clothes were crumpled and neither looked like they'd slept much, but their eyes were buzzing.

'I saw the news,' Dr Cornell said excitedly. 'I don't normally watch and I'm behind with the papers.' Artie Mullins had laughed at that, looking at the mountains of newsprint filling several rooms of Freeman's otherwise stylish house.

'The man, Craven, this Angel of Death.' Dr Cornell scrabbled around on the desk and pulled out a picture. 'Is this him?' He shoved it into Artie's thick hands.

It was a faded newspaper cutting, the picture grainy and worn. How old was it – fifties? A car in the background certainly suggested so. Two men were standing in front of a skyscraper, smiling as they held up a piece of paper that was obviously the subject of the piece. Dr Cornell punched his finger at a figure behind them whose head was turned slightly away from the camera. 'Him.'

'They look similar,' he admitted, 'but it's hard to tell. And it can't *be* him, can it, because this paper is old. But yeah, the bloke I saw yesterday could be his son or something. Same build, same features – same hair, as it goes.'

'I told you!' Dr Cornell's face had come alive. He grinned and slapped Brian Freeman on the arm. 'He's one of them! I told you.'

Artie looked from one man to the other. Whatever was going on here, he didn't want any part of it. He was happy running his own little empire, living with the small amount of knowledge he had. He was too old for whatever was firing Freeman and the junk collector. It looked too all-consuming for his liking.

'Well, whoever he is, he wanted to talk to Jones. He also wanted me to give him this.' He pulled the silver datastick out of his pocket. 'It's a token of his goodwill.' He handed it to Brian Freeman, despite Dr Cornell's hungry hand reaching out. 'I haven't looked at it.'

'Did he say what he wanted to talk to Cass about?' Brian

Freeman was already sliding the pen into the side of a MacBook perched on top of a pile of folders.

'Secrets. He said he had answers for Cass. Some bollocks along those lines.'

Dr Cornell was peering over Freeman's shoulder and both men frowned simultaneously. 'What's happened?' Dr Cornell asked. 'Why has the screen gone blank?'

Brian Freeman looked up at Artie. 'Did he give you any instructions to go with this?'

'No, mate.' He paused, suddenly awkward, as they fiddled with the Mac. Was he curious about the datastick? Yes. Could his curiosity wait? Too bloody right it could. Back home, his missus was choosing between three luxury holidays, and once he'd cleared with the coppers that he could leave the country then it would be sangria in the sunshine for him. By the time he got back, all this would have played out, one way or another. He'd get the story then. He didn't feel any need to be part of this action; he had no desire to get fucked with by the likes of the fabled Mr Bright.

'Maybe Cass will know what to do with it.' He sniffed and turned towards the door. 'Speaking of Jones, I think I'll be off before he gets back. Just in case.' He hesitated for a moment. The picture of Craven had thrown him. It had made him think of the few seconds in his office that he'd tried so hard to forget.

'One more thing,' he said. Maybe if he gave that moment to these two then he'd be able to bury it completely. He believed in solid earth and blood and grit. He refused to believe in what he'd seen.

'It'll probably sound crazy,' he continued, 'but Armstrong should have been able to nick him, no problem. He had a gun – Craven shouldn't have been able to bite him like he did.' His voice had lowered automatically. This wasn't something he wanted to speak out loud. He wondered if Armstrong had left it out of his statement, just as Artie himself had. 'But something happened in there,' he continued, 'something fucking weird. It was like, just for a few seconds, Craven was something else. He *became* something else.'

Both Dr Cornell and Brian Freeman were staring at him, the computer and the datastick completely forgotten for a moment, and it made him feel desperately uncomfortable. He'd hoped that they'd laugh at him, but they weren't.

'What?' Dr Cornell asked quietly. 'What did he become?'

'I don't know,' Mullins said. It was an honest answer. 'It was too bright. It made my eyes hurt. But I'm sure I saw metal in there, claws of some kind. And there was a terrible sound, like wings beating.' A flush ran over his face. It might be the truth, but listening to himself made him feel five kinds of crazy.

'Anyway, it was probably just my eyes playing tricks.' He turned to head back out to the hallway and raised a hand in farewell. 'Give Cass my best. I'm fucking off out of the country for a while. I'll catch up when I get back.'

He didn't give them time to ask any more questions. His gut was squirming like a barrel of snakes, and it was telling him to get the fuck out of there. He wasn't going to ignore it.

Chapter Thirty-Two

There were times in life when only brazening something out could get you where you needed to go. As Cass walked towards the main reception desk of the Charing Cross Hospital, head slightly down but a brisk confidence in his step, he was banking on two things: that the receptionist would be too busy to have her mind on more than the one criminal already in their hospital, and second, that most people never looked beyond the badge. He gave the woman a curt smile and held his police ID up, one finger slightly over the name, but with the picture clearly visible.

'I'm from Paddington Green,' he said quietly, 'here to see Toby Armstrong.'

'Third floor.' She barely looked up from her computer. 'If you see the nurse over there,' she nodded in the direction of a separate counter, 'she'll give you a mask and scrubs and gloves. There's a toilet just before the stairs that you can use. Please make sure you dispose of them in the clearly marked bins when leaving the ward. The scrubs go in one for washing and the gloves and mask are destroyed. Here.' She handed him a plastic ID holder. 'Put your ID in it and make sure it's clearly displayed. We don't want you mistaken for a member of staff.'

She smiled politely as Cass took it. 'Thanks.'

The woman at the second desk looked slightly harder at

his ID, but not enough to make Cass think she was in any way suspicious. She smiled tiredly as she gave him the items. 'Try not to be too loud, will you? The patients are very ill; they really need their rest.'

'I'll do my best,' he said and smiled back. He didn't feel the need to point out that they'd all be getting plenty of rest soon enough, so surely they'd want to be awake while they could. But then, what did he know of their hell? Maybe sleep was a pleasant respite – but, no, unlikely; he thought the sleep of Strain II victims would be filled with nightmares of death and the nothing that probably came after.

In the toilet he locked himself into a cubicle and pulled the green scrubs on over his clothes. He adjusted the mask over his face before tugging on the cap and tucking up the longer bits of hair. The ID holder stayed in his pocket. He checked himself in the mirror, slumped his shoulders slightly and softened the expression in his eyes. That would do. He stepped back into the hospital and walked with Dr Cromer's precise gait that he'd practised the previous night before rescuing Luke. Unless anyone looked right into his eyes he was unlikely to be recognised. He hoped.

He'd expected the third floor to be quiet, but the hush he found was so much more than that: this was the silent second before the last breath, the hanging moment between the final inhale and release, the expectant, trembling quiet that fell in the presence of death. There was a respect in that hush, and more than a modicum of fear.

Two officers talked quietly to each other by the doors as they swiftly peeled off their masks and gloves, eager to be away and back out in the freezing December air. Neither glanced at Cass as he passed them. He peered through the glass window of a door on his left. Inside, a man somewhere in his late fifties had his arm around a woman of a similar age. He was staring vacantly at the wall as she cried quietly into his shoulder. His fingers stroked her arm, but Cass wondered if either of them were aware of the contact. They were lost, facing a future that held no happiness for either of them. Toby Armstrong's parents looked so very middle class and ordinary that Cass' heart ached for them. Their son had been delivered a death sentence and they were now caught in that moment between life and death. All they could do was try to find the strength to say their goodbyes. A few seats and a respectful distance away, a young WPC sipped a cup of polystyrene coffee.

Cass left them to their grief. Despite the adrenalin firing through his system he felt slightly numb, and realised that until this moment part of him had been convinced that he wouldn't find Armstrong in this ward; that the attack launched on him by the Angel of Death hadn't involved infection. But Armstrong hadn't been that lucky, had he? An old cynicism gripped him as he moved through the ward. There was no luck. Armstrong's choices had led him here: his choice to go in without back-up, and a series of choices probably made prior to that. It was always your own choices that fucked you up.

He paused at the end of a bed and pretended to read the chart of the frail man sleeping in it. A nurse passed by without speaking to him and continued to the nurses' station at the entrance. As he flicked through the paperwork, Cass glanced around. There looked to be more private rooms at the far end of the corridor; he presumed that was where both Armstrong and Craven were being kept.

Two figures in scrubs huddled by a water cooler, though neither looked as if they intended to drink from it, and Cass realised that was likely all the police presence there was. If the Angel of Death had cancer, the ward would be

271

overcrowded with coppers ensuring no one could get in and harm the suspect, but that really wasn't necessary: who in their right mind would want to come into a Strain II ward, let alone get too close to the killer himself? It looked like not too many of the police did either, and no DCI or Commissioner could force anyone, not in these circumstances.

Unlike its originator, the more docile HIV, Strain II's ease of contagion – a sneeze, one drip of saliva inhaled, a droplet of blood – had gained almost mythical status. Cass figured if that were true they'd all be riddled with the bug by now, but he couldn't deny that underneath his fear of getting caught, his nerves were jangling at being in the presence of so much contagious death.

A door opened ahead of him and two immediately recognisable figures emerged, Tim Hask's physique was quite singular, his obesity so out of place in the midst of the skeletal figures dozing in the beds around them. The tall man he was talking quietly to was Ramsey, of course. They closed the door behind them and nodded to the two officers by the water cooler before going into a second room.

This was Cass' chance. In the bed in front of him the sleeping patient – whose features were so sunken he couldn't tell if it was a man or woman – drew laboured breaths through an oxygen mask. Cass picked up a liver tray and a small paper cup of water from the side-table and walked casually towards the room Hask and Ramsey had just left. His heart was pounding so loudly that he was certain the nurses could hear it from behind their desk, and behind his mask his cheeks were damp from his rushing breath.

He didn't recognise either of the officers who were so casually guarding the two rooms. He gave them a cursory nod. One of them glanced down at the items in Cass' hand, and then carried on with his idle chatter. Though he'd been shocked to see Hask and Ramsey so close, it was turning out to be a blessing; people invariably relaxed their sense of responsibility around their superiors, and these two were apparently no different.

The small private room was dimly lit, but it was as warm as the rest of the ward. Armstrong's eyes were shut, and there was a tube attached to his arm. What was that, some kind of sedation? Surely it couldn't be pain relief already? But now he was closer, Cass could see Toby Armstrong looked deathly pale, even in the golden glow of the side-lights. The sergeant had also lost weight – he knew Strain II was more aggressive than HIV, but surely it couldn't work this fast? Whatever Craven was passing on to his victims, it was carrying an unholy kick. He remembered the way Solomon had died: there had been nothing natural about that. So was Craven the same as Solomon and Bright? Were they all three of them something strange and ageless?

He put the water and dish on the table and then sat by the bed. There was an alarm button on a small pad just next to Armstrong's resting hand and Cass moved it to one side – well out of reach – before squeezing that cool palm.

'Armstrong,' he said softly.

The sergeant's eyes flew open and his head turned.

'Shh,' Cass said, gripping his hand, 'I just want to talk to you.'

Despite the frantic activity in his eyes, Armstrong's body had little strength, no doubt in part because of whatever the tube was pumping through his system. Cass pulled his face mask down. For a moment the two men just stared at each other. Cass wasn't surprised to see hate and resentment in Armstrong's face.

'What the hell are you doing here?' the sergeant said eventually. His voice was dry, but when he breathed, phlegm rattled in his chest. 'Come to watch me die? Apparently it won't take long. The doctors tell me they've never seen anything like it. Not in a good way.'

'I'm sorry,' Cass said. He knew the words were redundant, but Armstrong's bitterness stung, and he couldn't blame him for it: the young man was trapped in an *if only* moment that he couldn't escape: *If only I'd waited for back-up. If only I'd shot him when I first got there.*

'I wish I'd never seen your face. You know that, don't you?'

If only I'd never been assigned to DI Cass Jones.

Cass nodded. 'I can't blame you for that. I wish you'd never seen my face too.'

Armstrong's hand relaxed – giving up any attempt to go for the buzzer – and he turned away from Cass and looked up at the ceiling. Silence ticked by. 'I was looking for you.'

'I figured as much. You're a good detective.'

'I *was* a good detective.' Armstrong let out a sad, wet cough of a laugh. 'I'm past tense now. Just waiting for the body to catch up. Feels very surreal.'

Cass said nothing. The squeeze he gave Armstrong's hand this time had nothing to do with safety and everything to do with the ache he felt inside. Armstrong didn't squeeze back, but neither did he pull his hand free.

'That man – or whatever he is – Craven,' Armstrong continued, 'he said he knew you'd been set up. I heard him. You know how it made me feel?' He glanced over at Cass and there were tears brimming in his eyes. 'I felt *angry*: all that time I'd put in, all that evidence I'd found, and then you were going to make a dick out of me and my career by not being guilty after all.'

'You put together a good case,' Cass said. It was true. 'I'd have thought I was guilty.'

'You should have told me what you were doing,' Armstrong said. 'If you'd told me, then I wouldn't be here now.' He spat the words out, and Cass had to force himself not to recoil from the spray.

'If I'd told you, you wouldn't have believed me,' he said softly.

Armstrong turned away again. The truth in that didn't fit with his anger. He wanted someone other than himself to blame, and he wanted it to be Cass.

'It's all about you, isn't it? It's always all about you.' He sighed. 'Nothing good ever happens to the people around you, does it? You're like a curse – your family, Claire May, me – we've all been cursed by knowing you.'

The words felt like a slap in the face and this time Cass flinched. It *wasn't* his fault – this, Claire May, these were *not* his fault. He wondered who he was trying to convince. The dead still came after him in his dreams, and soon the cool fingers he held now would be clawing at him in the night.

'I wish that bullet had killed you.' Armstrong's voice was flat. 'I really do.'

Cass had expected Armstrong to hate him – after all, he hadn't *liked* his DI before all this happened. He just hadn't expected him to hate him so deeply.

'Did you tell Ramsey that Craven said I was set up?' he asked. Time was ticking away for both of them. Armstrong's parents would want to sit with their boy and as soon as he left the room, he knew his sergeant would start shouting the house down to get Cass caught. He was only containing it now because he wanted to vent his hurt.

'No.' He smiled. 'I left that out. They're already half-convinced you're innocent. Fuck them. Fuck you.'

275

'Fair enough,' he said. His heart picked up slightly. If Ramsey was starting to think he was innocent, then maybe there was a way back from all this for him. Armstrong coughed. It was weak and wet. There was no way back for him.

'Look, I know you don't want to hear this, not from me ...' Cass struggled to find the words – he didn't do emotional conversations, but he'd lost too many people without having the chance to say what he thought, and he needed to do it now. 'Toby, you *were* a good copper, and what you did yesterday – and I know you're regretting it now – but it was very brave. I've worked with a lot of people over the years and I can probably name on one hand those who would have done what you did. I'm sorry I was so fucking hard on you when you started. I'm sorry I kept comparing you with Claire, and I'm sorry I didn't tell you more about what I was doing.'

'You came all the way here to say that?'

'Yes.' It wasn't entirely true, but there was truth in it.

'There was something else I didn't tell Ramsey,' Armstrong said quietly. 'I don't think Mullins did either. They haven't asked me about it, so he couldn't have.'

'What?' Cass frowned.

'He changed,' Armstrong whispered. 'Just before he bit me. I had the gun on him but suddenly it was so bright and there was this terrible sound and I thought I couldn't breathe, and he moved so fast that I didn't have any time to react. Then everything was back to normal, he was on the floor, and back-up arrived.' He looked over at Cass, his eyes wide and, for an awful moment, filled with childlike wonder. 'You don't look surprised. What is he, Cass?'

Cass was lost in the memory of Mr Solomon, the Man of Flies, dying in the church: the light and the flies and the way he'd felt all the oxygen being sucked out of his lungs, and Mr Bright watching with silver tears running down his face.

'I don't know,' he answered. 'I really don't.' He felt the web tighten around him, pulling him closer to Mr Bright. Craven was like Solomon and that could only mean he was part of Mr Bright's Network. 'But I intend to find out.'

'I'll never know though, will I?' Armstrong said. The bitterness was back. 'I'm just a fucking pawn in this stupid game. My part is over and it's all your fault. I hope you rot in hell, Cassius Jones. I mean that.'

Cass recoiled slightly, not from the words themselves – he'd heard worse from people too many times – but from the sheer vitriol. Toby Armstrong wasn't just lashing out at the unfairness of it all; he truly *meant* what he said.

'*I'm* cursing *you*, Cass Jones.' Armstrong laughed a little. 'I'll be cursing you with my dying breath. Remember that. Now fuck off.'

Cass stared for a second. If he'd come here to try to make peace with a dying man then that had backfired. He'd had no idea Armstrong hated him that much. He opened his mouth to say something – *anything* – but Armstrong shut his eyes and turned his head away. Cass let it go. If his sergeant needed to hate him, then Cass would let him – not that he had much choice – but as he pulled his face mask back up over his mouth his heart felt heavy. Maybe Armstrong was right. Perhaps he was the curse in people's lives.

He got to his feet without another word and stood by the door, preparing to make a run for it once he was out of the room and Armstrong pressed the alarm. But just as he was about to step outside, all hell broke loose in the corridor. Someone – it sounded like Ramsey – was shouting in a room close by, and nurses rushed past Cass to get to him.

He peered out to see one of the two policemen rattling at the door ten feet away.

'It won't open! Sir? Sir? I can't— Oh fuck it, we need to try and kick it in!'

Behind Cass, Armstrong sat bolt upright. 'He's doing it again, isn't he?' His voice was filled with dread.

Cass didn't turn around. From under the other door, a terrible brightness streamed out through the crack. He knew he should run; this was the moment, while everyone else was focused on getting Ramsey and Hask out of Craven's room. No one would listen to Armstrong shouting in all this. He *knew* he should run, but he couldn't get his feet to move. His two friends were in there. He could live with Armstrong's death, though that sounded harsh, but he didn't think he could add Ramsey and Hask to the clinging dead – not like *this*.

He was about to run out and join the fight to open the door when suddenly the light was gone. As he blinked the last coruscating remnants away the door opened, nothing hindering it now, and Ramsey and Hask stepped out.

Gold glowed weakly at the edges of Ramsey's eyes. *He has the Glow.* Cass stared: it was watery, but it was undeniably there. After a second it vanished. Cass understood why, even if he didn't understand the Glow: he'd felt his own eyes burn – when he'd shot Macintyre, argued with Mr Bright, even when he'd seen Brian Freeman again that first time. For him the Glow came in times of extreme emotion, so maybe it was the same for Ramsey, even if he was oblivious to it.

'What the hell happened in there?' a voice asked.

'He's dead,' Ramsey said. He held up his hands, forestalling a rush of questions. 'We're fine. He just died, that's all.'

The expression on Hask's face said there was nothing *that's all* about it. The fat man was sucking in deep breaths as two nurses scurried over to check him.

His friends were fine; no death like Armstrong for them. As he turned his back on the scene and walked as quickly as he could to the exit, Cass thought that would make his sergeant bitter too.

He ran down the stairs. By the time he reached the main reception desk he wasn't even trying to be cautious. Armstrong would have raised the alarm by now, and he had to be out before some clever bastard called for a lockdown. He'd ripped off the gloves and mask, but the scrubs could stay on. He pushed through people coming the other way and then once through the doors picked up his pace to a jog. As he weaved his way through the cars and ambulances he took a moment to check behind him, half-expecting to see Ramsey charging after him, but there was no one. He grinned. He'd—

—and the thought was knocked away as two men came out of nowhere and grabbed him firmly.

Cass' eyes widened as he felt the sharp prick of the needle and cool liquid rushing into his veins. He opened his mouth to speak, but nothing came out. The world spun as a sleek car pulled up and the back door opened. *Not again,* Cass thought, moments before the blackness took hold, not a-*fucking*-gain . . .

Chapter Thirty-Three

Luke was tired, so after his hot chocolate and a sandwich, Father Michael took him upstairs to the spare room and tucked him into bed. The boy didn't speak, but he allowed himself to be undressed and put in a big soft T-shirt, compliant but not entirely complicit in the actions. He was old enough to get changed himself, but he looked to be in a daze. Father Michael wondered if it was more than shock; he could not begin to imagine what might be going on in the boy's head, having just been abducted from a place he knew by an uncle he'd never even heard of, let alone met. One of the Steves – he hadn't yet got clear in his head which was which yet – had run through the events of the previous night while they were tucking into bacon sandwiches. Cass' life was nothing if not eventful!

When he'd been a young man, Alan Jones had fascinated him with his wild stories and wilder ways. There had been something special about him then, and he could never quite understand why he'd been a little saddened when his friend had turned up on his doorstep years later declaring his own discovery of a love of God. Perhaps it was that Alan Jones had become a quieter, more subdued man, like a lot of the life had left him – as if the Glow had left him, the very glow that he – and then, years later, Christian – had talked about. Now he knew why, of course: Alan Jones had made a pact to give up a grandchild, and that was a pact with the devil if ever he'd heard one. And he'd left that legacy for his eldest child to put right. Cass had all of his father's early fire combined with his mother's inner strength, so perhaps all this was God at work. Who knew what the heavenly Father had in store for them all?

It was now midday, and the little boy still hadn't got up. The long night was catching up with the adults, who were half-dozing in front of the telly. Father Michael had peered into the room a couple of times, and watched the small figure twitching slightly, his eyelids fluttering as he slept. The dreams he was having didn't look like good ones.

'I've never knows such a quiet kid,' one of the Steves said. His face was troubled. 'It's not normal. Maybe he really is sick.'

'He hasn't got a fever.' Father Michael sat down and sipped his cooling tea. 'I checked. And he's eating plenty. I should imagine he's just stunned by it all.'

'I've got a nine-year-old. They don't stay that quiet, not for this long. They ask questions. It's what they *do*.'

Father Michael said nothing, but he saw Steve's eyes darting up occasionally from the television to the ceiling, and the room above their heads. He had to agree that there was something slightly odd about Luke – perhaps he was autistic? That would certainly explain his lack of communication. When Cass came back and all this was settled, he would suggest getting the boy checked out. If that was possible and the two weren't on the run. Just imagining everything that was going on in Cass' life right now made him feel tired. He was an old man, and on days like this he really knew it. His own adventures through the Middle East with Cass' father felt like a lifetime ago – more than that, they felt like part of a life that belonged to someone else.

He hoped Cass had been right to bring the boy here. He'd do all he could to keep Luke safe, of course, but he couldn't deny the arthritis that ached in his hands, or that it took him twice as long these days to get up the stairs.

The toilet in the hall flushed and he heard the heavy tread of the second Steve as he came down the corridor, and the sound calmed him. He recognised these men from his days in the Lebanon; there had been men there with the same purpose in their face and coldness in their eyes. He might not be able to keep Luke safe, but he was pretty sure that these two could. He'd let the boy sleep a couple more hours and then make them all some lunch.

Chapter Thirty-Four

The Experiment room was exceptionally hot, and even in his loose linen shirt, Mr Dublin could feel the first prickles of sweat. He didn't mind; he'd become used to it over the past few days while studying the Experiment. What he hadn't got used to was the screaming. He'd noticed several of the technicians wore earplugs to dull the sound, but they couldn't possibly block out the agonised shrieking entirely. Mr Dublin thought it would be enough to drive anyone mad.

He wondered how they could so calmly witness the suffering of their own kind for the sake of money or science or power. It didn't sit comfortably with him, and he had no intention of being present when Cassius Jones started screaming. Perhaps that was something they had got from *him*, their capacity for cold-hearted cruelty. They'd certainly got their capacity for pain from *him*, a most unwelcome gift, he imagined. He felt slightly queasy. He knew that what he was about to do was cruel.

He thought of his lost brother, Mr Rasnic, dribbling quietly in a cell not far from this room, separated from his *Glow* and with part of him stuck screaming out in the Chaos. This cruelty was necessary if it could end so much suffering and put all to rights. If it could find them a way home. He didn't have to like it, though, he decided as the door behind him opened and brought both Mr Escobar and a shiver of cooler air inside.

'Are they ready to start?' Mr Escobar asked.

'Nearly.' Mr Dublin didn't move from his seat but kept his eyes on Cassius Jones. He was starting to stir; he'd be awake within seconds now. Mr Dublin wasn't concerned; Jones was well strapped down. The monitors were being attached to his naked chest and the headpiece and eye mask were ready to be fitted on Mr Dublin's command. An ugly pink scar was knotted in the skin on Jones' shoulder. Mr Dublin resisted the urge to touch it. They were strange, these bodies, that knitted themselves back together after injury but left a mark of memory. Really quite fascinating. If only *he* knew just how remarkable these failures of *his* had turned out to be. Mr Dublin wondered what *he* would make of this one who had *his* blood flowing through his otherwise ordinary veins – would *he* want to destroy him, or accept him? It was always so hard to judge, but maybe now they'd find out. He wondered if this was what Mr Bright – still stubbornly refusing to speak – had intended for the boy.

Jones's eyes flickered open and his chest heaved as he dragged in a gulp of air. At first there was only confusion, then the adrenalin kicked in, his dark eyes widened and he started to struggle against his restraints. He tried to turn his head, but the strap holding it in place was too strong and all he managed was a grunt of frustration.

His eyes, though—

His eyed burned *gold*.

Mr Escobar inhaled sharply, and Mr Dublin wasn't surprised. This was the *Glow*, not some vague watery light occasionally glimpsed here and there; this was powerfully bright. Mr Dublin glanced at the technician who was attaching the final monitor to Cass Jones' skin. Her eyes were bland as she went about her task; she was oblivious to the streams of unusual light filling the room.

The *Glow* stopped as abruptly as it had come. Finally Mr Dublin stood up. He was more than a little surprised – he'd seen them with the *Glow* before, of course, but never like this, not with someone so aware of its presence – and he'd certainly never seen one of them able to turn it off like that. Cassius Jones was *controlling* his *Glow*.

Mr Dublin felt a small moment of sad admiration for Mr Bright, for how much work he'd put into tracking the bloodlines, creating this family. His jaw clenched. They needed the boy back – who knew what damage would be done to Jones when the Experiment started? They might need the boy to bargain with *Him* for a peace on their return ... *if* they found the Walkways, of course. *If, if, if* ...

'It's good to see you again, Mr Jones,' he said, softly. 'We were not formally introduced last time, when you were somewhat busy getting shot, and I was engaged in restraining Mr Bellew.' He watched as the dark angry eyes remembered him. 'That's quite a healthy *Glow* you've got there,' he continued.

'Where's Mr Bright?' Cass growled.

Mr Dublin was momentarily surprised – given the situation he had expected a more obvious question: *What the hell are you doing to me?* or *Are you going to kill me?* He'd obviously underestimated Jones' hatred of the Architect. As it happened, he didn't have exact answers to either of the expected questions; it very much depended on the Experiment.

'Mr Bright is no longer anyone's concern, least of all yours.' Mr Dublin pushed his fine blond hair away from his eyes.

Jones' eyes narrowed. 'Is he dead?'

'No. I'm not a monster,' he said, wondering why he felt the need to justify himself to this man. 'We will be deciding what to do with Mr Bright shortly, once he has told us what we need to know. If our Experiment doesn't work with you, then we will have no choice but to try it with him.'

'You're running the Network now?'

Mr Dublin could clearly hear the disdain in Jones' voice: he might think he hated Mr Bright, but there was a good measure of respect mixed in with it. Mr Dublin found himself smiling; this was not that far removed from his own feelings.

He brought his features back under control and said, 'The Network is not your business.'

'Mr Bright fucking with my family has made it my business.' Another flash of gold.

'That was unfortunate,' Mr Dublin said, 'but it was also necessary.'

'Go fuck yourself.'

The unexpected crudeness made Mr Dublin flinch, and Mr Escobar stepped forward, one hand raised, ready to strike him, but Mr Dublin shook his head. They were about to cause Cassius Jones quite enough pain without inflicting any more, and to be fair, the man had every right to hate them all.

A chilling scream cut through the walls, and Cass Jones froze.

'We call this the Experiment.' Mr Dublin waved a slim hand around the room. 'You've come across it before, I think, although not so closely as now, obviously. Those students who killed themselves had all taken part in it. Sadly for them, with the help of our equipment they saw things their unformed minds could not cope with.'

'Chaos in the darkness,' Cass said softly.

'Something like that, yes.'

'You fucking bastards,' Cass said softly but venomously. 'They were just *kids*.' The screaming along the corridor became more frantic and high-pitched, but this time Cass Jones continued his fruitless struggle against the straps.

Mr Dublin was beginning to see why Mr Bright had been so interested in the Jones boys.

'You can blame Mr Bright for what happened to them,' he said, 'and you need to know that we tried ourselves first – some of us, anyway. My own brother sits not so very far from this room after his attempt. Sadly, his mind was also destroyed.'

'I hate to break it to you,' Jones said, 'but whatever you're trying to do just isn't working.'

'We'll see,' Mr Dublin said more cheerfully. 'Maybe with you it'll be different.'

'Why should it be different with *me*? What's so fucking special about *me*?' Jones was beginning to sound agitated and Mr Dublin smiled softly.

'Let's find out, shall we?' He turned to the technician who had been waiting patiently by the bed. She picked up the eye mask and fitted it carefully, then reached for the headset, plugged it in and smoothed it over his skull.

Jones' breath was coming rapidly now, which reassured Mr Dublin: the man *was* afraid; Cassius Jones was human after all.

He leaned in. Jones smelled of warmth and sweat and blood and tears. 'Look for the lines,' he said. 'If you can't find them, then scream into the Chaos: scream at them to open the Walkways for you. Let them know you're *there*.'

'What the fuck is all this about?'

'I wish I could tell you everything you don't know, Cassius Jones – I do think you've earned that much.' Mr Dublin stood up. 'But we just don't have the time.'

The technician flicked the switches and the machines hummed into life. On the bed, Cass Jones gasped and his back arched against the restraints.

Satisfied that the equipment was working correctly, the technician left the room. She hadn't said a word, and Mr Dublin wasn't sure whether that was deferential politeness or self-preservation. Everyone who worked here knew the toll the Experiment took, and none of them wanted to end up on the sharp end of it themselves, so anonymity was probably wise.

He turned to Mr Escobar. The swarthy man was staring at Jones' juddering body in fascination and Mr Dublin wondered if he'd be so curious when Jones started screaming. He had no intention of being here for that himself; he would come back when this session was over. Cassius Jones wasn't going anywhere, and he had other business to attend to.

'You watch him,' he said, and gestured for Mr Escobar to take his chair. 'Call me if anything unusual happens. I'll be back when it's done.'

It was a relief to be back out in the cooler air of the corridor, but he didn't relax entirely until he'd left the Experiment floor behind.

People always underestimated the curiosity of the young. Although it had been a very long time since they had been home, Mr Vine was still young, certainly compared with Mr Bright and Mr Dublin. As Mr Bright sat against the wall of the white cell and let his body scream silently at him after the enthusiastic ministrations of Mr Dakin, Mr Bright wondered at Mr Dublin's stupidity. Leaving someone like him to be guarded only by someone like Mr Vine was a massive error of judgement. Or perhaps Mr Vine was Mr Escobar's choice; that would make more sense. Mr Escobar was a warrior; he was used to inspiring loyalty in the young – it was the loyalty of the young that had probably brought Mr Vine to them in the first place. But it was a long time since they had been warriors, and now Mr Vine was simply a Second Cohort who suddenly found himself in the company of those who were legends. It was likely Mr Vine would not have seen anyone other than his section leader since their arrival, and now here he was, guarding the Architect. Of course he was curious. He was also clearly out of his depth.

While Mr Dakin had been present, he'd no doubt stood tall, with his eyes straight ahead, but now that Mr Dakin had gone, Mr Vine was a different creature. The others had forgotten that in the eyes of the lower cohorts he and Mr Solomon and the First were magical; they were the stuff of myth. Familiarity may have bred contempt in those who knew them best, as proven by Mr Bellew and Mr Dublin, but to the rest they still *shone*.

Mr Vine had left the small hatch in the door open, and after Mr Escobar had gone – and once his breath had returned – Mr Bright had started speaking quietly. Mr Vine hadn't answered at first, but after a while his wide eyes had appeared in the window and it had become a conversation. He probably thought idle chatter wouldn't matter; he had probably told himself he was just showing the fallen leader a little of the respect he deserved; lying to himself that he wasn't actually doing anything wrong.

They had talked of the old days, the journey, and how they had all stood as one against *him*. Mr Bright had spoken softly – because he hurt too much to do otherwise –

and he had chosen his words wisely. When he mentioned Mr Dublin it was with affection, and a touch of pity. He maintained his superiority without ever mentioning it, and slowly he felt Mr Vine's uncertainty about the coup growing.

He remained sitting on the floor until Mr Vine ended his phone call outside, then he got to his feet, wiping away the smears of the blood that had leaked from his eyes during the questioning. It might have been a long time since they had been home, but Mr Dakin hadn't lost any of the extraction tricks *he* had taught all that time ago, and he had not been happy that Mr Bright was not succumbing to them. Mr Bright had been quite surprised himself. Mr Dakin was very, *very* good at what he did.

'What's happening?' he asked, when he reached the door.

'They've brought someone in.' Mr Vine licked his lips nervously, and the *Glow* flickered on and off at the corners of his eyes. 'For the Experiment.'

'Who?'

'Some policeman, I think – they didn't tell me his name. But they said he'd been at the hospital. Oh, and Mr Craven has died.'

The pain eased as Mr Bright's brain whirred. He didn't care about Mr Craven; his death had only ever been a matter of time, and he had become a nuisance, but he found he did care that they had brought Cass Jones in.

'It's a mistake, you know,' he said softly. 'Cassius Jones can't find the Walkways. The Experiment will destroy him.'

'Then why are they trying it?' Mr Vine's question was aggressive, but underneath Mr Bright could hear his uncertainty.

'Because he's the bloodline. I should imagine they are hoping that in the absence of the First, or the boy who's been kept pure – and only I know where they are – that somehow his blood will be recognised and the way home will be revealed.'

'Why won't it work?' Mr Vine asked. 'We need to get home – we need to stop the Dying.'

Mr Bright said gently, 'It won't work because even if the Walkways back were blocked from *His* end – and logic has started to tell me otherwise – *He* doesn't want peace; *He* wants to destroy us all. If Mr Dublin took five minutes to call the House of Intervention, he'd know this for himself, but Mr Dublin isn't used to having to manage everything by himself. He doesn't yet understand the necessity of always seeing the big picture – if I am to be entirely honest, though it pains me to say it, I truly do not believe that Mr Dublin is *able* to do what I do, especially not now.

'At this moment, more than in any other time in our history, *nothing* is as it seems.' Mr Bright voice was calm and steady, and he could feel Mr Vine hanging on every syllable. There was nothing that gave the young more confidence than knowledge, or at least the appearance of such. *Unanswered* questions scared them.

'There is an emissary here,' he continued, 'but she has come quietly, and she has not yet sought us out. Is that not strange? Perhaps they came because they were summoned? And if a message were somehow sent home, to whom would *he* respond? Whom among us here does *he* care about? There is a game being played here, Mr Vine, and you need to think very carefully about which side you wish to choose. Let me help you with that choice.' He paused and smiled.

'I am fond of Mr Dublin – and I harbour no ill will towards him for this unfortunate turn of events. He truly believes that he is acting in our best interests, but he is grievously wrong, and that is why I have declined to tell him all that I know. He would not use that information wisely. Mr Dublin is *not* the leader to deal with this situation. I must go further and say that *I* am the only one who can prevent Armageddon coming for us – but I cannot do it alone. I am going to need the help of the man now in the Experiment – and I am going to need yours.'

Mr Vine's eyes widened, but still he continued to listen intently.

'If we do not act immediately, the Experiment will destroy Cassius Jones, and then, no doubt, they will decide that it is my turn for that same fate, and I too will be left somewhere out there in the Chaos, screaming for all eternity. That is not your concern, but what should be is that very soon, as soon as he knows for a certainty that *He* can get home, *He* is going to arrive here with an army that we could never hope to match, and he will wreak such devastation here that he will leave nothing but a ball of sterile dust and a trail of broken bodies floating through space. *They* will die quickly. For us it will take longer – but die we shall; they will make it so, unnatural as that act is for any of us. *He* can and will kill us, and when he is done, *He* will turn his back and go home. His vengeance will be terrible, and it will be complete. Some – or at least one – might return with *Him*, but I can promise you that it will not be the likes of you or me.'

He leaned in closer through the gap, and his breath warmed the young man's skin as he spoke. 'Remember *Him*, Mr Vine; remember why we did what we did. And trust in me, like you did back then.' He paused to let his words sink in, then added, 'Oh, I should have said—' He paused and smiled, softly. 'There is no such thing as the Dying, Mr Vine. There is only *ennuie*.'

When Cassius Jones' first scream echoed along the corridors Mr Vine finally unlocked the door.

Chapter Thirty-Five

Dr Tim Hask stood against the wall as DCI Ian Heddings tore DI Charles Ramsey to shreds, and although the senior officer never once addressed him personally throughout the entire tirade, Hask knew it was meant as much for him, no matter if he was only a consultant, not a member of the team. He could understand why; he'd spent so much time and effort here he felt like one of the Paddington Green boys these days. And of course it was a matter of record that, like Ramsey, he believed that there was some doubt as to the matter of Cass Jones' charges of murder. On reflection, he thought it was quite an achievement on Heddings' part that he hadn't actively bawled him out yet.

'So let me get this straight, just for my own sanity—' Heddings paced from one side of his desk to the other. 'You came out of Armstrong's room and did not notice Cassius Jones coming the other way. He then had a nice cosy chat – for *ten* minutes, I believe? – with his ex-sergeant? And then he strolled out of the building and disappeared. And you didn't see him?'

'No, I didn't!' It was Ramsey's third denial, and his eyes were blazing. 'We were in with Craven when he died and all hell was breaking loose—'

'—and we'll come back to that craziness in a minute.'

Heddings poked a finger at Ramsey. 'Bright lights and locked doors – what the hell is wrong with you?'

'Listen, we weren't the only people there,' Ramsey started. 'There were two sergeants, supposedly watching Armstrong's and Craven's doors – and they didn't see Jones either!'

'They don't know him like you do.'

'To be fair,' Hask cut in, 'everyone in the building was wearing masks and scrubs – except for me, thanks to my somewhat obvious proportions, it is extremely difficult to identify anyone, police, hospital staff or otherwise.'

'Thank you, Doctor, but I did not ask your opinion. And now that Mr Craven is dead and DI Ramsey is suspended pending inquiry, I think perhaps it's time we terminated your current contract.'

'*Suspended?*' Ramsey jumped to his feet again. 'What the hell for? Because we didn't spot Jones while we were dealing with the death of a suspect? It won't stand up—'

'You let a man – an ex-colleague from a station already fighting corruption charges – walk in and then leave right under your nose. This is a man wanted on charges of terrorism and murder, and on top of that, he was your friend and you think might be innocent. How the hell do you think that is currently playing out in the offices upstairs? What do you think they had to say to me about *that*? They think you let him walk – and if they don't think that, then they think the newspapers certainly will, and you know what? *I don't disagree!*'

'What about Castor Bright?' Hask asked. He felt slightly sorry for DCI Heddings. It was clear he'd taken a roasting from his superiors every bit as harsh as the one he was currently dishing out to Ramsey. 'Anything on him?'

'Forget about Bright,' Heddings snapped.

'What do you mean – how can we? He's part of the investigation, regardless of Jones' guilt or innocence.'

'I mean, *forget* about him.'

'Does he work for The Bank?' Hask asked.

'Bright is irrelevant: that's what I have been told, that's what the Commissioner was told, and that's what I'm telling you.'

'Really?' Ramsey got to his feet. 'Because normally when there's that much *telling* going on, you find that the subject is really fucking relevant.'

Even Heddings flinched at Ramsey's cursing; it wasn't normally the soft-voiced American's style.

'Just what the hell is going on here?' Ramsey asked, 'because I sure as shit don't have a clue. Am I being suspended because Jones snuck into the hospital under my nose, or because I'm trying to find out more about someone who may well be responsible for several deaths, including setting Jones up?'

Hask watched the two men staring so angrily at each other. Did Heddings even know the answer, or was he just doing what he'd been told to do?

'Let's just call it a bit of both,' Heddings said eventually. His voice had softened, and maybe with those few words he'd already said more than he should. 'The point is, you can argue about it as much as you like, but the situation isn't going to change. But this will blow over in a few days, and you'll be back. For now, I'll assign Davies to the Jones case.'

Ramsey let out a derisive snort. 'He's got no chance of finding him. From what I hear he couldn't find his own asshole if he was buck-naked and standing over a mirror.'

Hask held back his own laugh, but Heddings shrugged wearily. 'Trying to find a police offer in this nick without a stain on his reputation wasn't the easiest task. He's the best

I can do. Now go and enjoy a few days' paid holiday. I wish to God I could.'

On the way to the pub they called David Fletcher. He too had been dragged over the coals, but at least he still had his job – the Commander of the ATD couldn't be suspended with the same ease as a humble DI. Hask thought it might just work in their favour; he couldn't believe Fletcher cared much for being told to back off from something so suspicious. He hadn't said outright that he'd continue his own investigation, but he had insisted he wanted to be kept in the loop.

Hask sipped his vodka and tonic as Ramsey half-drained his first pint. 'So, what now?' the profiler asked. He didn't suppose for one second that Charles Ramsey was about to go home and sit about watching daytime TV until he was allowed back into the fold. They had still to find out the truth about Mr Bright, but that fact didn't need to be spoken.

How could either of them walk away after seeing the transformation that Craven had undergone just before he died? Hask still hadn't really processed those few brief moments, the way he hadn't been able to breathe; the light and sound that had been so sharp and exquisite that it had hurt. Caroline Hurke had not been suffering from delusions – or if she was, then so too were Tim Hask and Charles Ramsey.

'I'm going to call a few friends in the media.' Ramsey took a long swallow of his beer, but his eyes were narrowed and focused, and somewhere completely different entirely. 'I want to make sure that the whole world knows I'm off the case.' He glanced at Hask. 'You too, if you don't mind.'

'My reputation can take it.'

'Good. You cost a lot of money, so you being dismissed by the Met will get a few headlines, especially if we make it clear that your contract was cancelled because you now think that Jones was set up by an unknown, very powerful man.'

Hask smiled. 'The Commissioner will then deny it, and that will make the story run for longer, yes?'

'Exactly.'

A flutter of excitement buzzed in his stomach. This could be fun. 'So talk me through your plan, Detective Inspector.'

'The way I see it, we need to find one of two people if we are ever to understand what the hell is going on here. And I also know that we're highly unlikely to find either Mr Bright or Cass Jones: Bright's a virtual ghost, and Jones isn't leaving any tracks behind him. However, there's a chance, that one of *them* might come looking for us if we play it right.'

'Cass Jones?'

'Exactly. He's out there on his own, and we know he's watching the news because otherwise he wouldn't have got to the hospital so fast. If he realises that we're on his side, then he might get in touch, especially if he needs us.'

'Or,' Hask said, leaning forward and resting his heavy arms on the table, 'he might think it's a trap.'

'He might do if it was just me,' Ramsey said, 'but not you: you're a civilian. Using you to trap him would give the Commissioner a huge headache – and on top of that I don't think you'd agree to something like that; it's not part of your normal observational and assessment role. I've looked at your file and you're always impartial, and this wouldn't be. Cass knows that as much as I do.'

'How nice that you think so highly of me.' Hask smiled. 'Do you want to make the calls now, or shall we have another drink first?'

'Let's have another drink.' Ramsey grinned. 'After all, it's your shout. And then after that, let's start this ball rolling.'

Chapter Thirty-Six

*N*ot just cold, but freezing black cold ... His soul ached with loneliness as he flew forward, stretching further and further into the empty darkness. He had no sense of time passing; there was no before the black, or if there was, it was simply the fragment of a dream he chased, but couldn't cling to. He had been here for ever, propelling himself endlessly across or through or around. He wasn't breathing, but his throat was raw. As he drifted in and out of consciousness, a strip of bright life tumbling through space, he wondered if he should be afraid. He was lost, and he would be here for ever, and yet he didn't feel afraid. There was something familiar about the darkness. He'd been here before, a long time ago, he was sure of it.

After aeons drifting in the depths he gasped as swirls of light and colour and terrible beauty filled the void ahead. He ached just looking at the glory, and he cried at his smallness in its presence. It was Chaos. There was Chaos in the darkness, and it tugged at something inside him, pulling him closer, and awe and fear threatened to rip his soul apart. The Chaos was shrieking, and it made him frown – the Chaos hadn't screamed before, and he wondered how he knew about before, and as he spun towards the hues that made his eyes bleed he no longer knew what was before and what was after. There was only now.

He could get lost in the colours that burned so brightly and rolled him around and pushed him from one thread to another, but even among their fierce beauty he could see patches of golden Glow sparking here and there. Unlike the dancing Chaos, the bursts of Glow didn't move, and an image filled his head: of flies, stuck in a spider's web. He trembled as he passed the golden haze, and it screamed, tormented. The scream didn't stop. He wondered if the scream would ever stop—

He tried to propel himself forward, looking for a path, but the Chaos moved him this way and that, trapping him in its maze. Colour was everywhere, confusing him and always peppered with the awful screams of the Glow. He paused and forced himself to be still. There had been a path here once, all white and glorious – he knew that, although he had no idea how he knew, or even who he was; all he knew was that there had once been a path, that they had built. Where was it now, hidden somewhere in the blinding, dancing colours? And who were they? Where did the path lead?

A strand of purple and blue and pink slid free from the mass and he gasped as it slithered stickily around him. He found himself screaming, an awful sound that grew louder as he shook it away. It was a trap; the Chaos would hold him here if it could, just like it held the patches of shrieking golden light now embedded within its colours. He fought the energy that propelled him forwards, instead floating free. He needed to get out. He needed to go back.

A distant sound teased him, music, just out of reach. The notes were pure and powerful, and he tried to look beyond the Chaos, to see through the colours, to find the source, but he thought the effort might drive him mad so instead he listened. It was the sound of trumpets, clear bursts of impatient music, and now it terrified him more than the Chaos did. Some part of him remembered the music, just like it had remembered the

Chaos in the darkness, and more colours stretched towards him and now he found he was too tired to fight them. He thought he might be crying. He thought perhaps he was here, and perhaps he might be here for ever, and the sudden end-lessness of eternity was shards of icy pain in his head.

The colours were coming for him. The Chaos was—

—and he gasped, sucking air into his raw chest, and the world spun in a mass of nausea and confusion and heat. Someone pulled off the eye mask and he found himself blinking rapidly – and for a moment he was purely sensory, his body reacting to his surroundings while his con-sciousness pulled back from the void. He was here and there at the same time— He wanted to puke.

'Get him out of there – quickly.'

'He looks terrible.' The hushed voice sounded shocked.

Confused and barely conscious, Cass turned and through the haze he saw a young man, a stranger, and he was yanking him free from the various monitors. He didn't recognise him – but he'd known the first voice; he would recognise that one anywhere. And in this moment he knew it better than he knew himself. *Mr Bright.*

And as the name registered, so his world fell back into place: *Cass Jones. Luke. The Bank. The dead—*

He groaned.

'That will pass,' Mr Bright said. 'We may have to carry him out of here.'

The straps on his arms came free and Cass struggled to haul himself up. He blinked through the black patches at the corner of his vision and his mouth moved with the ghosts of a thousand questions, but nothing recognisable came out.

Leaning heavily on the stranger, Cass turned his head to

see Mr Bright crouched by the body of a swarthy, well-built man. He was removing something from around his neck. When he stood up, Cass could see he'd been in a battle of his own; there were streaks of dried blood on his cheeks and his normally impeccable clothing was rumpled and stained. What had happened in here? And more importantly, what had happened to *him*? The room was baking, but he shivered. Cold had settled into his bones and his feet were numb – the cold from the void. He wondered if he'd ever be warm again.

'There are no Walkways,' he rasped, finally finding his voice. 'It's a trap.' Mr Bright and the stranger paused and looked at each other.

'We can talk about that later,' Mr Bright said. 'For now, let's get you out of here. We haven't got much time.'

Cass almost laughed. Go with Mr Bright? He'd rather take his chances here. He got to his feet. He'd rather—

—and the world spun and stars flashed in his vision—

—and a million miles away Mr Bright said calmly, 'Catch him. He's passing out.' The words sounded like trumpet music, and then blackness took him again.

The old man was like an excited child as they left the small attic apartment for the last time and headed towards the car she'd procured for them. He leaned on her quite heavily and their progress was slow, but his eyes were alive and his weakness was, at least temporarily, leaving him.

'I can't wait to see him,' he said, for the hundredth time. 'It's been so long – I can't wait to see him, and I can't wait to get home.'

'Me too,' she said, smiling. Her hair was shining, and a bright titian red again: as the First got stronger, so did they. She hadn't realised how much she had lost hope that they would ever get home again, until she got it back. Her nose stung and began to run in the biting cold. She'd be glad to be back in the endless warmth. She'd be glad to be herself again.

'And you think you know where Jarrod Pretorius is?' he asked as they turned off the main road and down a side-street. She didn't look at him as she pulled the car keys out of her pocket.

'I think so,' she said. He hadn't asked her about Jarrod Pretorius before, and for that she was grateful. In the end, she'd had to look for him in the old ways, and her abilities were so weakened that it had taken days before she got even the faintest of images. But since then, more and more had come to her – faces, places, buildings, names – until she had been left exhausted, and last night the old man had had to look after her instead of the other way round.

She wondered how much of the tiredness came from the search itself, and how much from the heartache it produced. She wondered if those who had marched off so long ago without a backwards look ever missed those they had left behind as they themselves were missed. Perhaps forgetting was easier if you were far from home ... She had never forgotten, though. He had always been a strange one, but she had loved him, even when they had taken different sides as they were duty-bound to do. He hadn't wanted to leave her, of that she was sure, even after all this time, but he'd done it anyway.

Inside the car, she turned the engine on and cold air hit her face from the vents, but she didn't close them; she *needed* the cold. She needed to be as strong as possible. Her strange new heart thumped loudly and she told herself it was the excitement of seeing the First, which wasn't entirely a lie. Now that their meeting was so close, her heart was leaping for it: it had been so long, and he had always shone so brightly – and she, like all the rest, had missed him.

But it was Jarrod Pretorius she needed her steel for.

She pulled away from the kerb and out into the traffic, then turned the volume up on the radio. She needed the festive good cheer. She found herself enjoying seeing the old man's foot tapping along as the singer screeched 'Merry Christmas!' at them, and then it was replaced with something older and mellower, but still full of warmth and love, and it made her think of Jarrod Pretorius again; it made her think of love. Perhaps *they* were right in that – perhaps true love never did really die.

She thought of the Architect, and all the others. She wondered if they would ever understand that *he* was so bent on the destruction of them and all they had achieved because *he* had loved them and *he* had missed them, and *he* would not ever forgive them for that.

Chapter Thirty-Seven

'I took it from the one who was guarding Cassius Jones in the Experiment.' Mr Bright held up the silver datastick.

'We have this one.' Brian Freeman held up a matching item. 'It came from your friend Mr Craven. He's dead now.' He delivered the last line with a smile, but it didn't appear to bother Mr Bright.

'That was inevitable given his condition. And colleagues we may have been, but I have never counted Mr Craven among my friends.' He returned Freeman's smile with more warmth than the one he'd received. 'I am glad you have it.'

The two men held the items up as if they were cowboys brandishing Colts in a duel. All Cass wanted was to sit down and wait for his terrible headache to fade. He was exhausted. The journey here had been a blur, and he had no recollection of giving the address to either Mr Bright or Mr Vine, as the stranger turned out to be, but at some point he must have done. He could remember seeing their faces, looming over him as he drifted in and out of consciousness, but the rest was a blank.

As reunions went, it had been a strange one. Cass had stumbled through the door supported by Messrs Bright and Vine, and the ensuing silence had been almost palpable. Dr Cornell had broken it: he'd crept up to within two or three inches of Mr Bright and then raised a trembling hand and touched his face.

'You,' he'd breathed eventually. Cass had thought he might have a heart attack with the shock, but instead he scuttled to safety behind Brian Freeman.

'You bastard,' Freeman had said.

'I've been called worse, and I suppose I've earned that,' Mr Bright answered quite cheerfully, 'but we did a deal, Mr Freeman. You took my offer. You can't blame me if for some reason you feel sour about it so many years later.'

Freeman had gone for Bright, but Cass forced himself between them, though his head almost exploded in agony at the sudden movement. The situation was fucked up enough without them fighting each other – right now, at least. Before anything else he needed to know why Mr Bright had rescued him.

'I have all the answers,' Mr Bright said, pulling the datastick from his pocket. 'I can tell you everything you want to know.'

And here they were, Cass thought, datasticks drawn at dawn. He let himself flop into an armchair as Mr Bright peered around the room at the photographs and documents that covered every flat surface. 'Although you seem to be doing a remarkably good job of trying to find them your-selves,' he finished, sounding almost impressed.

'Your friend Solomon killed my niece,' Brian Freeman spat, and Mr Bright's eyes widened slightly and then, after a moment, twinkled.

'Ah,' he said, 'and now this change of heart makes sense. I should have researched his victims more thoroughly.' He trod carefully over the piles of papers until he reached the large board of photographs and newspaper cuttings propped up against a wall. 'I'm sorry he did that to you.'

His voice was soft as he studied the pictures. 'Although I can't help but be pleased that even at the last, when he'd gone quite, *quite* mad, Mr Solomon didn't entirely lose his mastery of the game. I'm not afraid to say I miss having him by my side.' He turned back to Freeman. 'As things have turned out, your re-involvement might not have been the negative that Mr Solomon intended.'

'How do you see that?' Freeman growled.

'Because right now, and whether you like it or not, we're all on the same side.' Mr Bright came closer to Freeman. 'I'm sure you would like to kill me – or at least *try* to kill me – but I am also sure that you are a pragmatic man, Mr Freeman, and one who would not carelessly lose an ally with my knowledge and in my position.'

'What do the datasticks do?' Dr Cornell was oblivious to the tension between the two men standing on either side of him. His eyes glittered with obsession tinged with madness.

'What do you mean, we're on the same side?' Freeman didn't even glance at Dr Cornell, and neither did Mr Bright.

'Our own petty quarrels have been somewhat dwarfed by impending events,' Mr Bright said softly, 'and for now I suggest we put aside our differences and work together.'

'What impending events?' Cass asked.

'The small matter of Armageddon.'

Brian Freeman snorted a laugh. 'Yeah, right.'

'Yes. Right.'

'It's true,' Mr Vine cut in, speaking for the first time since his introduction. 'The House of Intervention saw it.'

'And I bet you have only his word for this?' Freeman sneered.

'I trust his word – I always have.'

'Interventionists,' Cass whispered, 'that's what Hayley Porter was becoming, wasn't it?' He rubbed his aching head and swallowed down another rush of nausea. Whatever that machine had done to him, it wasn't good. No wonder the students had killed themselves after being repeatedly plugged into it. Whenever he closed his eyes he could still see the universe of colours.

'Fucking Armageddon, my arse.' Freeman stepped in closer to Mr Bright.

'Charming as that expression is, it doesn't change the fact that it's coming.'

'There is something coming,' Cass said, suddenly, 'there was something there, on the other side. I heard trumpets.'

Mr Vine visibly paled.

'What the fuck are you on about, Charlie?' Brian Freeman said, unconsciously slipping back to the old name.

'I don't exactly know,' he whispered miserably. And that was true, partly because his brain recoiled in horror whenever he tried to think clearly about what he'd been put through and focus on what he'd experienced. 'But something's coming.'

'Why come here?' Freeman said. 'I may have an inflated sense of my own value to the world, but I doubt you'd share it, so explain to me: why rescue Jones and bring him here? You've got enough power of your own; you don't need us.'

'He's not running the Inner Cohort any more,' Mr Vine said. 'Mr Dublin has taken over. They were torturing him and I set him free.'

'*Inner Cohort?*' Freeman snapped. 'Mr *Dublin?* Inter-fucking-*ventionists?* Do you even speak English?'

Mr Bright flicked a hand to silence them, the gesture of a man used to being obeyed. 'None of that matters at the moment. What matters is that you have to get me to the boy – we're running out of time.'

Cass looked up, all memory of the chaos in the darkness forgotten. 'You want me to take you to *Luke*? My *nephew*? Are you crazy?'

'You haven't got your nephew.' Mr Bright spoke softly, and Cass' world tilted all over again.

'What do you mean? Of course it's Luke. He looks exactly like Christian. If he wasn't Luke, then why did you have him hidden away at that facility? You're always twisting things, but this time I'm not believing you.'

'I've never lied to you, Cassius Jones. I've played games with you, yes, and you may hate me for that, but I have *never* lied to you. I have been *very* careful not to.'

'That doesn't mean you're not lying now.' Cass' heart was racing. It had to be Luke. It *had* to be.

Mr Bright looked again at the photos pinned up on the board. His eyes lingered on the old black-and-white newspaper print of him with Mr Solomon and the broad, dark-haired stranger laughing outside the stock exchange.

'That's who you have.' He raised a hand and pointed at the central figure. 'The First. He's in Luke's body and Luke is in his. I imagine you found it easier than you had expected rescuing him. He will have made it so.'

There was a long pause and Cass felt as if he'd been punched hard in the solar plexus. It was *crazy*. Mr Bright had cracked – he must have done.

'You're out of your fucking mind,' he growled, 'and I'm not falling for anything as crazy as this.'

'The boy you have is not your nephew,' Mr Bright said, slowly and clearly. 'This situation was planned long before you were born – long before your parents ever met, even. Some among us had started to die. It was a concern, but they were few and the time between the deaths was very long. Also, none of them were First or Inner Cohort, so we thought perhaps it was a weakness in them rather than something that could touch us all. When the First suddenly began to grow older and weaker, however, we needed a plan: we could not lose our leader, and he had no intention of giving up his life, not after everything he had achieved. So I started to trace the bloodlines.' His eyes had narrowed and instead of looking at Cass, he browsed the events on the wall as he spoke.

'It was a long and arduous task, as you can imagine. There were a lot of false starts and dead ends, but eventually' – now he looked around and smiled at Cass – 'I found Evie and Alan and put them together. Their blood was almost pure, and their children? Well.' He shrugged. 'You know how powerfully you feel the *Glow*, Cassius.' He looked at Cass thoughtfully. 'I find myself wondering just how much *more* there is that you could tap into that you haven't accepted yet.'

'A body swap?' Brian Freeman stared at Mr Bright. 'It's like something out of a science-fiction film.'

'Science fiction is only ever fiction until someone achieves it. Look at everything around us that started as an idea in a book.' Mr Bright smiled. 'Your imaginations are so much brighter than *He* ever realised.'

'Who's "he"?' Dr Cornell asked. He had started pacing backwards and forwards, small shuffling steps, across a small patch of carpet. 'And what is on the datasticks?'

'Can we get back to Luke?' Cass snapped.

'*He* can wait for now,' Mr Bright said, ignoring Cass. 'The datasticks will answer every question you could possibly have about the First, myself, and perhaps more importantly, all of you. They are your *history* – the true history of the world.'

'So why can't we open it?'

'There are four. They all have to be inserted together to open.'

'These are the *scrolls*?' Dr Cornell's eyes had opened so widely he looked as if he was about to have a heart attack.

'The scrolls themselves are hidden in various locations around the world, places that are special to us. These are the modern version. The scrolls were scanned, of course, but on the four datasticks are stored the details of *everything* we have done here. Each member of the Inner Cohort wears one around his neck, and they are updated annually.' He turned to Cass. 'If you help me, I will give them all to you, and you can see *everything* – but you have to trust me. I have your nephew – he's trapped in an old man's body, and he's somewhere safe – for now at least. The others will be looking for him, just as they'll be looking for the boy. I'd rather Mr Dublin found him than the emissary, but something tells me she'll get there first.'

Cass' head whirled, and he thought of the woman with the red hair whose car he'd dived into as the bullet ripped through his shoulder. He remembered her voice on the phone – *The boy is the key. Don't let them keep the boy* – and the effect it had had on him. Was she the emissary he was talking about?

'We're going to run out of time,' Mr Vine muttered. Cass didn't like how afraid he looked.

'If what you say is true,' he said, 'then why are we suddenly on the same side? If you did all this for your First, or whatever you call him, why are you now so deep in the shit that you need our help?'

'It would appear that we've all become dispensable.' For once Mr Bright's eyes didn't twinkle as he spoke. 'It seems that a brush with death can bring out the worst in people.'

He looked back at the grainy pictures. 'And in some families, the worst can be very terrible indeed. But if it comes to it, then we will fight, you and I, Cassius Jones, we'll die side by side, whether you like it or not.'

'Why don't you call Luke,' Freeman said, 'and just check everything's all right?' The old gangster sniffed. 'Can't do any harm, can it? And I'll have a word with the boys, tell them to stay alert.' He handed Cass his mobile phone. 'Go ahead.'

Cass stared at the screen for a second and then punched in Father Michael's number. Why the hell was his heart racing so fast? Did he really believe what Bright had said? Could his nephew's body have been stolen? He thought of the *Glow* and Mr Solomon's death, and the sights he'd seen while strapped down on the bed, and he realised that maybe it wasn't that hard to believe after all. His stomach churned. The phone rang out in his ear, and with each second, his mouth dried further. At last he shook his head and handed the phone back. 'No answer.'

'I'll try Osborne.' Freeman said. 'That fucker has his phone glued to him.'

'He's gone,' Mr Bright said. His words were like a death knell in the silence. 'The emissary has found him.'

'How?' Cass was already reaching for the car keys as Brian Freeman frowned and redialled. 'How would she know where to go?'

'Was he sleeping much?'

'Yes.' Cass looked up. 'Why?'

'He was calling to her, using the old ways. It's probably why he's been so exhausted. He called her here from very far away.'

'There's no answer,' Freeman announced, 'from either of them.'

'I'm going back,' Cass said. 'I need to see what's happened.'

'There's no time,' Mr Bright said, his normal urbanity replaced with urgency. 'We need to find a man called Jarrod Pretorius – the First asked me about him when he woke. He's the key.'

'I'm going.' Adrenalin raced through Cass' veins and shook away the remains of his exhaustion. At least he had always thought of it as adrenalin. Maybe it had always been the *Glow*. 'It's an hour away if we push it,' he said to Mr Bright. 'I need to see what's happened. You can either stay here or come with me. It's up to you.'

'I'll get looking into this Pretorius,' Freeman said. He tossed Cass the mobile phone. 'I'll get my people on it. You stay in touch.' He looked at Mr Vine. 'And he can stay with me. As can that datastick.'

Mr Bright handed the silver stick over. 'So be it. But we'd better move fast. I hate to sound like a cliché, but for once the fate of the world really does hang in the balance.'

'There is no fate,' Cass muttered, and stepped back out into the crisp December air.

Chapter Thirty-Eight

Mr Dublin fought to keep his trembling hands under control as he reached for the ringing mobile phone. It had been thirty minutes since he'd realised how foolish he'd been in thinking that such simple methods as locks and torture could keep Mr Bright controlled, and since then, starting with the discovery of Mr Escobar's body, the situation had gone from bad to worse. The death of one of their own had shocked him, but he didn't have time to deal with it now; he'd left the corpse on the floor of the Experiment room where it had been found and locked the door. Mr Bright and Mr Vine were gone, and so was Cassius Jones. He had to keep this from the others for now, until he worked out how to put it right. He felt sick, nausea cramping his stomach – this was *fear*. Mr Bright's rage must have been very powerful indeed, for him to destroy Mr Escobar like that. Even in the great rebellion all that time ago very few of their kind had died. They were too strong.

Mr Bright's phone, taken from him during his capture, began ringing, and when Mr Dublin clicked to answer, the voice at the other end didn't even give him time to speak before releasing a stream of panic.

'They're not projecting the Rapture any more – they stopped an hour or so ago. Now it's Jarrod Pretorius – his face is everywhere, on all the screens. Does that mean *He's* not coming? Does that mean we'll survive? Or is Pretorius bringing it down on us?'

Mr Dublin waited for Mr DeVore to take a breath. 'What are you talking about? *What* projections?'

'Mr Dublin?' The panic was replaced by momentary uncertainty. 'I thought I'd called Mr Bright.'

'You did – this is his phone. *What* Rapture?' Mr Dublin asked.

'Didn't Mr Bright tell you? Didn't he tell you *He* was coming – that they've been projecting the end of the world? It's so terrible—'

'Send me the data streams,' Mr Dublin said. 'I want to see for myself.' He was pleased with the calm in his voice, despite his dry mouth, sweating palms and roiling stomach. 'I'll call you back when I've seen it.'

He ended the call, not wanting to have to answer any of Mr DeVore's questions. What was happening? What had he missed? What had Mr Bright held back from them?

He flipped open the laptop and waited for the file to arrive. As he watched, all else but the horror of the destruction in those silent images was forgotten for a moment. *He* was coming. That much was certain.

The morning's grey chill had never lifted and now, as Cass drove swiftly through the late afternoon traffic, not even the steady stream of headlights dispelled the gloom.

For a long time they sat in silence as Cass tried to process the information Mr Bright had shared while his heart was still pounding with worry for Luke and Father Michael – and even for the two heavies. He found he'd become fond of the Steves – they were straightforward, and honest in their own way: with them, what you saw was what you got, and there wasn't enough of that in Cass' life.

He glanced sideways at Mr Bright, who hadn't volunteered any conversation since they'd started their journey. He'd regained his composure and tidied his clothes, but Cass wondered if his quiet came from as great a need to regroup as his own. What had they done to him? He looked exhausted, not the relentless Machiavellian Mr Bright he'd come to know, always one step ahead of the game. In fact, the Mr Bright who had plagued Cass for the past year had always been *in control* of the game. Well, not any more: now he looked to be playing catch-up and surviving on his wits. Cass stared out at the road as he cut through the traffic to their exit. Mr Bright was down on his luck, so why didn't he feel better about that? Why did it disturb him so much?

'Why is my family so important?' Cass asked. 'If all you needed was one child, then why have you watched me all these years? Once you had the boy, why did you bother?'

Mr Bright had been so lost in his own reverie that when he looked around at Cass he appeared momentarily surprised to find himself in the car. He let out a long breath. 'I don't like to leave things to chance,' he said quietly. 'If something had gone wrong with the boy, we would have needed another, you or your brother, if it had come to it. I needed to know where you were – I needed to keep you safe.'

It was plausible, but it didn't ring true. 'When I was undercover, were you watching me then?'

'Of course,' Mr Bright said.

'Then why didn't you stop me from killing that kid?' The sentence sounded strange in his voice. He never talked *about* this; he talked *around* it – he and his wife Kate had talked around it for years.

'You weren't in any immediate danger.'

'How the hell do you know?'

A twitch of a smile played on Mr Bright's mouth: the old Mr Bright was fast coming back. 'Because someone else in the room that night would have shot Freeman before anyone hurt you.' His eyes twinkled. 'I told you, Cassius Jones, I've been looking out for you.'

Cass' head reeled again and the headlights of the on-coming traffic became the whites of a boy's terrified eyes as he stared down the barrel of a gun at them. He felt sick. The boy could have lived – Brian Freeman would have been dead, but Cass would have been spared all these years of guilt. How different would his life have been? Would he and Kate have still been married, or would they have gone their separate ways and gone on to be happy with other people? She'd still be alive, he was sure of that, and she wouldn't have had that destructive affair with Bowman. He'd pushed her into that with his endless coldness, always shutting her out.

He could barely breathe. He watched his hands, changing gear, turning the steering wheel, and they belonged to a stranger. His body was operating on autopilot, while the rest of him had been transported to the stinking back room of that snooker hall, where, in that single moment, the futures of so many lives hung in the balance while his sweaty, terrified finger sat on a trigger.

'You cunt,' he said eventually. 'You fucked up my life.'

'No, I didn't.' Mr Bright's voice was light, as if they were discussing pleasant weather on a sunny day. 'I *protected* it.' He looked over at Cass. 'You *chose* to shoot: you chose your life over the boy's. Your life is simply a sum of your choices, Cass, just like anyone else's.' He smiled. 'But if it's any con-solation, I did become more interested in you after that; I was glad that we hadn't taken you as a baby. I saw how you *struggled*, and it reminded me of my own struggles, I suppose.'

'This has always been more to you than just watching us – you've played too many games with me. You could have stayed hidden from me for ever, whoever you are, you've got that kind of power. So why didn't you?'

For a long moment, Mr Bright said nothing. His smile slipped into something wistful. 'I suppose I became affectionate towards you,' he said softly. 'I'd watched your family and seen you grow up so troubled, so reluctant to be who you really are. Even as a little boy, you were so determined, not wanting to see anything beyond this gritty earth.' He hesitated and for the first time in their acquaintance Cass thought he was struggling to find the right words. Was Mr Bright so used to talking in riddles he couldn't speak the plain truth?

'Our blood is so strong in you, Cassius Jones. I've seen it in others, of course, but not like with you. You're as close to family as we have here.'

'So was my father, and Christian – you didn't fuck around with Christian like you did with me.'

'I took his child. That was enough, wouldn't you say?' Mr Bright turned away. 'After that I made sure he had a good job, and prospects. I wanted him to be happy.'

'No.' Cass shook his head. 'That's *not* you. You took one child and gave him another; in your eyes I'm sure that was a fair swap.'

'Oh Cass, you think so badly of me. There are times when none of the choices presented can work perfectly. I hoped they'd have another child, or that Jessica would get pregnant during the time you were sleeping with her.' He winked at Cass, but the gesture didn't stop the words snagging Cass' heart like a barb. 'In fact, I will admit that I hoped for the latter somewhat more than the former. Still, I have a list of other eligible and appropriate ladies, so who knows? Perhaps in the future.'

Cass ignored his digression. 'It wasn't the same. You didn't fuck with Christian like you did with me. You didn't watch over him like you did with me or else Sam Macintyre wouldn't have been able to shoot them all.'

'No, I don't suppose I did,' Mr Bright finally agreed. 'But Christian wasn't like you. He saw the *Glow* – he loved it. He and Jessica both embraced the strangeness of it, the *other-worldliness*. Once I had the boy, I found them interesting, but that was about it. They had no anger, no passion. They didn't fight against anything.'

Yay! The boys see the Glow! One blond, one dark; one smiling, one frowning; one kind, one cruel: Cass and Christian, forever opposites.

'Not like you,' Mr Bright continued. 'I wanted to see what you were made of, all that anger and sense of injustice: I needed to know how much like us, like my old friend, you really were.'

'This is all because of my pissy attitude?'

'No, I think it was more because you didn't want the other-worldliness, even though it is so strong in you; you ignored it, refused to see it. You loved *this* world, and I, I suppose, loved you for that.'

Cass stared out at the road. The car was suddenly filled with the ghosts of his family, all pawns in this game of Mr Bright's. He was almost afraid to look in the rear-view mirror in case he saw Christian's bleeding eyes there, or his father's burned and tortured face. Of all the outcomes of this conversation, he hadn't expected affection to be at the bottom of everything.

'If this is how you treat the people you care about,' Cass

muttered, 'then I'd hate to see what you do to the people you hate.'

Mr Bright chuckled, a soft, humorous sound that invited company. Cass figured he could wait a lot longer if they were going to share a laugh together. There was far too much unfinished business between them.

'If what you said was true,' he said, 'and Luke isn't Luke but is this First, as you call him, then where is my nephew?'

'He's safe.'

'How could you have done that to him? A little boy?' The soft chuckle and the cruelty of that crazy act just didn't fit together. What was Bright, a psychopath? That wouldn't surprise Cass at all.

'I have had to do a lot of things that normal people would be ashamed of. After a while you learn not to think of them; instead you instead focus on the greater good.'

'*Whose* greater good?'

'That is the eternal question, isn't it? I like to think of it as the *global* greater good – both yours and ours, although sometimes it's more for one than the other, and although I would be lying if I said I ever put humanity's causes above our own – and I have *never* lied to you, Cassius – but I find that the two are often in tandem. What I did to Luke, however,' his voice softened, 'I did to save my friend's life. It was as simple as that. There were other benefits of course; he's our leader, but for me, I did it to save my friend's life.'

'It doesn't look like he's very grateful.'

'No.' Mr Bright turned away and looked out the window. 'But what's been done can be undone. And no one ever crosses me twice.'

They drove in silence for a while, only the bumps in the road and the throb of the engine punctuating their journey. Cass' head was still spinning, but he thought maybe it was whirling so fast that it was achieving some kind of stillness. Mr Bright was perhaps not the monster he'd believed all these years – could anyone ever be that bad? *No one ever crosses me twice.* Maybe they were more similar than Cass was ready to face. He couldn't deny that even with the story of Luke's body-swap he felt a strange comfort having Bright there, almost like a brother. Was that the Glow in him recognising one if its own? Is that what everything always came back to?

'He had no glow,' he said after about ten minutes. The words came almost out of nowhere. 'It's why I shot him. He had no glow.'

Mr Bright turned and stared at him. After a while he nodded as if what Cass had said had made perfect sense. He leaned forward and turned the radio on and Bing Crosby filled the car singing of chestnuts roasting on an open fire, and Cass' heart ached to enjoy it. He wondered if he'd ever get such simple enjoyment again – but had he ever? Memories of family Christmases flashed behind his eyes, his parents, his wife, Christian, Jessica and the Luke-who-wasn't-Luke, but he'd loved him anyway. His own laughter had always rung false, and he'd always felt a slight relief when the holiday was over and the world could settle back down to its uneasy discomfort.

'I love Christmas.' Mr Bright smiled. 'So many happy memories.'

Cass almost laughed aloud at the irony. The song faded and the news came on. Two minutes later, as the report finished, all thoughts of Christmas had been driven from Cass' head and his heart thumped, this time with a modicum of excitement. Ramsey had been thrown off his case for thinking he was innocent? And Hask's contract with the Met had been cancelled? They believed a powerful unknown man was being protected by both the government and the police? Suddenly Cass had allies. It made sense: he'd been in the hospital when Craven had died; he had seen the light under the door. Whatever Ramsey and Hask had seen in there, they knew it wasn't normal – none of this was normal, and so the idea of Cass being set up had stopped being so preposterous.

'Sounds like your friends are almost as dogged in their investigations as you are,' Mr Bright said with a wide smile. 'That's good. Why don't you call them? We need to know about this man called Jarrod Pretorius, where we can find him. He'll be in a facility somewhere – mathematics perhaps, science definitely.'

'Not yet,' Cass said. 'Not until I see what's happened at the house. If Luke is fine, then you're on your own with all of this.'

Mr Bright might have thought they'd bonded, but as far as Cass was concerned they were still standing on very different sides of the line. Mr Bright had taken Luke, and that was unforgivable. It had to be.

Chapter Thirty-Nine

C ass was still ringing the bell and banging on the front door when Mr Bright pulled his arm gently away and suggested they try the back door. 'You'll bring the whole village out if you keep making that much noise,' he added.

Without a word Cass turned away and jogged down the narrow pebbled path that ran alongside of the house. There was a waist-high wooden gate, only enough to stop a small child or a pet getting out, and as it swung open on well-oiled hinges Cass' heart ached. He could think of no reason why Father Michael wouldn't open the door, so someone must be stopping him. Or have stopped him.

He peered through the kitchen window, but the lights were off and all he could make out were a couple of mugs sitting on the table. His palms sweating, conscious of Mr Bright's cool presence just behind him, he twisted the handle. The back door was unlocked.

Inside the house, the heating was on and the warmth and the homely smell of cheese on toast came as a sharp contrast to the dread building in Cass' stomach. He flicked the hallway lights on. If there was anyone here, then they'd have heard Cass banging on the door; they'd have known he was intent on getting in and now they could fucking show themselves ... but his aggression was wasted. He had a terrible feeling that the house was empty.

'The emissary's obviously taken the boy.' Mr Bright was standing in the kitchen doorway. 'We might as well leave.'

'Father Michael?' Cass called up the stairs. 'Are you here?' He glared at Mr Bright before climbing the steps, taking them two at a time to the next floor. 'Steve? Wharton? Osborne?' No one answered.

'They must have taken all of t—'

But he stopped, mid-sentence, as the door to the second bedroom swung open, revealing the Steves in the corner as if they'd been flung there like discarded clothes. They were slumped sideways, their heads lolling unnaturally on broken necks. He didn't need to touch them to know they were dead; their cold, accusing eyes told him that.

'Jesus,' he whispered.

'We need to go,' Mr Bright said urgently. 'We need to find the boy.'

Cass didn't answer but turned, and with a heavy heart headed for the main bedroom. Maybe they'd taken Father Michael with them. Maybe Luke, or whoever he was, had realised he was just a kindly old man, and they'd just tied him up and left him somewhere. Maybe ...

'Don't go in there, Cassius,' Mr Bright said.

'Shut the fuck up,' Cass growled, glaring at the silver-haired man who was always so calm, so collected, and opened the door.

For a long moment he couldn't speak, couldn't even breathe, until eventually air rattled out of his lungs in something close to a wheeze. In his heart he had expected to find Father Michael dead – he'd hoped otherwise, of course, but ever since they'd arrived at the silent house he'd known. Neither Michael nor the Steves would have given up the child without a fight. And if the child – and as he stared at the terrible sight in front of him he found he could no longer think of the boy as Luke – had turned against them too, then they hadn't had much of a chance. He'd seen what Mr Solomon had turned into; he'd felt the power of the *Glow*. The three men he'd left guarding the boy wouldn't have known what was coming.

'Why?' he asked, when he could trust his voice. 'Why would they do this to him? He didn't hurt anyone – why not just break his neck like the others?'

Mr Bright moved next to him and they stood in the gloom looking up at the destroyed body hanging from the wall.

'Because of his faith, I should imagine,' Mr Bright said quietly. 'The First will want to distance himself from his complicity in everything we created.' He tilted his head sideways thoughtfully. 'He knows that cruelty and punishment always go down well with *him*.'

'I am *so* sorry,' Cass said to the naked man nailed to the walls. Rusty spikes had been driven through his palms and forearms, and picture hooks hammered into his forehead created a mockery of a crown of thorns.

Cass carefully pulled the masking tape from the old man's mouth. It was cold. No breath had warmed it for some time.

'You shouldn't touch him,' Mr Bright said. 'You're in enough trouble as it is.'

'I don't care. I don't care what happens to me after all this,' Cass muttered. 'As long as my nephew is safe they can have me.' He was tired of running; he was tired of being the pawn in games he never even knew he'd been playing. And he was tired of the people around him getting hurt because of their involvement with him. Not that there was anyone left, he realised with a wave of sadness. Everyone he'd ever loved was dead. Armstrong had been right: he was a curse.

324

'This will be no consolation to you,' Mr Bright said, 'but judging by what they did to his stomach, I would say that your friend did not give up his faith. For what such a belief is worth.'

The cut ran down from Father Michael's chest to his pelvis and from within, his intestines had been pulled out and allowed to slop onto the carpet: an old-fashioned dis-embowelling.

Cass left Mr Bright staring up at the crucified man. He was either going to be sick or faint, and neither was accept-able. Instead he forced his anger to overpower his shock and stumbled down the stairs to the kitchen, where he splashed cold water onto his overheating face and then went into the garden. He didn't want to breathe the air in that house any longer.

He lit a cigarette, and after two or three steadying puffs he took out the mobile phone and punched in Ramsey's number. During his first few weeks of recovery, when he'd been bed-bound and bored silly, he'd occupied himself memorising telephone numbers – Perry Jordan, Father Michael, Charles Ramsey, the few people he trusted. He'd thought one day they might come in handy. He hadn't wanted to be right this way.

A dark shadow passed across the kitchen window and as the phone rang out, Cass thought that pretty much summed up Mr Bright: a dark shadow, a *something* but *nothing* as well, a something that made you uneasy.

'Ramsey?'

The DI answered so quickly that for a moment Cass couldn't speak. His heart flipped. 'If you're tracing this call, then I'm going to find you and fucking kill you.'

It was Ramsey's turn to be silent for a second. 'Cass?'

'Is that shit about you getting suspended true?'

'Yes, Hask and I think there's more to all this. This Mr Bright—'

'I'm with him now.' Mr Bright watched him from the doorway and Cass turned his back.

'You're what?' Ramsey exclaimed. 'What the hell is—?'

'I can't explain everything now, but you need to trust me. I need to know where someone is: a man called Jarrod Pretorius. You might have to go to David Fletcher at ATD for this one. You still talking to him?'

'Yeah, he's as intrigued by your friend Mr Bright as we are. He didn't get fired, though.'

'That's a good thing. We need him.'

'Can you tell me anything else?' Ramsey asked. 'He's going to want more than just a name.'

'All I can say is that we need to find him fast. There could be catastrophic consequences if we don't.'

'What kind of consequences?'

'A terrorist attack – something huge. I'm talking end of the world kind of shit.' It wasn't a lie; whatever was coming was surely bringing terror with it. The bright colours of Chaos flashed behind his eyes and the trumpets sang in his head. There was an army out there somewhere, though his brain might not want to accept it, but he'd *seen* it. He couldn't fight that. 'We think he'll be working in some kind of scientific facility, probably government.'

'I'll call him. Keep your phone on.'

'Thanks.'

'And Cass—' He paused, and then said, 'Take care.'

'Thanks, Ramsey. I intend to.'

Chapter Forty

Mr Dublin was not a chain-smoker, but he lit his third cigarette as the Interventionists' projections played over and over on his computer. He froze the image of Jarrod Pretorius and stared. Jarrod Pretorius had loved the First, and he had loved the emissary who'd chosen a different side. He had always been quiet, and a touch strange; he'd never been a talker. Was that why they'd forgotten about him? Even Mr Bright had let him slip off to live anonymously, with no sector to manage, no reports to file – so when exactly had Pretorius disappeared? It was so long ago he couldn't remember ... Looking at the face on the screen, Mr Dublin wondered whether Jarrod Pretorius had ever actually chosen a side, or if he had just followed his best – his *only* – friend into battle. That was what he remembered the most about Pretorius: he was loyal, and he saw things in black and white. If you charged Jarrod Pretorius with a task, then he would do it, no matter now long it took. Had he chosen to go out into the wilderness, or had the First asked him to?

Mr Dublin sighed. His memories of the early days were so vague now; he'd been small too long. Sometimes he wondered if he was becoming more like *them* than one of his own. One day Jarrod Pretorius simply hadn't been there, and in the main, no one had cared. Those were the glory days, when their *Glow* was bright, and even Mr Bright and the First had seemed undisturbed by his leaving – but then, Mr Bright had always known that Pretorius was different. Pretorius had adored the First, although Mr Dublin was sure the First saw the strange youngster as some kind of pet rather than a friend.

And now it would appear that Jarrod Pretorius had been summoned back from the wilderness – by whom? And why?

His coffee was cold, but he drank it anyway, to soothe the dryness in his throat from the cigarettes. There were only two people who could control Jarrod Pretorius: Mr Bright and the First. Mr Bright had enlisted Mr Vine's help and now he was out there somewhere with Cassius Jones. As for the First, he was just a gibbering old man crying into his pillow somewhere. What could he do?

He thought of the day they'd stood by the bed, watching as he'd awakened. He'd been shocked, as had the late Mr Craven, and more than a little afraid. He sank into the memory, reliving it: had Mr Bright been as revolted? Mr Bright, the First's right-hand man: surely even he should had more of a reaction? Especially as the loss of the First could only impact badly on his own position ... No, Mr Dublin concluded, Mr Bright hadn't reacted, he had stayed calm ... it had been almost as if he had expected it.

Mr Dublin's brain raced: there was a bigger picture that he was missing. There was something about that wreck of an old man that Mr Bright had not shared with them – something that had clearly backfired on him, because he'd been ousted from his position and was now on the run, with Armageddon about to rain down upon them. *He* was coming – and only one person could have called *him*.

Him, the First, Mr Bright, Mr Solomon, Mr Bellew and Mr Dublin himself: this was the cast of characters who made up so much of their story. And as the figures danced in his mind, a cold realisation dawned on Mr Dublin: if he had to choose one of their own to trust in a crisis – someone he trusted to do the best for them and this world – then it would have to be Mr Bright. It had *always* been Mr Bright, the Architect.

Mr Dublin started cursing himself, for becoming side-tracked by fear, not just the others', but his too, and for losing sight of the wood for the trees. Mr Bright would die for this world – it was probably the only thing he would die for. If *he* was coming, then Mr Bright had been double-crossed.

He picked up the phone. 'I need to know the whereabouts of a man called Jarrod Pretorius. Fast.' He looked again at the screen. If the First was in England, then Pretorius would be as well. 'Check government records. He'll be working for one of the agencies.'

He hung up. A moment later, he lit his fourth cigarette and started making calls. It was time for them all to be on the same side.

'What do you mean, there's some kind of deep-space inter-ference?' David Fletcher asked.

The technogeek – Fletcher couldn't remember his name; he viewed most of the staff on this level more as one incom-prehensibly bright hive-mind – shrugged nervously. 'We're not sure,' he admitted. 'Whatever it is, we're not getting accurate data through from the satellites – *any* satellites, actually, not ours, nor any other country's. Whatever it is, it's a global phenomenon.'

'Something's knocking out all the satellites? What is it, some kind of meteor storm?' The call from Ramsey ten minutes previously had started small alarm bells ringing in his head, and now they were getting louder. For once he was actively interested in all the science stuff. He'd feigned disinterest in the DI's call – the last thing he needed was to get caught up in Cass Jones' antics – but Ramsey had warned him there would be some kind of massive terrorist event, and a few minutes later all hell had broken loose on the monitoring floor ... how exactly could that be a coincidence?

'We're not sure exactly what it is,' the technogeek said. 'Perhaps it's that.'

'You don't sound confident.'

'I'm not.' The man was sweating slightly. 'I've trained for years. I've got an IQ of 155 and I'm considered brilliant by other brilliant men. But even I don't understand exactly how SkyCall 1 works.'

'If all the satellites aren't working, then neither will SkyCall. Surely its function is to collect data from the other satellites?'

The scientist shook his head, a brief irritated action, as if he was talking to a child who wasn't listening properly, and slowed his speech in a way Fletcher found deeply annoying. 'You are misunderstanding what it is I am telling you. It's not that the satellites aren't working, exactly. We started picking up some strange deep-space activity, and that was when the satellites started to stop transmitting their usual information. In the past few minutes, the satellite TV signal in the United States stopped working. Ours should be gone shortly, if the satellites are going down in the same order that they started to malfunction. It'll be on the news soon. We'll say it's some kind of space-storm issue, that'll stall them for a while, but that isn't what's really happening.' He paused, looking very uncomfortable. 'The satellites aren't malfunctioning; all their systems are fine. They're just stopping their normal activities and then turning out-wards – towards space. It's as if—' He hesitated, and Fletcher wondered why he was looking so nervous. After a moment, the scientist said a little shakily, 'It's as if they're all waiting to start a new command program. *All* of them.'

'But that can't be,' Fletcher said, frowning. 'These sat-ellites, surely they all belong to different countries? And they all have different operating systems – they're not linked. So how can they be functioning as one unit?'

'But they *are* linked now,' the scientist said. '*We* linked them with SkyCall 1.'

'You think SkyCall is doing this?' He tried not to let his fear sound in his voice, but he wasn't doing a great job.

'I don't know!' The man's voice had dropped to a harsh whisper. 'I didn't program the virus it uploaded – *he* did –I didn't even understand it properly. What if—' He stopped and peered around him, to make sure they were not being overheard, then continued, 'What if there was a secondary virus under it? And we don't know what it does?'

Fletcher stood silently for a second, letting the techno-geek's words sink in, before turning and heading out into the quiet corridor.

He flipped open his phone and called the last number listed.

'Ramsey?' he said, when the voice answered, 'I don't have a Jarrod Pretorius, but I do have a Jed Praetorian. He might not be your man, but the names are close and my gut is saying yes. He's at the Harwell Institute, the Science and Innovation facility. We've tried to call him back here, because there're some problems with a satellite program he installed for us, but thus far we haven't got hold of him.' He paused. 'Tell Jones. And then pick me up on the way.'

Chapter Forty-One

T he old man's recovery had been short-lived, and they'd
had to stop twice on their journey as he coughed up
clumps of bloody matter and vomited loudly and violently
into dirty service station toilets. Gabbi stroked his thin hair
and spoke soothingly to him, but there was no doubt that
he was dying. The First was getting more impatient at every
stop; although he claimed it was simply his eagerness to get
them all home, she could sense his irritation and it made
her sad.

The old man had been so excited to see his friend again,
but it felt like that excitement was only one way. Perhaps it
would be different when they were home; perhaps the First
would be more relaxed, more like himself. She couldn't
quite adjust to seeing him in this strange child's body –
maybe that was affecting her judgement? He had been happy
when they'd arrived at the poor priest's house, and as she
dispatched the two men so ineptly guarding him he had
giggled and smiled and called them the *Angel Gabriel* and
the *Holy Ghost*, and that had made him laugh more, and
hug them tightly.

Then he'd told them what he wanted to do to the priest,
and all the laughing had stopped. When it was done, they
had washed and left, and she had avoided his eyes, as had the
old man. It had been so unnecessarily cruel. She wondered

when he'd become cruel – or had it always been there and they just hadn't noticed?

Beside her the First was sweating, his skin shining with damp, and she worried that he was stretching himself too far, especially given his recent weakened state. Where was he getting his strength from, the old man? It felt too much of a coincidence, that the old man was fading so fast while the First was getting stronger.

She quelled the thought as she turned the car through the gates of the Science and Innovation facility. There was a guard, but he appeared to be asleep, and the barrier was raised – so no wonder the First was sweating; it had probably been a long time since he'd used any of the skills that belonged to his natural body. This atmosphere made it harder as well – she knew that from the experience of calling for him in the old ways.

Jarrod Pretorius was waiting for them outside the small building that was his research unit, just past the shining metal and glass structure that housed the rest of the Harwell Institute. Her heart thumped: despite his changed form, she would have recognised him anywhere, just from his *Glow*, which had always been different, not gold, nor silver, but a strange muted silvery-purple. She had always been drawn to him, though so many others had been driven away by whatever it was that was so unusual about him. She liked his quiet; it was peaceful, and she could see beyond it to the strong heart and fearless loyalty.

It took all her will not to run to him, but instead to help the old man from the back seat first.

When they were finally face to face, his eyes rested on her for only a moment before turning to the First, and that broke her heart. She wondered if he even recognised her.

'I've been alone for such a long time,' he said softly. 'I waited, just like you told me too. I hid and I concentrated and I kept them locked in my head for such a long time. It was too much – it hurt – but I did it, until I could put the locks somewhere else.'

He had been damaged, Gabbi could see that; it was in his eyes. What exactly had the First made him do – how far had he pushed the loyalty of his gentle, puppy-dog friend?

'Are the Walkways opening? Have you unlocked them?' Even in his child's voice, the First's words were cold.

'I need to start the final sequence,' Pretorius said.

'Then let's go and do it.' The First smiled as more sweat dripped from his dark hair. 'There's only so long I can keep this place subdued. It's hurting me.' He strode ahead through the doors, and the old man limped along at his side.

'That family have always been so very selfish,' she said softly as she slipped her hand into his. The words were treason, but Pretorius had never repeated anything he'd heard; it was why he was so well used, she supposed. The First, who was more powerful than most by birth, had been concentrating for an hour or so at most. The old man was dying from the effort of finding him, and Pretorius had spent millennia keeping the universe locked in a riddle – and that had taken so much from him that he'd had to hide away in the quiet. They inspired so much loyalty, but beneath the surface charm they were cruel, and unutterably selfish.

Beside her, Jarrod Pretorius had started to cry. She stood on tiptoe and kissed him, and then led him inside. Whether for one or the other, she and he had vowed to serve that family. It was time to see their vows through.

*

'What the hell?' The man on the gate was asleep and the barrier was up. Cass had worried about getting access; he certainly hadn't expected it to be this easy.

'The First,' Mr Bright said, 'flexing his muscles.'

Cass didn't ask; he didn't want to know. He'd put his grieving for Father Michael to one side for now – the only way to honour that man was to find the people who'd killed him and deal with them, and to make sure that Christian's true son was safe. Part of him believed Bright's story must be crazy; that the little boy he'd stolen was really Luke, but that he'd become the focus of some ridiculous delusion of the Network's – but another, *deeper* part of him, the part who had seen the Chaos in the Experiment, who felt the *Glow*, that part of him was starting to believe, and what frightened him most about that was that it also meant that he was starting to accept the truth of the other things he'd fought so long against – the *Glow*, the Network, what Mr Bright and his colleagues really were – and how they resonated inside him. He closed that thought down and drove slowly past the main building. Ramsey, Hask and Fletcher would be on their way. *They* belonged in the real world – *his* world, the gritty, brutal world of murder and robbery and too-short lives. He belonged beside them, not standing with Mr Bright. He wondered what he'd dragged them into. He also wondered whom he was trying to convince.

'The whole place is asleep,' he muttered.

'There!' Mr Bright's finger shot up, pointing to a small building a couple of hundred feet away. Two figures were just disappearing inside.

Cass drove as close as he could get, his heart pounding, then started to climb out of the car.

'Wait!' Mr Bright caught his arm to stop him and pulled a gun from inside his coat. 'I have my own methods of defence, but you are not yet ready for those. We don't die easily – you know that now – but bullets will slow us down.'

'Where did you get it?' Cass released the safety, feeling better already.

'I took it from one of the two dead men while you went outside to call Ramsey.'

Cass wasn't sure what to say; he was glad Mr Bright had had the foresight to take the gun, but it hinted at a coldness that he couldn't trust. Perhaps it wasn't coldness, though. Maybe it was just that for a long time Mr Bright had been forced to think of every eventuality.

Rotor blades cut through the quiet and both men looked up.

'Who the fuck is that?' Cass shouted, watching the Bell JetRanger. The helicopter was approaching fast, and it was definitely coming down to land, and pretty much right where they were standing. Cass looked back at the door. 'Fuck it, let's get inside. Friend or foe, they can find us in there. We'll lose the others.'

Mr Bright was already ahead of him, and as Cass raced after him, he had a moment to admire how light on his feet the apparently middle-aged man was.

Two men were slumped over the reception desk, and Cass was relieved to find them both unconscious, not dead. After what had happened to Father Michael and the Steves he was expecting a trail of eviscerated bodies.

Mr Bright focused on the various security screens the CCTV cameras were feeling to the reception monitor, his eyes darting from one to the other until figures came into view. 'Downstairs,' he said. 'Lower ground.'

'And what's your plan, again?' Cass asked.

'Stop them.'

'I was hoping for a little more detail.'

'Sometimes, Cassius Jones,' Mr Bright said with a twinkle, 'even I just have to wing it, as they say.'

'I thought you might want a little help.' A shadow fell across the doorway.

'Mr Dublin,' Mr Bright said. 'This is a surprise.'

Cass automatically raised his gun: this was the fucker who had strapped him into that machine, the bastard who had almost stranded him in the Chaos. He could still feel that stuff sticking to him in the cold, and hear the screams of the lost . . . And he had so very nearly been one of them—

Mr Bright's hand gently pushed the nose of the gun down.

'Let's put our differences aside for the moment, shall we, gentlemen?' Mr Bright said with a smile. 'For my part, Mr Dublin, I am very pleased to see you.'

Cass said nothing, but turned and jogged towards the stairs.

Chapter Forty-Two

'Can't you go any faster?' Fletcher asked, punching more numbers into his mobile and tapping his foot impatiently.

'Not if you want us to get there alive,' Ramsey said, never taking his eyes off the road. The siren was wailing on the roof and he was going as fast as he could down the winding country roads. The motorway part of the journey had been fine – everyone got out of the way for a police car on a dual carriageway – but first they'd had to get out of London's endlessly gridlocked traffic, and now they were having to negotiate narrow lanes and farm vehicles with no sense of urgency. Ramsey could understand Fletcher's frustration; hell, he was feeling it himself, but he couldn't risk killing them, let alone any random strangers. He was a London policeman and he normally had a sergeant driving for him. His high-speed didn't get much practice.

'I still can't get hold of Pretorius, and all the receptionists at Harwell are on answerphone, saying lines are busy. Jones isn't answering either. Jesus fucking Christ, what the hell is going on there?'

'We'll find out soon enough,' Ramsey said, 'look, we're nearly there. Just another six miles or so. Couldn't you have got your people out there? Surely they could have helicopter'd in and be dealing with it by now?'

'I don't know what kind of power you think I have,' Fletcher flipped his phone shut and tossed it, disgusted, onto the dashboard, 'but I think commanding that kind of manpower on the say-so of a suspected murderer and a policeman just thrown off a case would be likely to get me fired too.' He sighed and looked out the window. 'And if Pretorius is a terrorist of some kind then there's a good chance someone in the ATD or the team he's been working with at Harwell is a traitor. I can't believe he's working alone, and I don't want him warned off so he's gone before we get there.'

'Cass and this Castor Bright are there.' Hask leaned his large bulk through the gap between the front seats. 'If Jones isn't answering his phone then I'm going to presume it's because he's too busy dealing with this situation to chat. And as for this Mr Bright . . . well, if he's half as Machiavellian as we think he is, we can probably rest assured that he's not the kind of man to rush into certain death without a well-thought-out plan.' He smiled. 'Let's not rule them out quite yet, shall we?'

The small room filled with computer equipment was hot, even though a fan whirred away somewhere. Lights twinkled on various panels and the air was almost humming with electricity. Gabbi eased the old man into a chair and waited for his coughing fit to end. Bright blood splattered the carpet, and he sighed as he wiped his mouth clean for the hundredth time that afternoon.

'There's no lock on the door?' the First asked as Pretorius settled in behind one of the many consoles.

'No one else knows how to use this equipment,' he said haltingly. 'They think it's some kind of maths experiment.' His voice sounded as if he hadn't had a proper conversation in a long time. 'Locks make people curious,' he continued. 'Everyone wants to know what happens in locked rooms.' His voice was different here, but it was still a deadened monotone, as if Pretorius couldn't quite release any of the emotion inside, even in the lilt of his words. 'Even at home.' His fingers tapped the keyboard and numbers flashed across a screen just above his head. 'I learned that from my father, a long time ago.' He glanced up. 'Two of the other rooms are locked. Not this one.'

'Clever.' The First granted him a small smile and then nodded at the keyboard. 'Is that it? Have you done it?'

'Not yet. It takes time. There are four sets of codes to enter and they need two minutes between each to allow the signal to function and the paths to open.'

'Why didn't you start it already? Why were you waiting for us outside?' The venom in the boy's voice was clear, but Pretorius didn't appear to notice it. He frowned slightly, as if confused. 'I needed to be sure it was you. You told me that one day someone might try and trick me. I had to see you to know.'

As much as she wanted to get home quickly, Gabbi smiled. Pretorius had always been so literal: the First had commanded his loyalty, and he'd followed his instructions to the letter, even though it had now slowed them down.

'You know it's me now,' the First said coldly, 'so get on with it.'

The old man burst into another hacking cough, and as much as she loved Jarrod Pretorius, a part of her wished that he was more like the rest of them and had just started the sequence earlier. When the old man's breathing was back to somewhere near the steady wet rattle which was the best he could manage, she left him and joined the boy and Pretorius at the console.

'Something's happening,' she said after the second number sequence appeared on the screen. 'I can feel it.' It was true, when she opened her mind to look for a way out, she could see white light in the darkness: the first shining paths. 'They're opening!'

Chapter Forty-Three

The door was open a crack, and they approached quietly, their footsteps muffled by the industrial carpet that lined the corridors. Cass wiped his sweaty palm against his thigh, then tightened his grip on the gun. At least there was no one keeping watch. They had that advantage.

Mr Bright gestured for Mr Dublin to stay outside, and then stared at Cass. This was it. Mr Bright slowly pushed open the door and stepped inside.

An old man was sitting in an office chair, his laboured breathing the loudest sound in the room. There was blood on his shirt and the dark, toothless hole of his mouth stood out against his pale skin. It took Cass a moment to recognise him as the violin-playing tramp of only a few months ago. He was so close to death that his body was mocking him with its corpse-like appearance. His smile was lost, and no music danced from him.

'I knew *He* would send you two,' Mr Bright said quietly, 'and part of me is sorry. I am fond of you.'

The three figures around the console had been so lost in what they were doing that they jumped at Mr Bright's voice. The sight told Cass all he needed to know. Luke – no, not Luke but *the First* – was peering intently over one shoulder of the seated man who had to be Jarrod Pretorius. When he turned to face them, his eyes flared with anger. They were old eyes, and any pretence of naïveté was long gone.

'Keep working,' he said, the child's voice a chilling contrast with his commanding tone.

'You disappeared,' Mr Bright said. His eyes were fixed on the man at the desk who had stopped typing, despite the First's insistence. Jarrod Pretorius was staring at Mr Bright, his dark eyes wide. 'Is this what you've been doing all this time?' Mr Bright continued. 'Keeping the Walkways closed?'

Pretorius nodded slowly. His eyes were full of trepidation, and something else – something Cass couldn't quite figure out. And then he got it: Jarrod Pretorius looked like a child who thought he was about to be told off. Could he be—?

'Oh, my son,' Mr Bright said sadly. 'I wish you'd talked to me. Why?'

'He asked me to,' Pretorius said. His voice was rough, and he spoke with a strong South African accent. 'He's my friend.' He rubbed his head with one hand. 'I had to go somewhere alone, to concentrate.'

'For all that time?'

'Do the next sequence,' the First cut in, and Jarrod Pretorius returned his attention to the keyboard. Cass stared at him. *This* was Mr Bright's son? How long had they been separated? He looked up at the girl on the other side of the First. He remembered her red hair, and he remembered the sound of her voice on the telephone. *The boy is the key*. Her hand rested on Pretorius' shoulder and her eyes kept flicking upwards to the ceiling. Her face shone with expectation and excitement. Whatever was happening, they didn't have much time to stop it – but Mr Bright was behaving as if they had all the time in the world.

'Why?' he asked.

'Believe it or not, I did it to protect us,' the boy said. 'After we started all this, after we got settled, an emissary came –

343

I never told you. *He* was angry; *He* wanted me to apologise and go home. As if I was still a child.' He laughed a little at the memory. 'I told her I'd think about it, and then I spoke to Pretorius. He said he could lock the Walkways back from here, but he couldn't do both routes.' He leaned back and crossed his arms. It was a manly pose, relaxed and easy; it looked wrong on the nine-year-old boy's body.

'I decided to close the return – not just close it, but booby-trap it so that anyone on the other side would hear the suffering of those stuck in the Chaos. It was the safest option – it meant that none of our number would be able to run back with tales of what we had achieved in the hope that *he* would somehow reward them. And *He* would know that anyone who came here would not be able to get back. It kept us safe from *Him*. *He* wouldn't send the army, not with no way out.'

'Why didn't you tell me?' Mr Bright said. He hadn't moved from his position by the door but from the corner of his eyes, Cass could see Mr Dublin just beyond him. The blond man's eyes were starting to *Glow*.

'Honestly? I didn't want to worry you. You were working so hard – building everything – organising our new society; this was something I could take care of. Afterwards, of course, when I realised the toll it was taking on your son, I decided that perhaps it was a secret I should keep to myself.' His eyes narrowed slightly. 'I think perhaps Mr Solomon suspected something, but he never asked. He was a loyal friend to both of us.'

'And now you're going to sacrifice us to *him* – after everything we did together, how we fought with you.'

The boy sighed. 'I'm sorry. I'm tired. I just want to go home.'

'Running back to Daddy?' For the first time, Cass heard

344

the stinging contempt in Mr Bright's voice. 'You do know what he's planning? You know what he'll do to the rest of us – those who aren't killed in the battle – and there *will* be a battle, even if we know we can't possibly fight the destruction *He's* bringing. *They* will all die, all of them, and we will die beside them. All this will be finished.' He gestured around him. 'And all because *you're tired and you want to go home?*'

'You weren't stuck in that old body for all those years,' the boy hissed. 'You weren't *dying!*'

Mr Bright laughed aloud. 'And you're not in the old body now, are you? I took care of that, just as we planned.'

'I was *afraid*,' the First said. 'I won't feel that way again.'

'I don't want you to fight,' Jarrod Pretorius said. He looked up. There was something strange about him, Cass thought. Was he autistic, was that it? 'I don't like it. I didn't like the fighting before.'

'Just finish the sequence and there'll be no more fighting.' The boy spoke to the man as if the man were the child.

Cass' head was spinning. Something *was* happening. The part of him who had travelled so far in the Experiment could feel it. The echo of trumpets was getting louder.

'One more,' Pretorius said softly. 'Nearly done.'

Cass looked from Mr Bright to the First and back again. Did Mr Bright really think they could *talk* their way out of this situation? Was he that stupid? And the answer came back at him immediately: no. No, he wasn't. He was keeping the First occupied with chatter, to the point that everyone else in the room was completely ignoring Cass. He wasn't one of them, after all, and definitely not in the First's eyes. He was so concerned with the wood, he couldn't see the trees.

The gun was gripped firmly in his hand and he raised it

suddenly. He might not be able to hurt them too much, but there was one thing he could do. Before the girl or the child had time to gasp out a warning, he fired two shots into the console, nearly taking off Pretorius' hands.

'*Nooooooo!*' the First shrieked as he stared at the ruined machinery, and his eyes burst into golden life. Pretorius had curled up in his chair, his hands clamped over his ears, the moment the shots had cracked through the room and the girl had jumped backwards. 'Do it from your mind!' the First shouted, pulling Pretorius' hands away from his ears. 'You kept it in your head all this time – you must know how! You *must*!'

Cass stared at the brightness in the boy's eyes as he started to change, to *become*. It was far more than anything he'd seen before; neither Mr Bright nor Mr Solomon had produced such blinding mix of gold and silver. And now Cass felt his own anger burning inside and there was heat running up his spine, and as Mr Dublin joined the fray and the world tilted once more, Cass raised the gun again. 'Sorry, Luke,' he muttered, and he fired again.

In the brightness that filled the room, Cass saw the bullet hit the child in the shoulder. The boy twisted awkwardly sideways and howled, but it didn't take him down. The old man was out of his chair and by the boy's side in a second.

'Try them!' the boy screamed. 'Try the Walkways!'

The beating of wings pushed Cass back against the wall and knocked the air from his lungs, but he stayed upright. The boy was changing and Mr Dublin – whatever Mr Dublin had become – was going to fight him. The room was too small for so much Glow. Cass' mouth dropped open.

'No, no, no, no!' Jarrod Pretorius' mouth moved as he stayed curled up in his chair, and although Cass could read his lips,

the sound was lost in the rush of air and heat and the beating of terrible wings. The thing that had been Mr Bright – the thing that was somehow still Mr Bright and yet not, all fire and wings and light, covered the chair, enveloping his son. Why didn't Pretorius change? Had he forgotten how?

Cass' own eyes burned and his heart thumped in time with the wings – his own wings. His skin itched and tingled and he wanted to tear it off and set free whatever was in his blood—

Two figures met in the middle of the room and their clash, like an underwater explosion, made Cass' ears scream.

Unable to stare into the nuclear flash that was the First and Mr Dublin (how was he so bright, so silver and gold and all the shades in between? How was he matching the First?) and unable to peel himself from the wall, Cass watched the two remaining figures. The old man's head was turned upwards, and his body was glittering and shaking. The girl was shouting something and tugging at him, but her words were to no avail. For a moment, a beatific smile spread across his face and his wrinkles fell away from him. His body filled out, reinvigorated, and his hair thickened. Even as he lost himself in the golden haze, Cass' heart chilled. Had the Walkways opened? Was this the end? The old man looked at the ceiling, and Cass was sure he heard him laughing, trumpet song in the sound, beautiful amidst the terrible throbbing wind from so many wings. But the laugh didn't last; the silver glittering across his skin turned to black, an empty black, the colour of the darkness before the Chaos, and suddenly the old man began frantically twisting. His eyes widened and he began to scream, a most terrible scream, as if music itself were dying, and these were its last throes. After what could only have been seconds, but felt like an eternity, he slumped in the chair and began to claw at his eyes. The girl tried to grab his hands, but he kept pulling them away and starting again.

347

From within the swirling mass battling in the air came tearing and slashing, and cries of rage and pain. Then the two figures broke apart as one was flung into the corner of the ceiling. Cass saw ice at its core and in its eyes, and across its wings. It was Mr Dublin. Cass had no doubt.

He looked over, squinting despite his own Glow at the other, the First. He gathered himself and with all his energy and will he fought the pressure that held him in place until his arm was free. He raised the gun again. Mr Bright had better be right: they'd better not die easily. He fired into the light and it roared and dimmed and Mr Dublin moved as fast as thought and dragged it, screeching, to the floor, slashing at it with claws of diamond ice. After a moment, the air stilled. The fight was over.

Black stars filled Cass' sight and his legs were so weak they almost collapsed under him. He blinked, pushing away from the wall. The girl sobbed beside the old man in the chair, stroking the bloody mess of his face, the holes where his eyes had been ripped out. Cass stumbled forward, his ears numbed and aching, and crouched beside the boy lying on the carpet. A small pool of blood was forming underneath him, from both the initial wound in his shoulder and the second shot that had grazed his side.

'I can't move,' the boy muttered. 'Why can't I move?' Even knowing that it wasn't Luke, not really, Cass' heart ached.

'You'll be all right,' he said. His voice was rough, dried out by the unnatural wind. He hoped he'd understood Mr Bright. He looked around at Mr Dublin, who was lying a few feet away. The slim man had lost weight in the fight. His clothes hung off him and his pale skin was streaked with blue where the veins beneath pressed against the surface. He breathed in rapid pants.

'Why can't he move?' Cass asked.

'He's restrained,' Mr Dublin whispered, fighting for air.

A well-manicured hand pushed the ash-blond hair from the man's face, and Cass looked up to see Mr Bright crouching on the other side.

'How did you do that, old friend?' he asked. 'You were so *strong*.'

'Old skills.' Mr Dublin tried to smile, and flinched with the effort. 'DeVore showed me the Projections and I sent the file to all the cohorts. It was a war cry. They joined with me to fight through me.' He sighed, and his gaze turned away from Mr Bright to the ceiling. 'It was good to use the old ways – to *become*. But it was better to feel we were united again, standing together.' His eyes flicked back to Mr Bright and his smile was full of joy. 'It reminded us all of why we are here. It's a good feeling, Mr Bright.' His slim hand rose up and Mr Bright took it. 'You should have told us,' Mr Dublin said. 'We would have stood with you.'

'I'm sorry.' Mr Bright smiled softly and squeezed Mr Dublin's hand. 'Perhaps I had forgotten our united honour. There have been so many betrayals of late; we have been dog-faced, constantly snarling at each other like wolves, not gods at all, and somehow we lost our way.

'And now I have betrayed all who stood together. I have just become so used to standing apart.'

'You have always served us all well, Mr Bright. *We* should have trusted *you*.' He coughed and a trickle of golden *Glow* leaked from his blue eyes. '*I* should have trusted you. But all is well that ends well.' He paused to catch his breath. 'I think I will end here. This is a good end.'

'Why?' Mr Bright frowned. 'If you have the cohort with you, how can you be ailing like this? Surely their strength will mend you?'

Mr Dublin looked at the boy. 'They're not with me, they're subduing the First. They'll hold him until you do what needs to be done.'

Cass looked over his shoulder at the First, twitching as he fought against his invisible restraints. The pool of blood beneath him hadn't got any bigger, and the graze at his side was healing as Cass watched.

'When I die, I will destroy this place.' Mr Dublin's voice was weakening. 'Going out in a blaze of glory, eh?'

'You will sleep well, and the stars will shine brighter for having you among them.' Mr Bright leaned forward and carefully removed the chain that hung around the slim neck. There were two small silver datasticks hanging from it. 'My life, however,' Mr Bright added, 'will be a little darker for your absence.'

'So we're not going back?'

Cass had almost forgotten Jarrod Pretorius. Mr Bright got to his feet and turned to face his son. He stroked the young man's face with a gentleness Cass hadn't known was within him.

'No, we're not going back – no one is. *This* is home now.' He leaned forward and kissed Pretorius on each cheek. Silver glittered in the corner of Mr Bright's eyes. 'I have missed you, my son.' He twisted Pretorius' neck so swiftly that Cass didn't realise what was happening until he heard the sickening crack and the body fell, slackly surprised, to the floor.

'No!' Gabbi left the lost old man and crumpled beside Pretorius. '*Nonononono—*' she murmured. Cass suddenly noticed her glorious hair had lost its shine, the Titian fire was fading. Her fingernails were bleeding. Her strength was clearly waning.

'Why?' Cass asked.

Mr Bright stared down at his dead son and the crying girl.

'For the greater good,' he said softly. Cass thought he could hear the anguish at the back of Mr Bright's voice. 'My son knew how to unlock the Walkways. He had transferred the keys to all of this' – he gestured at the equipment around them – 'but for centuries he'd had it all in his head. He was an *idiot savant*,' he said with a touch of pride, 'a genius.' He sighed. 'But the Walkways can never be unlocked. We can never risk that.'

For the first time in their acquaintance, Cass thought Mr Bright looked old. Shadows had fallen across his face, highlighting every wrinkle and frown line. As silver streaked from his eyes Cass wanted to cry *for* him, and the truth behind that emotion hit him like a slap in the face. He bore no hate for Mr Bright, not any longer. It had gone, vanished as if it had been nothing more than a wisp of smoke.

They were family, perhaps closer than his own had ever been. He'd felt it in the rush of the Glow as the cohorts had surged through Mr Dublin. He could feel it in the atoms of air around him. The world had changed for Cass Jones. He was becoming everything he'd ever been, and ever could be.

'You should go now,' Mr Dublin whispered. 'I think it will be soon.'

Mr Bright nodded. 'Cassius, you carry the boy.' He looked down at the girl. 'Gabriel. You have to come with us. We'll look after you.'

Cass swept the child up from the floor. Either Luke's body was absurdly light, or his own had become stronger. Perhaps it was both. He smelled warm and human, like Christian had when he was small. For a brief moment it had felt as if he held his nephew in his arms, until the twitching of the limbs and the rage in the boy's eyes dispelled that thought.

351

'Hurry,' Mr Dublin said urgently.

Cass looked at the dying man. Quietly he said, 'Thank you.' There wasn't anything else he could say.

'Gabriel?' Mr Bright took the girl's arm, but she shook it off.

'I'm staying here,' she said, her voice thick with snot and tears, 'with my *friends*.' She didn't even look at him. Mr Bright rested his hand on her shoulder, but she ignored him and after a few seconds he sighed and walked away. Mr Dublin began to shine, and as the light flooded out into the corridor Mr Bright and Cass started to run.

The JetRanger had barely taken off when the fire burst through the first floor and flames illuminated the windows of the building. The First had lost his hold on the people in Harwell now and as the helicopter rose higher and the employees started to evacuate they looked like ants as they scurried around, running out of the main building and towards the blaze. Cass looked down at his abandoned car and hoped that Freeman had been wise enough to have had it registered in someone else's name and reported stolen. Probably, he decided; Brian Freeman had never been a fool.

The helicopter turned away and as the scene below receded Cass felt he was turning his back on an old life, somehow. He closed his eyes and rested his aching head against the seat. Thinking could wait until later.

Chapter Forty-Four

Charles Ramsey, Tim Hask and David Fletcher looked on silently as the final flames were extinguished and the building stood dripping in the cold evening. Emergency services personnel ran here and there, brandishing hoses and protective suits. Staff members wandered about, dazed, as the ambulance pulled away with the last of the injured, the receptionist from the smaller facility. Everyone said he'd had a lucky escape; he was suffering from smoke inhalation, but it could have been much worse. The Commander of the ATD, the Detective Inspector and the internationally renowned profiler had been standing there watching for almost two hours with barely a word between them until Fletcher's phone had broken the silence a few moments earlier. He finished the call.

'The satellites are all functioning normally again. All across the world. Whatever was happening, it's over.' His voice was dull, exhausted.

Hask nodded, but said nothing.

'So what made all these people pass out?' Ramsey asked. 'Some kind of sleeping gas?' His eyes stayed on the burned building.

'I guess so. Time will tell.' Fletcher didn't look at him but stared as the final jets of water closed down. Several firemen ventured into the building.

'Maybe he wasn't in there,' Ramsey said. 'It's possible.'

'That's his car,' Hask said, pointing to the abandoned Range Rover. 'His cigarettes are still in it.'

'Doesn't mean he's still here,' Ramsey said.

A woman brought them hot mugs of coffee that they accepted gratefully but didn't drink. Eventually, a smoke-streaked fireman emerged from the wreck and pulled his helmet from his head as he walked towards them.

'There's four dead in there: three men and a woman, we think, but it's hard to tell. They're not in a good state. It looks like the fire started in the basement room that they're in. It's a mess. I'm sorry.'

None of the three men spoke, and the fireman nodded and then walked away to join his team.

There was a long silence. 'Shit,' Tim Hask said eventually. 'Bloody shit.'

'There was something else,' Fletcher said, after a moment. 'A chopper.' The other two men turned to look at him. 'According to reports it left moments before the blast. Normally I'd have satellite images, but not today so we don't know how many or who were on board, but someone got away from here.'

'You think he could still be alive?' Tim Hask asked. No name was required. Cass Jones hung in the air between them, as he'd done for such a long time. Fletcher didn't answer and the three looked once again at the destroyed building.

'Oh, I'd put money on it,' Ramsey said eventually. 'Wouldn't you?'

Chapter Forty-Five

A drawn curtain separated the two patients. Cass didn't want to see the body Christian's son had been transferred into when the First took his. When he first saw Christian's boy – looked him in the eyes and *saw* him – he wanted him to be in the body he'd been born in. Mr Bright had respected his wishes.

Now, sitting by the boy's bed, he wasn't sure what he'd been expecting – tubes and wires, definitely, gas masks and noisy machines, definitely. Perhaps they were required for the ageing body hidden from view, but whatever was making the exchange happen must be being done by something else.

Cass watched in awe as a nurse examined the boy's shoulder. He was sleeping deeply now, in a medically induced coma to get the process under way. The bullet wound wasn't yet healed, but the flesh was already knotting together and it looked as if it had happened two weeks ago, not a few hours. Within a few weeks there might not even be much of a scar.

The nurse left quietly, without looking up.

Cass didn't move from beside the bed as night rolled into dawn and into day, and back to night again. People brought sandwiches and drinks at regular intervals, but most went back untouched. He wondered if it was the same for Mr

Bright, on the other side of the curtain. He hadn't seen him emerge.

The transfer was being effected by the power of the cohorts, Mr Bright included, and it was nearly complete. It had apparently taken much longer the first time, when they were experimenting, but the serum had been injected and he'd been told the boy was ready. Certainly his breathing was regular and even.

Now Cass saw machines being wheeled past him to the area behind the curtain, ready for when the other patient woke – to keep him alive as long as possible, Cass supposed, although he didn't pretend to understand why. For his own part, he wanted the First dead – he'd told Mr Bright that in the helicopter. The enigmatic man had simply smiled and said gently, 'But he's family – *your* family. You have the same blood.' The faint twinkle that had risen in his eyes faded. 'And there's been too much death for now, don't you think?' he murmured as he turned and looked out of the window.

As he listened to the machines blipping and bleeping away he wondered if that had been the whole truth – or perhaps there really *were* some fates worse than death. Why should the First escape so easily after he'd been so willing to bring Armageddon, to destroy them all? Maybe that's what Mr Bright and the cohorts were thinking.

He closed his eyes for a moment and rolled his head to loosen his aching neck. He was exhausted . . .

When he opened his eyes again the air had stilled to silence. Cass frowned. Had he fallen asleep? The yellow lights overhead were dimmer, and shadows stretched across the room. The hairs on the back of Cass' neck prickled: someone was in the room with him. Something caught his eye and he slowly turned his head to the right.

Polished black lace-up brogues. Bright splashes of crimson.

356

Dark trouser cuffs. Cass' breath caught in his throat and he blinked several times. The shoes didn't move. He dragged his eyes upwards: a pale blue Armani shirt, half untucked. Tie, loosely knotted. Cass wasn't sure he wanted to go further. Would Christian's eyes be bleeding, as they had in the monastery? Would his face be wrecked and the back of his head missing, as it had after his brains had been shot out?

Cass sighed. He had no choice. He looked up.

Clear, blue eyes looked back at him from under blond hair. Christian's ghost was whole. Cass rose to his feet, his exhaustion forgotten in this moment of frozen time. His little brother smiled at him, and Cass' heart sang. They stood face to face for a moment, Cass grinning like a fool, and then Christian turned and moved down the other side of the bed. His footsteps were silent. Cass stood on the other side, mirroring Christian, and the Jones brothers stared down at the boy lying between them. He had the pale skin and blue eyes of the one and the thick dark hair of the other. Christian leaned forward and his dead lips brushed Luke's cheek. He drank in the boy, one long, wistful look, and then turned to Cass.

He smiled again, an easy, happy grin, and Cass saw all the kindness and goodness he'd tried so hard to ignore while the other had been alive, shining from his brother. He *loved* Christian, his baby brother, and now he'd love his son for him too, as if he were his own. He smiled back, tears bright and burning at the corner of his eyes. On the other side of the bed, Christian raised his arm and pointed, his smile spreading. For a second, Cass wasn't sure what he meant, and then he saw the gold in his brother's dead eyes and he gave in. He'd spent his entire life denying the truth, running from it, and that had brought him nothing but trouble and heartache. It was time to accept who – *what* – he was.

'I see the *Glow* too, Christian,' he whispered. 'I *feel* it. I'll make sure Luke does too.'

Christian nodded and lowered his arm. He turned, and without looking back, walked out of the room, disappearing just before he reached the door.

Cass stared after him. 'Goodbye little brother,' he muttered. 'Sleep well.'

In the bed, the child muttered something and Cass spun round, his heart suddenly racing.

'Luke?'

The child's eyes flickered open. He looked around, dazed, then he focused on Cass. He looked afraid and confused. He looked innocent. He didn't recognise Cass at all.

'It's okay,' Cass said, 'I'm your uncle Cass. It's all over now.'

Luke raised his hand and stared at it. 'Am I normal now?' he asked, his voice trembling. 'I was so *old*. I was trapped.' He looked at Cass. 'Are you really my uncle?' His eyes were drifting shut again.

'Yes, I am,' Cass said, and stroked the boy's hair. 'You go back to sleep, Luke. It's all going to be okay from now, you wait and see.' For the first time – in all the time he could remember – Cass had a moment of pure contentment. It was a good feeling.

'It's like we've been reborn. Reinvigorated.'

Cass turned from the sleeping boy to see Mr Bright standing at the end of the bed. He was smiling.

'The cohorts have done well.' He tilted his head and looked at Luke. 'When they were with me, as they had been with Mr Dublin, I felt a new hope in them. We all know there's no going back now. I think perhaps that has brought us a measure of peace.'

Cass stared at Mr Bright. Things had shifted during the

course of the day and Cass was confused – tired and confused. He didn't know quite how he felt about anything any more. Where did his future lie – did he even have one? After the events at Harwell would Fletcher and Ramsey be looking for him? Had Fletcher told anyone that he'd been involved in that? Perhaps all his future held was a long prison sentence. He looked at the child in the bed. No, prison could not be an option.

'I imagine you have a lot of questions,' Mr Bright said.

'Oh, yeah.' Cass almost laughed. 'I have so many questions I don't know where to start. Who the hell are you? That would be a good place to start.'

'Take the boy,' Mr Bright said, 'and go to Mr Freeman's place. Luke will be fine now – he'll sleep for a while, but that's not such a bad thing for the next few days while things settle down. I'll see you there tomorrow.' He looked at the dividing curtain. 'I have a few things here to take care of. I will come. I promise.'

An hour after Cassius had taken the child Luke, the nurses called to say everything was prepared, and they could transfer the old man back to the room at the top of Senate House. Mr Bright followed the discreetly unmarked private ambulance in his normal car. Dawn was breaking. It was Christmas Eve.

Outside, the ground was covered in a hard grey frost that matched the colour of the buildings and the sky. A street cleaner shuffled past slowly, scarf and hat almost covering his face against the cold as he cleared the rubbish from the gutters.

Despite the early hour, yellow lights illuminated office windows and fairy lights twinkled around their edges. He wasn't sure if it was just his own feeling of calm, but it was as if the whole of London was somehow more tranquil this morning. Two pedestrians, strangers, smiled at each other as they passed. Mr Bright was certain that this world of his, of all of *theirs*, had never looked more beautiful. Sacrifices had been made – he squeezed away his pain; that was for another day – and he would make sure that those sacrifices had not been in vain. The car came to a halt and he stepped out into the freezing air. It felt fresh and invigorating in his lungs. He smiled and lit a thin cheroot. He had a few moments before he had to go inside.

He had sat by the First's bed many times when he'd been sleeping, talking quietly to him as if to a Father Confessor. He'd found a measure of peace there, surrounded by the quiet hum of the machinery and the silent presence of the nurses. Now it was different. For a start, the First was no longer sleeping. Mr Bright saw the watery eyes in the sunken face flare with life as he leaned forward and carefully pushed a wisp of white hair out of them.

'I know you hate me,' he said. 'I can understand that.' He dipped the small sponge on the bedside table into the water cup and squeezed a little onto the cracked lips. 'But I will look after you, just like I always have, old friend, for as long as it takes.' He smiled fondly, remembering everything that they had once been: how *glorious* they were. The eyes raged at him silently, but they were different now. There was no *Glow*.

He looked more closely and wondered if there was more than a touch of madness there instead. He put the sponge back beside the cup. Perhaps, given the situation, the First losing his mind might not be such a bad thing. Mr Bright had a feeling that young Luke had woken up with more than his own share of *Glow* after the transfer. Time would tell, but he was sure he had a lot of the First's too.

'Try and rest now,' he said, heading to the door. 'I'll be back to see you soon, I promise.'

Within an hour the Experiment was being dismantled and the separate components destroyed. Mr Bright sipped strong coffee and listened to the news in the same office Mr Dublin had summoned him to not so long ago while he waited for the doctors.

They handed over the injections and he thanked them courteously and dismissed them. This was something he had to do himself. His heart heavy, he made his way through the corridor to the rooms where Mr Rasnic and Mr Bellew and all those others who had tried so desperately for the Walkways sat slumped and lost, surrounded by their padded walls. He moved from one to the next, kneeling down beside each, talking softly, reassuringly, as he slid the needle deep into their veins. The poisonous liquid was strong enough to kill a hundred men instantly, but still they fought. Mr Bellew took fifteen minutes, and Mr Bright waited with him, holding his cold hand tightly in his, giving whatever measure of comfort he could. Perhaps the screaming in the Chaos would stop now. He hoped so.

When it was done, he went to the rooftop and looked down at the city he loved. Times had changed; there were things they must stop fighting. Perhaps the Dying was simply a sign that this was truly their home now: they and it and *them, the children of those who'd come with them,* were all one. They would have to learn to accept that death would come to them all, in the end. The cold began to numb his nose and he smiled as he headed back to his car. They might have to learn to accept it, but he for one had no intention of dying, not for quite a long while yet. Not in these new, exciting times.

Chapter Forty-Six

Cass was lost in the computer. Christmas Eve had turned into Christmas Day and the night hours were ticking their way towards morning. A dull ache had settled into his neck, but he barely felt it. Dr Cornell and Brian Freeman were sitting either side and Mr Bright was ensconced in an armchair, smoking a cigar and sipping brandy, but Cass felt entirely alone as he absorbed the information in the silver datasticks.

As soon as Mr Bright had inserted all four into the computer the screen had come to life, opening up a world of documentation – so much of it: financial and legal records, images of paperwork long-since destroyed: a paper trail of the world's history. He looked past it, digging deeper for what he really wanted: the story that would let him understand. And then—

It was Paradise. Everything dazzled. Everyone Glowed. They lived wanting nothing, having everything. He, the Lord God, ruled over them as he, and his forefathers, had for ever and ever, before and after. There was music and laughter and light. His kingdom, for those who lived within its walls, was magical. He was kind and forgiving. He was wise.

At first.

Change came as endless time passed, and He became cruel.

Perhaps He *had always been that way, but in the first hot flush of* His *reign the cohorts and the Emissaries and the Heralds and the Archangels and all those beyond the gleaming walls of Paradise who lived in the dusty sands of the cities of Heaven, didn't want to see it.*

Debate ceased as those who raised issue with the Lord God disappeared, taken and tortured. Some returned, cowed and corrected, but others were never seen again, their wealth stripped and families ruined. He grew fatter, rarely travelling, except in a golden Chariot pulled by the Flight of the Army. He toured the cities of all the suns until they bowed to His will. There would be no more Leaders of Harmony; they were dispelled back to their States of Heaven. Instead of the Leaders of Harmony, representative of all the peoples of Heaven convening in Paradise to bring their grievances and concerns to the Lord God and his Inner Cohort, now He would instead send an emissary to each of them with His demands. They would fulfil them or He would have his terrible vengeance. He no longer forgave.

He grew fatter.

His first son grew up.

They were light and life and courage, the young. The first son was everything the Father was not: he was filled with easy charm, if a little arrogant and spoiled at times, but he was good and he drew others to him, the young men of the cohorts, the quiet Architect, and the rest. They bathed in his confidence and the cities smiled as they watched them soar beneath the suns as only the people of the cohorts could. They were brave and brilliant. And the first son and the young saw the Father, the Lord God, for what he was and they agreed they would no longer tolerate the cruelty of His whims. They would go to distant places and talk where they could not be heard.

Trouble brewed.

With the peoples subdued, Paradise was still filled with music and everything glittered and Glowed, and as long as He was happy, all was well. But it became so hard to tell when He was happy, and it could change so very swiftly. His ministers and the Inner Cohort were quietly relieved when He started a new project, locking himself away for days at a time with His scientists. Platters of food and wine disappeared inside at regular intervals, but the Lord God rarely emerged. It was a pleasant time in Paradise and it reminded them that there could be something other than luxurious fear as a way of life. More of the cohort, the élite residents of Paradise, the ruling class, the flyers, gathered to the first son and those who stood with him. They wanted their honour back; they did not want to be the representatives of a Despot.

When the Lord God eventually emerged, at first He didn't notice the trouble. He barely noticed that the young had grown and were no longer children, but men. The Architect had a child of his own, a strange little thing with a peculiar damp Glow. He saw these things but they didn't register; He was too filled with his own achievement.

He had created new life, He declared. It was His first attempt and the results were crude, but they would be His slaves: they could work the mines in the lands before Chaos. With a flourish He presented them to the court: two feeble bodies that did not shine or Glow. They looked shy and awkward under the scrutiny of the cohort.

'I tried to make them in my own image,' He said, stuffing grapes into his mouth. He laughed a lot at that irony, for these pathetic beings had no wings and were so very small, and the cohorts politely joined in, but none matched His guffaws. 'Aren't they so innocent?' He said. 'Look at their dull eyes.' He nodded to himself. 'Stupid. Just what I need them to be.'

He let them live in the palace garden, where He could watch

364

them from the windows of the throne room, but He soon grew bored. Their bodily functions were crude, and they weren't as pliable as he'd expected. As soon as they could speak, all they had were questions. And they were eating all His *fruit*.

After a while, He *no* longer looked at them. He *couldn't* destroy them – not yet, at least – because He *would not show* himself *fallible. The creation had been a success, but* He *would* attempt a more successful one. He set the scientists the task of creating a better HuMan, as He *had named his experiment.* In the meantime, He *declared all female cohort second-class* citizens. It amused him.

Trouble rumbled.

It could no longer be ignored.

Father and son went to war, and it was terrible: the skies above all the cities of Heaven burned as the two sides fought. The Lord God even flew himself, *and although* He *had grown fat,* He *was still powerful – the most powerful – and although casualties fell on both sides,* He *would not be dominated.*

The first son could see that they were losing, and he knew the penance for his sins would fall on his friends, for the Father loved his *first son, and that was* His *weakness.* He *thought the first son had acted in impatience and ambition and* He *could understand those traits more than any desire for kindness and justice, for the Lord God considered* Himself *kind and just.*

The first son and his friends fought harder as those around them fell, but they were too young, and there were too few of them. The Lord God and His *armies were crushing the rebellion.*

As defeat stared them in the face they made a plan: they would not stay here to be humiliated and paraded as part of his *victory; instead, they would travel. They would go far from here and start again, build their own civilisation – the Architect would build it. Many wanted to come with them,* and while the first son returned to Paradise to speak with his father they waited, out at the edge of Heaven, with instructions to leave without him should he not return. The Lord God was angry; He told the son to go and never return; He didn't care about him. The first son was a disgrace and He had a second son. His roars made the palace shake.

As he left, quickly and quietly through a side-door, the first son saw the HuMans, the failures, in the gardens sitting beneath the apple tree they loved. He took pity on them and called them and their children, for it appeared the HuMans bred quickly. He would take them with him. They could be failures in his father's eyes together.

And so they travelled, out to the furthest reaches of the suns of Heaven. They made a path of their own, the cohorts and the women and the HuMans, through the endless fields of Chaos, and found their way to the unchartered Hell beyond. They would find their new home here, somewhere beyond the cold darkness, the first son was sure of it. His enthusiasm kept their tired spirits raised on the long journey.

Finally, they found somewhere. The Architect studied it thoroughly and started to build.

They called it Earth, after the first son's dead mother.

For a long time they stayed in their natural shape, but the HuMans bred fast, and soon they began to question those who were different, so the cohort became small. It was wisest.

After a while, the HuMans, with their short life spans, couldn't remember that anything had ever been different.

But somehow, perhaps he had programmed it into them, they started looking for a Lord God – a deity. A creator. They had questions.

The cohorts contemplated long and hard on the appropriate course of action. Some wanted to tell them the truth about the creation, about the terrible Lord God, and how they had all come to be here. But the Lord God hadn't been entirely wrong about the humans, as they now called themselves; for all that they were capable of great cruelty and anger, they had a belief in goodness and they needed to look up to something greater than themselves, a father figure who would judge them. The truth would destroy that. They would run to ruin.

Eventually the first son – the First among them – came up with a plan: he would take their own story thus far, but change it slightly to suit. He would be the Messiah they craved, the son of the benevolent God, and he would say he had been sent among them to die for their sins. He would pick some from those among them who now had the Glow – for the cohorts had spread their seed among humankind – to be his disciples, and they would use their long lives to spread the word and it would grow.

And thus it was that Lucifer, once the first son, the First among them, became Jesus of Nazareth and brought the word of God to the lost.

He was very good at it.

Afterwards, when it was done and the Good Book was written, there was celebration and merriment. The Architect, always the more serious of the three who had led the way, thought perhaps the rising again on the third day was a little elaborate, but he smiled as he watched the seed of the religion grow. Around the globe they repeated the stories, variations on a theme, until all the people of the Earth had a Lord God they could believe in.

As time passed and the cohorts sank into the background, pulling the strings of the world quietly from within their Network, the First and Mr Bright and Mr Solomon and many others were shocked at how like their original Lord God His creations could be. How they could be so cruel to each other, *and all in the name of the kindly God the First had fabricated for them. Perhaps He had made them more than a little in his own image after all.*

They bred and the world filled.

Mr Bright settled in his first city, Pandemonium, Londinium, London. He liked the cool air, so different from the heat and sand they'd left behind.

Time passed.

'All the proof is here!' Dr Cornell was pacing the room, unable to contain his excitement. '*Everything.* All I've researched, all I've believed in while the rest of the world called me mad – it's there on that computer!' He laughed a little maniacally. 'I'll be reinstated. They'll probably make me a dean. Don't you see?' He looked at Cass. 'It's all *there.* The entire history of a conspiracy. We have to show the world. There is no choice! Just do it! Why are you hesitating?'

Cass said nothing. His eyes were still focused on the screen. Dr Cornell was right; everything was there. It might take people years to go through it all, and it would certainly shock, but it could not be denied as truth. The command on the screen flashed at him. 'Send?'

He lit a cigarette and stared at it. Why was he hesitating? Sending the information out over the Internet had been his immediate suggestion; Dijan Maric would be able to turn it into a virus and it would be in every inbox in the world within days: the ultimate virus. The truth.

From the kitchen came the sound of ice tinkling in a glass. Brian Freeman had left them to it. Unlike Dr Cornell, he wasn't interested in wading in with his opinion.

'This is your choice, Cassius,' Mr Bright said. He hadn't

moved from the armchair during the hours Cass, Freeman and Dr Cornell had been sifting through the overwhelming mass of information. One leg was crossed casually over the other and he had recovered and his composure. His eyes twinkled merrily. 'You can send that out to the world, open their eyes – that's up to you. But you know this human race as well as I do: they are insatiably curious. In fact, you sum up their curiosity, the way you wouldn't stop coming after me, the way you had to *know*.' He smiled. 'What do you think they will do with all this knowledge?"

Cass looked over at him. 'What do *you* think they will do?' He was surprised to find that he wanted Mr Bright's opinion.

'I think at first the focus will be on the finances. No one will truly believe in men who have lived for ever, and so they will presume each of us is a code name for some corrupt society or other. The careful balance we have built will crumble. The Bank will fall, definitely. Governments across the world will fight for the money in the X accounts. More than likely, we will have an Armageddon of our own making. If not, then finally someone, somewhere, will look for the cohorts. They will want to bring them down. They will see all this as some kind of deceit, which of course it has been. What will start as curiosity will end in a witch-hunt, and perhaps we will be forced to fight.' Mr Bright got to his feet and went to the window and looked out. He couldn't see the houses beyond Brian Freeman's gates, but he knew they were there.

'They will not forgive us for being *different*. Ultimately we will probably have to *become*, to assert our authority through physical might – but this time the weaponry you have invented means we will probably die. As will a great many of you.'

369

Brian Freeman came in with four glasses of whisky on a tray. Mr Bright smiled his thanks as he took one.

'And all of that, Cassius Jones, I could live with, if you'll excuse the pun. Perhaps we have been too controlling. Perhaps we should never have changed the story of our journey, but we did. If we had to fight and die because of it, then *c'est la vie*. Things were always thus. But that wouldn't be the end of it, would it?'

'What do you mean?' Cass asked.

'Don't listen to him!' Dr Cornell snapped, brushing Freeman's offered drink aside and sending the glass clattering to the carpet.

'Take it easy!' Freeman put the tray down and grabbed the old man, forcing him down into a seat. 'Take it fucking easy, mate.'

'People have a *right* to know the truth,' Dr Cornell shouted. 'I have a *right* to be vindicated!'

'The truth,' Mr Bright said calmly, 'is often only a matter of perception.'

'No, the truth is right there in that computer,' Dr Cornell snarled.

'And for a long while, people will still think that is madness. It'll only be the money that interests them. Maybe for as long as your lifetime.'

'You're wrong. There's too much information there. And the original scrolls will be found and carbon-dated. It'll be enough.'

Cass could see the desperation in his eyes. He was close to cracking. Releasing these files would never restore his life, but they would give him peace. Cass looked back at Castor Bright and repeated his question. 'What do you mean?'

'Once the fighting was done here, you know what they'd do – in your heart you know: finally, maybe not this century, but eventually, they will look Heavenwards. They'll want to find it.'

'But the Walkways are locked.'

'Yes, they are, for now. But you all have such tenacity: you will die trying to find a way, until you succeed. What is *here*, all that has been built, that we have all worked so hard to create, will become worthless, because everyone will want Heaven. And when they do find a way to undo the locks, then they will meet their Lord God. And he will destroy them.'

'Don't listen to him, Jones.' Dr Cornell leaned forward in the chair. 'You *can't* listen to him – I'll send it myself. I'll—' He lunged forward, but Brian Freeman pushed him back again.

'Don't even think about it.'

There was a long pause.

'Sometimes,' Mr Bright said, so softly Cass could barely hear it, 'it is only the greater good that matters.'

Cass looked from Mr Bright to Dr Cornell. *The greater good.* They were Bright's words but Cornell no doubt thought that what he wanted Cass to do was also in every-one's best interests. Cass wasn't so sure. Was releasing the truth for the greater good? Was Cornell right? Did the world have the right to know? Or was the old man driven simply by his own need for vindication and that was a good argu-ment to hang it on? Cornell might believe his motives were altruistic, but Cass wasn't so sure. The Network had been his life's obsession and he had been ridiculed for it. This was his opportunity for a moment of glory. Then there was the power, Mr Bright – always in the shadows, pulling strings and making decisions that affected them all. Was he acting in the greater good?

Cass thought of the students who had killed themselves

after the Experiment. They had been innocent and Bright had used them. Their truths had been lost and their families would never know the true circumstances of their deaths. Could he live with that? Would releasing the truth to the world actually make any difference to them now? He looked at the silver haired man whose eyes had lost a little of their sparkle over the past nine months or so. He found that he didn't believe that Bright had acted in malice, no matter how terrible his deeds. What had those decisions cost him? And now that the Walkways were closed for good, how would Bright and the Network change? Was there an opportunity to really make them work for the greater good now? Cigarette smoke burned the back of his throat. He thought of the Glow. He thought of Luke. He thought of everything he had learned about himself. He thought about the world he realised he loved in all its grittiness.

The greater good. He stared at the screen and then looked into Dr Cornell's desperate eyes. He knew beyond certainty that if he deleted the files it would destroy the man, just as surely as if he were to shoot him between the eyes.

The greater good.

He knew what he had to do, and his heart raced with the relief. His choice was made, and he thought that perhaps it was the only choice he'd ever had.

He pressed the key.

Dr Cornell yowled like a broken animal when he saw Cass delete the files, and he yowled until Brian Freeman chloroformed him. Cass had known he would be destroying the old man when he'd made his decision.

'What do we do with him?' Freeman asked.

'Keep him unconscious,' Cass said, before Mr Bright

could speak for him. 'Get him and all this stuff back to his house. When he wakes up, who's going to believe his story?'

'They're going to have to put him in the nuthouse,' Freeman muttered. 'He's snapped, poor bastard.'

'Yes they will, and yes he has,' Cass said. 'It can't be helped.' He looked at the old gangster.

'Haven't you got anything to say about this? About what I've done?'

Freeman drained his whisky. 'I'm not so different from him.' He nodded in Mr Bright's direction. 'I've lived a lot of my life in the shadows. I understand the need for secrets. I'm all for knowledge, Cass, son, but not for everyone. Just for me.'

Cass smiled. He was coming round to that point of view himself.

Epilogue

It was New Year's Day, and the two men stood side by side at the vast windows and looked down over the sprawling city of London as they listened to the news on the radio. One smoked a cigarette, the other a thin cigar.

'Investigators still have not been able to locate the cause of the devastating fire at the Harwell Institute in Oxfordshire last night. They have, however, confirmed that one of the dead bodies is that of Cassius Jones. Detective Inspector Jones had been on the run from the police after they sought him for questioning over the deaths of two men earlier this year. Jones was responsible for uncovering a network of corruption in his own force only eight months ago, but there has been speculation that he suffered some kind of mental breakdown in the aftermath of the violent deaths of his brother's family. The other bodies have yet to be identified, but are—'

The elder of the two men clicked a button on the small remote control in his hand and the woman's voice was cut off. From upstairs somewhere came the sound of a computer game being played, and the room started filling with the scent of rich, expensive coffee as hot liquid filtered through the machine on the table between the offices. It was a brand new year. It was a brand new era.

'Are you ready to get to work, Mr Jones?' he asked, his eyes twinkling.

'Yes I am, Mr Bright.' Mr Jones smiled too, but he continued to stare out of the window for a little while. He no longer had to look up. There was nothing to look up for. Everything that mattered was here on Earth. He turned and paused, automatically adjusting his expensive new suit, and enjoying the feel of the silver against his chest. The history had never been deleted. How could it be? But Cass had passed that final test. He'd made the choice that he'd always been destined to make. Beneath it, his shoulder moved with ease. There was no longer even a scar to show that he'd ever been injured. Mr Bright had been right; Cassius Jones was beginning to learn what the Glow could do for him. He smiled as he looked at the office doors. The brass plaques had been taken down and replaced with more stylish aluminium. Mr Solomon's name-plate was now lying in Mr Bright's desk drawer, a nostalgic memento. Cass looked over at Mr Bright's door, and then back to his own. MR BRIGHT and MR JONES. He smiled again, and rocked on his feet, enjoying the feel of the thick crimson carpet beneath his Italian leather shoes. He hadn't changed much, including the large painting of the fallen Angel on the wall: Mr Solomon had had good taste, and he liked the sense of history that came with it.

Behind his desk, Mr Jones took a deep breath and turned on his computer. He had a lot to get through before taking Luke for lunch, and then after that he had the first meeting of the new Inner Cohort. He looked at the small silver ornamental engraving sitting on his vast desk. The words shone out at him, reflecting in the winter sunlight pouring through the glass behind him:

Better to Reign in Hell, than serve in Heaven.

Wasn't that the truth? he thought, as he lost himself in the morning's work.

THE END

Acknowledgements

It's so hard to know where to start with these now that this trilogy is done. There are, I'm very lucky to be able to say, just too many people who have helped me on the way. Of course, as always, huge thanks to Jo Fletcher and Veronique Baxter and all the team at Gollancz, especially Gillian Redfearn, my new editor, and Jon Weir, my publicist and drinking buddy. For inspiration I need to thank Michael Marshall (Smith) and John Connolly whose work made me realise you could write crime that was still a bit on the weird side. A big thank you to Tony Thompson for writing books that give me so much of my research, and I still owe him a dinner. Ray Marshall at Festival Films for liking it so much he bought the TV rights – a man of taste obviously, who has also become a friend, mentor and colleague over the past two years. Stephen Jones for making sure I got a meeting with Jo Fletcher way back when, and all at the British Fantasy Society for making this writing journey less lonely. You all totally rock.